Shadow Protocol

A Navy SEAL's War Against the Deep State

Thomas Boyle

Copyright

Shadow Protocol: A Navy SEAL's War Against the Deep State

Published by Defiance Press & Publishing, LLC

Bulk orders of this book may be obtained by contacting Defiance Press & Publishing, LLC. www.defiancepress.com.

Defiance Press & Publishing, LLC

281-581-9300

info@defiancepress.com

Prologue

Capitol Building, Washington, DC, 08:30

Outside the Capitol, Tyler Cox, soon to be the Deputy Director of Special Operations and a lifetime CIA deep-state swamp creature, exited his cab and began the long walk into the Capitol. He dodged the high-velocity suits talking to themselves, rehearsing the morning's lines from their never-ending production of the taxpayer-funded *Gone With the Wind.*

He grabbed a triple espresso café Americano at the coffee wagon, dumped in five packets of raw sugar, and stirred anxiously. The first pull was a desperate attempt to stimulate some adrenaline, if there was any left. It wasn't long before a couple of drops of the vital juice squeezed out from his overworked adrenals and gave him the illusion of energy.

Cox started his long trudge into the Capitol Building. He recognized several people he had called friends or colleagues in the past, but on this day, he acknowledged none of them.

Inside the Capitol, he made his way to his SCIF. He started to panic about being so far underground. He quickly washed down a green Xani-bar and started his deep breathing technique, and with Big Pharma on board, he slipped into a droopy diazepine daze.

The place card holders took their seats on either side of the conference table, while their aides were largely relegated to the outer ring of chairs.

Cox was crashing the meeting at the request of his boss, CIA Deputy Director for Special Operations Warren Trask.

The meeting director reminded everyone, “Only personnel with Q-level clearance are permitted to remain in the SCIF."

Political lightweights set sail quickly, while some of the older Capitol Hill lackeys argued.

Tyler Cox tried to look busy and inconspicuous at the same time. One of the CapPo officers asked Cox to leave, and the image of an angry Warren Trask materialized in his head. He pulled out his CIA credentials and held them up in front of the woman in an oddly public display of his Langley club membership. For CapPo, it was a bridge too far.

"Sir, you are not Q-level cleared," said the officer. A rush of adrenaline surged through Cox and triggered a quick Xani dump that obliterated his impulse control.

As a devotee of no-limit Texas hold 'em, Cox decided to go all in. He rose from his chair to his full height of five feet nine inches and pushed in all his chips. "Young lady, I was jumping into hot LZs a week before—after 9/11! Before you were old enough to—"

Cox stopped mid-bluster. He realized he’d screwed up his hot LZ line and searched the room for a potential ally. Tim Lawrence, a White House Operations guy who had helped out in times past, cut Cox a break and cleared him to stay as part of his staff.

The soundproof doors shut, and the SCIF’s sound dampening and signal jamming engaged. Inside, Admiral Martin Corbett, the senior naval officer with more gold braid than almost anyone else in the SCIF, pointed to Rear Admiral Ulysses Gable, who saluted in return. Gable stood, and the crowd instinctively fell silent.

"Ladies and gentlemen," Gable began, "today's briefing focuses on the identification of a high-value individual, Mullah Attah Kassem. Kassem, who has assumed the role of CFO for the entire Taliban movement, has performed nothing short of miracles in securing hundreds of millions, even billions, of dollars despite the most stringent economic embargo and forensic accounting barriers ever created. The CIA and NSA have data indicating that Kassem may control nearly two billion dollars."

Gable scanned the row of senior officers until he found Admiral Corbett, who was caught shuffling papers, and returned the nod. His aide handed him the sheet he was looking for.

"Thank you, Rear Admiral. Some of this money has surfaced in Pyongyang, Tehran, Damascus, and Mogadishu, in amounts large enough to appear on our radar, which is a problem. The fact that this money has been used to buy a large weapons cache compounds the problem exponentially. The CIA has tracked the weapons through the Himalayas, along with Mullah Atta Kassem, to the village of Darbart, in the Korengal Valley, on the Pech River at the base of the Hindu Kush. Darbart is a stop on an unofficial highway, a treacherous route that winds through countless canyons and passes in this section of the Himalayan Mountains. Drugs, foreign fighters, spies, intel, and weapons are just some of the illicit cargo that makes its way through the Hindu Kush. This area is an extremely violent region that has been heavily militarized due to its value to smugglers and the Taliban alike.

"Mullah Attah Kassem—don't bother trying to recall his name; he's a recent invention. Following the termination of the last exchequer, he became the new finance minister for the Taliban. He has funneled money along this highway to terrorist cells operating in Afghanistan and Pakistan. Kassem has forged connections with many of the biggest weapons dealers, and his reported billion-dollar terrorist slush fund has bought him some friends in high places. We have reports Kassem's money was part of the same tranche of funds the Obama administration provided to the outlaw regime in Iran. It's worth noting that this payout was supposedly intended to temporarily curb Iran's nuclear ambitions; however, no consideration was given to the deadly consequences created by handing the world's largest state sponsor of terrorism such a massive tranche of money. In a somewhat similar operation, the Obama administration handed Mexican cartels large amounts of fully automatic weapons in their Fast and Furious operation, which only served to destabilize our southern border, where one of those weapons killed a border patrol agent. One can only surmise the reason for engaging in such harmful policies. It's important to note that Iran is only a proxy for the real sponsor of worldwide terrorism, the CCP, which funds not only Iran but also North Korea, Venezuela, and Cuba, to name a few. The failure to eliminate Iran's nuclear program aside, the incalculable damage to the U.S. and the suffering endured by thousands of American servicemen and women in Iraq, Syria, and Afghanistan, caused by directly funding a terrorist state with 1.5 billion in cash, seems to be just the tip of the iceberg."

"The question that continues to baffle the intelligence community is: who is Mullah Attah Kassem, where did he come from, and how did he achieve such overnight success?"

Admiral Corbett gave a theatrical shoulder shrug. "We were operating in the dark until last week when we received vital information from our friends across the pond at MI6. I'm sorry, Lady Carrier, I mean SIS. Before that fortuitous communiqué, we had data on Kassem but little to no background."

Corbett motioned toward a tall, dark-haired woman in a Savile Row tweed suit. She removed her tortoiseshell glasses and stood. She was six feet tall in her stockinged feet, showcasing an impressive stature, and when she flashed her pearly whites, the men in the room reflexively smiled back.

"Thank you, Admiral Corbett. As the Admiral noted, I am a member of Her Majesty's Secret Intelligence Service, or, as Hollywood likes to call us, MI6. My name may be familiar to some of you, but for those who do not know me, I am Mary Carrier, Deputy Director-General of International Counter-Terrorism at SIS."

She moved to the table from her seat in the outer ring. She stepped between two placeholders, put her knuckles on the table, and leaned into her briefing.

"Traditional funding for Islamic terrorism has almost exclusively come through an informal, sometimes underground, Hawala finance network. Low tech and low volumes serve as its firewalls. The Hawala utilizes retail shops and merchants of various shapes and sizes to move money and valuables through an unconventional pipeline for asymmetrical financing. Historically, the number and size of the transfers have been limited by the Hawala's capacity to hold and move treasure. Its hallmark is the absence of electronic transfers and any real evidence of its existence. So, when Dr. Hasan Mudgizzen, a former professor and chair of Middle Eastern Economic Theory at the distinguished London School of Economics, tried to move a large sum through the Hawala system, klaxons sounded at Her Majesty’s Revenue and Customs. Mudgizzen left the LSE when he was found to have established back-channel funding mechanisms for terrorism. He financed camps in England and France as far back as 1980. He financed a series of training camps across the western European countryside, as well as here in America; 22 camps, from New York to California, were found to be financed by Mudgizzen. We believe the CCP began financing the radicalization of Islam after the USSR folded. Islam was the perfect tool for the CCP; inexpensive, malleable, and economically vulnerable soldiers were madrass indoctrinated and terrorism camp educated in the skills of terror before they were sent off to attack the West, especially America, the Big Satan.”

Several people nodded their agreement with Carrier's description. “At present, elements in both our intelligence and investigative branches of our governments are aligned with progressive and globalist elites across Europe and here in the States. These deep state actors use the power of their offices to provide cover and intel to the enemies of the people. Lives lost, millions left with their world in ruin, but always the legions of the International Military-Industrial Complex, their political mouthpieces, and their globalist elite masters walk away unharmed with trillions of dollars in their pockets. War will never stop in our world until profit has been taken out of it.”

Todd Nadler, one of the State Department representatives at the meeting, objected, "You're saying that members of your government conveyed information to known terrorists?"

"You sound surprised, Mr. Nadler," said Lady Carrier. "Globalist elites have for decades worked tirelessly to secure

China most-favored-nation trading status while granting it developing nation trading status and a seat as a permanent member of the World Trade Organization. Payback for the globalists was access to a workforce that was, in some cases, prison labor or, worse still, concentration camp labor, where rape, murder, horrible violence, and psychological warfare were just some of the blatant civil rights abuses inflicted upon a Chinese workforce and population that has no say in their lives."

Does the name Tiananmen Square or the Uyghur genocide mean anything at the State Department?"

Major General Grant leaned into Admiral Corbett and said, "I like her."

An extraordinary level of side conversations and low-level objections broke out.

Troy Gill, a former SEAL who was an outspoken pit bull who worked as an advisor in the Trump White House, was included in many of the Biden administration's National Security briefings as an investigator for the Senate Oversight Committee. He slammed his fist down on the table. "Let's have some goddamn order. Ladies and gentlemen, if Lady Carrier has come all this way to help us, we should give her the courtesy of listening to what she has to say."

Mary Carrier smiled at Gill and continued, "Mudgizzen was released despite being an overwhelming flight risk. Once on the street, Mudgizzen vanished. He surfaced in Waziristan, then resurfaced in Afghanistan. All of it a part of a pre-planned victory tour. During his run from justice, he took the nom de guerre, Mullah Attah Kassem."

"If Mudgizzen, or for the sake of uniformity, Mullah Attah Kassem, has been obtaining miraculous sums of money," said General Grant, "and he is guilty of funding terrorists, we need to bring him in, Admiral Corbett."

Corbett was caught in a side consultation with his chief of staff and nodded in agreement before he said, "ONI puts the Taliban war chest at a little more than two million. How far off could we be?"

"The long and short of it is that Lady Carrier's intel is a stunning revelation," said Troy Gill. "Mullah Kassem is not looking for funding; he's looking for a war to fund."

The side conversations picked up, and General Bull Grant, a four-star general with a slow-paced Kentuckian demeanor, raised his hand to put the brakes on the chatter.

The room quieted as the old warrior stood. "Admiral Corbett, I think we should discuss this situation," said Grant as he peered over his gold-rimmed glasses.

Corbett got up and walked over to Grant. He took the aide-de-camp's chair and leaned in. "Agreed, General. A mission to the Korengal Valley almost always requires numbers. If we're talking about using my SEALs, we have two SEAL platoons under Lieutenant Commander Kane at FOB Chapman and two more platoons scheduled to rotate out at the end of the month.

It's pretty rare to have that many tier one operators in-country and not involved in a mission," said Grant. "Did the White House have some sort of heads-up on this Kassem guy?"

This is no place to discuss a mission, General Grant; it's filled with deep state assholes, who use confidential information as entrees to the Georgetown cocktail party circuit."

Chapter 1

Darbart, Korengal Valley, Afghanistan. 03:00

Four platoons of Seal Team Six, Gold Squadron, haloed in two miles from rally point Razor. They began their march with strict light and sound discipline.

Kez Littlefoot, Quinn to the rest of the team, led the unit through the mountains using Ground Panoramic Night Vision Goggles and his innate ability to navigate any terrain under any conditions. Cutting trail was a gift from his Inuit ancestors, as well as his parents and grandparents, who were Alaskan wilderness guides.

He raised his fist, bringing the entire team to an immediate halt. Whispering into his neck mic, he said, "I have a slight rise in the ground over a long and straight axis, over."

"And?" Kane asked.

"No straight lines in nature, over."

"Can you neutralize it, Kez?" Kane asked as he looked around the dark moonscape.

Kez scanned the area. "Yes, it looks like a simple pressure plate, over."

"Simple means look for a secondary. Measure twice, cut once, Quinn." Kane replied.

Quinn the Eskimo, as in the Bob Dylan song The *Mighty Quinn*. It was Littlefoot's team name since BUDs.

"Son of a bitch, you're right. The pressure plate's a primary, sir. I've got questionable soil on either side of the path. I'm standing in the middle of the kill box. It'd be a bad day for me if there's a remote trigger nearby. The whole thing's probably daisy-chained together, over."

"How long to neutralize?"

"Five minutes minimum."

"Mark it, back up twenty yards, and cut a trail around it."

"Roger that, Actual, out."

***

Two clicks later, the squad assembled in a ravine at the base of the everywhere mountains that formed a near insurmountable wall all the way around the village of Darbart.

All four of the roads north out of the village converged into a single dirt road at the beginning of the Hindu Kush.

Gold Squad was 64 operators strong. It was split into two teams: Gold Team, with thirty-two operators, remained in position, while Blue Team's thirty-two operators would cross the same ridge to a point on the southeast side of the village.

Comms Specialist Donny Urban, a lanky twenty-eight-year-old who had played guard for Division 1 basketball powerhouse Seneca College, set up his comms unit and established their CP.

Lt. Moe Epstein and Lieutenant Commander Kane monitored the village and the roads leading north out of Darbart.

"Lieutenant Commander," said Urban, "Comms are deconflicted; no enemy traffic, just positive communications, sir."

"Good job, Donny; continue to deconflict any incoming comms," Kane replied. Specialist Urban nodded while listening intently to his headset.

Kane leaned toward one of his platoon commanders and remarked, "Moe, this is going to be interesting," all the while scanning the village with his night vision spotting scope. "I can't understand why we need four platoons for this mission. We could have handled this with three 8-man squads and a pair of Apaches."

Epstein lowered his night-vision binoculars and said, "I have never seen sixty operators in the same province, let alone on the same mission."

“Tora Bora,” Kane interjected. “They let Bin Laden get away. If he was captured by us, he’d have spilled the beans and given up the guys who set up—

“Don’t say it, boss; if the CIA’s anywhere around here, they’re probably listening in on our comms,” said LT. Morris as he took a sip of water from his camel. "Your team had probably just arrived in-country when that clusterfuck happened."

Kane looked at him and laughed. "Yeah, I had a full ride at Slippery Rock; not that college wrestling is any way to enjoy the college experience. I was starting my junior year when 9/11 happened. I left school and signed up with the Navy.

"Halcyon days, Boss, halcyon days."

Specialist Urban interrupted them with a comms message. "Skipper, Wolverine One is in position, on standby, and awaiting your orders, sir."

Kane’s mind wandered, frozen. He looked up into the inky night sky. Urban attempted to ask him a question, but Kane hushed him with an outstretched hand.

"Do you hear that? Right—right there, there it is," said Kane.

Urban listened carefully and nodded. "That's a reaper, sir," he said.

"It's a goddamn Reaper, Donny! And it's on-station, goddamn early."

"It's below the mission hard deck; I'm sure of it," said Epstein.

"If we can hear it—so can the damn Tallies," Urban replied.

"Damn straight, Donny," Kane said. "Get me Captain March on the horn—now. Tell Wolverine One to launch their —"

Before Kane could finish his sentence, two loud explosions from Blue Team's position lit up the night sky. “Contact,” shouted out instinctively across the valley.”

"Who the hell started firing?" Kane exclaimed. A brief silence was followed by a barrage of tracer fire. A DShK, a Soviet-made Cold War-era heavy machine gun, opened fire, raking Chen's position, accompanied by a half dozen RPGs that exploded all around.

Kane snatched the radio headset from Donny Urban. "Wolverine One, Wolverine One, this is Wolverine Actual. What is your status? Over."

"Wolverine Actual, this is Perez. Wolverine One is down. I've taken over Wolverine One's team. The tangos opened fire on Wolverine One's position just before we received the order to engage.

"We're neck-deep in a firefight, over."

"Roger that, Bear," Kane said into his mic. "I'm trying to reach whoever's controlling that drone overhead!"

"We'll maintain our rate of fire, over."

"Be ready, Perez, to drop and exfil on my orders." Kane wiped the sweat from his face and continued, "What's the condition of Wolverine One? Over."

There was a pause before Perez replied, "KIA, sir—one's gone, sir; he's dead... sir."

Kane's mind went blank. Everything fell silent, like the three monkeys: his eyes, ears, and mouth closed off. Rounds were cracking off everywhere, creating a laser light show of multicolored screaming-hot tracers.

A second deadly DShK unleashed rounds up and down the line, zeroing in on Kane's position and forcing everyone into the dirt.

Gold Team, the two platoons set to intercept the package, held their fire.

Kane's mind spiraled. He struggled to halt his descent into the void.

***

Children's furniture is everywhere: little tables, chairs, and even pint-sized recliners. Pastel colors and cartoon character murals fill the space, accompanied by toys, books, and all things related to kids. This is the Pediatric Cancer Ward at Doctor's Hospital.

She has the face of an angel, my little Gabby. So little time, so very vulnerable, so very alone. Lifeless little hands cradle her head; her hair was lost months ago to radiation.

Chemotherapy has stolen what little joy she had. Helpless and holy in her innocence.

Dead, not even a year past her first birthday. The last time I saw her, I had to let her go—alone.

***

"Sir, they're probing our POS!" shouted Urban.

A second later, Hector Perez crashed down over the berm, sending dust, scree, and sand flying. He landed hard on his plastic kneepads and came face-to-face with his confused lieutenant commander.

Perez had crab-walked through 500 yards of no man's land to reach Kane. "I've been trying to reach you, boss; I tried several—"

Urban caught Perez's eye and shook his head. The Bear nodded his understanding. He said to Kane as calmly as he could, "My comms are a bit glitchy, boss. You good?"

Kane broke out of his malaise and snapped back into the battlefield reality, the real insanity. He handed the radio headset back to Urban and looked at Perez. "We lost Chen."

"Yes, we did, sir," replied Perez. "I came from his command. One of Blue's platoons executed a fire pivot, flanking the Tallies and driving them into retreat."

Kane nodded blankly. “That won’t last long.”

"No, sir, it won’t, so we need to move; the point of attack has shifted, and the package is on the move," said Perez.

"How do you know this, Perez?" asked Kane.

"Wallace, our CIA strap, spotted the package heading to the north side of Darbart."

"How?" Kane pressed.

"Wallace has some sort of satellite drone feed," Perez explained.

"One of those drones could be a CIA asset," Urban interjected.

"How is the package traveling?" Kane inquired.

Perez shook his head. "Right now, they're on foot, but that could change at any moment."

Kane turned to Donny Urban. "Who's controlling those drones? Do we have confirmed communications?"

Urban nodded. "There are two drones up there. One of them is ours, loitering at high altitude. I'm trying to determine who's controlling the other."

Kane rose to the level of the berm and scanned the village, where a significant small arms battle illuminated the night sky alongside the burning buildings. "Bring me Wallace, Chief Perez."

"Not possible, Kyle. Wallace is on the run, Sir."

"Gone?" shouted Kane. "What do you mean, gone?"

“He showed Chief Jackson an iPad monitor displaying a man Wallace identified as Kassem, moving north with a five-man security team. Wallace charted his path and then used a sat phone to relay the data."

"Wallace relayed data—to whom?"

"Don't know, Sir. He's on the run."

Kane thought for a moment. "We’ll move north to intercept any traffic leaving town. Moe, send two guys to watch the northeast in case he tries to slip away."

Urban and Perez exchanged glances, wondering what was going on with the commander.

Kane raised his night vision binoculars and scanned the area north of town. "We’ll converge on the roads leading north and intercept Kassem as he attempts to exfiltrate into the Hindu Kush."

"Master Chief Perez, you're with me. Epstein, take your platoon across this ridge to the point where you can support Blue Team’s exfil. Bear and I will each take an eight-man squad and cover each of two roads with a four-man fire team. There are really only two passable roads that can support a high-speed run for the Kush. Clear?"

"Roger that, sir," said Epstein. He stayed in his crouch and moved to the line, where he motioned with hand signals for his men to circle up on him. There was a short discussion before the entire platoon started their crouch-run across the ridge. This running skill, crucial in a firefight, was designed to enhance agility and speed while maintaining a crouch for long distances.

Kane looked at his friend. “Bear?”

“Yes, sir, boss. Good copy, five-by-five.”

Chapter 2

North of the Village of Darbart, 03:23

Kane and his men quickly moved away from the firefight on the southwest side of Darbart.

The command post was established on one of the four roads. Kane gathered his men for last-minute instructions.

“As you know, these four roads are the only routes away from the firefight in the village. Only two of them are passable by four-wheeled vehicles. Heading south would take the package through the firefight. Use your spike strips first, and LAWS as a last resort. Take down anyone attempting to leave town."

As the team began to disperse, Kane called out, "Watch for decoy vehicles. Maintain fire discipline; we need this package alive and able to talk."

Each of the four-man teams split up and headed to their designated road. It was a five-minute run to the farthest point. The other three teams radioed in that their roadblocks were set up, and it was game on.

Kane and his team positioned themselves on the high side of the road. One direction led to Darbart and the firefight; the other plunged into the endless rock, river, and scree that waited for anyone who dared to venture into the profoundly lawless dark of the Hindu Kush.

One man worked on the spike strips while two others positioned themselves on either side of the road with a SAW and an M72 LAW rocket. Linskey and Moss provided overwatch and covered the front and back doors.

The firefight seemed to be getting closer to Kane's position. He maintained contact with the other squads as they took down a pair of vehicles.

"Wolverine Actual, this is Perez. Two stops—no joy, over."

Urban responded to Perez, "May the odds be ever in your favor," just as a call came in on the VHF.

"Roger that, Thor. Go for, Wolverine Actual." Urban patched the comms through to Kane.

"No, sir," Kane said tensely. "I do know who this is—"

"Yes, sir, Deputy Director ... No, we do not have control of the package yet, over. No, Wallace is not with me. I don't know where he is, over."

"Yeah, he briefed me on the interrogation of the package. Over," said Kane, completely out of patience.

"Dick." Kane handed the handset back to Urban. "A real jerk who thinks we should be babysitting his fake operator."

"If he's an operator," Urban replied, "I'm Michael Jordan."

"I've seen you play; you're good, but nobody's MJ."

"My point exactly, sir."

Kane's night vision goggles flared as headlights approached the hill from Darbart. He raised his desert camo Mk12.

"Who was that, sir?" Urban asked.

"He said his name was Cox, and he's looking for Sir William Wallace," Kane replied. "Did you say his code name was Thor?"

Donny Urban shook his head. "Yeah, the idiot's hitchhiking on our Marvel Comics theme."

"I'll bet he's the jerk who sent in that drone ahead of the mission," Kane said.

"So why is he asking us where his boy Wallace is?" asked Urban.

At that moment, two white Toyota Hilux pickups—the favored vehicle of terrorists everywhere—rolled over the crest of a hill, sixty yards away.

The fast-moving vehicles were retrofitted with mounted Soviet PKS machine guns. They reached the ambush and hit the spike strips dead center. The front tires of the first Hilux blew out completely, causing it to spin hard toward the downhill roadside ditch. The second vehicle lost both left-side tires, crashing into the uphill berm along the opposite edge of the road. The two Taliban militiamen seated in the truck beds were thrown through the air, along with several others who were ejected through the windshield.

The gunfight lasted only a few seconds. The machine gunners in the back of each truck were both taken out. Two men, foreign fighters, jumped from the downhill truck but were dropped before they could reach cover.

A couple of quick taps finished it. Two more men emerged, and Kane targeted the one nearest to him. The second leveled his AK-47 at Kane and fired, sending rounds that sprayed the berm behind him. Kane dropped him with a center mass shot. A red spray erupted from the entry, and the back of the man was blown out in a massive exit wound. One of the remaining men threw down his AK and raised his hands. Spider and Beyer flex-cuffed him and led him away.

"Secure the technicals!" shouted Kane. He rolled over the nearest man and held up his cell phone, displaying an ID shot of Kassem. "Shit, it's not him."

"Clear!" shouted the others who were checking the cab of the truck in the ditch.

“Clear. The truck’s empty.” All guns were trained on the Hilux that had slammed into the opposite side.

"There's a body inside!" shouted CPO Troy Walker. He moved to the side of the truck and pulled open the door and found a man trying to hide under the dash. The man's head and face were covered by a long white Pashtun headscarf. Walker attempted to grab hold of him, but the tall, thin, gawky figure sprang up and, with surprising speed, broke free from Walker's grip like a Big Ten fullback.

The man sprinted through the chaos of the scene. Everyone, caught off guard by his quickness, failed to shoot him before he disappeared into the darkness. Unfortunately for the fleet-footed fugitive, the darkness concealed a set of spike strips. The scarf-covered man, using all his awkward, levered-up power, executed a downstroke and stomped down on a spike.

Everyone stopped and watched in amazement as Professor Mudgizzen, a.k.a. Mullah Atta Kassem, the financial genius of the Taliban, suffered a catastrophic blowout and cartwheeled across the Afghan moonscape in an ungraceful manner.

Kassem ended up in a heap, adrenaline pumping, arms and legs flailing, with his scarf wrapped around his head like a mummy. He screamed in agony as Chief Beyer cuffed him.

"Did you see that?" Urban asked anyone within earshot.

"I did," Beyer replied. “Even the Russian judge would have given him a 10.”

"I can't believe no one shot him," Perez said. “He looked so pathetic that I couldn’t bring myself to do it."

Perez stood Kassem up to make a positive ID.

"It's him, Boss, and he's got a serious hole in his foot." Perez examined the wound. "I see metatarsals, Boss."

Urban knelt next to the man. "Oh, that's gotta hurt."

Walker, cross-trained as a corpsman, began packing the large hole and bandaging the through-and-through wound in Kassem's foot. Perez pulled up a picture from Kassem's days as a professor at LSE.

"He's had quite the makeover at Casa de Tali, Boss, but I'll wager Urban's next month's salary it's him."

"Donny, are you good with that?" asked Kane.

"Sure. I’ll give him a shot of vancomycin.”

"Mullah Kassem?" Kane asked. The man’s eyes widened with fear.

“We need to get this guy under the lights as quickly as possible. Mullah Atta Kassem, you are now in the custody of the U.S. military."

Kane activated his throat mic and issued the mission success call sign: "Tippecanoe." “Tippecanoe."

Three other squads confirmed Kane's call. "Be prepared to move to rally point Razor for extraction," Kane instructed.

Urban handed Kane the VHF handset. "Tippecanoe, I repeat, Tippecanoe." Kane tossed the handset back.

"Donny, get command on the line; they need to know we have the package in custody."

"Send confirmation, Wolverine Actual?" Urban asked. "That's coming from FBI Deputy Director Karen LaVette."

Kane rolled his eyes. "What the hell is the FBI doing in on this?" He approached the prisoner.

Perez had pulled a large black hood from his kit and placed it over Kassem's head, securing him for transport.

Kane looked at Kassem and said, "Cuff him in front. Mudgizzen's squirting days are over. And those black hoods —they're just too Dark Ages, Master Chief."

"Experts say taking away one of your captive's senses, like vision, generates fear and feelings of impending doom. Breaking a prisoner down is fair game, boss."

"I understand, Master Chief; now shine your light on Mudgizzen's face." Kane moved to lift the hood from Kassem's head when the unmistakable snap of a large-caliber round whizzed just past his ear. The report echoed through the darkness. The massive round grazed Kane and seared a line across the inside of his forearm and simultaneously ripped the hood from his grip. Kassem screamed and fell back.

Kane's immediate reaction was to dive on top of the package and cover him with his body. His men dropped into shooting positions and scanned the angles.

"Anyone spot that muzzle flash, anyone?" shouted Kane, reaching for his throat mic. "Overwatch, this is Actual. Did you see anything?"

"Sir, I did; big flash," replied Linskey.

Master Chief Ludlow, with his distinctive southern drawl, said, "That was no AK-47, sir."

"Boss, this is Moss. The round was fired from inside our perimeter. It came from the direction of the village. Big muzzle flash, 12.7 or bigger."

Eight men watched and waited under the moonless night, made even darker in the lee of the mountain. It was nearly impossible to spot a concealed shooter.

Kane realized Kassem was still alive as he pulled him upright. His forehead had a similar mark. "Imagine the odds of that."

Several operators gathered around Kassem to assess his condition.

“Let’s go; Blue Team is holding the line," said Perez as he checked the vehicle for SSI.

Kane leaned in. "Look closely; it could be something as small as a memory stick."

"Pee Wee, you're on point. Max, you and your SAW will be the tail gunners. Farrell, you and Doc assist Master Chief Perez with SSI."

"It's all right, Boss, I've got this," Perez replied.

"Farrell, take the two prisoners and ensure none of their own people take them out. Doc, pack up your 240 and prepare to escort the prisoner."

"Tail gunners, stay frosty; we're going to become real popular, real quick. In fact, Lawrence, you keep Max company as the tail gunner. Anyone with LAWs, pass them to Max and Lawrence," Perez shouted. "Light and sound discipline!"

"I found a laptop in a knapsack under the front seat," Perez added, "along with a ton of greenbacks and euros, sir."

"Rack it, pack it, and stack it, Master Chief,” said Kane. “Widows and orphans fund. Quinn, take us out. LZ Zulu."

Kane reached for his throat mic and said, "Overwatch, this is Wolverine Actual. I'm calling Tippecanoe, heading to LZ Zulu!" The sound of an intense gunfight filled his ear when Wolverine Three came on the line.

"Roger that, Wolverine Actual. We're in a mad gunfight, sir. Seems like more than three hundred tangos in this freakin' village."

"Wolverine Three, be aware, danger close. I repeat, danger close—C-130 Gunship inbound. Three, direct fire as necessary."

"Good copy, Actual. Nothing like a dance with the Dragon."

"Blue Team, this is Wolverine Actual. Keep up that rate of fire; keep their heads down until we exfil across the ridge and up the mountain."

Blue Team held the line for another eight minutes, which seemed like eighty. The firefight was building when Wolverine Three called down a pair of Hellfire rockets to cover Blue Team's withdrawal from their position on the southeast side of Darbart.

***

Gold Team was halfway to LZ Zulu when Blue Team exfiltrated. Some Taliban fighters pursued Blue Team up the mountain as soon after the Hellfire effect subsided.

The village militia moved quickly; they knew the terrain like the back of their hands and had superior conditioning, having lived at this altitude and navigated the mountains all their lives.

The militia closed to within two hundred yards when the AC-130 Specter gunship descended through the moonless night sky and prepared for a gun run to saturate the target area. A pair of Vulcan M61 20mm cannons and a single Bofors L60 40mm cannon fired alongside the 105mm howitzer. The combined firepower of the weapons platform, enhanced by the FLIR radar computer targeting accuracy, delivered their barrage with devastating effect. The pursuit ended, and Blue Team reached the high country and the extraction point, LZ Zulu.

SOAR Night Stalkers, the best helicopter pilots on earth, roared in through the night and hovered on station until Donny Urban called them in. They descended onto LZ Zulu, where prisoners were loaded up. The sixty-three men, to a man, nodded as they walked past Chen's body.

Kane looked down the mountain, not more than a few hundred yards below LZ Zulu, and watched the explosions and listened to the overzealous fighters as they went up slope into the thermal imaging array of the AC-130 gunship. They were painted, plastered, and posthumously celebrated in tales and songs by the same people who had sent them into the flames of the dragon.

Perez and Kane lifted Lt. Chen's body onto the deck of the last bird. Chen had always made it a point to be the last man on board, and Perez and Kane were almost always there with him.

Kane and Perez took seats across from each other. The dozen men on that bird, every SEAL on Green Team, felt the weight of grief as they stared down at the dark green body bag, at the man all of them called brother.

Kane reflected on the good times he had shared with the teammate everyone called Charlie—Charlie Chen. The distorted lump before them, his body having taken a direct hit from an RPG-7, was not the Lt. Chen they knew. The guy who made BUD/S seem easy, who pulled half a dozen potential ring-outs back from the edge, and who helped them earn their tridents. He was the coach, the caretaker, and the coolest guy to ever carry the DEVGRU's current.

The powerful rotors lifted the helicopters high over the Pech River Valley, far enough to evade most ground fire. Still, the occasional round that struck the airframe had everyone praying.

Kane glanced over at Chief Durrell Moss and signaled to Master Chief Perez to get Moss a pair of headphones.

"Durrell, did you see the sniper?"

"Yes, sir," replied Chief Moss. "I saw a big muzzle flash north of your position. The report was unusual," he continued. "I would have returned fire, but I had no positive ID."

Kane nodded and pointed to Master Chief Ludlow, while Moss passed the headset among several operators.

"No one saw Wallace, the CIA spook?" Kane asked. The general response from those who could hear him was negative.

"I saw him," Ludlow replied. "He hightailed it out of here before the Tallies launched their first RPG. Did he make the exfil?"

Perez shook his head and looked at Kane, who also shook his head.

"He was not at LZ Razor," Lt. Epstein said.

Kane turned to Lt. Kalish, the co-pilot responsible for headcount and overall helicopter payload capacity. "I contacted the other five birds, and William Wallace is not aboard. Oddly enough, sir, he is not listed on our headcount manifest."

"Roger that, Captain."

"What about that sniper shot? Any idea what kind of round could do this?" Kane asked, holding up his forearm.

"That's a nice graze, and it's not a Dragunov SVR; it's not large enough to leave a burn like that, sir," said Ludlow.

Perez suggested, "Maybe an M200 .408?"

"A fifteen-grand sniper rifle in the middle of the Korengal, Master Chief?" Ludlow replied. "You'd be more likely to find a Ferrari pulling a goat cart down Main Street, Kandahar. If it had been just an inch either way, you or Kassem would be one body part short."

Chapter 3

FOB Chapman, Khost, Afghanistan, 05:06

A staggered formation of SOAR Blackhawks roared in over the mountaintops, flanked by their Air Cav Apache escorts. They thundered down onto the runway with impressive skill.

"It's like a beehive got kicked over when we arrive," said Ludlow, staring out the open door. "Chocks down, and the trauma boys roll in."

Two ambulances rolled onto the tarmac and pulled up to the helicopters. The six injured men from Blue Team were transported to the Combat Support Hospital. In contrast, Lieutenant Chen's body was removed from one of the Blackhawks and loaded into a Humvee.

“That's how Chen would have wanted to go out—in a Humvee, not in one of those meat wagons,” said Kane as he climbed out of the Blackhawk and thanked the crew. His heart was heavy, and his temper was at a flashpoint as he made his way to the TOC.

Out of the corner of his eye, he caught sight of the prisoner exchange. Mullah Atta Kassem, with his black hood, was handed off to a group of mercenaries who seemed to appear out of nowhere.

“Who the hell are those guys, a couple of Blackwater types taking custody of our HVT?” Krause said. “I guess that's just our new world protocol.”

***

The mood was somber as the men filed in for the debriefing. There were no outbursts or chairs being thrown around the room. SEALs, as a group, were professionals who worked hard to maintain their composure until the commanding officer arrived.

They waited for their CO, who was the last to enter. He removed his chest rack and dropped the forty-five pounds of gear onto one of the Aeroflot recliners in the front row.

"First off, men, I want to say the mission was for the most part a success."

Grumbling from the back row was quickly silenced by Master Chief Perez.

"Quiet down while the lieutenant commander is speaking."

Kane scanned the room and began again. "Lieutenant Chen's death is a terrible loss for us all." His eyes reddened, and his voice reflected the pain. "We will find out what happened out there; I promise you that."

"We need to understand what that spook was doing out there and who was running his operation," said Chief Jung. "Sir."

"That first salvo of RPGs started just before our assault, Lieutenant Commander."

Petty Officer Mack Tilford reported. "An RPG hit right on Chen's position. Art Gaus was hit too."

Petty Officer Kenny Moss, the most outspoken member of the team, could no longer hold back. He interrupted the CO's next words, exclaiming, "We were set up by that CIA shithead!"

"Moss, stow that until the CO tells you to speak freely," Perez replied, his dark eyes narrowing and the veins in his twenty-two-inch neck bulging to emphasize his point.

Moss hung his head and said loudly enough for everyone to hear, "My apologies, sir. Charlie, I mean Lt. Chen, was a great leader—a friend. Whatever it was, Charlie was the best operator I've ever known—sir."

"No apology needed, sailor; my heart is full. I just know that whatever we do, we need to be cautious. We can't rush in blindly. We'll lose our standing in this fight, and anyone involved could find cover in the bureaucratic mess over at CENTCOM—and I refuse to let that happen. Now, speak freely, but remember, we keep this between ourselves until I file a formal inquiry."

Kane acted as a referee, toning down the revenge rhetoric several times. He concluded the debrief and dismissed the men.

On his way to his plywood condo, a sentry stopped him with a message to return to the TOC.

Higgs, an Army corporal monitoring radio traffic at the Comms Center, approached Kane. "Sir, we have an emergency PRC signal coming from a unit about eight miles south of Darbart," he said.

Kane sent a specialist out the door to locate Master Chief Perez somewhere on base. Five minutes later, Perez arrived, jogging over between desks to Kane and Higgs in the Comms Center.

"Master Chief, is that little puke calling us for a ride?"

Perez didn't hesitate. "Wallace, the CIA spook, went out on his own, and now he wants us to mount a rescue—sir."

The corporal looked uncertain. "Should I scramble SOAR?"

Kane shook his head. "No, Corporal Higgs, that'll draw too much attention. I'll follow up on the situation myself."

Kane contacted the senior Air Cav officer on base. He was in a poker game and agreed to meet Kane. He caught up to Lt. Colonel Renzi outside of the TOC.

"Lieutenant Colonel, I was hoping to keep this off JSOC's radar and the CIA's, for that matter. It'll just spiral into a huge shitstorm."

"So what you're asking is," said Renzi "can we pick up this asshole with the least amount of fallout?" He paused for a moment. "If he's not being used as bait, we can do it. I'll dispatch a single Blackhawk with an Apache escort. They can scan the area using FLIR, and if we encounter an ambush, they'll make the call. Chocks up in thirty."

The two men shook hands. "I owe you one, Lieutenant Colonel." Kane then walked back into the TOC, where the decision was made to pick up Wallace. The dawn light made the mission infinitely more dangerous.

"Every time one of these CIA assets is assigned to a mission, something goes wrong," said Moe Epstein as he took a seat next to Kane in the TOC.

Chapter 4

Tactical Operations Center 04:50

Kane sat down with his second cup of wickedly strong Ethiopian coffee, determined to stay awake until the golden-haired child from the CIA returned to Chapman.

"I didn't like the deal then, and I like it even less now, giving Wallace first crack at Kassem. It smells like politics," Kane said to his new second-in-command, Lt. Morris Epstein. "Every minute that passes, Kassem regains his composure and rehearses his story."

Kane slammed his Steelers mug down on the battleship-grey desk. The noise was enough to draw attention but not enough to provoke a reaction. He stood up and pushed his chair in with a bang. "These CIA characters cut deals with the enemy to get intel. They cut deals, and the American military pays the price. We're told to stand down and the enemy gets a pass, and we have to give it to them. The bad guys operate with CIA immunity, and we're forced to take a back seat to these shitbags."

The death of my good friend, one of the best Seals I've ever known, and I'm carrying the weight. I want some payback."

The whole situation started to gnaw at Kane, really eating away inside him. The walls of military discipline, training, and procedure, drilled into his DNA, were cracking. He felt tempted to exercise some demons with a bit of enhanced interrogation but quickly realized it was a bad idea.

"After all, it was his fucking people who killed Chen, and if there was a setup, I want to know about it."

***

Mulla Atta Kassem was already at the Intake & Interrogation Center on the opposite side of Chapman. The airbase at Khost was a sizable installation built by the Russians in the 1980s and expanded in the following decade. The current US expansion included the military base known as Forward Operating Base Chapman.

Chapman was one of the most secure and secretive bases in the theater, where special forces and intelligence units from the CIA and several other agencies operated in unison to target high-value targets (HVTs) and other vital objectives.

Kane realized he needed a vehicle to reach the flight line and retrieve the strap. He walked out onto the staging area beside the airfield. It was sunrise, and soon the sun would rise over the Afghan mountains to the east.

Kane called over to a soldier on duty. "Specialist, can you call me a Humvee?"

Specialist Marco Zeldin, who had been in-country for less than six weeks, attempted to reach one of the roving Humvees but unfortunately received no response.

"God damn it," Kane said. "I've got places to be." The young man grew nervous, and Kane felt a pang of sympathy. He looked down at the ground, took a deep breath, and tried to rein in his edgy demeanor.

"Listen, troop, I'm feeling pretty frazzled right now. It's hard to keep everything together."

The young freckle-faced kid looked at Kane. "It's okay, sir. I heard some chatter about your mission."

Kane smiled at the kid and asked, "You pulling a long shift?"

"Yes, sir, eight to eight. We're all on Bravo alert status, sir."

Kane nodded and walked inside. A few minutes later, he returned with a large Styrofoam cup of steaming hot coffee, handing it to Specialist Zeldin.

"Be careful, kid; that stuff will put hair on your chest."

The young man laughed. "Too late, sir. I've been drinking your special ops coffee for a couple of months now."

Zeldin took the cup and smiled. "Thanks."

He then received an RF message and relayed it to Kane. "Sir, we have choppers on approach."

Kane nodded and said, "Scratch that, Humvee Specialist; I'll hot-foot it over to the helipad."

Lieutenant Commander Kane sprinted toward the helipad, stopping half a mile later as some of his anger dissipated. He reached the cautionary yellow line that surrounded a row of twenty 40-by-40-foot crosses painted bright white on the tarmac.

The SOAR Blackhawk descended in front of Kane, while the Apache positioned itself on the other end next to the ready room shed, preparing for QRF duty.

Wallace jumped off the helicopter and attempted to brush past Kane, only to find himself on the ground after a quick straight punch to the chest and a leg sweep.

Looking up from the deck, Wallace saw Kane standing over him. The crew completed their post-flight check and walked past Wallace without a glance.

"Where the hell did you go, asshole?" shouted Kane.

"I was confronted by a roving band of Taliban," he said, choking. "I ha—ha—had to double-time it—into the desert." Wallace glared up at Kane with false bravado.

"I lost a man in Darbart, and six other operators were wounded, fucking Wallace," yelled Kane. "Lieutenant Chen—my friend—a great fucking soldier—is dead! All because of your chickenshit CIA cloak-and-dagger crap. Do you understand me, A-g-e-n-t Wallace?"

Wallace rolled around, trying to get to his feet, but Kane kept him on the deck with a stiff arm.

"Damn it, man—it was no picnic for me," Wallace said, fumbling with his words. "I got lost out there trying to evade those idiots."

"What are you saying, Wallace? It was your fucking drone over Darbart and your stumbling around that tipped off the Tallies. They killed Chen—goddamn you," Kane shouted. "They killed my friend!"

Wallace shook his head. "I didn't know. I don't think so, but—"

"You better start figuring it out, you fucking cockroach. Shit like you pulled out there might not get you in trouble with the CIA, but if my boys catch a whiff of double-dealing in Lieutenant Chen's death, you'll fucking vanish," Kane warned. "Believe it: a little trip into the desert and you'll be just another star on the Langley wall, maybe."

"Is that a threat, Lieutenant Commander?"

"The stakes are life and death out here. If you get caught cheating, death will be your punishment. I'm on the verge of doing it myself. Are we clear, CIA case officer—asshole?"

"Crystal," Wallace replied.

Kane reached down and pulled Wallace up by his collar. Wallace winced and tried to shake off Kane, not wanting to appear too much like a coward.

"I think I cracked a vertebra. I fell twenty feet from a plateau," Wallace said.

Kane leveled his gaze. "You want me to feel sorry for you?"

"That's real funny," Wallace retorted.

"It's not funny, or anything like it. You're going to tell me what really happened out there, or I'll put you down like the dog you are," Kane said.

Wallace sized up the man who had just threatened his life and considered a sucker punch. He weighed the likelihood of failure against the potential bodily harm Kane could inflict.

Kane marched William Wallace over to the I&I Center. The two men standing guard at the front double doors were mercenaries. Kane had never seen them before, but he noticed that Wallace recognized them and grew nervous.

"Intake and Interrogation Center," Kane said. "That's a handy euphemism for a black site on a US base."

Wallace looked at him with furrowed brows. "This is not a black site; no torture is done here, none. Technically, this building is not part of the base. It's just outside the property line."

"That's convenient, Wallace. Did you come up with that?"

The two mercenaries stopped Kane and Wallace at the double doors. Wallace pulled out his CIA ID. One of them reached for it and scanned it into a handheld reader while the other reached for one of the doors. Kane looked them up and down.

"Hired guns watching Kassem?" Kane asked as they entered the site. "It's starting to make sense."

"You CIA pricks don't want anything blowing back on you."

Kane glanced around; his first impression was that he had walked into a grade-B office building, complete with rows of cubicles, desks, credenzas, and even a few plastic plants. The one giveaway was the dozens of recessed cameras covering every possible angle in the space.

Wallace led the way to what appeared to be a janitor's closet. He opened a light switch faceplate, revealing a numerical touchpad. Wallace entered a code, and they stepped into another room filled with outdated radar and communications equipment. It was yet another facade meant to deceive anyone inspecting the building.

"Are you aware that someone took a shot at Kassem while he was in our custody?"

"No, absolutely not. There was a lot of shooting going on; it could have been a stray."

"Maybe, but the angle was all wrong," Kane said. "Besides, I have it on good authority that it wasn't an AK or a PPK or any other 7.62 round."

Kane noticed a strange look on Wallace's face.

He really doesn't know.

They cleared another cleverly disguised security door and entered a series of high-security cells and interrogation rooms all connected to a central control panel.

"This place is impressive, Kane," said Wallace. "It features a video stage. We can dose the package with LSD-25, scopolamine, or heavy barbs, and then put them in an environment designed to trigger a psychotic break. They can be made to believe they are anywhere, in virtually any situation, and we can extract all manner of intel… but I digress."

Wallace took a seat at the control panel, which was equipped with monitors and audio-video recorders covering every room.

Kane glanced at the monitors, which displayed empty rooms except for one. Inside room six sat a hooded man, flex cuffed to a steel table. He was shaking and babbling in Farsi and broken English.

"Get that goddamn hood off."

"Why?"

"We don't need to torture him, Wallace; he'll give it up."

"If you're not up for this, Kane, I can handle it—"

"Say that again, cockroach, and I'll knock your teeth out."

Wallace looked as nervous as a long-tailed cat in a room full of rockers.

"Let's just brace him hard," said Kane. "Good cop, bad cop. You know what I mean."

"No," Wallace replied. "Let me try a couple of techniques. Things have changed a lot in the interrogation biz."

"His bio shows he's kind of timid," Kane pointed out.

"Good cop, bad cop might shut him down. Let me—" Wallace started, but Kane cut him off.

"I'll give you three minutes," Kane said, "and that's only because I was ordered to. That's the only reason you're getting first crack at Kassem. Any funny business, any drugs, and I'll throw you in one of these cells, capisce?"

Wallace said nothing, simply passing by Kane and entering Room 6. Kane took Wallace's seat in the control suite.

Wallace sat in front of Kassem. The Taliban's financial genius had turned pale and began to tremble. Before Wallace could speak, he reached into his pocket and produced a cell phone. He fiddled with it, and the next thing Kane saw was a blinding light that filled the entire room. A concussion grenade followed, knocking Kane to the floor.

The observation suite and all the interrogation rooms went dark. Kane, on the floor, struggled to regain control of his hyper-excited senses. He got to his knees and tried to stand, but a blow from behind to the back of his head sent him into darkness.

***

Boots on the floor—dozens of them—were the first thing Kane heard as he returned to a blurry consciousness. He struggled to open his eyes; the blow had stunned his occipital nerves, and the flashbang had overwhelmed him.

Ten Rangers had pushed into the room in two groups, clearing every corner. The emergency lights flickered on, and Kane watched the smoke and dust waver in the dull beams of the auxiliary lights.

Another minute passed before a soldier helped Kane onto a chair. He fought to stand. One of the Quick Reaction Force Rangers brought him an ice pack, broke the chemical pouch inside, and pressed it against his neck. The cold slowly revived him.

"Room 6, terrorist, high value!" Kane shouted, his voice straining to be heard outside. His hearing was as compromised as his vision. He coughed and shook, desperate to make himself understood.

A shout came from Room 6, and Rangers rushed past Kane into the back rooms.

The sergeant leading the QRF called, "All clear!" He stopped in front of Kane and attempted to speak to him. Kane strained to hear, but the words were lost on him. Eventually, he got up and pushed past the sergeant into interrogation room 6.

"Fuck me," he said, unaware of how loud he was. Across the table, still handcuffed to the steel surface, sat Kassem. His arms stretched as far as they could go, and his head tilted back, exposing his throat, which had been cut ear to ear.

Kane pounded the table hard enough to make it bounce, causing the old man's tongue to slip out of one side of his mouth. Kassem's completely dilated brown eyes reflected the terror of his final moments.

"Shut down the base," Kane said, controlling his volume as he rushed to the nearest MP with a radio.

Before Kane could speak, the radio crackled to life. "Sgt. Becker, this is Colonel Cowell. Transport Lieutenant Commander Kane to my office ASAP, over."

Kane replied into the radio handset, "Roger that, sir."

One of the Rangers, assigned by Sgt. Becker, was waiting to attend to Kane's injuries.

A medic stopped Kane as he headed for the door and shouted, "Before you go, let me slap a couple of butterflies on that gash."

Kane walked out of the I&I Center, his head bandaged, marching across the flight line like the Spirit of '76. He felt like he'd been called down to the principal's office.

Moe Epstein exited the TOC and stopped Kane as he was en route to the base commander's offices.

"Kyle, what the hell happened to you?" he asked, examining Kane's head closely.

"I got jumped in the I&I center. The HVT gets a Colombian necktie, and that

Shitheal Wallace is in the wind—again."

"The hell with that; I'll gather the men, and we can scour the base."

"He's a spook, Mo. He's all about not being found. Someone, somehow, got to him, then to Kassem, and cut his throat. They silenced him, big time. Hell, Wallace could be dead too."

"What about the SSI, the laptop?"

"Operative word: 'was,' as in there *was* a laptop. If they went to the trouble of killing Kassem, they certainly wouldn't leave the SSI for us to decrypt."

"Roger that. Are you heading to sickbay, Kyle?"

"No, I'm going to the head shed to get a new asshole ripped."

"Yeah, for some reason, boss, one's just never enough for those assholes."

Chapter 5

FOB Chapman, Senior Staff Offices, 07:30

Smoke poured from the crack at the bottom of the CO's door. Kane mused to himself about the possibility that everyone inside Colonel Joseph Cowell's office was on fire.

The U.S. Army Commander of FOB Chapman was engaged in some very heated discussions on the other side of the door.

Cowell and the senior CIA officer on base, Meredith Betts, were bemoaning the evening's events to a figure on a large flatscreen. The talking head on the secure satellite feed was Army Lieutenant Colonel Archie McLeish from Army CID in Quantico.

Kane overheard the team discussing HUMINT, HVTs, and geospatial intel, a term he had heard only once or twice before. They talked about the loss of the highest-ranking Taliban target since Hassan Akhund. All that made sense to Kane, but geospatial intel did not.

Kane fought the urge to sleep. His higher faculties were frayed by the concussion and sleep deprivation he was experiencing. The last time he'd felt this bad, he was sitting in two feet of very cold water in the dark of night just off the beach. It was hell week, and he and his buddies were halfway through. Today, it was compounded by a ragged Ethiopian dark roast jag; he preferred it to caffeine pills. Add it all up, and Kane was in a downright dark mood.

He focused on the anteroom wall and its Waterloo print, depicting a four-squares fighting formation.

How insanely symmetrical war was back then and how insanely asymmetrical it has become. I wonder if a CIA spook setting me up is considered asymmetrical.

Thoughts of his wife, Maria, and their two-year-old daughter, Gabriella, played in his mind, reminding him that he had lost Gabriella to a true asymmetrical terrorist—cancer—six months ago to the day.

The same painful images of her lying on the hospital bed, intubated, with tubes and wires crisscrossing her fragile little body, tortured him.

Kane felt his emotions overwhelming him and quickly tried to stifle them. He slammed his fist down on the empty desk as he tried to change the vector of his anger.

The door opened immediately after the thump, revealing Meredith Betts, a scowling woman with a hollow look, dressed in old-school mommy jeans and a Georgetown Law T-shirt. She was a chain-smoker with a bad haircut, embodying every bit of a DC bureaucrat queen—a lifetime card-carrying member of the DC Swamp.

She was there to ensure everything went according to plan. A wave of cigar smoke enveloped her, as if she were on stage at a Kiss concert. She gave Kane a long, hard once-over.

***

Colonel Joseph "Smokin' Joe" Cowell sat behind a sprawling mahogany desk covered in military memorabilia. In a previous life, he was a linebacker for the Black Knights of the Hudson, and as a lieutenant colonel, he commanded Fort William D. Davis in Panama before its closure. Fort Davis was known in the special operations community for two things: intense balls-to-the-wall jungle training and world-class cigars, both of which became synonymous with Smokin' Joe.

"At ease, Lieutenant Commander Kane," Cowell said, his strong West Texas twang evident. "Please come in and tell us your side of what happened."

Cowell's request to share "your side of the story" struck Kane as amusing. He approached the desk, with Betts taking a seat to his right. Captain Walter Marcus, the ranking naval officer and JSOC liaison for Chapman, sat to his left.

"Son, can you recount for us exactly what took place over the last two days?" Cowell asked.

"Sir, is this a formal investigation?" Kane inquired.

Before Cowell could respond, a voice on the speakerphone interrupted, "Lieutenant Commander Kane, this is Rear Admiral Tommy Griggs, JSOC Command."

"Sir," Kane replied, snapping to attention.

"At ease, Lieutenant Commander," said Griggs. "This is not a formal investigation; Colonel Cowell and Ms. Meredith are trying to gather as many facts as possible."

Sounds familiar: Comey and McCabe, the top officials at the FBI, lied directly to the president and then set up General Flynn, telling him it was an informal fact-finding meeting. McCabe met with the president and claimed he didn't need a lawyer.

"We're just trying to piece together the situation," Meredith added. "There's no need for JAG to get involved."

Kane listened as Griggs and Cowell exchanged remarks. While Meredith spoke very little, she made it clear that the CIA had no connection to the loss of the high-value target (HVT) and the missing intel. What was even more telling was that she hadn't mentioned Wallace once.

"But you're trying to determine what led to the loss of an extremely high-value intel source, murdered by what appears to be a rogue CIA agent who is now on the run," Kane pointed out.

The CIA base director cleared her throat loudly and said, "Admiral, we don't know for sure if Case Officer Wallace has gone rogue or if he is Kassem's assassin. Furthermore, I would like to—"

Before Betts could finish her sentence, Admiral Griggs cut her off. "Ms. Betts, take it from an old sailor: when you're in rough seas, don't hoist sail—not just yet."

Betts turned away, said nothing, and lit another long, skinny cigarette.

"Now, Lieutenant Commander Kane, please proceed with your unofficial report on what took place during the last two days. Include anything that you think brings clarity to this situation."

Kane looked at Meredith, then Cowell. "Sir, our mission, as I'm sure you know, came directly from Admiral Corbett's office, via JSOC Command," said Kane.

"Yeah, ah—that's being reviewed. There's some question as to the validity of the orders.

It seems there was some sort of problem with verification," said Admiral Griggs. "We're examining every aspect of these missing orders."

"Sir, did you say missing orders? There's some question about the orders themselves?"

"Yes, Lieutenant Commander, everything is on the table. Everything is being reviewed. Now please continue."

Kane detailed the events of the last two days hour by hour. No one interrupted him. As soon as he finished, the admiral concluded the meeting by thanking Kane for his candor and his exemplary career as a member of SEAL Team Six, DEVGRU.

Kane was dismissed. He nodded to the other three and backed out of the room. His first thought as he left the smokehouse was that he'd just been stiff-armed by his own command, and every thought thereafter was about Admiral Griggs' remarks, thanking him for his career at DEVGRU, which was at best irregular and, at worst, a cast-off into the rough seas the night watch at JSOC had just warned the CIA about. For Kane it was uncharted waters.

Every step was a struggle until he reached his billet. He pulled the flimsy door open and sat down on his bunk. He cleared his Mk 12 assault rifle. He fully planned to clean and oil the Mk12 and his Sig P227 after he set his boot piece, a . 45 ACP Derringer, onto the plywood desk.

"A good soldier never sleeps without cleaning his weapons," he said aloud. "A soldier who waits until the next day is failing at his duty." He struggled to draw energy from anywhere.

His Sig Sauer P227 broke down easily. He cleaned everything with a pre-oiled rag. He tossed it onto the desk, where it landed on the keyboard of the old IBM PS/2 desktop. The screen lit up, which surprised Kane.

"Security breach," he joked. "I'm sure I shut that damn thing down before I left for the op."

He dragged his tired body off his rack and sat in the creaky old swivel chair. Sleep deprivation was taking its toll, but something just didn't feel right. He typed a passcode into the secure email server, the same server that almost everyone with a rank of lieutenant and above had access to.

It took a few minutes; he nodded off twice, and finally his encrypted emails came up. He scrolled through them for the last two weeks and found nothing.

"It was a JSOC-directed email. What the hell happened to it?" said Kane as he stared at the wall of his quarters. It wasn't long before he fell back onto his bunk and started to think about the twenty-four-hour period before they were wheels-up: *I was sitting right here, on my bunk. It was zero two hundred hours, and the stack of after-action reports and assessments on my desk was staring me in the face.*

An old IBM desktop sat next to the pile on a two-by-four-framed plywood desk, which was covered with graffiti. The more I focused on it the more I saw in it. The countless initials, messages to loved ones and friends, not-so-kind words for other officers, and icons—lots of icons. There was iambic pentameter and some very blue haiku. I started to see a sort of history left in the carvings, the graffiti, and some surprisingly talented drawings. The soldiers and sailors, marines and contractors, and even a few spies, who could very well have set up a dead drop or coded message to some other asset. Whoever they were, they had inadvertently created a timeline, a totem from one generation of the committed to the next, marking their passage through the war on terror on that desktop, memorialized in plywood wood around the beginning of the twenty-first century.

I remember thinking about starting up my navy-issued Toughbook, but that impossible wireless security is such a pain in the ass. I just used the old PC, however archaic it was.

And yes, I had to deal with the last vestige of the ancient LAN system, possibly installed by the Zoroastrians or Alexander on his way back to Macedonia. It was still working. All the good tech left Camp Chapman when JSOC moved over to FOB Salerno. All I had to work with was that shitty dinosaur of a computer.

The piles of backed-up paperwork appeared larger every time he looked at them. I got started, and halfway through, thoughts about home crept into my mind. It happened like that. It always started when I was sitting alone in my little pressboard cubbyhole.

I tried not to worry about life back home; it was the kind of stuff that could get me killed. My soon-to-be ex-wife and my oversized colonial with its oversized mortgage were a burden, and my wife, Maria, had become angry and hostile toward me. I became persona non grata ever since I DD'd out on this deployment.

Outrageous hospital bills for experimental cancer treatment and travel expenses to and from the Mayo Clinic, NIH, and Johns Hopkins were huge problems. I had to find novel ways to distract myself from these thoughts. My mind was trained to subdue pain, both physical and psychological, to compartmentalize it and lock it away until it was time to use it.

I could handle physical pain; I'd been shot, stabbed, and blown up more times than I could remember, but I could always count on one particular memory popping up. It was early in my career, during a Southeast Asian training exercise. We were blowing off steam in a Bangkok fight bar with our new Thai partners.

Too many shots of tequila was my excuse when I climbed into the ring with the club champion. Standing in the center of the ring, bare-chested and ready to brawl, I felt both loose and tight at the same time.

It just seemed like the right thing to do—the frogman thing to do.

My opponent was Saechai, the house champion for as long as anyone could remember. I should have Googled him.

When the fight started, I took it to him like a Seal would. The combination of moves from various disciplines created a kind of unpredictable style. Seal hand-to-hand combat confused Saechai, and I caught the Thai fighter flat-footed. I really nailed him with a spinning elbow—right on the button. I was the first and only man to knock down Saechai, and in his bar the crowd was so quiet you could hear a pin drop. At that moment, I realized something monumental had happened.

As I came to find out, Saechai was a Muay Thai world champion from years past. I remember him getting to his feet. The look on his face, aside from his eyes going side to side, was one part stunned and nine parts really pissed off. I remember thinking, what's the big deal?

What's the big deal about this Saechai guy? So he owns the fight club.

It cost me three hundred baht for a cornerman. The guy was all of five feet tall and carried a bucket, a towel, and a stool. All he would say in English was, "Watch for sins, big boom-boom sins."

Less than a minute later, I was staring up at the lights, my jaw feeling strangely on the other side of my face, relocated by Saechai's rock-hard shin. It was at that moment I understood what the big deal was and what my cornerman kept trying to tell me: watch for the shins, big boom boom shins.

I started to stare up at the knots in the plywood overhead. I tried to imagine different constellations or solar systems—anything to occupy his mind. I knew what was coming. I began pleading with fate.

If I could just go back and somehow make my little girl well, or get the ferryman to take me instead. I knew the witching hour was upon me; the darkest hours brought forth the darkest thoughts, and when those bad dreams came calling, the gut-wrenching images of my vulnerable little girl, the door to my ironclad mind was breached.

I started asking myself, why did she have to die? Why couldn't I do something to help her? Why? I stood by and watched as the most precious, innocent little girl was taken from us. That moment was the most painful I have ever endured. I wanted to rip the feeling right out of my soul. Then the thoughts of her in the cold, dark ground, lying in that earth, scared and alone, with no one to guide her, no one to take her through the formless void.

I remember trying to stop the images, erecting mental roadblocks, and putting up the circular thinking traps, but once the tapes began to run, there was no stopping them. The memories flickered in my mind like a torturous zoetrope, running around and around until my emotional well ran dry.

At that point I reach for the bottle of Jack beneath my bunk. I drank enough to slow images down, and when I joined the void, it was mission accomplished.

I woke at O-dark thirty, just as lost, and that's when I began my ritual of racking the slide on my Sig and looking into the darkness; I started telling myself time had run out.

Like so many times before, I stood up, ready to do something, to run or go work out. I caught sight of myself in a reflection in the creased stainless steel mounted on the wall. The truth was all there, written across my face like a roadmap of the last twenty years—a whole lot of hard living in the land of bad. A shit ton of hard miles that were staring back at me. Most of the real truth was obscured by my thick, rust-brown beard, worn by an operator to buy a moment's hesitation. It's an opportunity that a world-class gunfighter will exploit, because when your job is killing other killers in the land of bad, there are no runners-up.

I dropped the clip, racked the slide, caught the round as it ejected, squeezed back into the stack, and last night's battle for my soul ended with the same easy-peasy click of the clip. And when a loud knock came at my door, my Sig P227 was back in my hand.

Who?

Corporal Getty, sir. There's a call for you at the TOC, sir.

I told our new comms corporal that I'd be with him straightaway. I threw on my chest rack and grabbed my MK12, a real dinosaur bone from decades before. Corporal Getty was standing in the hallway, ramrod straight. He had just come in from the world and was in desperate need of an in-country skill set.

I told him not to stand at attention around anyone, no calling anyone sir, and never ever salute anyone outdoors. Those were tells the enemy would use to ID officer targets. Understand whether it was a sniper or a local Tali posing as a translator or guide, they are looking to kill us.

Dust devils whirled across my path as Getty and I walked to the Tactical Operations Center. It's the head shed on this sprawling campus. I remember using the five-minute walk through the maze of trailers and buildings to gather my thoughts.

Master Chief Hector Perez, my senior enlisted man, met us halfway to the TOC. Six-foot-three, burly, barrel-chested, he was a warrior with a black-as-coal, Brillo pad beard and eyes to match. He could easily pass for an edge-rushing mullah until he opened his mouth. He hailed from South Central LA, and occasionally, after too many tequila shots, he would tell us about his gangbanger thug life or go off on a tangent about his mother's unsettling devotion to Santa Muerte and how it disturbed him. He had the thousand-yard stare long before he ever set foot in a real firefight.

He kept asking me if we could move back to FOB Salerno. Chapman gave him the creeps. I told him that the Navy did not care about evil spirits on base and that JSOC wasn't going to consider a spooky place or lots of bad Soviet juju valid reasons for moving us.

We reached the Tactical Operations Center, and when I pulled open the plywood door, I was stopped dead in my tracks by a wall of icy cold air.

I asked Bear if the Navy was terraforming the Middle East on the taxpayers' dollars. It was hell's half-acre out here, and we're hanging meat in the TOC. We navigated the maze of desks and dodged the map holder and the sand tables before we reached the center of the comms center, where several soldiers and sailors were sitting in front of two banks of six flat screens mounted in two rows on the wall.

They were monitoring drone feeds, CCTV feeds, body cams, and low-grade Asian porn, which probably garnered the most attention. Banks of landline phones, cell phones, sat phones, and radio sets sat in their cradles waiting to be deployed.

I remember Charlie wearing his trademark Chicago Cubs baseball cap with a miked-up headset over it, telling me he had Langley on the line. I remember him telling me that it was the CIA and that they don't even know what they want.

When I took the headset, I got a Mr. Cox from Langley, and he asked if I had received his communique. I looked at Charlie, and he nodded. So I told Cox we had and that I reviewed the file. We were already aware we would be receiving one of his men from FOB Salerno.

I gritted my teeth and told Mr. Cox I would assist his man any way I could.

I handed the headset back to Chen and picked up a stack of briefings and crypto messages. "Sir, should we start the mission briefing?"

I told Chen that's why I was here and that perhaps we can begin the briefing before our CIA strap arrives.

Chen printed out the bio of Cox's case officer and handed it to me with a smile and told me good luck with this one. He looks like Alfred E. Neuman, which made me think Charlie wasn't old enough to have read Mad Magazine.

The briefing center attached to the TOC was a box of reinforced concrete with high ceilings and fluorescent lights hung in rows from front to back. The seats were filled with pipe hitters who as a group dressed more like a Montana militia. Most days, they resembled a bar league softball team from Maine, sporting baseball caps, mismatched uniforms, Middle Eastern sand scarves, Oakleys, and plenty of hard-earned attitude. To call them alphas, this group of the finest warriors on the face of the earth was a galactic understatement. Often copied but never replicated.

Operators went nowhere without their weapons. They were in hand virtually every second of the day. The style and manufacturer were chosen by each operator, tailored to their job and their individual needs and strengths, and of course the mission. Almost all of their long guns, with the exception of their sniper rifles, were full auto. They all had Picatinny rails and rail gadgets, scopes, laser sights, silencers, and tactical lights—lots of tac lights. They had options, but most used the Colt M4A1 Carbine, some with the M26 underbarrel 12 gauge as a modification to their base model, or the SCAR H MK17, an FN creation, a popular CQB weapon.

My MK12 was a multipurpose assault rifle with sniper capabilities out to 400 meters, which I upgraded with a Nightforce 5.5-22x56 NXS scope. I carried it like Linus' blanket.

All of the 64 operators, four 16-man SEAL platoons, despite their rugged individualism, trained and fought with more unit cohesion than Bobby Clark's line. Individually, they were a force; together, they were a tactical nuke. An eight-man squad could hold off a company in a pinch or a battalion if they had enough claymores and a little time to plan.

Senior staff officers never invited SEALs on a hunt. White-tailed deer, grouse, or waterfowl—none of it. SEALs never miss, and if there's one in a blind with other hunters, no one else will get a shot off.

I remember having to tell this group not drop those spitters or leave them in ambush positions. The Pashtun cleaning ladies are on a war footing, talking about real tribal violence. You do not—I repeat—you do not want to go hand to hand with one of these Pashtun women. They'll liberate you from your nuts, okay? All you Copenhagen freaks, you know who you are, leaving your spit cups in ambush positions, cease and desist. Are we clear?

Inshallah, boss, inshallah was all I got back.

I told the team that Team Taliban had a new player: Mullah Attah Kassem. It was a recent development from the NSA. Using their formidable SIGINT gathering capabilities. Kassem is the latest high-value target. I'm sure they combined their flawless SIGINT with the superb field intel from the CIA to reach this masterful conclusion. A few senior team members expressed their doubts about the accuracy of either source.

The intel had pinpointed the location of Dr. Hasan Mudgizzen, a.k.a. Mullah Atta Kassem, a former professor and department chair at the London School of Economics, as

Darbart Village in the Korengal Valley, north of Kandahar. Apparently, he had amassed one point five billion dollars, and it triggered alarms over at His Majesty's Revenue and Customs, who took an interest in him and involved the SIS, and he had to leave his life of academic bliss.

Troy Walker, a breacher and all-around pipehitter, raised his hand and asked how he was able to serve as a professor at the London School of Economics while also working for a terror organization.

I told them we should ask our SAS friends how this guy managed to establish such a network right under their noses the next time we see them around the barn. As of now, he is the Taliban's chief of finance, and he's on the job.

When I told them he's living in the Korengal Valley, there was an audible groan. In the Korengal, Mullah Atta Kassem believes he is untouchable. It is a very hostile, remote environment where we will change that perception.

I displayed on the screen a drone view of Korengal Village, Darbart. There will be, at any given time, up to three hundred Taliban fighters. Expect a significant number of highly trained foreign fighters, like Chechens, and that their numbers are growing in Darbart. It's a stop on their way south to join up with the growing Taliban presence around Spin Boldak. In terms of ordnance, we can expect AKs, RPG-7s, Dushkas, Dragunovs, PPKs, and the more common 80mm mortars, possibly some 120s."

We HALO into the drop site, which will be two miles out from the X. We'll hike into visual range of the target village and launch our diversion at 03:00, and in conjunction with a member of the intelligence community, we'll engage the village's defense force with a two-platoon-strength diversion. A third platoon will back up the diversion, and the fourth platoon will monitor movement in the village and take Kassem when he squirts.

We will have a Predator Drone in high loiter over the village. If we need sustained heavy ordnance, there will be a Specter gunship twenty mikes out.

Wheels up at zero one hundred hours; the package is known to travel with a laptop; if we lose the package, the laptop becomes the mission.

Mr. GQ, Will Wallace, the strap, took over the briefing and told everyone he predicted that Kassem's security team would form a secret service-type defensive circle around him, with Kassem in the center, and move him south to Kandahar. The SEALs, all hardcore veteran operators, quickly sized up the strap—from his off-the-shelf, pressed, and creased hunting gear camo to his fake-ass window-glass, military-issue black frames. He was swiftly identified and classified as a smarter-than-thou jerk who had learned all his tactical skills and tradecraft in the Boy Scouts.

A handle circled the room right off the bat—Abercrombie.

His CV, sent over to us by his boss, lists him as a paramilitary case officer. I told everyone his CV and case notes on the package were on the secured computer in the ops center. Only one man raised his hand: Colt "Old Man" Ludlow, a Tennessean known for not being the best-conditioned operator in the group but, without question, the finest shot on Green Team. His southern drawl could give cold molasses a run for its money. He asked Wallace if he could tell everyone where he obtained that impressive bit of intel before he spat a big wad of Red Man chew into his empty Yoo-Hoo bottle.

Wallace told Ludlow that the intel that Kassem would flee south to the Afghan capital came from the CIA's Central Asian Desk and that it originated from a source inside the ISI, Pakistani intel.

Someone asked if all they had was some HUMINT from a notoriously hostile intelligence service.

Wallace looked perplexed and wanted to know why this intel was inherently untrustworthy. And then he asked if we were in the habit of challenging the brass, JSOC, these days.

Several people challenged Wallace's authority by asking him who the hell he thought he was and if he knew where he was standing and who he was talking to at that moment.

I had to cut that short. I told the team that if anyone had a problem, anything that's going to keep any man from max RPMs, I wanted to know about it. The Korengal Valley is the land of bad, and right at the top of the list of AOs you don't want to parachute into.

After the briefing, Lt. Chen told me Wallace doesn't carry our unit's current. Krause wanted to know what current he was talking about, and Charlie, and this is why I love the guy, gave a completely off-the-cuff explanation that every unit has a current, and it runs through every business, organization, or family. For example, if you're on a guided missile cruiser, it's the engineers and the surface warfare officers on up to the captain; they all carry that boat's current. Their work is measured in watts, calories, and joules. It's the fucking current, brah."

I asked him what DEVGRU's current was?

Come on, boss, DEVGRU? They'd have to rewrite that XY graph going forward. Our unit's current grades out better than 99.99% of humankind, et al. Maybe the best pro cycling team charging up Mont Ventoux in the Tour, they might be close—but we do it under fire.

And Quan Mingus asked what Delta's current was.

And Charlie tells Quan that Delta and SEALs are different. We're under the same genus but different species. SEALs are generally younger and better conditioned, while Delta operators are usually more experienced and intellectual gunfighters. Another way to put it: if you're blowing up an Iranian gunboat with hull-activated ordnance and you've got to swim four miles of seasnake- and shark-infested waters, that's us. If you're infiltrating a Russian military soiree to take out a target, you go with Delta. Why, you ask? Because Delta knows a salad fork from a dessert fork when the dinner service starts.

God, this world has lost one of its best. RIP, brother Chen.

Kane allowed his eyes to close, and the next thing he heard was a loud knock on his flimsy pressboard door.

***

Smokin' Joe Cowell was a judicious soldier, if nothing else. He always acted quickly to eliminate any bad news from his command. He did give Kane a fair six hours of sleep before sending the base MPs to deliver a new set of orders, direct from the Pentagon.

The knock came early enough to catch Kane in the depths of a powerful dream. His head snapped off the pillow, thick with fog. The Sig was out of its holster and aimed at the door before his first thought registered.

He kept the gun pointed upward. "Enter." The door opened slowly, and the two MPs standing in it motioned for Kane to lower his weapon.

Kane dropped his Sig back into the holster and adjusted himself, pulling on his pants as the senior MP stepped inside.

"Your boss doesn't waste any time, does he?" said Kane.

The older of the two MPs stood stone-faced while Kane signed the receipt for his

orders.

Kane read the orders as he put on his Oakley boots. He looked at the two men. "Is the rest of the team shipping out too?" he asked.

He glanced at the time and date stamp on the orders. "Are they serious?"

The older MP, a staff sergeant with enough hash marks on his forearm to know better, stepped into the hall and looked up and down the particleboard corridor. He stepped back in and shut the door.

The shoe-leather-tough old warrior dropped to one knee close to Kane's ear and said quietly, "Sir, I'm in the Army, and as such, I'm no fan of the Navy, just on principle. But SEALs are a different breed. I'm going out on a limb here, sir."

Kane nodded. "Whatever you tell me, Sarge, it stays in this room."

"Okay—those CIA rats are scurrying around trying to get out from under this thing, whatever it is, sir."

Kane began to speak, but the sergeant raised a finger to stop him. "I don't want to know specifics, sir; I just want to fade back into my gig." The old soldier rubbed his chin.

"Lieutenant Commander, for what it's worth, the music has ended, and you need to find a chair."

Kane looked past the sergeant and stared at the wall for a second before shaking his head.

"So it's come to this. You put your life on the line fighting for your country, and some jerk throws a monkey wrench into the works, making you the scapegoat." Kane stood up and extended his hand. "Thank you, Staff Sergeant; you are a good man."

"I know a good soldier when I see one, sir."

The second MP broke his stony stare and looked down at Kane. "I'm with him—on this one—sir."

Kane shook hands with both MPs as they left his room. It took him less than an hour to gather his gear. He gave the room a last look, threw his seabag over his shoulder along with his knapsack, and came face to face with a navy seaman who was ready to knock on his door.

"Sir, I got a note from Master Chief Perez for you." Kane took the note and thanked him.

“Boss, I have no idea what's going down. They rousted us after only

four hours of sleep. They're sending us on a bullshit training op to

Diego Garcia. WTF! We were told you've been

recalled stateside and would rejoin after the training operation. Stay frosty, sir.

Visit Compton if you get a chance; it's where my people are. Just saying.

MCP Perez

Kane looked at the note for a second, then folded it and shoved it in his ODs. The last line gave him pause. *Why is he telling me where he comes from? I've heard all of his of his gangster stories.*

He marched over to the TOC, humping all his gear through the ridiculous heat. By the time he reached the ops center, the sun had topped the Sulaiman Mountains, and a hot breeze rolled in.

He reached the flight line in time to watch a C-130 transport carry his men up and over the Khost-Gardez Pass, into the burning orange and fiery red sky.

"God damn it—this is getting fucking deep, fast!" said Kane. He walked away from the strip toward his home away from home, the TOC. He approached the entrance, and when he reached for the door handle, he heard a woman's voice.

"Lieutenant Commander Kane. Kyle Kane."

He stepped away from the door. *Canadian or a New Yorker*?

He considered the voice as he turned toward the row of Hesco barriers that lined the left side of the TOC.

"Lieutenant Commander Kane, if I may, a moment of your time, please?"

Kane smiled and said, "Let me guess, Mata Hari."

He walked toward her position, shouldering his MK 12, never taking his eyes off her.

"What are the odds?"

"Excuse me?" she said.

"You're a sight not often seen here at FOB Testosterone: skintight BDUs, a smoking hot bod, cherry red lipstick, and a perfect—"

The woman raised her hand. "I get it."

Kane stopped less than a foot from her and said, "Something out of a Le Carré novel or Graham Greene, no?"

"Could be, Lieutenant Kane, if this were Hanoi. Let me cut to the chase—because I believe in being honest with a man in your position."

"A man in my position; you mean a man walking on the edge of a razor?" Kane said. "A razor stropped with firsthand evidence of CIA misconduct."

"What are the odds—me wanting to help you?"

Kane looked away, smirking. "A mysterious, tall, red-headed woman with intriguing emerald green eyes and a body to die for, skulking around quite possibly the most high-security military facility in this hemisphere—and this woman, who'd be a shoe-in as Ilsa Lund in the remake of Casablanca, wants to help me with my classified mission problems? I'd say the odds are about the same as the dolt king Joe Biden sitting in his basement and winning a presidential election.”

The woman looked around cautiously. "Bad odds indeed, Lieutenant Commander, but be smart, like George Bailey when he’s thrown a lifeline in *It’s a Beautiful Life;* don’t throw it back."

Kane scanned the airfield. "I've been on deployment here for four months, and I have never seen you or anyone who looks remotely like you around, and you're definitely someone I'd remember."

"It’s my job not to be seen, Kyle Kane. What I don't know, what I’d like to know, is what information, if any, Wallace got from Kassem."

Kane rolled his tired eyes. "How the hell do you know about Kassem?"

"I operate in a world where knowledge quite often can be the difference between being quick or being dead." She looked around anxiously.

"Okay, Miss—"

"Call me Daisha."

Maybe I can use this opportunity to extract some information about Wallace that I don’t already know.

"We could horse-trade."

"You have me at a loss," said Kane, trying to buy time to think. "How about you tell me your real name?"

At that question, the woman looked at Kane crossly. "Are you daydreaming, or just trying to come up with a workable question, or are you thinking about retirement?"

"Say what—retirement?" Kane replied awkwardly. "Do you know something I don't?"

Daisha frowned. "I haven't heard anything—official. Now you tell me, who gave you your written orders?"

"You're going big-ticket item right out of the gate. That’s just not cricket."

"I think we both know you don’t have a lot of time to dance around," Daisha replied. "We could go back to my hooch, have wild first-time sex, and then play the guessing game, or just—"

"They came out of JSOC Command," Kane interjected, "by way of Admiral Corbett's office."

"Was Langley involved?"

"You could say that," Kane continued. "A case officer shows up in the middle of my confidential mission briefing and throws down a resume—a real pile of bullshit. Then, after he's strapped onto our mission, he gets my best operator killed."

"Just showing up like that, is that in any way normal, Kyle Kane?"

"Not at all. There's nothing normal about this whole damn thing. This place, Chapman, is ten steps from the Pakistani Tribals. We're surrounded by the Taliban, terrorists, and sundry other tangoes that want nothing more than to collect the bounty put on Americans. Nothing here is normal. Insanity is the norm."

Kane smiled at the young woman. "And I still don't know your name?"

"Daisha Willows is my real name; they call me Lady Di. I'm a tech who sets up surveillance for field ops. You haven't seen me around the barn because my job takes me off base. Lately, I've been attached to a group in Kandahar. I was working with CSIS, Canadian Intelligence, embedded with a Canadian news crew as our cover."

"Really," said Kane, "that sounds interesting."

"It was pretty thin, and things got chaotic toward the end of last month. ISI, I believe, blew our cover to the Taliban. They used a car bomb to bring down the building we were set up in," Daisha explained. "Just their way of saying, 'Welcome to the neighborhood.'"

Kane smiled. "Yeah, they're funny like that—a regular welcome wagon. Did you lose anybody?"

Daisha smiled back. "Funny you should ask. It was 01:00 hours, and we had one tech on duty, Albert DeLamielleure. He was surveilling a restaurant from the top floor of our four-story vacant building. A powerful car bomb collapsed most of the building, except for the back wall and the plumbing chase with over-spec cast iron sewage pipes. Luckily for Albert, he was on the toilet, and that particular bathroom fixture was bolted to the back wall. He sat there on the toilet, clothes blown off, covered in roofing tiles and concrete dust for nearly six hours before the fire brigade got him down."

Daisha opened a flip phone and showed Kane a video of the man on the toilet, fifty feet in the air, screaming obscenities in French.

Kane was starting to like this woman. "Well, Lady Di," he said, "I gotta tell you, this whole op stunk from the beginning. Last-minute William Wallace, unidentified drones overhead, a sniper trying to kill Kassem in my AO, my lieutenant getting killed when Wallace tips off the Tallies. He gets lost, and we have to go find him. Kassem gets offed, and Wallace is gone, along with the intel."

"The interrogation?" Daisha asked.

"What interrogation? I was in the I&I center and saw Kassem for less than a minute before someone dropped a flashbang on me, thumped me when I tried to get up, and killed the package. When I came to, the package was dead, our SSI was gone, and the wonderful William Wallace was in the wind."

"What about the laptops? Did you copy the drive?"

"Yeah, we copied it in the middle of the Korengal. No, we didn't; it's all gone," Kane replied.

Daisha looked around nervously.

"It's not good," Kane said, staring at her full, buxom chest for a moment too long.

"Been on deployment long, sailor?"

"Yeah, it's been longer than I want to admit."

"You pipe hitters really don't pay much attention to the political overtones around you, do you?"

"Wanting to have mad, passionate sex with you—is that a political overtone?" Kane asked, laughing. "Seals set the tone, the overtone, the undertone, the tides, tsunamis, the gravitational pull of the earth—everything, all the time, wherever we go."

"Land, sea, or air, right?"

"You know what would really scare me?" said Kane. "A Langley company picnic, you know, a real old-fashioned work picnic."

"I'm going to give you something for free, Lieutenant Commander, because I like you. Once you become an *officer* in the military, it's no longer about fighting for the man next to you. It's a universe of one, and your senior officers will run for cover if the Pentagon comes looking for scalps. Your best friends will always be the enlisted men."

Kane nodded as Willows patted him on the shoulder and walked away.

He paused for a moment. "That's why I never took the cake-eater option. I was offered a promotion to captain and a job at the Pentagon—a rear admiral in five years. When I retired, depending on how many contracts I pushed across the goal line for the defense industry, I could have had a job with a nice seven-figure salary, along with all that country club living."

"Be well, Kyle Kane. I'll be watching for you in the funny papers."

"Never seen a woman look so damn good in fatigues." He watched her full, round bottom bounce from side to side as she faded into the shadows.

For the first time since he left home, Kane felt a pang of guilt. Wanting to have wild sex with a woman he had just met was something he hadn't felt since his college days at Slippery Rock.

He began singing, "She's so fine there's no telling where the money went." Kane turned toward the TOC and double-timed it back to the door. "She's so fine—"

Chapter 6

Pentagon, Washington, DC, 14:35

Lieutenant Commander Anne Cathcart, the executive assistant, called in the captains and vice admirals waiting in the anteroom outside Admiral Martin Corbett's office.

The officers of the carrier task force, excluding the two attack submarine commanders, took their seats in the office, admiring one of the Pentagon’s most coveted commodities: an unobstructed view. A set of windows like the ones in Admiral Corbett’s office was a luxury reserved solely for senior officers and high-ranking bureaucrats who had triumphed in the E-Ring's battle for supremacy.

The admiral's prized office became the topic of conversation among the captains until Admiral Corbett rose from his desk and brought over his handcrafted, Spanish cedar-lined, Honduran mahogany humidor, along with its coveted contents.

Admiral Corbett flipped it open. "Sailor’s choice, the smoking lamp is lit," he announced. "Cohiba, Partagas, Romeo y Julieta." Everyone selected a cigar and lit up.

"How do you get away with smoking in here?" asked Rear Admiral Toth, the carrier commander and task force XO.

"The room is surprisingly clear of smoke, right?" Corbett replied, snipping his cigar.

"Thanks to my recently installed, state-of-the-art smoke removal system. It was created and installed by one of our biggest defense contractors."

"Does it pass the smell test, Admiral? You know how nosy CID can be."

"It's part of a beta testing agreement," Corbett explained. "The manufacturer, GDC, benefits from product testing through my use of the equipment."

All the officers nodded in agreement, admiring the admiral's ingenuity, fine cigars, and general good fortune.

"So let's discuss the deployment of Carrier Group 3 to the Straits of Hormuz."

"I thought we were getting underway this week," Toth said. "We're already two days behind schedule, and the weather excuse is wearing thin."

Anne Cathcart knocked on the office door, and Corbett barked, "Enter."

"Sir, you have a call from your doctor at Walter Reed."

"Thank you, Lieutenant. Please tell the good doctor I'll be right over," Corbett said as he turned back to the command officers of Task Force Jupiter.

"Marty, why don't you use the doctors at the DiLorenzo Health Clinic here at the Pentagon?" Toth asked, exhaling a cloud of cigar smoke.

"I have an appointment with a very attractive podiatrist at Walter Reed," Admiral Corbett replied. "She rubs these tired old dogs without being asked." He donned his dress blue uniform jacket. "Besides, avoiding the Pentagon rumor mill, with all its wagging tongues, can't be undervalued."

Toth, Corbett's friend, thought his superior officer's response was a bit out of character.

"That about wraps it up, gentlemen. As I've mentioned several times last week, delaying the departure of Carrier Group 3 was both a strategic and tactical decision. If we take our time and begin the mission in seven days instead of yesterday, the additional time on station will cost Iran money and resources they don't have."

"You're going to catch hell from lawmakers on the Hill, sir. Pelosi will have a cow."

"If she still has a uterus," Corbett replied. "I can't imagine she hasn't sold that along with the rest of her soul."

"If we unilaterally change our departure date without discussing it with them," said Elijah Moore, captain of the USS Bainbridge, the first nuclear-powered frigate, "they'll ruminate, fly to some luxurious location, spend taxpayer money, and do absolutely nothing—all in the name of democracy."

"That's all past history, gentlemen; I believe the Speaker's position on the military and most other matters in this country is influenced by a particular Asian nation."

"That would make sense," Vice Admiral Toth said skeptically.

"Finish your cigars, gentlemen," Corbett said. "We'll convene again next week to discuss strike packages and strategic responses."

A few junior officers attempted to raise questions, but Corbett was already on his way out the door.

Admiral Toth raised his hand. "Run your questions through me; if we can't work them out, I'll bring them to the old man."

***

Outside the Pentagon's Riverside Entrance, a well-polished black Chevy Suburban pulled out of the expansive parking lot, often referred to jokingly as Ground Zero. This dark humor dated back to the Cold War, when those who worked in the Pentagon understood they were a primary target for the Russian nuclear ICBM program.

The large truck rolled up to the portico, which overlooked a lagoon and a small boat dock on the Potomac. Corbett motioned for his driver, Petty Officer Rick Garner, to roll down the window. "It's okay, Donnie. I'm going to walk down to the dock and smoke this cigar." Garner chose not to insist that the old man ride with him; instead, he parked as close to the dock as possible.

At the boat dock, Corbett settled onto a bench that faced the Potomac and the city of Washington across the river. He noticed an unusual amount of helicopter traffic going in and out of Bolling Air Force Base—strange for this time of day.

“Bloody loud machines," he muttered to no one in particular.

"We'll soon have ones that make no sound at all," said a tall, lanky man with a hard, angular face who seemed to appear out of nowhere.

He sat next to Corbett as the admiral exhaled a thick cloud of smoke.

Garner had cracked open his night school books and logged into his online course. Before he began studying, he glanced up at his charge.

"Where the hell did you come from?" Garner asked. "Two men sitting on the same bench, and one of them is my senior staff admiral. Damn." He considered driving over the lawn but decided it was faster to get out and run.

Corbett looked at the man, who was dressed in black rain gear from head to toe. He had a dark complexion, and Corbett struggled to place his face.

"Why are you dressed for rain? There isn't a cloud in the sky," Corbett said.

"Apparently, Admiral, your command of this most important mission has become somewhat of a sticky wicket—gritty, like sand in your gun's receiver. Quite the sticky wicket," said the Middle Easterner.

"Do you know who you're talking to?" Corbett asked.

“Oh, I do.”

Corbett leaned forward and looked at the man. "This conversation has come to an end."

"It has, Admiral Corbett; Apex considers you a significant impediment to our progress," the man replied. With astonishing speed, he drew an NAA Black Widow .22 revolver equipped with a Switchback 22 suppressor. He was like a Black Mamba, striking from the shadows of the tall grass with deadly accuracy.

One of the highest-ranking naval officers in the most powerful country in the world never left his seat. His final thought was to close the distance between himself and the assassin, but that never happened. The dull thud marked the end of his forty years of distinguished service.

Garner was still a hundred yards away. He didn’t see the shot, and when Corbett fell back, he came to rest in an upright position.

He was as dead as a stone. The round had entered his skull, and because it had expended most of its energy, the jagged edges of the flattened projectile remained inside the skull and caused catastrophic carnage as it dissected the old sailor's brain.

The assassin moved away as if nothing had happened, and to anyone watching, the admiral appeared to be napping.

A cool breeze blew in off the river, tossing his wispy grey hair. Without signals from his brain, Admiral Corbett's body shut down, organ by organ, as he sat on a long bench along the sunny shoreline of the Potomac.

With the calm precision of a professional killer, the tall, lanky man in a black rain suit walked away. He was aware of the cameras on one side and the lumbering Navy Chief, sidearm drawn, on the other.

Garner sensed that something terrible had happened but had no visual evidence of foul play.

The swarthy man cast off the lines and jumped aboard a 28-foot Bayliner, stolen from a Washington marina less than an hour earlier. The powerful speedboat sliced through the wide, fast-moving Potomac.

Garner reached his fallen charge just as the killer sped out of range, through the chop, leaving his horrific act behind.

Chapter 7

Hoover Building, Washington, DC. 15:30

The J. Edgar Hoover Building in Washington, DC, was typically a bustling place. Today, at 3:30 PM, the seventh floor—designated as the Director's floor—was experiencing an unusually high operational tempo. Among those present was Cole James, the FBI Director, regarded as the most powerful law enforcement officer in the US outside of the Attorney General.

James was adept at maneuvering the agents and departments under his authority, working closely with power brokers within Washington's law enforcement and intelligence communities.

As he stepped off the elevator on the seventh floor, he reflected on a recent meeting with a California congressman, during which they discussed their planned dissemination of disinformation regarding January 6th and the use of FBI agents and the hand-picked Obama-and-Biden-appointed judges to crush anyone that attended the January 6th protest. In the same discussion, Cole James acknowledged the investigation into the 2020 elections would go nowhere under his watch.

The congressman, however, neglected to inform James about the significant return of taxpayer money from Ukraine. He also omitted another crucial detail: the investment firm serving as a clearinghouse for the domestic distribution of the quid pro quo billions that was coming in from the Ukraine war. These funds had found their way into the hands of numerous senators, congressmen, and unelected bureaucrats throughout the government, the deep state actors, poised to contribute to the "Chinavation" of America's government.

As James walked past his secretary, she sprang to her feet, signaling that his office was not empty. In fact, it was filled with high-ranking intelligence officials who had just arrived.

"There's a fly in the ointment, Cole?" said Warren Trask, seated in the spacious corner office, calmly thumbing through his travel magazine.

Chuck Bogner, Director of National Intelligence, was a clumsy bureaucrat who benefited from Trump's inexperience. The illegal transfers of wealth from foreign governments into a revolving line of offshore accounts had created an army of willing administration employees.

"Chuck, are you comfortable over there? I know Warren can find the sweet spot in any setting, but you're all spread out on my conference table and looking a bit unzipped." Bogner immediately checked his fly. Cole James winked at Trask, who smirked at Bogner's lack of sophistication.

"It's so nice to see you all," said James. "Very unexpected, I might add."

James saluted Bogner, a former Army general and staff officer at the Pentagon, who worked as the Obama administration's hatchet man, going after generals and other staff and line officers the administration deemed an impediment to their plan to bring woke to the armed services, after which he was rewarded by being bounced up to the DIA.

Bogner was tasked with crafting waves of orders that confused members of his staff that were not aligned, nor ever would be, with the Chinavation of the US. He was sowing as much surreptitious chaos in the government as possible.

"What kind of problem, Warren?" asked Cole James. "Is there a mutiny over at the CIA?"

James sat at his desk with a look like somebody had just broken his favorite driver. Like the other two, he had spent his day signing off on orders that reassigned the agency's best agents—whom he dismissed as constitutional dinosaurs—to positions of little importance.

His motivation was to move America's top law enforcement agents into unfamiliar roles. He was assigning his lapdogs to run down the J6 visitors while shunting the FBI's best off the front line and into ineffective positions, reallocating agents to investigate bank robberies in the Yukon, pursue domestic terrorists in select gun clubs in the South, or chase nonexistent kidnappings in states along the Canadian border.

"We've lost control of Kassem. That tough-book-toting Taliban turd," said Trask in his refined northeast Virginia accent, "lost that damn laptop he carried with him everywhere."

"He's in the wind?" asked Bogner.

"He's dead," said Trask, with his usual droll detachment. "The data, the laptop—it's in the wind too."

James's expression went from unhappy to a look like he was ready to snap his favorite driver over his knee. "Quantify for us, Warren, what you mean by the word 'too,' as in 'also."

Trask, Deputy Director of the CIA and, by all accounts, soon to be Director, finally put down the copy of Conde Nast he'd borrowed from his plastic surgeon's office earlier that day.

"Let's determine our exposure."

"It's hard to tell, Warren," said Bogner. "Corbett's guy at Naval Intel says the laptop is deeply encrypted. It's either AES or RSA; the government uses AES, I believe, so let's suppose it's AES."

"So who was the last person to have control of the laptop?" asked James.

"Wallace, one of my agents, got the assignment," said Trask.

"Agent? That's a seismic semantic stretch. He's a fucking analyst. Why trust him with such a critical operation like this?" asked Bogner.

"To hell with that, Chuck. It was you and Cole," said Trask, pointing to Cole James and Bogner, "who lectured me expressly on keeping it inconspicuous, on the DL. Those were your exact words."

"Okay, Warren, what does that mean?" asked Bogner.

"Send someone you can control," said Trask, before he returned to leafing through the thick, slick travel magazine. "A CIA field agent—had I sent one," said the Deputy Director, "would be like putting a fox in the henhouse.

He closed the magazine before he flipped it into the center of the conference table. “Without giving them a top-down briefing, they'd be reading our intel, our secure server dispatches, and accessing any of their agency sources or outside contacts to try and piece the plan together, then making decisions on their own. We could end up reading about this mission on YouTube. What I’m saying is that it would be a total roll of the dice, and not your type of loaded dice, Chuckie. Our field people know to investigate their exposure in any given situation, and that’s doubly so when you have a black bag op with so much upstream exposure. When they’re handed a suitcase nuke like this one, one of the first things they’ll consider is whether there will be a cleanup crew dispatched to tie up any loose ends. Field agents are big on self-preservation, and they’ll set up a safety valve that could threaten our exposure if they believe they will be purposefully compromised.”

“Makes sense,” said James, “wanting to stay off the wall at Langley.”

Trask's last statement elicited a laugh from the other two. He looked at the two and said, “So, we’re clear on this particular issue: sending Wallace was the best choice.”

Cole James looked intently at his cohort and nodded. "Anyone else on this op?"

"I used an agent who was in-country. She had been attached to the embassy in Dubai then in Qatar and worked in Afghanistan for the last three years. She went in to confront the Seal Team Commander," said Trask.

"And?"

"Nothing conclusive."

Bogner spat his chew into a Styrofoam spit cup positioned on the conference table.

James sneered at Bogner. "General Chuck, do me a favor: don't drop that nasty shit in any of my wastebaskets.”

"Are you serious, Cole? I've been chewing since I was a cadet on the Hudson. I commanded an Abrams A1 M1. We used to booby-trap other units with full spit cups. You know, a nice big juicy—"

"That's enough, Chuck; we get the picture," said Trask, feeling nauseous at the idea.

"I spent this whole morning working on canned responses to obfuscate our actions," said James. "Does the loss of Kassem change the overall dynamics?"

"No, we've spun it as a dereliction of duty with terrorists inside the wire at Chapman," said Bogner. "Everyone will stay clear, like a polonium cocktail."

Cole James signed off on a few more reassignments and then asked, "What about your analyst, Warren? Has he been addressed?"

"Working on it, Cole."

"That's not the response I was hoping for. Will this become a problem? If Operation Misanthrope goes south, we can expect to be in the public eye five by five."

"With all of our disinformation, coded documents, disorienting orders, restrictive rules of engagement, and massive redeployments, I've thrown everything in the playbook at it. Hell, I stopped backing agents who get in difficult legal situations. How can it fail?"

"Playbook, Warren, what playbook?" asked Chuck Bogner.

"Seriously, Chuck, where did you think the concept of *woke* came from? Do you think it was just something Obama dreamed up? Woke, Antifa, transgender for everyone, open borders, the attack on God and country and the nuclear family, normalizing porn, and voter fraud, just to name a few, are all part of the asymmetrical attack plan that began well before we became a part of the federal government. When I say "we," I mean the members of the permanent federal government who can be counted on to act in their own best interest in every situation, who have signed on, and when I say "signed on," I mean taken sufficient cash, gifts, or favors, and whether they choose to believe it or not, are captured by the CCP, and when I say the CCP, I mean the CCP's Ministry of State Security and their minions throughout the country. When we talk about the number of espionage operations going on across the United States, not to mention around the world, at this moment, it's absolutely diabolical, and I say that in the most positive way possible. Between us and the academic institutions across the country, we've passed on more military or industrial secrets to the MSS than probably every spy agency across the globe for the past fifty years. And there are two reasons for this grotesque tsunami of seditious subversion: greed and peer pressure. When the boys and girls at the top, the presidents, the senators, the congress, and the cabinet members steal from the American taxpayer, it becomes endemic. Significant parts of both the federal and state governments are controlled by the CCP.

The other two men looked surprised. Cole James said, "When I joined the Bureau, we chased corrupt agents down and arrested them or drove them out. Now we're chasing the good guys out."

"Why are we hiding our connection to the CCP, guys?" said Trask as he displayed his usual overconfidence. "It's been posted on every one of the federal government's message boards. They're disguised as DEI training class schedules, gender norming agency-sponsored conventions, GSA sensitivity training, and rules committee meetings, among other things. We've utilized HR message boards and event boards in every HQ, field office, local station, and safe house. Just kidding about the safe houses, but we've left our people the crumbs necessary to implement the resistance once the mission begins in earnest."

On a typical day, Trask and Cole James were crosstown rivals for intelligence, rarely sharing information. James had done his best to navigate the treachery on his side, but Trask's brand of narcissism rubbed the FBI director the wrong way.

"Are you sure we've used every tool at our disposal?" James asked. "Failing to bring about the required change could give those pious red-state dogs like Nunes or Jordan a way into our plan."

"And?"

"That could be catastrophic. If we focus on the mission of Chinavation, gather the weak-minded to our side, and isolate the conservatives," said Trask, "then our mission and our globalist cover story will hold."

"Speaking of cover stories, should we invite the media?" Bogner asked.

"No, no need. The legacy media are owned by or act in unison with our pro-Chinese globalist billionaires, who are receiving huge sums of taxpayer money from various government sources like USAID and our network of fraudulent NGOs. It's such a glorious scheme, an entire government involved in stealing the American people blind. It's the biggest RICO case that could ever be imagined."

"And our propaganda mouthpieces tailor a unified, monolithic message that covers everything we're doing. Who cares if they sell their souls to their national audiences?" said James. "Look at that pair of idiots, Mika and Beaker."

"Who's Beaker?" asked Bogner.

Trask shook his head. "Scarborough; he looks like Beaker the Muppet."

"They have the same IQ," said James. "You never see them in the same room together."

Bogner looked confused at James' last line and shook his head. "What happens if something catastrophic occurs, like Trump getting reelected?"

"That'll never happen," said Trask. "Remember, Chuck, we control the high ground. We are Main Justice. We will put him in jail or—"

Both James and Bogner looked at the deputy director and said, "Or what?"

Trask stopped short of saying what he knew. "The legacy media is a real case study as to the corruptibility of the human soul."

"Attacking the former president like fucking piranhas is a cover for us?" asked Bogner.

"It is, Chuck," said Trask with a crooked smile. "I love how they generate cross-thought of fact and fiction, half-truths and lies, and mix it with their MSS propaganda, and extrude their brand of bull-chip sausage."

"They've even enlisted the guilty parties—the liars and leakers—to be part of their nightly sideshows."

"My favorite California congressman has done an outstanding job, performing his best political vaudeville," said Bogner. "He reminds me of Charley McCarthy."

"He is a virtuoso sociopath," said James.

"Okay, enough of the team building," said Trask. "When Misanthrope's success is assured, we'll activate our cells in embassies around the world, and they will release as much damaging confidential documentation as possible. I've sent coded messages in the daily traffic to advise them of this part of the plan.

“If Trump had any governmental experience, he would have fired the entire State Department; it’s a virtual democratic shadow government, rife with fraud, graft, and corruption. It serves as a release point for confidential material to gain influence with the governments we seek to control.”

“And it makes for great gossip on the Georgetown cocktail party circuit,” said James.

“Hey guys,” said Bogner, “here’s some good news. Wallace was identified two days ago by a US Customs and Border Patrol facial recognition app at a Canadian-US border crossing.”

“Two days ago,” said James. “Why’d it take so long?”

Trask shook his head. “There are a certain number of agents and assets that are not in the system. Wallace left under an alias when he flew out of Andrews for Afghanistan.”

"All of these moving parts," said Cole, "the media, the Resistance, members of the cabal, the professor, the elites here and in Europe, all brought together by the—"

Cole James' secretary buzzed him. “Carrie Gould.”

"Send her in." He turned to his co-conspirators. "It's Carrie Gould; be gentle. She’s an ivory tower ideologue and, as such, is oversensitive and triggered by just about everything."

"She doesn't like dirty hands?" asked Trask.

"Not true, Warren. She flew jets, F-18s," said Bogner, as Carrie Lynn Gould walked in.

"It's true, I flew Hornets off the Gipper, CVN 76," said Carrie as she walked into the frat house, cutting a striking figure. Tall and athletic from her college soccer days at South Carolina, her strong presence seemed to ruffle the egos of the overly confident intel gurus, who overlooked Gould's abilities.

Gould stood in the center of the room, not surprised that this bunch of frat boys were noticeably lacking in civility. When no one stood or invited her to sit, Cole James made a half-assed attempt and stood. She took a seat in one of the leather chairs against the wall. James went around the room and introduced the other two, who merely nodded.

"Guys, this is Carrie Gould, the NSA's Chief of Foreign Affairs. She's an agent of influence and an integral part of our movement. She's developed apps that intercept and misdirect nosy probes, like inquiries from Congress, the press, and various other snoopers. Her work has successfully insulated our intelligence agencies. She's taken the art of MASINT and elevated it to a new level, mastering the amplification of disinformation that further confuses the already bewildered."

"Have you heard from Apex?" asked Gould, chuckling at the idea of calling the leader of their movement Apex.

"What's so funny, Carrie?" asked Bogner.

"Calling the boss 'Apex' sounds so very Specter. I mean, come on guys, does he look like Ernst Blofeld or have a caddie named Oddjob?"

"I know things aren't as critical at the NSA," Trask said condescendingly. "At the CIA, we operate under critical tolerances and best practices. That means encryption, codes, and tradecraft discipline. What we are doing, the other side calls treason. If phase one fails catastrophically, we'll be hunted down like rabid dogs."

"By whom?" Carrie asked. "Not the President; he’s so controlled he’s bowling with the bumpers up. The White House handlers will shut down or at the very least actively work to obfuscate or slow-walk any investigation. Global socialism is the only way to unite the people of the world."

Bogner looked at Cole James, who glanced up at Trask, and they all smirked.

"That's wonderful, Carrie," said Trask.

"You don't believe that crap, do you?" Bogner replied.

James put his pen down and frowned at Bogner. "Carrie is a true believer in the goodness and inherent fairness of our movement."

Bogner frowned at Cole James. "The reality is, honey, we're trying to gain a permanent hold on the U.S. government —a single-party system to implement lasting changes and resolutions. Not this back-and-forth nonsense of desperately trying to sway an inherently corrupt political system of Democrats and Republicans, who sell their souls in the same old sham game of bipartisanship while stealing trillions through fraud. Nothing of substance ever gets done, and if it does, it results in a bill packed with so many fraudulent NGO payoffs that it ends up becoming just a revolving wheel of corruption. Someone's always paying off someone else. The whole system is morally bankrupt."

"I get it," said Carrie Gould. "The resulting masses of money and control will give us—the Democrats—the ability to rewrite history. You heard the speaker after 2020 about how they can finally change the world, ultimately allowing us to usher in a new global system of governance."

"Yeah, I think he was talking about stealing Junior's cheesecake recipe."

"That's a good one, Chuck," said Trask. "Rewriting history: the sins and indiscretions of our past administration, from the president down to his pages, will be swept under the proverbial rug."

"That will be some biblical shit coming, Carrie, biblical," said Bogner.

Carrie cringed at the notion. "We can't be that cynical."

Cole James received a call from the former Attorney General, Casius Crumb. The conversation was brief and straightforward. "Let's meet tomorrow," James said into his phone. "Yeah, in a couple of days, we can watch it on CNN." He laughed as he ended the call.

Carrie Gould's mouth hung open in disbelief. Realizing it, she quickly closed it. "So what's the general upside for the American public and, eventually, for people around the world?"

James set his pen down and looked up at Carrie. "You're worried about the middle class? Seriously? This movement would die on the vine without the privileged, whose sole desire is to destroy everything their fathers built."

"You don't see the Chinese or the Japanese, for that matter, tearing down their way of life because the world won't let them sit back and play single-shooter computer games while eating hot pockets," said Bogner.

"That's very cynical, Director Bogner," Carrie Gould replied. "I think there's a lot more to their unrest."

Cole nodded. "It's about the CCP wanting to undermine America's democratic process. They aim to establish an oligarchy with communist-style control over our populace, particularly the middle class."

Carrie Gould tried to respond, but no words came out.

"Not getting cold feet, are you, Carrie?" Warren Trask asked with a grin. "We conducted extensive vetting to identify the leadership council for our interim transition team. If you have other ideas, now is the time to share them."

"No, no—no second thoughts. Just tell me what to expect when this thing kicks off."

Cole turned to the other two men in the room. "Gentlemen, could you give us a moment?"

Trask looked at Bogner and said, "Absolutely; I believe I saw an open-faced meatloaf sandwich with onion gravy on the lunch board."

Chuck Bogner nodded in agreement and replied, "Yes, I noticed it too. We can mingle with the troglodytes."

The last few comments surprised Carrie, and she struggled to keep it from showing on her face.

"So tell me, Cole, what's this thing going to look like? I got the polished, sanitized version from Crumb's associate, Rosen. He pitched this to me back in 2015, I think at an interagency softball tournament."

"That's right; you played college soccer at South Carolina. What did they call you, the Lady Cocks?"

"That's correct, Cole," said Carrie, swallowing a terse comment she felt James deserved. "We lost in the super region—"

"Listen, Carrie," James interjected, not acknowledging her words, "I think you know this, but I'll say it for clarity's sake: the transition to a global society is going to be messy—very, very messy."

“Will minorities suffer disproportionately as they always do? Will they be represented equally when the dust settles?” asked Carrie. "Messy implies loss."

"Carrie, you need to understand this is a process; people will try to cling to their old lives, holding onto their guns and bibles. Old ways of thinking will lead to chaos. It will inevitably become a mess."

"Save the children's version, Cole. I've been a lifelong socialist, and nothing's going to change that. Give me real-life statistics. I know Apex ran a statistical outcome projection. He wouldn't be involved without it."

"You're right, and there's a strategic outcome assessment that includes both wins and losses."

"I can imagine what you're referring to: numbers of dead, displaced refugee populations, infrastructure damage, and a focus on medical facilities. What do you mean by wins?"

"Think about control over the world's natural resources. The global community shares in the wealth of chemical and mineral riches found in Venezuela, Russia, Greenland, and throughout Africa, just to name a few."

"Who will control these resources?" asked Gould pointedly.

Cole James briefly displayed a moment of impatience but quickly regained his composure.

"Initially, the council will have complete control. Once the government transitions from capitalism to an oligarchy with authoritarian rule, it will evolve into a socialist globalist government."

"How much bloodshed, Cole?"

"Only as much as necessary to quell the outliers."

"Statistically?" asked Gould, losing patience.

Cole James paused for a moment. He considered providing a false number but quickly reconsidered, aware of Gould's sharpness.

"Anywhere from sixty to three hundred."

"Thousand?"

"Thousands, Carrie? We're talking about global assimilation. It's millions—three hundred million."

Gould was speechless but managed to nod. "So, what's our opening move?"

"Operation Misanthrope is stage one," said James.

"Okay, the briefing I received at the club stated that the Middle East is a starting point, and Homeland Security would suppress any significant dissent or backlash flashpoints across our country, while similar groups in Europe would take control. Asia and the Pacific Island countries will fall under the thumb of the CCP. Central and South America will fall into chaos and remain so until we can institute globalist rule."

"As the process progresses and various population centers come under control," asked Carrie, "will regional autonomy be restored?"

"Provided they enforce our new Magna Carta Liberatum Veritas. Failure to enforce the MCUL will result in punishment by the PGC," said Cole. "The Progressive Global Council?"

“Nothing was mentioned about three hundred million dead."

"That's a worst-case scenario. It could go much smoother—it should go much smoother. Focus on phase one: the wresting of power from the states," said James. "Just 72 hours, and we will be at the beginning of a new world order." James glanced at his watch.

He thanked Carrie for her candor as she picked up her valise and tried to appear calm.

"Be well, Carrie Gould; we'll be in touch," said Cole James with his usual nonchalance.

A minute after Carrie left the office, James leaned out and asked his secretary, “Can you get ahold of Paul? I need him ASAP.”

***

"Paul, we need to get up on a wiretap," said Cole James. "Can you get us a FISA warrant on Carrie Gould, like now?"

"Why's that, boss?" asked Rosen, a little surprised.

"She seems like a bleeding-heart Georgetown sorority type; I don’t think she can be trusted."

"She's all about emoting," said Rosen. "I'm not a progressive, and neither are you. If I've read you correctly, you and ninety percent of federal employees don’t care about global warming, transgender bathrooms, or any of that special interest crap Obama trumpeted."

Cole looked at Rosen and said, “Yeah, we're pragmatists. I’m just in it for the money too.”

“Really?” said Rosen. “You could have fooled me.”

“I’m glad to see hubris and arrogance are alive and well in the brief writing trade,” said James. “If we win, we will become the new founding fathers.”

"The left didn’t say founding fathers; they'd rather we be the founding eunuchs."

"Okay, we, the founding eunuchs, will hold office in perpetuity, receiving a portion of every US taxpayer dollar and controlling the world's resources and treasures indefinitely."

"It's a beautiful sound, Director, in perpetuity. Now, queue up our favorite FISA Court song and dance, get our best judge, and roll out a USC 1803. Oh, and send a team over to Gould's DC condo; set up a full audio and video surveillance system, and don't forget the bedrooms—I want some real J. Edgar Hoover stuff."

"Shouldn't we wait for the judge to sign off on the 1803?"

“What? We’ve submitted hundreds, maybe thousands, of requests. I think we've had only about ten applications denied, probably due to poor penmanship."

"Roger that, Cole. Carrie Gould and her partner are living together in their Dupont Circle love nest. I’ll bet she’s a dirty girl."

"I look forward to seeing proof of that," said James. "If you need documentation, I'll have what's-his-name whip up a 302 and fax it over to you. Now, get me my FISA warrant."

Chapter 8

Bagram Air Base, Afghanistan. 06:10

Kane sat back in one of the uncomfortable jump seats that lined the C-130 transport. Alone on the long ride from Bagram, he tried his old standby, Ambien, but even that couldn't summon the sandman.

A few weeks prior, he had started reading a Michener novel; it provided a distraction from the painful thoughts of his daughter, Chen, and the countless other casualties lost on his watch—ghosts that wandered the dark corridors of his mind.

Thoughts are often unreasonable and unfair, as if my mind has a mind of its own.

Kane nodded off, then jolted awake to the muffled roar of the four Rolls-Royce turboprops. He drifted between wakefulness and a sluggish, Ambien-induced haze, a sort of somnolence that plagued him throughout the night.

Senior Airman Anthony Tasaris was hitching a ride back to his duty station at Travis. The crew saw an opportunity to haze the young airman. They spun tales about the psychopathic SEAL assassin sleeping in the cargo section, claiming Kane had just returned from an insane mission and was on edge, ready to snap at any moment.

The co-pilot asked Tasaris to wake Kane, and the crew captain even urged him to bring the man a cup of coffee.

Nervously muttering to himself, Airman Tasaris prepared the cup. He approached cautiously, finding Kane in a fitful sleep. Gently, he nudged him awake.

Kane jumped back into consciousness with a violent start, and in one quick motion, he was on his feet with his SOG Tano blade drawn.

Tasaris, just a little more than a year off his Iowa farm, yelled and stumbled backward, spilling coffee all over himself. The three crewmen who watched from the shadows started laughing, hooting, and hollering.

"Please don't kill me!" shouted Tasaris. Kane quickly sheathed his knife.

"Sorry, buddy," said Kane, struggling to read the kid's name patch. "Tasaris, I see your buddies have stretched your leg pretty far."

"Yyyyeah, I mean yes, sir. They've been razzing me for a while."

"It's okay; I went through the same stuff," said Kane.

"We'll be touching down at 06:30 Pacific time, sir," said Tasaris.

Kane looked out the small window and caught the sun cracking the sky at 0-dark-thirty. "Roger that, Senior Airman. Now go back and give those boys a taste of their own medicine." Kane reached for his thermos of coffee.

Chapter 9

Silver Strand Training Center 15:00

The moment Kane touched down at Coronado Naval Air Station, a strange nostalgia crept into his mind, even though he believed he could still salvage his career. He couldn't shake the feeling that he had lost a part of his life, something so integral to his self-image that it felt unreal. He thought about the first days of training and how intense the instructors were.

He caught the first ride he could to the Silver Strand Training Complex (SSTC), an impressive military facility in San Diego County that had grown substantially since he'd been there last.

Kane asked his driver, "Can we stop at the NEX for a minute?"

The driver glanced in the rearview mirror and replied, "Aye, aye, Lieutenant Commander. Silver Strand is kind of a beachside resort of sorts, complete with its own gift shop."

"It depends," said Kane. "It also houses one of the world's toughest training pipelines, the grinder. It smelts down the hardest ores on Earth over months of heat and pressure, ultimately pouring out a white-hot magma free of the learned and earned impurities from previous lives."

The driver adjusted his mirror and noticed the trident. "You'd know."

"I do know; I was a student-athlete and summertime surfer bum when 9/11 hit. I went through Navy basic training at the Great Lakes facility, then straight into BUD/S.

"Everything I thought I knew was burned away during the crucible of BUD/S training. Months of crushing physical and mental challenges were followed by training, education, testing, and repeat. It created a constant level of physical, mental, and emotional stress that nearly broke me. Some evolutions, like Hell Week, allowed for only four hours of sleep for the entire week."

Kane stared out the passenger-side window. "So much has happened in my life since the last time I was at the SSTC."

Graduation from Hell Week, an early and temporary crescendo, proved that you could endure. There was always a physical and mental war going on in BUD/S. If the intense physical challenges didn't injure you along the way, or if the psychological warfare didn't break you, we were subjected to a mix of high-tech training on communications, weapons—every kind of weapon—trauma medical care, intelligence, interrogation, hand-to-hand combat, close-quarters combat, and tactics, always more tactics. All of this was conducted on land, sea, and air while enduring relentless pressure from a squad of professional ballbusters.

Kane looked in the rearview mirror and said, "Attack, success, next evolution, repeat; that was the mindset of every BUD/S trainee. It's funny; I used to think I would never make it to the end, and at the same time I knew that ringing out was an impossibility. I lived those days somewhere between those two mindsets. When I look back on it, I realize that I had invested too much of my soul and endured too much pain on the grinder, on the sand, and in the ocean to just walk away. But that never-give-up mindset, inherent in every BUD/S trainee, persists right up to the mental breaking point—the sudden crack that could drive you across the tarmac of hard times and the macadam of misery—prompting you to ring out and walk away from one of the greatest accomplishments of modern times. I can't remember how many times I told myself it's ten minutes at a time out here. If I get through the next ten minutes, I've won. Thank you, Seaman Wanzer."

Kane jumped out of the LSSV, a navy-colored Chevy Tahoe that had dropped him on the doorstep of three pivotal years in his life. As he approached the SEAL training center, he caught sight of the current class of BUD/S trainees enduring one of the real joys of BUD/s: the sugar cookie. They were getting wet and then rolling in the sand, caked from head to toe, to be enjoyed for the remainder of the day. They carried phone poles, rolled camper-sized ship fenders up and down the dunes, and some teams were hauling their instructors in Zodiac inflatables along the beach like they were pharaohs of the dunes, as these same instructors launched into tirades of invective and obscenities through their favorite communication device, the bullhorn.

Kane smiled, momentarily forgetting about the meeting with his JAG attorney the next day. The sights, sounds, and smells of the place pulled him deeper into a time where every kind of pain was softened by the thrill of success.

It's like a walk down memory lane in your best, worst nightmare.

Kane stepped onto the blacktop but quickly jumped back as if he'd burned the soles of his feet. The blacktop was hallowed ground. It had been a long time since Kane had been to the grinder or the West Coast Naval Special Warfare Command.

The entire BUD/S training facility was just a short run from a pristine Southern California beach.

Kane watched the instructors as they sought out every possible weakness in a trainee.

Seal instructors are the Torquemadas of the dunes; they lived to pour salt in your wounds, poke at the difficult moments in your life, and work you like pathological oyster shuckers, digging into your humanity and stomping around inside it until it was a bloody mess. Anything to push you to ring that bell.

"Hell week, boys?" shouted Kane from the porch of the instructor's quarters. The class of fifty or so trainees had returned to the blacktop in their sand suits. Instructors needled them every step of the way back, always with a bullhorn in hand to drive home the message.

Kane stood by, needing to be invited onto the grinder. Violating that rule would have resulted in severe consequences.

"Holy shit, boys, look at what the land crab has dragged in," shouted Master Chief Robert 'Rad' Radanovich over his bullhorn.

"As I live and breathe, it's Captain America!" exclaimed Senior Chief Otis Washington, known to his friends and enemies as the Freak.

"No—tell me it isn't so—the king of the SEALs arrives for another week of hell?" shouted Master Chief Hawkins.

Kane looked at Hawkins. "You know something I don't, Hawk?"

Hawk smirked. "The unofficial story?"

The instructor closest to him, Master Chief Radanovich, waved Kane onto the grinder with his twenty-four-inch arms.

"I know one thing," Kane said. "Fleet Admiral Corbett's not with us anymore. Whacked...on the Potomac, in front of the fucking Pentagon."

"Some Iranian slag, I heard," said Hawkins.

"You think so?" Kane asked. "It just seemed so impossible."

"This is a discussion that calls for a wee bit of the Irish," said Radanovich. "The tongue-loosening truth serum."

Kane knew well enough that his friends would engage in the time-honored search for the truth. He held up a rucksack containing a pair of half-gallons of Paddy's Irish Whiskey, purchased at the PX on his way over. He raised it high and shouted, "Up the rebels and Viva Zapata, Hawk."

Rad laughed and called to his men to get to their feet. "Master Chief Hawkins here, whose mother was indeed from Guadalajara, believes he is a descendant of Aztec warriors."

"Dismiss the men," shouted Senior Master Chief Radanovich. "The Grinder's closed for the day."

Hawkins shouted, "Senior Chief Washington, take them out—one up, one back, and everyone comes in under thirteen, or we do it again."

After a couple of quick instructions, Washington led the class off the grinder and onto the beach. Hawkins, Werner, and Radanovich greeted Kane with bear hugs and headlocks, roughhousing for a minute or two.

They were giving Kane a hard time until their emotions broke through, and they shared genuine happiness at seeing their old friend and CO.

The three tanned fitness enthusiasts—honest-to-God killing machines, not unlike the Terminator T-800—pulled their friend off the grinder and led him over to their hooch.

Kane had been the commanding officer for each of these men at some point in their careers. It was rare for an operator to spend so much time in the Developmental Group, DEVGRU, but Kane managed it by sidestepping the promotions in Washington, D.C., that he knew he didn't want. For an operator accustomed to the highest operational tempo, a desk job at the Pentagon—where asses got fatter and men of honor became men of greed—was yet another reason his wife, Maria, pulled the ripcord and yanked him out of their freefall.

As he stepped onto the porch of the instructor's hut, a sudden rush of nostalgia washed over him. He recalled every stab wound, gunshot, shrapnel injury, and broken bone he had suffered in his nineteen years before the mast.

He looked at the surrounding trainees' barracks, a modified example of textbook military austerity—nothing fancy, just pure utility, laid out as simply as a summer camp cabin.

The four aging warriors settled into their instructor's quarters, which featured several personal upgrades typically frowned upon by the Navy. Anything that caused friction within the teams, such as comfort, was discouraged. Regulations allow for comfort only if you are a CMH winner.

The current occupants—Hawk, Rad, Washington, and Chief Werner, the new junior instructor—used their quarters for relaxation and frequent poker games.

The centerpiece of Radanovich's austere design scheme was a large cable spool turned on its side. After a few drinks, Rad would threaten to launch his own interior design brand. The half dozen bar stools, a masterstroke of design, were donated by the ALL Inn Bar, hoping that when the instructors got too drunk—not if, but when—they would shelter in place.

Rad tossed down a dozen tins of smoked mussels and some Ritz crackers in the middle of the table. "Nothin' sits better than salty, oily shellfish on a Ritz, boy."

"Nice touch, Rad," said Kane. "You've always been such a genuinely progressive guy." The master chief flipped him the bird.

Hawkins poured four glasses filled with four fingers of whiskey from the handle of Paddy's.

Rad raised his glass. "To the Admiral." They downed their shots and began eating the smoked mussels. “How does something like that happen? He’s a fucking admiral and our boss of bosses.”

"Lieutenant Commander Kane, sir, permission to speak freely," said Chief Oscar 'Oz' Werner, call sign Frankenwerner. He was still wearing his dress whites, fresh off a PR trip to a Sand Dog public school.

As the senior sailor on deck, Kane replied, "At ease, Chief. Speak your mind. You look frazzled, Oz. Did those middle school kids get the better of the Frankenwerner?"

Werner untied his black neckerchief and flopped it down on the table. "The kids were great, but their fucking teachers —when did they become such lunatic, radical, left-wing nut jobs? As soon as I got there, this creature—I mean, she looked like a cross between the Bride of Frankenstein and Gloria Steinem—went after me about drone strikes and illegal killings. She even had the audacity to ask if I committed any war crimes. During our initial contact, she acted like a pissed-off warthog, tusks and all."

Kane choked on his drink. "Get used to it, Oz; the American education system has become a grand experiment in dumbing down. We're seeing adolescent Marxist reeducation that graduates completely confused and misinformed juveniles into an insane, anti-Western university environment."

"It's all popped smoke," said Hawk. "Education has always been a pit of corruption. Every administration is eager to scream for more money, dumping as much as they can into education, knowing that most of it will be funneled to the teachers' unions, which in turn support Democrat politicians.

Just like Planned Parenthood, they receive taxpayer money and then give it to Democrat politicians."

"And nothing gets better," said Kane. "The US invests far more in public education, yet the quality has dropped from the top five to 25th in the world, and it keeps sliding down the scale."

"Why?" asked Rad, looking for paper towels to wipe his face.

"Inverse reality curve: while the money spent on our schools increases every year, the quality of education declines. This inverse relationship can only mean one thing: rampant, systemic corruption. Combine that with a ridiculous Marxist curriculum and a completely corrupt national union led by a crooked hag for a union boss, and you have rings of corruption operating in perpetuity."

"True that, Kyle," said Hawk. "Everyone at the top is either taking a piece or working for someone who is."

Kane laughed and replied, "The liberals get elected with promises of free everything—education, welfare, housing, anything and everything. The bigger the bill, the better, because it never reaches the poor folks. Congress attaches ridiculous and absurd pork to it before it gets approved; that bit of deficit spending they call bipartisanship. The treasury prints the money and sends it to the bullshit NGOs that kick back to the bureaucrats and elected politicians. If the bill involves a big city, the Democrats in charge steal it."

"That has a ring of truth, Citizen Kane, but lecturing a group of cromags like us isn't why you're here," Rad said, smirking.

Kane nodded. "You heard something, didn't you?"

"Boss, it's that whole officer-enlisted man thing."

Kane nodded again. "Not a thing, dawg. That tune's been playing everywhere I go lately."

Rad leaned over the giant wire spool table and poured Kane another generous four fingers. "I'll get more ice; this weather is hell on a man's drink."

Master Chief Radanovich, a SEAL for sixteen years, walked with a slight limp. One of his massive thighs bore the entry wound from a Dragunov SVD-63.

He packed his five-foot-eleven, two hundred eighty-pound frame into a pair of spandex navy shorts stretched to the point of catastrophic failure. He walked with a bit of a waddle, which always drew comparisons to Captain Hook, Long John Silver, and everyone's favorite, Tennessee Tuxedo.

"Speaking of the head shed, I stopped by at zero dark looking for a trainee file on a medical drop. Your name came up, along with words like negligence and dereliction of duty."

Rad pulled a bag of ice from the freezer, causing a couple of vials of HGH and D-ball to tumble onto the floor. "Damn it, I keep forgetting I put my juice in the freezer."

"Are you serious, man?" Kane asked anxiously.

Radanovich paused for a moment. "You think I got this ripped drinking protein shakes?"

"No," Kane replied, walking over to the freezer to help pick up the dozen or so vials. "I was asking about the discussion down at the head shed."

"Oh yeah, boss, there was some concerning talk, no doubt, but no direct implication of you." He leaned closer to Kane. "I've been having lots of fully unbelievable carnal knowledge with the CO's secretary, the awesome Toni Nabila."

"You mean that hot gal down at command?" Kane said. "I think I've seen her pop in and out of a few zoom calls."

"She's straight-up 100% Sicilian, a dark-eyed vixen, fiery as hell, and she's got curves, bro," Rad said with a wide grin. "We may even tie the knot."

Kane smiled. "Wow, Rad, that's fantastic. I'm happy for you, brother. You deserve it."

"Was there a report?" Kane asked tactfully.

Radanovich nodded slowly, then shot Kane a look as he realized where Kane was headed. "Rad, they're hanging me out to dry; I need some intel."

"You're crazy, man. You want me to sweet-talk the future ex-Mrs. Radanovich? Get her to snag a classified document—from her boss—the fucking rear admiral?" Rad looked at the other two SEALs and flipped them the bird. "Hell yeah," he said, "let's get started."

Kane almost fell over backward laughing. "You big bastard, you had me."

"Yeah, I did, didn't I? I owe you from that smash and grab in Tunisia; you carried me out of that mess." Kane nodded. "Kyle, you can't buy what we share, bro. I can't count the times you've saved my life. You're the finest, fastest fucking gunfighter I know, and that says a lot. I'd do anything for you, brother."

The two high-fived and downed their shots. Werner poured them both another round. They polished off a couple of tins of smoked mussels and all the crackers.

"What, no ritz for you, Werner?" asked Radanovich.

"No man, it's a keto thing."

"Get the fuck outta here, Oz," Kane said, holding up the empty half-gallon of Paddy's, "all carbs, bro."

Rad downed his drink and belched. "These smoked oysters give you some seriously foul breath, but she loves me anyway."

"Kyle, you and Werner head down to the ALL Inn and grab a table," Hawkins said. "We'll be with you in half an hour."

Rad reappeared, pulling on a shirt and a pair of flip-flops. "I'll need to do some sexual healing first before I submit a request for espionage," Rad said, gyrating his hips and singing, "Sexual healing, baby."

Kane, Werner, and Hawkins all rolled their eyes.

"No, no, no, that's not right. I can't unsee that, man," Hawkins said. "I'll be scarred for life."

***

The ALL Inn was a West Coast biker bar fifteen years ago, known for its reputation as an outlaw establishment that welcomed few outsiders. One Saturday night, five legendary SEALs, on a bet, entered the bar and cleared it. The rest is history.

Dark as a cave and cold as a meat locker at any hour, the ALL Inn had all the essential elements of a SEAL bar: beer served just above freezing and a never-ending supply of good tequila, poured by a bevy of Southern California's finest surfer chicks.

The walls were adorned with flat screens and Navy lore. The military channel played continuously, showcasing clips from WWII, Pacific Theater island assaults, D-Day, Bataan, Korea, Vietnam, and the Iraq War. The Navy and Marine Corps were prominently featured, while other favorites like men's and women's MMA, Aussie Rules Football, and NASCAR were squeezed in wherever possible.

Hawkins grabbed a table with Werner, while Kane was stopped every few steps by old friends. They exchanged pleasantries, and by the time Kane reached the table, he had a few more rounds on the cuff.

"So you and Maria are done?" asked Werner as he sat down.

"Yeah, I guess. Losing our baby hit hard. She needed me, and I needed the war," said Kane as his face darkened. "I should have told command to shove it."

He looked down as Werner placed his hand on Kane's shoulder. "Kyle, you gotta let it go, man."

"It's not easy, bro," Kane replied. "Gabriella was always the brightest star in our orbit. Losing her was a gut punch."

“Woe never changes,” said Oz. Everyone understood his sorrow. Pain was an experience they all shared.

Radanovich walked through the door, and as usual he circled the bar, greeting what seemed like everyone. It took him at least fifteen minutes to reach the table, where he sat down with a fresh half-gallon of Paddy's Irish and one glass.

The bartender rolled his eyes upon seeing the handle. The bar had stopped carrying Paddy's because of Radanovich, but for that reason, Carson turned a blind eye when the big man brought in his own.

Rad looked at the other two glasses on the table and dumped their contents on the floor before refilling them with Paddy's. Carson shook his head hopelessly.

"Ya big galoot," said Oz, "that was a perfectly fine Long Island iced tea."

Rad turned to Werner and furrowed his brow. "That's a secretary's drink, not a proper drink for a frogman; we have a lineage to live up to. Put some real navy grog in your belly, boy, and you'll be feeling fit as a fiddle."

Rad turned to Kane and raised his glass. "To mission success, Lieutenant Commander Kane."

"You got it, Rad. The document?" Kane asked, laughing.

"I attained situational awareness within a half-hour of operational coitus. I Haloed in, with my English hood securely in place, in broad daylight no less, penetrated deep into the target AO, and exfilled, package in tow."

Rad pounded the table and said, "How's that for success?" He looked at his two friends with disbelief. "There was a time when that meant something, boys."

"Shit, you're a class one stud, Master Chief," Kane said. "Did you read it?"

"You know Rad can't read," Oz replied with a straight face. "It's a perishable skill."

Turning back to Kane, Radanovich said, "Basically, you're screwed, bro."

Kane read the document carefully. "Oh, this is bullshit; I had orders authorizing me to turn the package over to Wallace for interrogation. I didn't do it on my own."

Radanovich nodded. "Do you have the orders?"

"I did; the bloody CIA chief called me several times, reminding me of my duty to turn the prisoner over to Wallace. I received an email from him stating just that, but the last time I checked my computer in my hooch at Chapman, I couldn't find the orders."

"Oh brother, you're doubly screwed," said Werner.

"According to this, I am," said Kane. "I'm going to need a good lawyer."

"You may need more than that, Kyle," said Werner.

"What are you talking about, Oz?"

"You may need to consult the savior of SEALs, down through the ages—the man, the myth, the legend, Freddie 'the Friar' Carpenter!"

Chapter 10

Naval Air Station North Island, Coronado, 07:00

Lieutenant Commander Kyle Kane, dressed in his navy whites, entered the outer office of Senior JAG Counsel Captain Freddie Carpenter.

Kane felt uncomfortable in his dress whites. He could swear the same cigar smell lingered in his uniform from the last time he met with Freddie. The thick, acrid smoke seeped under the crack of the office door, and Kane experienced a wave of déjà vu.

"Kane," shouted a gravelly voice. Kyle stood up and entered the office. The walls were covered with photos and memorabilia from famous California politicians, left-leaning coasters, and other Hollywood types.

Freddie Carpenter's serious demeanor served as his professional facade. He was a man with an incredibly droll sense of humor, a penchant for the bottle, and a love of fine cigars. His brother ran a movie production company in LA.

Freddie was likely the most sought-after lawyer in the JAG Corps, largely due to his work with the SEALs.

He offered Kane a stubby Cohiba from the humidor on his desk. Kane nodded and took one of the fat little cigars.

"Thank you for taking the time to meet with me today, Freddie," said Kane.

Freddie lit his cigar and savored the first deep pull, releasing a cloud of smoke.

"Kyle, how long have I known you?" asked Carpenter. "Ten years—at least?"

"Yeah, sounds about right. The mission in Chad, where we brought cosmic justice to the Junkgiwy."

"They're called Janjaweed, and your cosmic justice line was quite a stretch at the time. It hasn't improved much with age. Even the Chadians, who hate them with a passion, considered one hundred and twenty-three dead Janjaweed militia in twelve minutes an excessive use of force," said Freddie.

"That's the Chadians for you; they're a country that outsources their best soldiers," replied Kane.

"You're talking about the Foreign Legion?" asked Freddie.

"Janjaweed are murderers who continue to commit heinous crimes against the most innocent people in Darfur and Chad, Freddie. They deserve my boot on their throat and more."

"I know, but explain that to the world—a world filled with people who hate their fathers and whose sole mission is to destroy America."

Kane leaned forward in his chair and tipped his cigar. "Those Janjaweed attacked a convoy moving orphans from Sudan to safer accommodations. I didn't disobey orders; I just didn't ask for a green light. I made a command decision and unleashed the hell of my sixteen apostles on them. Hence the term—'cosmic justice.'"

"We went from God's justice to cosmic justice; you have to keep that straight," said Carpenter. "I still can't find God or cosmic justice in the Navy Code of Conduct." The stocky carpenter sipped his 32 oz Dr. Pepper. "The State Department saw it a little differently. They said you single-handedly destroyed years of discourse and diplomacy with the Janjaweed."

"Who parlays with genocidal murderers of women, children, and infants. Diplomacy, really," said Kane. "There is no such thing as diplomacy with those khat-chewing psychopaths. Our State Department uses our taxpayer money not to feed the starving Chadians or the desperate Black Africans in Southern Sudan; no, they buy off these Janjaweed and pay them to stay out of the State Department's favorite NGO's hair. It's all about allowing those NGOs to continue exploiting the poor and the weak, literally stealing their oil and minerals while donating to certain corrupt politicians in DC. It's their birthright—those natural resources found beneath their land."

Freddie knew to leave well enough alone and waited until Kane finished venting. "Those resources could have changed lives and futures. Had they not suffered enough?"

Kane leaned back in his chair. "Our rules of engagement were clear: if opposition forces shoot at us, we are free to engage—a green light to go weapons hot. If there were five hundred of them, we'd have just piled the bodies higher."

"Sounds like you were fighting at the *Hot Gates.*"

"Then we'll fight in the shade," said Kane with a smile. "We took down every one of those bastards who carried a gun, and more's the better, so the story goes."

"They were all carrying guns, Kyle. Your actions aligned with the Janjaweed ethos: If it breathes, kill it," Captain Carpenter said as he leafed through Kane's file. He smiled a few times, then abruptly snapped it shut.

"I love reading your case files, Kane; they're filled with so much righteous payback." Carpenter leaned forward and rolled the ash off his cigar into a deep blue and gold glass USN ashtray. "The current file has a different spin, a different group of assholes—much more of a looking-for-your-scalp kind of thing."

"I can't help it if I'm popular, Freddie," Kane replied. "Really, this whole thing was above my pay grade. I was a pipe hitter leading a group of pipe hitters; we just did what we were told—there was no ad lib or ad hoc—nothing."

Carpenter then asked Kane, "Where's the email? The one Corbett's office sent you, directing you to undertake this mission in connection with the CIA?"

Kane looked at the end of his cigar and tipped it into the same blue ashtray. "Whoever is behind this had the skill, the clearance, and the access to get it done."

"I can go on and on, Kyle, about how difficult it would be to delete an encrypted email from a secure military server, Freddie."

"Who comes to mind?"

"The Agency," Kane replied.

"That's funny, Lt. Commander?"

"The NSA comes to mind, along with some Silicon Valley NGO specializing in espionage."

Captain Carpenter put down the file. "Precisely, and that's why you should consider the early retirement package... coupled with the honorable discharge that the Navy's Judge Advocate tossed in."

Kane shot Freddie a hard glare before crushing his cigar into the ashtray.

Freddie leaned forward and emphasized, "Listen, sailor, I read tea leaves for a living, and the bottom of this cup tells me someone wants your scalp. From the data, I can't determine who's behind this dirty work." He raised the brief. "These culprits have gone to great lengths to make you look culpable, or at the very least, negligent in your duty." Carpenter pushed Kane's file over to him.

"Who, Freddie? Who has that kind of influence? I mean, who in particular?"

Freddie leaned in and, with a serious expression, said, "Warren Trask, the CIA emperor in waiting.

He's a very anti-American bureaucrat. Open a thesaurus and look up 'truculent'; you'll find a list of pretty terrible human traits. Warren Trask embodies every one of those."

"Why would that asshole have it in for me? We never crossed paths."

"You messed up his mission inside your mission."

"I didn't; William freakin' Wallace did."

"Braveheart, that—"

"No counselor, the CIA puke who murdered my HVT stole the SSI and got my best officer—my best friend—killed!"

"William Wallace, that's his name? It's redacted in my file. If he did what you said he did, then there are people in the CIA operating against the wishes of Pope Trask."

"So the enemy of my enemy is my friend?"

"Yeah, something like that. Listen, there are stacks of references regarding your fitness to serve, unit and individual commendations, and you've received enough medals to fill a Russian general's chest. However, there are one or two statements—unnamed references—regarding daydreaming and loss of focus during the last four months, specifically concerning this mission."

"Well, that part has some merit; I found myself thinking about my dead daughter." Kane paused. "Listen, Freddie, I was starting to get a grip on it, and it's bound to get better; it just takes a little time."

"Kyle, time is something you don't have."

Kane looked around Freddie's office, trying to focus his thoughts. "So that's it? I've got no other avenues?"

"What about President Obama? He personally met with me after Yemen; we had a beer at the White House—in the Rose Garden."

"That little tidbit wasn't included in the prosecution's brief. If you think that's going to sway a board of Navy leftovers, you're kidding yourself, Kyle. When Al Jazeera got a hold of the Janjaweed massacre, the Speaker of the House nearly shit her adult diaper in a fit of joy, and a creepy congressman from California jumped for joy like Ted Bundy at a sorority mixer."

"Bundy might find that offensive," Kane replied, "if he were alive."

Freddie laughed and said, "Bundy does remind me of that wacko. Anyway, couple the Sudan screwup with the shitstorm we currently find ourselves in; that screwup is tied directly to the Navy, Admiral Corbett to be specific. By the way, he overruled the decision to charge you with dereliction of duty and court-martial you. If you retire, your record will be clean."

"Admiral Corbett saved my bacon?"

"How did you get this brief, Kyle?" asked Freddie. "On second thought, don't tell me; I don't want to know."

"No, you don't want to know; it would just piss you off even more."

"This went all the way up the line. The mere fact that Corbett gave you a way out and sweetened the deal speaks volumes about the kind of operator you are and that they may believe you regarding the orders. It's an inter-agency thing, and the CIA is forcing the Navy's hand."

"They need to appear strong on this; looking weak in the current political atmosphere could end their careers. Obama got rid of the career officers with a spine, and under Biden Obama is making sure everyone tows the woke line. The ones that are left don't fight for anyone."

Kane leaned back in his chair and tried to relight his cigar. "Maybe there's still enough time left in my life to start something new. I'll pick up the pieces and make something out of it."

"That's the spirit, Kyle."

"Yeah, hell yeah, it's time for a change," Kane replied. "If I had the chance to do it all over again—two Silver Stars, a Bronze Star, a Navy Cross, a few Purple Hearts—add up the hardware, divide that by eighteen years of blood and guts, death and destruction, throw in one dead child and one marriage on the rocks—and does that equal forty-eight thousand dollars a year? I say it doesn't, but if I'd still become a SEAL, without question."

"You and I should have gone to Wall Street, like my father always told me to," said Freddie.

He glanced at his Fordham law degree on the wall and smiled. Turning back to Kane, he continued, "I've calculated the cost of staying with the JAG instead of joining my father's Wall Street firm; it cost me over twenty-three million dollars, but it saved me countless years of therapy and a ton of grief from dear old Dad."

Kane motioned for his lawyer to pass him the resignation of commission document. He signed it with a flourish, as if afraid he might change his mind. He pushed it across Freddie's desk and pushed back in his chair.

"Hoorah," said Kane. "Hoo-fucking-rah!"

Kane rose from the leather chair, and Freddie Carpenter stood to salute Lieutenant Commander Kyle Kane. They shook hands.

"You're still one of the best who has ever worn the Trident, Kyle. You've got nothing to be ashamed of." Kane nodded and left Freddie Carpenter's office.

Chapter 11

Parking Garage Hoover Building 16:30

The concrete ramp of the FBI garage was where Carrie Gould, thin as she was, had to shimmy into her special edition Tahoe. She hoisted herself up and fell into the plush leather seats. Staring into her visor mirror for what felt like an eternity, she could sense her father's eyes on her, even though he had died six years earlier. He too had been a carrier pilot, flying F-4 Phantoms.

Her phone rang, startling her. It was Lizabeth Holcum, and she said into the phone, “Yeah, I'm okay. Just feeling like I’ve been snarked by a couple of snarky assholes."

"Anyone in particular, girlfriend?"

"No, I can't say, and yes, I'm coming home."

"Grab a bottle or three of Pinot."

"I will. We need to talk."

***

An hour later, Carrie walked into their spacious Dupont Circle condo. The two-story, open-concept space featured a restaurant-grade range, a steam oven, and a huge Zero King fridge.

She slid her vacuum-packed sea bass into the sous-vide drawer and began working her magic on a four-star bouillabaisse.

Carrie slipped in behind Lizza, inhaling the savory steam from the Marseille fishermen's stew simmering on the SKS eight-burner.

"Hey girl, what's cooking? I smell some real ooh la la."

Lizza, whisking up a rouille—a mayonnaise made with olive oil, saffron, garlic, and cayenne pepper—dipped her finger into the steel bowl and sensually slid it onto Carrie's tongue. Carrie playfully patted Lizza on the bum.

"That is heaven-sent, Lizza-girl. It needs a little more cayenne pepper.”

"That's my killer rouille, and we're going to slather it over some grilled slices of French bread.”

Carrie wrapped her arms around Lizza's hips.

"What's bubbling away in the stockpot?"

"A traditional bouillabaisse," Lizza replied.

"And you are nothing if not traditional, Lizza," said Carrie. In truth, Lizza was a Cordon Bleu-trained, Michelin three-star chef. She had all that talent and none of the ego.

"I'm using red rascasse, sea robin, European conger, a few clams and mussels, some sea urchin, langoustines, and vegetables."

"Okay, girl, I think it's time for a little vino."

Lizza rummaged through their everything drawer, which contained digital thermometers, acidity meters, kebab skewers, and assorted hand tools. As she pushed everything around, something beeped.

"Is that a smoke alarm?"

"Not unless there's smoke in the everything drawer."

Carrie shuffled through the utensils until she found her FEAYEA digital bug sweeper.

By sheer luck, Lizza pressed the sweep button. Carrie hadn’t thought about it since she swept their new home six months ago. She lifted the device out of the drawer and pressed the sweep button.

"Hold on, girl," she said. "Hold those naughty thoughts."

"What's going on?" Lizza asked as she flipped the toasted French bread on the indoor grill.

A couple of minutes later, Carrie returned holding a smoke detector and a handful of devices. Some were little boxes, and others were the size of a quarter with a wire tail. She dropped them on the kitchen table and continued through the rest of the house, finishing in the bedroom.

"What the hell are those things, Carrie?" Lizabeth Holcum asked, looking down at the blinking device.

Carrie pressed her index finger to her lips and pulled Lizza into the living room. She switched on her Macintosh bookshelf system. Lizza began to protest, but Carrie took her by the shoulders, and they sank into the loveseat.

"There are two of them in our bathroom," she whispered in Lizza's ear.

One was integrated into the shower, and the other was hidden in the woven palm laundry hamper. There were seven more throughout the other rooms.

"Our bedroom? Carrie, what are all those things doing in our home?"

"They're listening devices and video cameras." Lizza felt a tightness in her chest, and Carrie rushed to find her inhaler.

After two puffs, Lizza struggled to speak. "Why?"

Carrie rubbed her chin. "The little boys' club doesn't like women."

Chapter 12

Naval Air Station Oceana, Virginia. 11:11

“The air is much thicker in Va Beach. Sand Dog was the perfect place,” said Kane as he stepped off the red-eye flight from the West Coast.

He grabbed his seabag and backpack from the baggage carousel and carried them out to the curb.

He tossed them into the back seat of his Uber for the drive to Naval Air Station Oceana. His DEVGRU digs were just a stone's throw from NAS Little Creek, where the rest of the East Coast team trained.

"Back to the world?" asked the driver.

"Back for good."

Kane's arrival went unacknowledged; there was no send-off, no handshakes with the brass at Oceana or Little Creek, and no small party in a conference room.

He spent a day or two catching up with friends before finally scheduling his discharge meeting. He emptied his cage and turned in all the gear he couldn't keep. Then, he met with his benefits coordinator and received his VA card.

Kane felt a jolt as he pulled onto his street, an unexpected rush of emotion. If he were operational, he would push it deep into the darkest corner of his soul. He parked in front of his three-car garage, stepped onto his front yard, and expected to see a lawn suffering from too many bargain basement bags of seeds and not enough watering. Instead, the transition to deep and plush was thanks to his neighbor, Jerry Destoto, who was Kane's drinking buddy when he was at home with Maria. A few beers and laughs later, a day before Kane left for deployment, Jerry promised to take care of his grass until he returned.

I never thought he'd turn my lawn into an Augusta fairway.

Destoto was a general contractor who built houses all over Southern Virginia. His wife, whom he met at the University of Richmond, was an executive at a cell phone company. The two had befriended Kane and his wife, Maria, during better times, and when things turned difficult, the Desotos remained steadfast.

Kane stared at his house. It was more than he could afford on his retirement pay. His wife, Maria, who taught oceanography at the Virginia Institute of Marine Science, moved to her mother's place across town a couple of months ago—around the time Kyle began his last deployment—and she abdicated any responsibility for their three hundred thousand dollar mortgage.

Kane wasn't scheduled to rotate home for another four months, right up until the US Navy cut him loose. For the first time in almost twenty years, he had nowhere to be and no one to answer to.

"Kyle Kane, you're home, bro!" The voice boomed out from the stand-alone, four-bay garage with all of its doors up. Kane knew it as Desoto's workshop, and it had every tool imaginable, and with that much equipment and that many jobs going on came the appearance of confusion, but Jerry, like most all successful GCs, employed the time-honored tradition of robbing Peter to pay Paul and pooling his resources from other jobs; his employees pulled his project across the line.

Kane tried to remember if he had left on his last deployment without having returned any of the many tools Jerry had lent him. *Being on the Teams was a constant source of life lessons, and borrowing tools was no different. It happened all the time on the Teams, and loaning a teammate a roll of matte black duct tape, or a spare pair of tac-gloves —something that simple—could save someone's life, and not returning it as soon as possible could just as simply put a crack in the bond that was the reason it was loaned in the first place. Between teammates, one crack begets two, and two becomes three until soon enough the bond is gone.*

Kyle turned to see Jerry Desoto bounding over the newly planted privet hedge. The big man, who once weighed three hundred pounds during his playing days at Richmond, had lost a good bit of his fit form.

"Hey, neighbor! How's the work of making the world safe for democracy going?"

"Jerry, it's going well. How are you, Siobhan, and the kids?"

"They're great, Kyle! Before I forget, I got a dozen tickets to the Spider's season opener. We're playing the Tar Heels, and I'm sure they're taking us lightly."

"Jerry," Kane laughed, "I should be taking you to a game. You watched my house and turned my front yard into a putting green, and I don't know how to repay you."

"No worries, brother. It's just our way of giving back."

"Well, your sacrifice is not lost on me."

"You can repay me by joining us for drinks and dinner."

Kane nodded in appreciation.

"Okay, how about six?"

"That works perfectly."

"We'll see you then."

***

Kane unlocked the door and pushed it open, greeted by the smell of stale, stagnant air. A layer of dust had settled on everything, a telling sign of neglect.

"New construction houses shouldn't have this much dust," he muttered. He bent down to grab his duffle bag, but as he stood up, a flashback halted him in his tracks. He remembered Gabby running to greet him, her adorable, awkward steps, pudgy little arms, and tiny hands reaching out for him. The memories washed over him like a firehose.

Kane had attempted to speak with his estranged wife, but his mother-in-law urged him to give her some space, and he reluctantly agreed. He told Edith he still had the same cell phone number and that if Maria wanted to talk, she should call.

After an hour-long workout in the basement gym, Kane took a quick walk around the house and compiled a punch list of a dozen repairs that needed attention. With his schedule now permanently open, he had no excuse left to bring the house up to speed.

One reason Maria had left was that Kane was slow to tackle the home repairs on his to-do list. He began by cutting and nailing down a few loose clapboards that had cracked and fallen. The mailbox, which hung precariously by a roofing nail, received a new support. For the day's finale, Kane straightened the cupola on the garage roof and positioned its weathervane in the correct direction.

Sitting on the peak of the garage roof, he surveyed the neighborhood.

Standing on the roof peak, he balanced himself as he picked and pulled at the splinters he had acquired.

I was the one at fault, eager to jump back into the fight and its two hundred mile per hour ops tempo, never once considering how Maria was coping—left alone and vulnerable, the person I vowed to love, honor, and protect. I had left her hanging; I had failed her utterly and completely.

Kane climbed down from the roof and sat on the steps of his back patio. *She was facing the loss of a child while I was running away.*

At dinner time, Kane pulled out a pizza and added a few frozen burgers before throwing it in the oven. He poured himself a fifty-fifty Jim Beam and ginger, intending to drink himself to sleep. Halfway through, he decided to turn on his laptop.

He found dozens of emails from SEAL Team operators around the globe. A few of his brothers were sending him mercenary job websites. He spent some time browsing the listings. After reading about the salaries, he stopped.

"I should look for a job," he thought.

He opened a website run by Derrick Ross, a former SEAL who advised veterans on how to translate their skills into post-military life. Kane explored the site and sent Ross an email detailing his qualifications and experience, keeping it non-specific and omitting personal information.

Next, he moved to LinkedIn and created a profile. *Maybe I can reinvent myself as a corporate security suit-and-*

tie guy. Life in a cubicle? No, I've been chasing the wolves too long to be comfortable resting with the flock. Besides, AI is going to make gone whole swaths of middle and upper management positions, a jobs genocide, and the soulless tech billionaires who will be the lords of this most hated technology will become the targets of the unemployed masses.

Kane returned to his emails, sifting through half a dozen more before spotting an unfamiliar name.

Ronald Brunswick—who the hell are you? Kane read the email and leaned back in his chair. "You're a self-proclaimed Spec Ops guru."

"What the hell, I've got no other prospects. I suck as a handyman, and I'm too old to start as a cop." He took a long pull from his glass of bourbon. "What do I do with my skill set? Professional door kicker? International man of intrigue?"

It was late, and he felt the need to unwind, so he closed his laptop and sank into the faux leather sectional. He turned on the flat screen and kicked back.

He glanced at the remote. *That's new, and the damn TV has doubled in size. So that's where my hazardous duty pay went.*

***

The sound of automatic gunfire pierced the darkness. Kane reached for his Springfield XD. "Shit, where's my fucking burner?" he yelled as he rolled off his bed and onto the floor.

He searched the room for his Mk12. Nothing was where it should be. Rounds crackled around him as he crawled across the floor, desperate to secure a weapon. Suddenly, the door to his room burst open, revealing a Taliban fighter clad in black from his turban to his Jaguar trainers.

It's an RPG-7 at my head! That's it, I'm dead!

***

The sound of his own voice shattered the scene. The fog of his dream state, clouded by his buddy Jim Beam, lifted with a surge of adrenaline. He rolled off his bed and hit his head on the corner of the nightstand, sending him back into the dark world of unconsciousness.

Loud pounding opened Kyle's eyes to the sunlight flooding the room. The same loud banging that had jolted him awake now throbbed in his head. Unsure if it was real or just in his mind, he heard the knocking again and realized it was coming from his front door.

"Asshole... pounding on my door at this hour," shouted Kane. He pulled on his PT shorts and stumbled through the wreckage of his bedroom. Reaching into the nightstand, he found his trusty Springfield XD and racked the slide.

The loud knocking came again as he approached the front door, half-naked with his 9mm in hand.

Kane yanked open the door with more energy than he intended. He stood ready to deliver a scolding rebuke but found himself face-to-face with a very pretty college-age delivery girl.

Another cover-girl beauty in uniform; this could be a trend.

The delivery woman, dressed in the gold and brown uniform of a courier service, smiled at Kane. He could only smile back as his dehydrated, oxygen-deprived brain struggled with misfiring neurons.

"You have to be the most beautiful woman I have ever seen," said Kyle Kane, trying to straighten up. He noticed she was staring at his bare chest, which bore the scars of his travels through the sandbox. Crisscrossing shrapnel marks, three 7.62 mm bullet holes, a six-inch gash from a scimitar across his sternum, and a couple of well-placed stab wounds told the story of a life lived on a razor's edge.

The young woman, with the name Sophia stitched across her ample chest, smiled and said, "Thank you, Mr. Kane. I'm sorry to have woken you."

Her face turned a slight shade of red as she attempted to hand Kane an electronic receipt to sign. She didn't flinch when he had to pull his pistol from behind his back to take hold of the e-pad.

She caught a glimpse of the gun but remained surprisingly calm.

Kane smiled and waved his hand. "It's—I'm a Navy guy," he said. "Old habits die hard." He set the gun down on a small table in the foyer.

Kane signed the digital pad and handed it back to the young woman.

She nodded and handed him an overnight letter envelope. He opened it quickly and found a black eight-by-ten card embossed in silver. Kane spun it around in his hand and smiled at her.

"It's okay, Mr. Kane; I dated a SEAL for a couple of weeks. He was a cool guy. So I know how attached you guys are to your guns—kind of like how sane people feel about their golf clubs."

Kane smiled as he tried to process her last comment. *Sane people?*

Sophia handed him a receipt before turning to walk back to her van.

"Hey, hold on for a second!" Kane yelled as she began to pull away. He jogged barefoot up to the driver's window and said, "I'm sorry, but there's no return address."

"It didn't come with one," she replied. "It's not the norm, but I have delivered a few without a return."

Kane nodded and backed away from the van. The cute delivery woman appraised him from head to toe before smiling. As she took in his rugged, scarred six-pack, she winked at him.

Kane was both amazed and amused by the boldness of the young woman.

Nothing like being checked out by a lovely little Lolita; things must be looking up.

He looked down at the matte black envelope in his hand, impressed by the quality of the stock and the hand-embossed silver lettering: "Lieutenant Commander Kyle Kane, USN Retired."

He checked his mailbox but found nothing. His curiosity piqued during breakfast as he stared at the big black envelope propped up in a napkin holder on the lazy Susan.

Kane reached over, spun it, and watched the enigmatic letter revolve around and around. After finishing his coffee, he pulled out his SOG Tano folder, took hold of the letter, and cut a fine line across the top with the razor-sharp blade.

"Could this be a letter bomb, ricin, or maybe Publisher's Clearing House?" Kane gingerly slid a single piece of black cardstock out of the envelope and laid it on the kitchen table. Once he cleared it, he read the silver-embossed calligraphy:

Lieutenant Kyle Kane, USN, SEAL Team Developmental Group, Retired.

You are cordially invited to the 14th Annual World Warrior's Draft &

Combine Evaluation and Full-Contact Hand-to-Hand Combat Tournament.

October 21, 22 & 23

Woodford Mountain Lodge and Resort, Thunder Cloud, Montana

RSVP: WorldWideWarrior@GGIU.org

Kane examined the card and envelope, but they yielded no answers. He sat down at his desk in the den and used Maria's Dell desktop to pull up Google Earth, recalling how he had previously used it to show his wife where his deployments were.

He searched for Thunder Cloud, Montana, and Woodford Lodge. A sizable river and several large ranches appeared on the map. The resort was expansive, boasting world-class fly fishing, four Nicklaus-designed golf courses, horseback trail riding, and a large indoor arena for concerts, rodeos, and other major events. It featured pools, saunas, spas, and massage therapists—everything one could imagine. It was an impressive place, set in a wooded, mountainous area, and, for all practical purposes, quite remote.

"Maybe it's the Taliban looking for payback, or ISIS trying to frame someone with a staged online beheading. Now I'm starting to sound paranoid. I should just finish the siding, have a couple of drinks, and sleep on it," he chuckled to himself. "It's 08:00, and I'm already planning my drinking for the day."

Kane worked throughout the day, frequently checking his emails. After finishing his tasks and tidying up, he decided to go out.

***

This is the only way I'll avoid checking my email every ten minutes.

Kane was headed to the Cigar Emporium, his favorite spot for great steaks, good conversation, and exceptional cigars.

He drove the three miles to the waterfront, arriving at the impressive hundred-and-fifty-year-old refurbished warehouse that sported a large retro sign proclaiming, *Cigar Emporium*. The building was half the size of a football field, combining a bar-restaurant with an old-school tobacco warehouse.

Antique and vintage equipment used by stevedores to move the hogsheads of bright-leaf tobacco and bales of local wrappers to the ships that were docked alongside the original warehouse owned by the tobacco trader, J&S, was set up around the retail area where crates and cases of cigars, cigarettes, and loose tobacco were stacked behind the display cases.

The original wood-plank walls and floors were shored up with I-beams and a new steel roof, and the warehouse that had sat vacant for decades before Harvey Schwartz purchased the condemned structure. He saved a historic building and gave it a new purpose with café-style dining and a hundred-and-fifty-foot sports bar where dozens of big screens ran sports day and night in the forty-foot-tall, open-architecture space.

Kane opened one of the glass double doors and stepped into the damp, slightly chilly atmosphere, maintained by state-of-the-art climate control.

“I love this place, like Panama on a winter's day.”

Kane walked through thousands of square feet of deep, aromatic shag, leaf, and snuff tobacco, surrounded by floor-to-ceiling crates stamped and labeled from around the world.

He admired the cigars, loose tobacco, and gold-embossed cigarettes displayed in glass cases that ran the length of the building. Beautiful briar, meerschaum, and clay bowls complemented an array of lighters, cutters, crocodile pouches, and ashtrays.

Kane looked over the cedar boxes of Arturo Fuentes X, Cohiba, H. Upmann, Gurkha Black Dragons, and King of Denmark cigars. He chose an Upmann, which would be waiting for him at the bar.

Threat assessment was a perishable skill, but it was one Kane kept sharp with constant observation and evaluation no matter the environment from the moment he stepped out of his front door. Once inside the building, he evaluated the fifty or so potential targets around the Cigar Emporium's happy hour in the first minute.

He looked for anything or anyone that seemed suspicious or out of place. Eyes were the key; they were the windows on the soul, and for Kane they were the lead indicator, followed by head movement and posture.

He made his way to the far side of the warehouse, where two hundred feet of back wall had been blown out to create a restaurant with a large glassed-in terrace.

Kane scanned the dining area. He rarely took a seat at the bar; he usually stood with his back to the wall, but this time, he chose to sit. He settled at the bar because his friend Otis Childress, an all-state defensive tackle in the Virginia's Patriot Conference, was behind the stick.

"Nothing like a military discount," Otis said, a wall of a man. When they shook, Kane's hand disappeared in Otis's giant paw. Above Otis's hand, barely visible on his forearm, was a faded Marine globe and anchor, with the Force Recon skull and wings beneath.

"It's good to see you, Otis," Kane replied.

Otis pulled a bottle of Jim Beam from the speed rack, but Kane waved it off. He had purchased an Arturo Fuente and was looking for an eighteen-year-old Macallan single malt.

"Sometimes you just gotta go big," said the three-hundred-pound bartender.

"Or go home, eh, Otis?" Kane quipped, pouring a little water into his glass of scotch.

"I thought you were on deployment."

"I was," said Kane, as his eyes dropped to his glass. Otis Childress had been a bartender long enough to know that some guys can't share much.

As he walked back down the bar, Otis scratched his 60s-style afro.

Kane felt bad about showing off in front of his friend and considered saying something.

But it is what it is; when you're a Seal, your life is a closed fucking book. It's one of the reasons I'm now on my own.

Kane started to think about calling Maria. Unsure of what to expect, he finished his drink and left a fifty. Otis was halfway down the bar, engrossed in his favorite fishing story, when he noticed Kane pushing in his bar stool.

Otis shifted his momentum—an act of special relativity —and bounded the fifty feet to the other end of the bar.

"Kyle, I got that dog," he shouted. "Drinks are on me!"

Kane waved his hand and called out to his friend, "Semper Fi, big man, Semper Fi," before cutting hard right and heading out of the restaurant.

Outside, he took a deep breath of the evening bayside air, reached for his keys, and started toward the far end of the parking lot.

"Something isn't right," he thought. Decades of experience with the unseen and the unknowable had triggered his sixth sense.

"Too many shadows near those cars? No one else in the parking lot." He couldn't quite put his finger on it. Something was off.

Kane's master control alarm lit up when he saw a group of three, maybe four, individuals get out of a car and gather on the far side of a parked pickup. He quickly calculated a response.

He stopped and took a long drag on his cigar, using the moment to assess the potential area of operations. He blew the ash off his twenty-dollar cigar, revealing the bright orange ember, and made a swift tactical evaluation.

Removing his SOG folder from his left back pocket, he snapped it open and secured it at the small of his back.

Without looking, he gauged the distance to the first and immediate threat.

Close the gap, remove their leverage, and extend it. He felt for his tactical baton in his front right pocket and began his approach. It was just light enough for Kane to make out three potential combatants gathered around a body on the ground.

Whoever's on the ground looks hurt, but there's no blood. It's a ruse. If they all come at me at once, it's going to get crazy.

Three men broke off from the group.

Three more steps, and they'll be in range. First man on me. Kane extended his ballistic baton and delivered a blow to the man's head.

Before he could take another step, the other two assailants split and moved in on either side of Kane.

"All I can do is turn and run," said Kane as he offered up a decoy.

He watched as the man on the ground got up and staggered over to the pickup.

A third man joined in against Kane. *Three against one, a sucker's play.* His thoughts raced. Anger surged through Kane's body. *Three assholes coming for me on my home turf, my bar, making my decision to stay and fight for me.*

"A fucking trap, a setup here at my favorite bar!" shouted Kane. One of the gang, with high cheekbones, deep-set dark eyes, and a pointy chin that made him look like the devil himself, flashed Kane a toothy smile.

Fuck me, this is gonna hurt.

Kane swung his baton, which had a half-inch steel ball bearing welded to the tip of a set of telescoping, high-tensile steel rods. It was a formidable tool for those trained to wield it, and Kane was surgical with it.

"One direct blow and you're out; two and he'll kill you," said the swarthy man, who apparently controlled the gang.

Who the fuck would be coming for me in the States?

They look tough, trained, and military. They're spread far enough apart to draw me in, then they all collapse on me.

The biggest man moved first, and Kane flicked his cigar at him. It struck him on the bridge of his nose, exploded, and sent embers into both eyes. He screamed and fell to his knees. Kane finished him with a head shot.

The second assailant swung an ax handle from behind.

Taking the easy cheap shot is a display of weakness, thought Kane as he ducked.

The wild roundhouse sailed over his head, striking the wounded assailant as he stood up from Kane's cigar attack. The loud crack said it all.

"Cracked skull, one down, three to go!"

Overextended, the weak-minded ax-handle man was wide open for a head blow with

Kane's baton. "Never take the obvious headshot, asshole!" shouted Kane.

Kane's momentum carried him out of the center of the deadly circle. "Two down, two to go—fuckers," he shouted. "Cockiness always has a price."

The man on Kane's immediate right yelled, "I'm going to kill you, motherfucker!" He came at Kane with a short staff and jabbed at his midsection. Kane blocked it and drove a palm strike into the man's face, crushing his nose and knocking him down.

Another man moved to Kane's blind side and got around his neck. A fifth assailant appeared out of nowhere and kicked Kane's knees out from behind.

Kane went to the ground. Normally, he'd be right at home in a jujitsu guard, but three well-trained assailants working together on top of him posed a serious threat.

Body blows landed, and the man on Kane's neck secured a rear-naked choke. Kane's breathing was restricted, along with the blood supply to his brain.

I gotta get this mutt off my neck. Kane felt the lights starting to fade. I'm choking out; then come the head blows, and it's jello and soft food till the end.

Suddenly, the pressure around Kane's neck released. Through the fog of hypoxia, he saw what he thought was a body lifted off him and sent flying into space.

A loud crunch was followed by a bunch of heavy thuds. Kane made out shapes and sounds, dark figures blocking out the parking lot lights. He sensed a presence standing over him.

"It's the big man," mumbled Kane as he lay on the ground. It was the big man who fought like his childhood hero, Big George Foreman. He dispensed punishing blows that emanated from his tree trunk core and were delivered through his huge jaw-busting fists. Kane tried to pull himself together and get back in the fight.

Otis stood his ground and countered every attempt to break through. He absorbed axe handle blows and knife slashes, returning fire with devastating punches, hooks, straight rights, and uppercuts. All Kane could do was watch in foggy amazement as it all unfolded.

Sirens rose from the distance and cut through the salty night air.

One of the men shouted, "Trouble close!"

The tall, swarthy man cursed and shouted, "Bokon!" He drew a small-caliber silenced pistol and pointed it at Kane's head as he lay on the ground. Otis fearlessly shifted one of his tree trunk legs, blocking the shot.

"Bokon… you Farsi bastard!" shouted Kane. "He's Iranian."

The man smiled a chilling, toothy grin and cocked the long-barreled Black Widow revolver. He aimed down the barrel at Otis's face.

"Pull that trigger, asshole, and you'll have a crater in that ugly-ass face of yours." It was the half-crippled cigar genius, owner of the Cigar Emporium, Harvey Schwartz, that was staring through wire-rim glasses that made his eyes look three times their size, down the long barrel of his M1 Garand battle rifle. Otis's boss, a member of the 1st Marines at seventeen and one of the Chosen Few, had survived one hundred and twenty thousand Red Chinese and North Korean soldiers at the Chosin Reservoir, and he wasn't about to let this son of a bitch harm his friends.

"I won't say it twice, Omar Sharif! I'm inclined to shoot you just for the ruckus you've caused, but you'd bleed all over my nicely restriped parking lot."

The Iranian considered turning his pistol on the old man, but Harvey Schwartz's hands weren't shaking. He also recognized the weapon as a large-caliber battle rifle that could literally separate his head from his shoulders.

"It's been more than sixty years since I killed someone, asshole, and I killed a lot of people. Take my word for it, Omar; shootin' one more rabid dog like yourself ain't gonna change my handicap with the big guy. Now, get the fuck outta here before I change my mind!"

With a face like the devil himself, the man, dressed in all black, sneered at the old marine. He weighed the galactic odds against him as he stared down the barrel of the rifle. Schwartz hopped down the steps, never taking the iron sights of his M1 off the Iranian's head. He motioned for the other four thugs—bleeding and beaten—to leave his parking lot.

The four men hustled across the pier to a gangway that led to a floating dock. Seconds later, a cigarette boat sped out into the intercoastal waterway. Otis took the M1 from his boss and considered putting some rounds downrange until he thought about the potential for collateral damage.

Kane pushed himself up to his knees and said, "Otis, I knew it was you."

Kane looked over to the glass double doors, and Harvey was gone. "You saved my life, big man," said Kane, getting to his feet. "I thought it was the second coming of George Foreman banging away."

The big man checked his wounds, a few gashes on his head and forearms. "It's the least I could do for a brother who drops me a fifty."

Police cruisers arrived first, followed by an ambulance and an unmarked car. A short, stout man with a round face and a perpetual silly smile climbed out of his blue Crown Vic and pulled on a tweed blazer.

Kane sat on the back of the ambulance as he prepared for a concussion protocol exam. He refused to go to the hospital for a CT scan. Instead, he went back inside and took a seat at the bar, where Harvey, the sage old tobacconist, brought out a few raw steaks and a bottle of Johnny Walker Blue.

"Strange kind of assault, Kyle," Harvey shrugged. "But you must be doing something right for someone to send five scumbags."

***

Kane walked into his large, empty house and sat in his spacious, vacant kitchen. The contract for realty services lay on the table in front of him. Beyond the boilerplate document was the black invitation, as vague and enigmatic as the moment he first opened it.

He had considered signing on with Blackwater, attracted by its seven-figure salaries.

Working as a paramilitary for a covert agency like the CIA doesn't seem half bad. Given how I left the Navy, that doesn't seem like a likely option.

This situation is a horse of a different color. They want me to try out for a team, but what kind of team? I'm pretty sure I know what a full-contact hand-to-hand tournament entails, but a player draft?

Kane reached over and signed the realty agreement. He picked up his cell phone and entered the number from the mysterious black invite.

Before long, a phone number was texted back with a European prefix, +33, and a French number. He dialed it and waited for the call to connect. No voice came through, only a series of electronic beeps and sounds, followed by a prerecorded message. It was a very pleasant voice, a French woman's voice:

"Monsieur Kane, please be available for transport at 06:00 tomorrow. You will need only toiletries and the clothes on your back. Everything else, including a contestant's fee of ten thousand dollars, will be provided if you are not chosen.

If you are chosen, your contract will serve as your remuneration.

You will be responsible for your own negotiations.

Compensation in the past has been closely tied to success in the combines and the hand-to-hand tournament, followed by the GGIG's World Warrior Draft. Press one to indicate that you understand and accept these terms. Press two if you need to reschedule your pickup. Press three if you wish to decline this opportunity entirely. Au revoir."

"I could sit around and wait for those mooks to take another shot at me. They might show, and they might not. I can't go around using tactics from the sandbox here in the real world. I have to get used to letting the cops do their job."

He pressed the first key and waited for a response. A second later, the call ended.

Kane looked at his cell phone in disbelief. "So much for French etiquette."

Chapter 13

Virginia Beach 05:30

The shrill sound of the alarm clock shattered the early morning peace. Kane reached it in an instant and silenced it with a decisive slam. He jumped out of bed, still half-awake. Like every other day of his adult life, this one began at zero-dark-thirty. He bolted out of the bedroom and hopped into the shower. The bed was made, and the house was tidy.

Kane stepped outside and quietly shut the door behind him. It was that time of morning, just before dawn, when the faintest hint of light began to chase away the night.

He raised the red flag on the mailbox and hesitated before placing the signed realtor's agreement inside. Thoughts of his wife and baby daughter held him back. When he finally dropped the letter and slammed the mailbox shut, he felt something precious. like a spirit that was attached to his house, like his family, or maybe his warrior spirit and how it had begun to slip away.

He returned to the raised concrete and brick porch that spanned the front of his house. He sat on one of the Adirondack chairs, closed his eyes, and tried to block out his emotions. Kane had read a lot on the lives of the American Indians. He thought about the braves, the Cheyenne Dog Soldiers who fought the US Army in a war they could never win. It was a fight that their warrior spirit demanded. He imagined their thoughts as they sat bareback on their mustangs across from the line of blue. He wondered if that was his warrior spirit that he had felt slipping away.

Just then, a pair of headlights cut through the foggy morning, prompting Kane to stand.

The black Mercedes 600 pulled into his driveway, and Kane was on his way.

***

It took only three and a half hours from the moment Kane was picked up until the Gulfstream 5 taxied to a stop at Teterboro Airport in Northern New Jersey.

A black Suburban pulled up a few feet from the Gulfstream's staircase as it descended from the fuselage.

The back door of the big black Chevy opened for Kyle, and the strong midday light blacked out the interior of the truck. Kane squinted as he climbed inside.

He settled into the cool leather seat, which felt almost clammy. The light filtering through the heavily tinted windows was barely enough to see, certainly not enough to make out the two very attractive women waiting inside.

One sat right next to him while the other leaned over the seat from behind, running a long, sensual finger along his neck.

Kane suppressed his instinct to react. "Well, this is an unexpected... pleasure. I had envisioned something a little less, ah, civilized."

The woman behind him giggled and draped her arms over Kane's shoulders.

"I could get used to this."

A sultry French voice came from the passenger seat directly in front of him. "Bonne journée, Mr. Kane. Welcome. We are representatives of the Groupe de Guerrier's International Guild, the GGIG. As you may have guessed, you have caught the attention of several organizations seeking someone with your talents. My name is Francesca Renaud, and I am your contestant liaison."

"All of a sudden, I'm a popular guy," Kane said. "But looking at the three of you, I feel a little overmatched."

"And you should, Commander," replied the beautiful Asian woman behind him.

"We are not here for your entertainment," said the woman next to him. "We are here to conduct a full assessment of your physical capabilities."

Kane glanced at the woman beside him, a stunning blonde with deep blue eyes.

Three beautiful women examining me? Things are getting strange, but it's a good kind of strange.

He looked out the tinted windows and considered his situation. *For sure, these women know more than they're letting on.*

"Okay, what's my position in all this?" Kane asked the three of them.

"Lieutenant Commander Kane, we have all the background information on you that exists," said Francesca Renaud from the front seat, passing a half-inch-thick folder to Kane, who leafed through it.

"I'll be damned, you have the names of my high school girlfriends in here. Oh no, you got this wrong; my high school wrestling record is 103-8-0, not 102-9-0."

The three women exchanged glances and began to laugh.

"We did that on purpose," said the tall 'Uma Thurman' type, shifting onto Kane's lap. Her ice-blue eyes locked onto his as her perfect alabaster skin gleamed, slipping out of her jet-black leather miniskirt suit.

She leaned forward, her plump breasts straining against the top button of her suit jacket. She caught Kane looking and smiled, her full red lips curving enticingly. She had him, and he knew it.

With her pure London accent, she said, "Like what you see, Sub Commander Kane?"

“Reminds me of a Christopher Lee vampire movie," said Kane. "What's not to like?"

"A second woman—is that a fatal flaw, QB One?" asked the lanky Asian girl, who began the sensual ritual of unbuttoning her top. As she leaned over the back seat, her large, perfect breasts swayed enticingly.

"Noooo, absolutely not," Kane said. "As for QB One, I think we’ve jetted well past the high school cheerleader references and into deep space."

"Speaking of getting behind," said the tall blonde as she spun around, raised her skirt, and shook her perfect china-white backside in Kane's face.

Francesca Renaud smiled as if none of the antics behind her bothered her at all. She faced forward, writing in her daybook while whispering to the driver.

"By the way, Mr. Kane, we're not heading to Montana," Renaud said, glancing into her compact mirror. "So, try to take care of business in the next forty minutes."

Kane pushed himself up from beneath the tangled bodies. “Forty minutes—where are we headed?” When he received no answer, he returned to the two women, who were bumping, thumping, and gyrating around him.

"MetLife Stadium, where else? I’m sure you didn’t think we were going to Montana, Mr. Kane?"

"No, Ms. Renaud. I make it a point to know what the possibilities are. Why the ruse?" Kane asked as a long, lustful hand reached up and pulled him back into the writhing twist of bodies.

Renaud smiled and snapped her compact closed. She climbed from the front seat of the Suburban into a second blacked-out Suburban. On her way, she said, "You're entering a world where nothing is as it seems, Mr. Kane. Always remember, I'm here to guide you through this competition."

***

The Suburban drove for forty minutes, the wildest forty minutes of his life, before the driver pulled into the stadium parking lot. An ornate portico for VIPs led to an escalator that likely took wealthy clients to their super boxes.

Kane decided to pay the driver a couple of hundred dollars to park along the reed-lined service road. “As ordinary as it seems,” Kane said, “it’s not every day an everyday guy like me gets to do the horizontal mambo with two beautiful women. So an extra twenty minutes could make all the difference.” He was lost in a punchbowl of lust, slithering around like an eel with his two new friends, Mia and Anna, both covered in sweat.

As Anna grabbed a towel to dry herself, Kane said, “Don’t. I love the scent of a woman; like your sweat, it’s filled with pheromones.”

Half an hour later, the Suburban stopped at the stadium's player entrance. A line of men waited to check in, all turning to watch as Kane struggled to climb out of the dark cave that was the back of the vehicle. He was pulling on his pants just before wrestling his shirt away from the two naked vixens, who were trying vigorously to pull him back into the shadows of the back seat.

He said to no one in particular, “This lends new meaning to the term ‘grinder.’”

The two dozen contestants and their support personnel began whistling and applauding Kane, who stood barefoot and shirtless as he fought off the grabbing hands and long, silky legs wrapped around him.

Kane managed to straighten himself and slip into his loafers, sending the ladies off with a fond farewell.

Just as Kane got his feet under him, Francesca Renaud emerged from the stadium. She took him by the arm and led him past the line of smirking and laughing men. The security personnel nodded their approval, allowing Ms. Renaud to skirt around the checkpoint.

The two walked out onto the mezzanine section and looked down upon the spectacular playing field. “The stadium floor is sectioned off into four areas,” said Francesca, “along with a fully enclosed shooting range in the basement. Over there is a live ammo kill house for CQB, covered from all angles and displayed on the Jumbotrons.”

Next to the combine area, at the end of the forty-yard sprint lane, stood a group of mysterious-looking voting booths. "What goes on down there?" asked Kane.

"That's where cognitive, tactical, and spatial relations testing is administered," said Renaud.

Kane noticed three fighting octagons folded up and stored at one end.

"Those are waiting to be rolled out for the hand-to-hand combat tournament, the World Warrior Championship, Mr. Kane."

"Quite impressive, Ms. Renaud. Impressive to the point of intimidation; it makes a man wonder if he has what it takes to compete at this level."

"I know what you're thinking, Mr. Kyle Kane," said Francesca Renaud, her sexy French accent adding a playful edge. "You wouldn't have received that kind of reception if my boss didn't believe you to be, how do you say, the real deal."

Kane stood inches from Francesca's slender, curvaceous body, perfectly fitted into her Vera Wang dress. *If hot were a characteristic, she'd be the face of the sun.*

"You have what it takes, Kyle Kane. GGIG does not make mistakes."

Kyle smiled at Renaud's opinion of him. "I'll try to remember that, Francesca."

They shook hands, and Kane turned to head back to one of the tunnels that led to the locker rooms. An officious-looking young man with a security ID around his neck and a clipboard in hand stopped him.

"Have you checked in?"

"No, I've had way too much fun not checking in," Kane replied.

"Back outside and at the end of the line, soldier."

Kane glanced back at Francesca for a bit of help, but she had vanished. He looked down at the dozen documents he needed to complete before he could head to the ground-level locker facility.

***

Kane made it to the locker room and changed into a pair of navy blue camo pants and a Go Navy T-shirt supplied by Renaud's people. He walked out of the tunnel and onto the field, performing a few kick stretches, lunges, and hurdlers, and with effort, he worked his way into some splits.

A group of men in black slacks and black polo shirts sporting the silver GGIG emblem approached Kane. "Your name?"

"Kane, Kyle Kane."

From behind, Kane heard his name called over the PA system.

He glanced at the man's clipboard and saw: Kane, Combine 10:00. He nodded and jogged over to the open area he had scouted out earlier with his new friend.

"Lieutenant Commander," said Renaud, who appeared out of nowhere again. "I understand that you are on the first flight?"

Kane spun around and came face-to-face with Renaud. "Always nice to see you, Francesca. I was just getting warmed up."

The slender woman touched his shoulder and said in her sultry French accent, "Bonne chance, mon ami."

Kane smiled and walked over to the desk. He signed in and took his number. Ms. Renaud pinned it to his back.

"Russian Spetsnaz, French Legionnaires, South Korean Rocs, Polish Groms—there's a lot of talent here," he said, standing up and looking around. "I wonder if there are any other SEALs?"

Kane found a spot on the field and sat down, focusing his mind.

"Competitors with names beginning with the letters A through H," the PA announced, breaking his concentration, "will head to the firing range. Competitors with names beginning with the letters I through R go to the combine field, and those with names beginning with letters S through Z go to the CQB kill house."

The PA sounded: "The competition begins in ten minutes." Kane looked around the stadium, where several thousand seats were filled, along with many of the executive boxes.

"This is going to be a long day," he said.

Each of the three stations lasted two hours. The contestants competed in the 40-yard dash (three attempts), vertical leap, and a 100-kilo bench press.

Kane ran a respectable 4.8 seconds in the last 40, and his thirty-inch vertical leap surprised even him. He expected to complete twenty-four reps on the bench press, as it had been part of his weekly workout routine for the past twenty years.

He felt he had maximized the potential of his 38-year-old body, but that confidence waned when the PA announced the two-mile run. Kane shook his head and jogged over to the end zone, where the umpire was giving race instructions.

He took his place on the starting line, which began at one of the end zones. Everyone in his group was required to run around the outside of the stadium floor ten times. Back when he was an enlisted man, on his first placement with the teams, he ran a couple of miles with gear four or five days a week. However, as a senior operational officer, his fitness too often was left to his off-hours.

Finishing somewhere in the top third, Kane pushed himself hard to gain ground. He was near the back but made up distance in the last two hundred meters. He was sweating profusely when he crossed the finish line.

Shit…that takes my lungs back ten years.

Kane guzzled a couple of electrolyte drinks and downed some energy gels before being led to another area with twenty-four other warriors.

I wonder if their legs are twitching as badly as mine?

Everyone approaching the CQB Kill House had experience with staged house-clearing gunfights.

Kane had spent much of the past twenty years training in various kill houses. The purpose of these facilities in SEAL training was to sharpen perishable skills. When an operation was planned, replicas of mission-critical structures were created so SEALs could practice in the most realistic mock-up situations possible. In special operations, muscle memory could be the difference between life and death.

Kane surveyed the kill house. *I've run hundreds of mission preps in spaces just like this a thousand times.*

He had helped write the book on current SEAL stack tactics. When Kyle scored a 9.6 on his first run through the kill house, Kane was surprised. This was followed by two 9.7s.

Kane and his group headed to the shooting range beneath the stadium. Along the way, he struck up a conversation with a recently retired French Foreign Legionnaire, Eves Safiatu.

He grew up in Liberia and chose the Legion as a way to escape the violence of his childhood. Safiatu was built like a linebacker and had some very serious training. In fact, he had finished his twenty years as an instructor at the Legion's French Guiana Rain Forest Training Center. Retirement from a career as a professional operator left him, like most, in search of a second career that wouldn't bore him to death.

"Must have been a Russian judge in there somewhere," said Safiatu. "You hit every bad guy in the kill house, and they still docked you three-tenths?"

"Yeah, I thought I had a perfect score."

"That fits with their national ethos: win at any cost, but winning unfairly is the most fun."

"You've had some run-ins with the Alphas?"

"That's right."

The two talked about their different training. Before becoming an officer, Kane cross-trained as a sniper, explosives expert, and small arms specialist.

Bart Togal, a retired special forces operator with the Senegalese Company Fusiliers Marine Commandos, approached them and began discussing the marksmanship competition.

"Respiratory and cardiac control during the shot," Kane said. "That's the key. Leading the target, the curvature of the earth, and its rotation are constant variables. The farther the shot—"

"Is that not an oxymoronic statement, Mr. Kyle?"

"Yes, Mr. Togal," said Kane. "It's true that the curvature and rotation of the Earth are constants. However, for shooters, anything beyond a certain distance becomes a variable. The farther the shot, the more factors to consider, beyond just distance and wind speed."

Eves Safiatu nodded. "Controlled breathing and a slowed heart rate are essential physiological factors that must be mastered before you can adjust for distance, drop in trajectory, wind, rotation, and the curvature of the Earth. Leading a target involves chance. Combine all these elements in an instant, and you have a world-class shot."

The shooting competition was conducted in groups of five. The range was set up as a half-mile-long chase that ran beneath the stadium, wide enough to accommodate three shooters competing simultaneously.

Each group used Ruger Hawkeye FTWs, chambered for 6.5mm Creedmoor rounds. Kane shot in the last group of five and won his round. The competition lasted two hours, and when they emerged from the basement, the crowd cheered.

The scoreboard displayed the day's results. Several groups moved between challenges, and Kane's team was directed to the mysterious booths lined up in rows of five, closed off by black drapes.

Safiatu tapped Kyle on the shoulder and said, "Check out the Jumbotron; you’re in second place in the overall standings."

Kane smiled at the sight. "There's still a long way to go, my friend."

A tall, professorial-looking gentleman introduced himself as Professor Kilgore.

"Gentlemen, please pick up one of the wireless headsets hanging on the rack in front of the group." With that, Kane moved into the comprehension testing area.

Togal, Safiatu, and Kane, along with the 22 other men in their group, approached a rolling rack containing rows of virtual reality goggles and accompanying over-the-ear headphone communication gear.

"You will please take a set of VR goggles and your headphones," said the announcer, "and find a seat. The computer will register you by your optical biometrics. Place the headsets on your head and the VR goggles over your eyes. Pay close attention to the reticles in each set of goggles. Listen to the instructional video, after which you will begin the comprehension portion of the test."

Kane put on the VR goggles and headphones, and after a few seconds, a woman's voice provided a new set of instructions. Before long, Kane was deeply engaged in the Specially Modified Psychodynamic Competency Evaluation.

MPCE was a computerized test that alternated between battle simulations, tactical command decisions, strategic theory, abstract logic questions, and a series of unrelated and disjointed questions. These were included to challenge the test taker's ability to ignore psychologically probing questions designed to identify weaknesses.

I feel like a skin job from an off-world hit team forced to undergo a void comp test.

Some tests lasted forty minutes; Kane's lasted three hours. After finishing, he removed his virtual reality goggles.

The stadium floor was nearly empty, except for himself, a couple of GGIG administrators, and a group of security personnel.

One character from an earlier group, a hard-looking Russian named Yevgeny Medved, remained after completing his test. Medved was a top competitor at the end of the first day and had finished the MPCE test earlier, but his immense ego drove him to see who was still testing so late in the afternoon.

When Medved heard the test was over, he rushed to Kane's booth and pulled back the black curtain. He stared down at Kane with a steely dark look.

"Can I help you, pal?" Kane asked, sweeping his dirty blond hair back.

The Russian, speaking perfect English, replied, "I wanted to see who my competition was. But I must say, I'm surprised to see such an old man in the hunt for the belt."

Kane stood up and faced the Russian. "You're joking, right? Are you really going to stand there and call me an old man?"

The Russian cocked his head and stepped toward Kane. Attempting to assert his dominance, he executed a leg sweep, but Kane effortlessly stepped over it and delivered a straight right to the Russian's solar plexus. The blow landed cleanly, compressing his heart and doubling him over. Medved staggered back for three or four steps before charging at Kane again.

This Russian's as thick as a bison, but he seems to lack impulse control—that's an exploitable weakness.

Medved was robust and powerful, known to have torn a heavy bag with a single leg strike. When the Russian responded with a straight left, Kane blocked it.

Before the two men could engage in a serious fight, six GGIG security personnel pulled them apart. They had been watching the Russian since he started a brawl earlier in the competition.

"You fucking cheat! All Americans cheat! No one has superior skills to me. You manipulate tests!" He shook off the four men restraining him and cursed at Kane in Russian.

The whole situation took Kane by surprise. He flipped Medved the bird and shouted as he walked away, "Fake-ass Ivan Drago!"

Kane began to laugh and added, "Bobby Fischer's the man, and Boris Spassky's his bitch, you Sputnik asshole."

Medved stopped and turned back to Kane, disbelief etched on his face as he shouted something angrily in Russian.

One of the older GGIG men, Angus Walsh, positioned his burly self directly in front of Kane. "Sputnik, asshole—I think you really hurt him with that one, Yank."

Medved spat on the concrete floor, turned, and stormed off into another tunnel.

Kane looked at Walsh with mild annoyance and said, "It's okay; I know my way around a locker room, Scotty."

"My name's Angus Walsh, and one of my jobs is to make sure you hotheads don't kill each other—at least until tomorrow night."

Kane stood a few inches from Walsh, who was as big as a Neanderthal. His head was abnormally large, as were his shoulders and arms.

“Were you ever stationed in Ukraine, like Chernobyl?”

Walsh crossed his arms, waiting for the dig.

“I mean—you look like a genetic mutation—a cross between Mankind and Shamus.”

“Is that some professional wrestling crack, little man?”

“That thick mane on your head and those eyebrows—they're like some sort of a crazy Brillo pad made of rusty steel wool, all of it perched atop that abnormally large bucket head.”

Walsh's eyes narrowed. He stared hard at Kane, who started to think he was gonna have to fight this huge Scottish bear of a man.

It took a second, but the larger-than-life cartoon character started to laugh. "Did you just compare me to Mankind?"

Kane started to laugh. "Yeah, I did, didn't I? But I threw in Shamus to kind of counter the whole mutant hillbilly, Texas Chainsaw Massacre look."

"Somehow I think you're gonna run afoul of that Medved twat."

Kane looked at Walsh quizzically. "Oh, you think Sputnik is gonna take me out?" He noticed a faded SAS tattoo on the man's Popeye forearm.

"Aye, I do. Keep your head on a swivel, Kane; some of these competitors are a special kind of foul git."

"So you work for GGIG?" Kane asked.

"Aye, I'm a member of GGIG; it's a union, the Group of Warrior's International Guild. Operators that retire from their military can join. The top prospects are invited to compete in the World Warrior Draft. My job is normally to provide security on tankers passing the Horn or ride shotgun on a few Saudi oil rigs," he said with a wink. "I've worked for BP and Aramco on and off for a few years."

"Did you do any other merc work?"

"Merc work, I like that. Aye," said the big Scotsman, "I carried the gun for Blackthorn for nearly ten years."

"Where?" Kane asked, pulling off his fatigue shirt and then his shorts.

"Be easier to say where I haven't worked. I covered the hot spots: Jo-burg, Ivory Coast, the Congo, Sierra Leone, and the Sudan—just about everywhere in Africa; I worked for those soulless NGOs."

"Have you come nose to nose with those shitbags, the Janjaweed?"

"They're some real sweethearts," said Angus Walsh. "I've seen firsthand examples of their savagery. I signed on with more than my share of convoys, hoping to get a crack at those murdering bastards."

"Did you meet up with any?"

Angus was silent for a moment before replying, "There's more to being a corporation than just murder and mayhem."

"What do you mean?" asked Kane.

"Nothing, mate. You're quite the chatty bloke, Lieutenant Commander."

"Sorry, I've recently re-entered the workforce. That's how you say it—right?"

"If you're looking to deliver phone books out of the back of a lorry—ah, scratch that."

"Tell me, Mr. Angus Walsh, how's GGIG to work for?" asked Kane.

"GGIG is really just a union. The quality of the work depends on which company you work for. That Russian guy, he's a textbook CCU Special Branch schmuck."

"I've never heard of GGIG or CCU before this week, and definitely not the Special Branch," said Kane. "Special Branch sounds like Ned Kidney's department?"

"Come again, Yank?" said Angus. "You're talking about Ben Kidney, the head of Special Branch? That's from a Johnny Depp ripper movie called 'From Hell."

Kane shook his head and walked toward the showers. "Lately, I've found that the Iranian spec ops are in the game. You must have heard about Admiral Corbett's murder."

"The story I've heard is that Corbett was working for the Iranians. That's why his battle group is still in port and not in the eastern Mediterranean."

Kane turned on a dime. "What did you say?" He was steaming his way over to Walsh when an impeccably dressed little man stepped between them. "Pardon me, are you Mr. Kyle Kane?" He asked with a noticeable Italian accent.

He handed Kane a business card. Kane took the card and examined it for a long moment, recalling something he had learned during training operations with the Japanese special forces, the Tokushusakusengun.

"My name is Corrado Petrozzi, and I'm your tailor." Another man with a similar bearing pushed in a six-foot-tall rolling pilot case.

Kane looked back at Angus and shrugged. "Do I need a tailor?"

"It's required," Angus replied.

"I'm taking the measurements of all ten top finishers after today's competition. The top twenty semifinalists will receive a tailored suit, Mr. Kane. The draft is the gala affair of great significance, attended by influential power brokers," Petrozzi explained. "You must be dressed in a fine, crisp, perfectly tailored suit."

"Why?" Kane asked.

"Does Tom Hanks or Leonardo DiCaprio accept an Oscar in a potato sack?" Corrado countered.

"Generally speaking, no," said Kane before turning to Angus. "And I'm not done with you, buckethead."

"You will feel like—come si dice—a moth, clad in a perfectly tailored Italian cocoon. In front of thousands of fans, your comrades, you will burst forth from your chrysalis like a beautiful butterfly."

"Whoa there, Corrado, go easy on the butterfly analogies."

"As you wish, Signore." Corrado smirked and began measuring the half-naked Kane, moving with the speed and skill of an old-world artisan.

"My entire adult life has been spent in camo, navy blues, dress whites, or ODs. I once had a sports coat—navy blue."

"Indeed, Signore Kane," said Petrozzi, opening his Pelican case to reveal a sewing machine and a rack of suits. "I have Versace, Armani, and Yves Saint Laurent."

"I'll meet you outside, governor," said Walsh, passing Kane and his tailor as he headed for the door.

"Stick around, Walsh," said Kane. "I believe you need a new suit as well." Kane glanced at Corrado.

The little Italian man paused, looking at his box of suits, then back at Angus, and then back at his suits. "It's a task that may be beyond even the skills of Corrado."

Angus looked back at the tailor and laughed. "So if I don't fit your skinny-fit, pajama-boy, Euro-style mold, you can't find enough material to make me a suit?"

Kane placed a hand on the little tailor's shoulder and asked, "Corrado, are you telling me you can't craft a suit for a man of such grand gargantuosity?"

Corrado stared nervously at the formidable form before him. He approached Walsh, who had grown up competing in the Highland Games across Scotland. He let his rolled tape drop to the floor and began measuring Angus's broad back.

Kane shook his head. "Those poor loom operators in Glasgow are going to have to work night and day to manufacture enough worsted wool to cover your big ass."

Corrado shook his head and said, "I think Signore Walsh has too much good living for one of these suits, but," he raised his index finger, "I just happen to have a fine, bespoke suit made for a man of your impressive stature."

Angus smiled widely. "Have a drink with us, Coronado."

"It's Corrado, and thank you, Signori Walsh; I'll be working right up until the draft."

***

Outside MetLife Stadium, a freshly showered Kyle Kane surveyed the empty parking lot, a sea of tarmac, concrete, and chain-link fence.

My entire career has been about accomplishing the impossible: life-or-death operations run on split-second timetables with a team that would follow me into the fires of hell. We possess the skills and mental toughness it takes to win an Olympic gold, pitch an MLB no-hitter, or make the Pro Bowl. But there's no multi-million dollar contract or stadium full of screaming fans until now. Nobody will ever see the incredible things my men have done. Only another tier one operator can relate to a job where death awaits you every time you buckle up for a plane ride.

Kane stepped off the curb as a shiny Suburban approached him. It was one of a couple dozen lined up in the stadium parking lot. He tried to see through the dark window tint and considered seeking cover, having just taken down the top Russian Alpha dog.

The window slid down with predictable sluggishness, revealing his newest BFF, Angus Walsh, behind the wheel.

Kane jumped in. "If you're my bodyguard for the evening, I need to know your full rank and your last post."

"Cheeky American."

The two made their way to a Masterson's Steakhouse.

"We could have eaten anywhere, Command Master Sergeant."

"Aye, Laddie, but this establishment serves the nectar of the gods."

"I prefer Johnnie Walker Blue."

"Ah, a blended Scotch of the finest variety."

"You're a purist, Angus?"

"Aye, that I am."

Angus Walsh leaned over to Kane and said, "Your new friend, Ivan Putsky, is a real foul git."

"You mean Medved? I'm starting to get that impression. So, why do you say that?"

"He's a stone-cold killer. I had a look at his folder, and he's made Chechen genocide his life's mission."

"Are you trying to cheer me up?" Kane asked.

"I don't want to rain on your parade, but your compensation for this rodeo will be determined by your draft position, which is directly related to how you perform in tomorrow's hand-to-hand combat tournament."

"A draft? Is this a real thing? It's really going to happen —like a real NFL-type draft?"

"Aye, laddie, that's exactly what it is. And understand this: last year's top pick received a four million dollar signing bonus and a two million dollar annual salary to lead a security team for a prominent NGO."

Kane's jaw dropped. "Did you say—millions?"

Angus signaled his newest best friend, Mandy the server, by holding up his empty glass.

"The teams that work for the members of the GGIG are mostly corporate-owned. Some are security firms; more than a few are multinational conglomerates."

You'll find a few billionaires mixed in, complete with their own security details, along with the occasional deposed dictator.

"Dictators, like who?"

"Mugabe, Morales, and Viktor Yanukovych, to name a few. Oligarchs fall into that category as well. Some teams are independent mercenary groups, like Blackwater. The president of the GGIG is quite the shadowy figure himself."

"Where did he get his money?"

"Where else? He inherited it. They built the Moreau dynasty through currency manipulation and post-war profiteering. The modern-day scion, Roland Moreau, manipulated currency and capitalized on some manufactured crisis," said Angus. "In earlier times, it was called international banking, but now it's simply naked currency manipulation, usually involving small countries with fragile economies. A little foul play—like talk of crop failure, nationalizing industries, or a coup, or an invasion by a hostile neighbor—causes currency values to drop. You can see the sordid history of international banking throughout the ages."

"How does the GGIG fit in?" asked Kane.

"Holding on to the best warriors in a security force has become far too expensive. It's become, for lack of a better term, cutthroat. Operators regularly jump ship mid-contract to sign on with other firms. It's a real mess." Angus motioned for another scotch. "Are you ready for another?"

"I'm in training, remember?" said Kane with a smirk.

Angus glanced down at his glass. "You're driving."

"I liked you better when you were the Ghunga Din of single malts."

Walsh raised his hand. "Good on you, Lieutenant Commander Kane. It warms my heart to know at least one Yank is familiar with Sir Rudyard Kipling."

"Why is it that Kipling is so important? His writing always seemed a little stiff to me."

"Britain is truly the cradle of civilization."

"They may have looted the cradle of civilization. When the sun never set on the British Empire, they released their favorite killers, The East India Trading Company, and they sure as hell knew how to rob it."

"Did you bring your gold card?" asked Angus as he raised two fingers. "Let me give you a quick history of the Groupe de Guerrier's Internationale Guild. It began as an old-school French mercenary group, founded in earnest by a group of former Legionnaires in the 1970s. One of them was Moreau Sr.

"After France suffered a terrible defeat at Dien Bien Phu, they were unceremoniously driven from Vietnam. It became clear to businessmen, diplomats, and wealthy plantation owners throughout Southeast Asia that they would need military-level protection.

"Other regions were becoming hot spots as well. Africa, South America, and the Middle East were rapidly devolving into authoritarian, tribal, or religious conflicts. Government-backed terrorist cells were robbing, hijacking, and kidnapping businessmen, merchandise, and even armored cars." Angus paused for a moment to gather his thoughts and grab another MacCallum's from the waitress's tray.

"The first private military company was created by a Scotsman, Colonel Sterling, a former British soldier who established the commando unit that became the SAS. He incorporated soldiers of fortune seeking work."

Kane interrupted Angus, "In my opinion, the first private military entity was the British East India Company, a model of brutal efficiency that thrived by employing paramilitary operators to extort poor nations of their natural resources. Vietnam under the French was no different; businessmen employed French Foreign Legionnaires to terrorize the Vietnamese. This is all very interesting, Angus, but how does that tie into GGIG?"

"Roland Moreau's grandfather, Claude Moreau, fought for France in World War One. When he returned to a very different France, he started snapping up properties of the soldiers and civilians that were killed in the war. With his post-war profiteering, he built a steel mill and started a manufacturing company that built heavy machine guns, rail guns, and tanks, at the time all very cutting-edge weapons. After World War Two, Vietnam was returned to the French as part of a post-World War Two deal to get Germany into NATO. The result was a brutal French repression of the Vietnamese. CCU had grown exponentially, and Moreau's father decided to join the French soldiers who fought in Vietnam. He was lucky to survive the self-inflicted wound that was Dien Bien Phu. When he returned to the family business, he expanded the weapons manufacture with its own R&Dcompany. He was a soldier to his core and started the guild, GGIG, to allow the unemployed soldiers around Europe to find work.

"The Groupe de Guerrier's International Guild was formidable—comprising many ex-legionnaires from Spain, Morocco, Germany, Poland, Tunisia, and various African nations. Many unattached warriors joined GGIG, which was a somewhat reputable union until Roland, took control twenty-five years ago."

"Same old story: the good sell out to the bad. Let me guess, the son never served."

"Just so, laddie, but the World Warrior Championship and the World Warrior's Draft were Roland's ideas. His family's ruthless business acumen, which built his multibillion-dollar conglomerate, CCU, was evident in his role as chairman of GGIG."

Kane looked interested and shared his views: "The rich are getting richer than ever, thanks to the political class. Look at the 2008 financial crisis, where the rich bailed themselves out. That was the catalyst that allowed a smaller CCP invasion to expand its invasive attack.

Angus sipped his favorite adult beverage and asked, "How did they manage that? Who managed that?"

Kane shook his head. "I don't believe in coincidences. Obama appeared out of nowhere like a Manchurian candidate and skipped through an entire career of achievements in a few years. Look at the seminal events that happened during his administration and now under his puppet. Most of the extreme events have been manufactured by the CCP backed globalist uniblob party in DC. In the states the CCP has gone from a beachhead, Illinois, New York, and California, to a full-blown systemic capture, all the way to the top. And how does the CCP maintain their control? Through a captured, corrupt corporate America, globalist intervention, and the crown jewel of the CCP's spy apparatus, voter fraud. I've seen too many coincidences, like the zero interest rate policy, quantitative easing, trillions in deficit spending, most of it going to NGOs that kick back billions to the mechanism that created them. The globalist elites, who control democrats and RINOs are trying to install a CCP-backed oligarchy that will be inside every American home, monitoring every American's life in the most invasive, authoritative way anyone, even, George Orwell, could ever imagine."

"How did you pick all this up?"

"I read, Angus. It's the lost skill of self-education. I have always read when I could. It's all out there waiting to be understood."

"Aye, laddie. I was never a good student, and so, my old man always put my shoulder to the grindstone, literally. After the Paras, he returned to the family business, stone masonry. When we weren't building foundations and walls, we travelled to festivals around Scotland and competed in their Highland Games competition. We were a couple of terrors, known around the UK as the British Bulldogs."

"I'll bet you were. I've heard that the SAS were more brawlers than the super-soldiers they are now, chosen for their fearlessness in a fight."

"That's an accurate picture of me."

"I heard a lot of mercenaries were making bank... some making millions," said Kane. "I think I need an agent."

"Right you are, boy-o; you're just an old sailor trying to stay solvent."

"Solvent? I'm selling my house to avoid debtor's prison."

"Aye, Laddie, ducking a stint in some dodgy Tolbooth."

"Tolbooth?"

"It's an old-school Edinburgh debtor's prison," said Walsh. “The Scottish version of the Black Hole of Calcutta. You win this competition, or even place in the top ten, and you’ll see a significant improvement in your financial situation. But mind yourself, laddie; there are millions on the line and a championship belt that every spec ops warrior would kill for."

"Belt?"

"The World Warrior Championship Belt, Kyle."

"Right. Do you think I have a chance?"

"No," said Walsh, without hesitation. "You, Mr. Kane, not a bloody prayer."

Kane shook his head. "I've been in quite a few places I never thought I'd return from, but like so many warriors throughout history, I convinced myself I was already dead. So you see, Angus, it’s just a matter of being in the right frame of mind."

"That’s a tough place to be," said Angus.

"I can do this, Master Sergeant, I can."

"Aye, Laddie, then you can, and I wouldn’t want to be anywhere but in your corner."

Chapter 14

MetLife Stadium, Meadowlands, NJ, 10:00

The tournament began at 09:00, and the stadium's parking lot was already a field of braziers grilling brats and burgers, with barrels of beer flowing to tailgaters enjoying it like an NFL home game.

Angus navigated the big-block Chevy through the parking lot to the contestants' entrance, and the sheer volume of fans amazed them both.

***

They cleared the security gate and walked to the mezzanine seats. "This is really something, an amazing transformation, Angus."

Three octagon fighting rings had been set up on the stadium floor, along with about fifty circular eight-top tables. They were covered in black linens, bone china, and Waterford crystal, all monogrammed and embossed with the GGIG logo. The goal of this grandiosity was to secure the best professional operators in the draft: warriors who had just retired from the military. These professional soldiers were the physical equivalent of some of the finest athletes in the world

The preliminary bouts had already begun, and while the private floor party was still fairly sparse, the stands were beginning to fill up.

Several thousand people jumped to their feet and roared at an early KO.

Angus Walsh looked up from his copy of the tournament brackets and competitors' bios. He glanced at the stands and then at the carpeted area of the stadium floor. "Take a look at the aristocracy, as usual flaunting their wealth and inaccessibility. The A-lister area," said Angus. "Bunch of bloody tossers."

The early rounds were mostly entertainment, while the real contests were taking place at the fine dining tables on the stadium floor. Deals were being cut among many of the GGIG team owners—personal security titans who had built impressive private armies employed worldwide to secure NGOs, private citizens, and heads of state in smaller foreign countries.

Billionaire casual was the attire: bespoke slacks, button-downs, and sport coats that probably cost more than the average soccer mom's new electric minivan. The larger-than-life Moby Dicks were great white whales that swam around the bar and sucked up Grey Goose bloody marys like they were buckets of krill.

The galactically rich mingled with security industry suits, while some officers from the Pentagon discussed defense with military-industrial insiders; all of them looked to make deals, whether it was lining up a post-retirement gig or pitching the sale of an additional one hundred main battle tanks. There were even a few third-world governments seeking to secure a world-class operator, a leader atop their secret police strike teams, vying for a higher draft choice.

Caviar, blinis, and rosé champagne were served by tuxedo-clad servers circulating through the crowd with their silver trays, just feet away from the vicious hand-to-hand battles fought amongst the beautiful, genteel people.

The wealthy felt they needed a high level of security. Some, in their obvious naivete, chose seats close to the rings, where they were introduced to blood spray, sweat, spittle, and even the occasional molar, all part of the visceral reality unfolding before them. They were willing to spend tens of millions of dollars to avoid the violence and mayhem of the streets but wanted to be ringside for the brutal battles inside the octagons, as if the proximity to real violence gave them some referent tough-guy image.

Captains of business, guided by their favorite talent scouts, navigated the array of tabletops that comprised the ringside seating. They renewed old acquaintances and forged new connections, feeding the rumor mill for their own benefit. Some simply tossed out gossip grenades—lies and half-truths—while others, like the worst types of gossipers, asked unsuspecting individuals leading questions to turn them into sources for their ugly gossip.

The four-star hospitality and the competitive atmosphere of the event had become a much-anticipated joust during the relatively young World Warrior Draft.

However, the real business—the selection of a leader for any security team, which could serve a variety of purposes—was as serious as life and death.

The people in the know, the best judges of mercenary talent, looked for that rare alchemy of split-second decision-making, high-functioning mental acuity, and world-class physical prowess, all combined with master-class martial ability. Industry insiders considered it a rare blend of complementary extremes—extremes tested each time a leader issued orders to a team of elite alpha-male warriors.

The positions at the top of the competitor rankings were shifting. "Check it out, Angus, my name's up there on the Jumbotron," Kane said, sipping some OJ. "I'm near the top, me ol' mucker."

"Me ol' mucker?" Angus Walsh replied. "Where in the blazes did you hear that?"

"From an SBS operator. It's like being a grunt, a grunt can take anything."

"Aye, Kyle, you're right. Now it's hand-to-hand combat time, and what you see up there is one of the four tournament brackets. You're at the top of one of them. Your combine numbers, except for that two-mile effort, which you phoned in, were very good. You ranked in the top five for CQB and marksmanship, and you aced the competency section with top marks."

"Phoned it in? I ran a good, well-paced race."

"Well-paced indeed."

Kane shrugged and said, "My scores are good enough to put me near the top."

"Bob's your uncle, Lieutenant Commander—retired. Do you know who your competition will be?"

"Well, for one, there's the German KSK guy, Heinz Kohl. He's a former Olympic decathlete, so he must have better combine numbers than I do," Kane replied, catching sight of Yevgeny Medved. "And what about Ivan Drago over there?" he added, rolling his eyes. "What a jackass."

"He's the top-seeded Russian. Like you, he won't see hand-to-hand combat until the semifinals," Angus said, unwrapping a snack from the concession area.

"What the hell is that?" Kane asked, looking visibly put off. "It smells pretty strong, Master Sergeant."

"Yeah, but it tastes soooo good. It's haggis, Laddie—a Highland delicacy."

"Is there such a thing?"

"Don't be a tosser, Kyle. Go grab yourself an Egg McMuffin or a Hot Pocket," Angus said with a dismissive wave. "Or better yet, a hot dog; that's a real American delicacy."

"Okay, okay, Angus; there's no way you can hold out British food as anything more than culinary leftovers."

Angus, with his mouth full of haggis, smiled and gave Kane a reverse peace sign. The British bird dated back to the days of the English longbow archers. They were so deadly that captured archers would have their index and middle fingers cut off.

***

The first rounds of fighting commenced with expected ferocity. As is typical in early tournament matchups, the extreme mismatches led to some explosive outcomes. With all three rings going at once, fighters were literally being knocked out of the ring while other bouts went into triple overtime.

"There were some real underdogs showing out, Angus. Eves Safiatu just knocked out his first-round opponent."

Kane left Angus to his choice of blue-chip stadium food. "Meet me in the locker room. I'm up in an hour, so I need to get my game face on."

Kane was warming up in the locker room when Angus joined him with his tape guy. Initially, he planned to go with just fight gloves, but Mickey Kirk, a professional tape man, advised him that split knuckles could quickly end his tournament run. It took thirty-five minutes to tape Kane's hands, after which he worked up a good sweat.

With just a towel over his shoulders, he prepared for his first bout in the semifinal round. His opponent was the former top operator from the Grom, Tomas Wojohowitz, a Polish Greco-Roman National Champion in the 98-kilo class and one of two competitors from the Polish spec ops teams. Wojohowitz had defeated his first two opponents by knockout.

Kane entered the center ring just behind the card girl, who strutted with an exaggerated, sassy strut.

"Whoa, you don't see that walking around Ft. Bragg," Kane remarked as the tight-bodied young woman circled the cage. Cheers and catcalls followed her until she stopped in front of Kane. He was working his way into a full side split when the card girl caught his eye.

"After the fight," Kane asked, "maybe we could grab a drink?"

The tall Aussie beauty smiled, revealing her pearly whites. "In your dreams, yank!"

Kane's jaw dropped, and he slumped back against the cage. He started to laugh as she winked and sashayed past him. He tried to refocus when the down-under stunner bent over directly in front of him, looking between her legs at Kane, who couldn't help but stare. "Only kidding, mate, the old man put me up to it. Cheers."

Her ample bust strained the seams of her micro-kini, and when she bobbed up and down, Kane silently prayed for a costume failure.

She strutted past Kane, through the open gate, and off into a sea of tables. Six hundred guests, six thousand spectators in the stands, and another thousand or so partying in the super boxes had their eyes fixed on the center octagon.

"Kane, Kane, watch the low leg kicks."

"I don't fucking believe it," Kane said, his head spinning almost 180 degrees. "I know that voice." He focused on a man waving to him from the first section of the stands.

"WALLACE," he shouted. "Wallace, you traitorous bastard!" He threw off his towel and turned to the crowd.

Tomas Wojohowitz, Kane's opponent, was passing through the cage door just as Kane shot past him and out of the ring. He crossed the stadium floor and pulled himself up into the stands.

By the time Kane reached the spot, William Wallace was gone. Kane spun around, searching, bare-chested among the fans, dressed only in his spandex fighting pants. The crowd eyed him with a mix of concern and curiosity. When he stopped his search, he looked down at the empty seat. A tournament program and a recently poured beer rested in the cup holder.

Kane examined the program closely. The words "Cheers, Kane" were scrawled across the cover in red china marker. He grabbed the program and struggled to open it with his fighting gloves.

"Did any of you talk to the guy who was sitting here? Did anyone see where he went?"

Everyone within earshot either shook their heads or tried to look past Kane at the fights taking place in the other octagons.

"Kyle Kane to the center octagon, Kyle Kane to the center octagon," announced the PA system. "Last call, Kyle Kane to the center octagon."

Kane hustled down to the octagon, passing an oddly unfazed Angus Walsh. "Glad you could make it."

His opponent was slightly taller and much younger. With a neck as thick as a fire hydrant and arm muscles that were veined blocks twitching with anticipation, he presented a formidable challenge. Kane touched gloves and readied himself for the onslaught.

His mind was still on Wallace when he instinctively raised his left hand.

What could be inside that program?

A hard left jab followed by a straight right knocked that thought right out of Kane's head, slamming him back into the cage. He almost went out.

The referee stepped in to check Kane’s eyes. Kane shook his head and adjusted his trunks. He raised his gloves, and the referee gave them a tug. Following the referee’s instructions, he pulled them back. Kane got on his bicycle, jabbing his way out of trouble until his legs got back under him.

Tomas Wojohowitz, or Wojo, was young, strong, and ready to bang. Kane's first instinct was to rope-a-dope Wojohowitz. His arms took a beating, but he managed to avoid the game-ending blows.

"Jesus, I just drew freaking Dolph Lundgren!" shouted Kane as he got off the fence.

"You're fighting one of the Expendables," shouted Angus. Kane shoved Wojohowitz back, and instead of getting off the cage and dancing into the ring, he laid back on the octagon fence and snapped out a jab when Wojo waded in. The blow flattened the big man’s nose, and Kane waved for Wojo to come on in.

Kane smiled broadly, revealing his blood-streaked mouthguard. Wojohowitz was now a menacing mass of muscle and veins, consumed by an overwhelming desire to smash Kane’s face.

"Kid's not a fighter," said Angus.

"He'll do until a real one gets here, Angus."

"If he figures out your strategy," Angus cautioned, "he's gonna punch your ticket."

"It's okay; he's punched me everywhere else."

Kane nodded as the big man repositioned himself in front of him. The nonchalance infuriated the former Grom operator, causing his eyes to darken with anger.

Wojohowitz began raining down blows—big overhand roundhouse punches. He launched a few barroom hooks that skimmed the top of Kane’s head.

Kane continued to hide behind his gloves and thick forearms, both of which he wished were a bit thicker.

All of this only served to anger the big Pole, changing the pace of the fight. Kane tightened up his defenses, and two minutes later, Wojo started to slow down. His punches left most of their sting on Kane's gloves, and when the first round ended, he looked back at Kane, bewildered.

In the second round, Wojo continued his relentless barrage. Lactic acid had built up in his shoulders and arms, which caused his hands to drop. When the big man let his guard fall to his waist, Kane saw his opening.

After one more big hook from Wojo, Kane ducked it and roared off the fence with combinations until Wojohowitz was back on his heels. He shot a sneaky straight right through and stung the big man, catching Wojo flush on the button and snapping his head back.

Instinctively, Kane executed a textbook Jordan Burroughs running double-leg takedown.

Once in on Wojo's legs, Kane picked up the bigger man, skied him, and dropped him hard onto the mat. The powerful impact knocked Wojo silly, and his eyes reflected the damage.

A testament to his training and toughness, Wojo forced himself to stand. Out cold on his feet, he barely raised his gloves. Kane was tired and pretty well beaten up, but he had enough left in the tank to throw a couple of jabs. Wojo shook off the blows and plodded forward.

Kane unleashed an old punch—one that, if executed correctly, could drop a grizzly bear. He delivered a powerful liver shot, and Wojohowitz froze for a moment. It took that brief pause for the pain receptors to register the devastating blow, and when they did, he dropped like a Polish redwood.

There was no standing eight count in World Warrior Championship rules. Wojohowitz tried to get up, but Kane pushed him back down. He didn't want to hurt the kid any more than he had; Wojohowitz was dangerously vulnerable.

"Stay down, big man; you're done for today," Kane said.

The referee was prepared to call the bout when a ringside judge beckoned him to the edge of the octagon. Kane watched as the ref stopped in front of the judges' table, where one of the bout officials handed him a cell phone.

It was odd, to say the least, but nothing could prepare them for what happened next. The referee returned the phone and walked to the center of the octagon, motioning for the bout to continue.

Kane shook his head. "Ref, he's out; just call it."

"Finish the bout," shouted the referee as he glanced up at one of the super boxes. Kane followed the ref's gaze and saw a shorter man in a suit pointing down at the ring.

"Finish the match, Kane, or I'll disqualify you."

"This is bullshit!" Kane exclaimed, approaching Wojo, who was still struggling to get up.

Kane dropped onto Wojohowitz, took the big man backward, and applied a rear-naked choke.

Wojo tried to fight it but had nothing left. Realizing Kane wasn't applying pressure, he tapped out.

Kane helped Wojohowitz up and steadied him. The official raised Kane's hand, and the two men shook hands as they exited the ring. Kane received a round of cheers from fans who stood and applauded. He saluted them and walked off.

Before leaving the stadium floor, Kane glanced up just in time to see the same little man staring at him from the super box window. Kyle was surprised by his strange smile.

Several competitors stopped Kane to congratulate him on his sportsmanship.

Kane reached his locker, threw a towel over his head and shoulders, and immediately pulled out Wallace's program, leafing through it. He found letters and numbers circled on different pages.

"That was a fine fight, me boy-o," said Angus as he caught up with Kane at his locker, dumping the spit bucket down a nearby sink.

“'Boy-o' is Irish slang, Angus Walsh.”

“Scots-Irish, boy-o.”

"Did you get a chance to look at this?" Kane asked, holding up Wallace’s program.

He handed it to Angus. "Just some random numbers and letters. It has to be a code." Frustrated and angry, Kane watched as Angus examined it carefully before rolling up the magazine and placing it in Kane's locker.

"You're through to the finals, Kyle dearie; don't lose your focus. It could get you hurt."

Angus paced anxiously around the locker room area.

"What's got you so anxious, Sarge? We won; I'm in the finals."

The crowd outside roared, prompting Angus to hustle over to the door.

"Maybe I should go back out to see who I'm facing in the finals," Kane suggested.

"Don't bother, Kyle. It's Medved."

Kane brushed past Angus and hurried down the tunnel, asking, "How do you know?"

"I just do," Angus Walsh replied, resigned. They stopped at the end of the tunnel.

"If the guys on the teams could see me now." Kane reached the end of the tunnel just in time to see Medved's hand raised. His opponent remained on the mat while several trainers tended to him.

One fan, standing in front of Kane, turned, walked past, and remarked, "Bloody animal, tore him to pieces."

Another man brushed by Kane in the tunnel. "He could have ended it in the second round, but he carried him, beating the poor bastard to a pulp."

Kane shook his head in disgust. "That guy is a psychopath."

Angus approached from behind. "You find them every once in a while in the military. They use the fog of war to cover their sadistic tendencies." Walsh nodded toward the octagon.

"It was Eves, and he was up and on his feet. He’s moving under his own steam."

The big Scot stood face-to-face with Kane. "Be mindful, Kyle; this Medved bloke is a real hampton wick."

"Roger that, Master Sergeant. I read him loud and clear. I've got something special in store for this son of a bitch."

Angus nodded. "The finals are a few hours away, so what are you doing until then?"

"I've got some work to take care of," Kane replied. The two men shook hands, and

Kane walked back to the shower.

Before he had taken two steps, he stopped and called to Angus, who was still watching the crowd. "Are you going to be there tonight?"

"There’s nothing in this world that could keep me away, Kyle dearie."

"That's great! Is your truck here?"

“It’s in contestant parking.”

Chapter 15

Metlife Stadium 19:43

Kane left the stadium and made his way through the crowds tailgating in the parking lot, heading toward Angus's dark green Tundra.

He turned on his phone and opened his contacts.

Kane spoke into his cell, "Jerry, it's Kyle Kane. That's great to hear, and how's the family?" He inquired about work and asked if Jerry had seen any realtors showing his house.

"Thank you, yes, if you could. Listen, Jerry, I need a favor. Could you ask your wife to look up a cell number for me? I know it's illegal, but I wouldn't ask if it weren't really important. Yeah, yeah, national security. I'll explain everything later. Thanks, Jerry, you're doing me a huge favor, and I won't forget it."

Kane laid his phone on the dash and reclined his head against the headrest. His eyelids grew heavy as he watched the sun set over the Jersey Meadowlands.

***

"Bam, bam—bam!" Explosions erupted all around him, his instinct to secure his weapon was followed up with panic. Kane searched for his Springfield XD and found it in the truck's side pocket. He pulled it out. *"We're surrounded by* tangos." His entire body tensed. Only the blast of a nearby car horn jolted him from the chaos of his dangerously foggy dream state.

***

"Someone popped smoke? I can barely see." He moved his finger off the trigger guard as he pulled himself back into reality. He recognized familiar faces—just everyday folks—

walking and talking as they moved toward him, past him, and into the stadium.

"Oh, thank God," he said to himself. "I'm at the tournament. They're just going to the fight." He cleared his weapon and dropped it back into the door pocket, taking a deep breath.

"This isn't Afghanistan."

Kane entered the arena through the general admission gates. It took some effort, but he finally convinced the gate security that his credentials were valid and that he was fighting in the finals.

"So what if I'm supposed to fight in twelve minutes?" he said to the GGIG officer. "I'm here now." The woman called into security HQ, and Kane was cleared to go through.

He ran from the security checkpoint toward the locker rooms.

I've done shit way harder than this! Time to man up and get it done.

Inside the locker room, Angus Walsh was pacing a rut in the tile floor.

"Where the hell have you been, you bollocks? Rasputin's almost walked away with the bloody trophy."

"It's a belt, Angus, not a trophy."

"The point is the same, and you're this close to defaulting."

"I know; I fell asleep. It was quite enjoyable. You should try it sometime," said Kane.

"A bloody nap? A couple of hours before the biggest payday of your life, and you're napping like a bairn? Either you're knackered, or you have balls of steel. Whichever it is, you've got five minutes to get ready, so get yourself sorted, you bloody bampot!"

Angus walked away, shouting, "Where's the tape guy?"

The lights dimmed, and the music roared. It was ELO's *Fire and Ice* that roared through the concert-grade sound system as Kane made his way down the tunnel. Angus hustled up from behind and got in front of Kyle to lead him out.

"Stay on your toes, Kyle. Medved is always a rage in a cage in the first round, and you've got to throw him out of the club if he tries to go chest to chest."

Kane was wearing the same blue navy camo pants, with only a towel draped over his shoulders. A lone spotlight illuminated Angus Walsh as he led Kane through the crowd.

The center of the octagon was occupied by a lean Bruce Buffer lookalike in a tailored tuxedo. He began his introduction as Kane reached the stairs to the cage:

"Ladies and gentlemen, welcome to the GGIG World Warrior Hand-to-Hand Combat Championships. Entering the ring from Virginia Beach, Virginia, a nineteen-year Navy veteran, retired from the elite SEAL Team Six, and boasting impressive stats in tactical warfare—considering his hours in the field. Fighting out of the blue corner—Lieutenant Commander, United States Navy, Retired, Kyle Kane!" The crowd erupted.

"Hours in the field?" said Angus. "That's a nice way to put it."

"Tell it like it is, bro. I'm old as dirt, my feet hurt, but I do love Jesus," said Kane.

The announcer smiled at Kane. "And he's as old as dirt." His words were drowned out by the roar of the stadium.

From the opposite end of the arena, Medved charged onto the floor, waving a red hammer and sickle flag. He wore the light blue beret of the Spetsnaz and had a large red Soviet star tattooed on the center of his back. He raised his arms, urging the crowd to cheer for him.

Kane glanced at him and spat into his corner bucket. A majority of the crowd began booing and hissing at the imposing Russian.

Kane got into it. He nodded and raised his arms to engage the crowd. "He looks like a puffed-up peacock."

Angus shouted, "Stay focused, Kyle. He's a southpaw; remember to stay outside his right. If he throws a lazy jab, come right over the top with yours. Make him pay. Bang him if he gets stupid—because he's going to get stupid." Angus worked on Kane's traps, trying to keep him loose.

Kane watched Medved as he stomped around outside the cage.

“I don’t think that’s going to be difficult.”

Medved ripped off his tearaway warm-up pants as he reached the stairs, showcasing his powerful legs and ripped upper body to the crowd. He pointed at Kane and cursed at him in Russian.

The Russian leapt into the octagon as the announcer declared, "Fighting out of Saint Petersburg, having taken an extended leave from the Russian Army's special forces, with ten years of active duty in the renowned Spetsnaz Alpha Unit, and fighting out of the gold corner, with the highest point total ever in GGIG Combine history, Major Yevgeny Medved…Medved!"

The stadium erupted in boos and jeers, which only brought a smile to Kane's face and further irritated Medved, who cursed him even louder.

A round of indoor fireworks exploded, and the two men approached the center. There was no handshake, just a slap of hands. Kane could see nothing behind the dark eyes glaring at him. Medved's face formed a hard V shape down to his chiseled jaw, and his thick brow made Kane think he was descended from some kind of caveman.

Kane returned to his corner. “I’ll bet even money that he's descended from Cro-Magnon. His brow looks like Mt. Rushmore, and he has muscles in his disturbingly shaped face."

"Be ready, Kyle; this is going to kick off quickly, and it’s going to hurt."

Kane pushed himself off the cage as Angus climbed out of the octagon.

"Kick his ass, Kyle!”

The bell rang, and Medved stormed across the canvas. Kane stepped just far enough away from the fence to avoid being driven back into it. He tried to touch gloves, but Medved slapped his glove away. Kane threw a jab, catching Medved on the nose. They exchanged a few quick punches, testing each other's distance and speed.

I can't stand in front of this jamoke; I’ll get hammered.

Kane feigned right and moved left. He hadn't landed a solid shot on Medved since his first jab, but he had also managed to avoid any big shots himself.

"Stick and go, stick and go!" yelled a voice that Kane thought was from his corner.

"Jab him, take him down; he's got no leg defense!" called out another voice from the front row. The sound of that voice struck a chord.

Medved threw a haymaker that sailed over Kane's head, prompting Kane to challenge the big Russian. He stepped in, locked his arms around Medved, and lifted the larger man off the mat, causing the crowd to roar. Kane executed a suplex, dropping Medved backward over his head. The impact was thunderous as Medved slammed onto his head and neck, resulting in an audible crunch, followed by a frantic struggle for control between the two men.

"How the hell did he walk away from that?"

"Nice one, Lieutenant Commander," came a voice from somewhere in the front row. "Great lateral drop. Keep it going!"

Kane spun behind Medved, momentarily taking his eyes off his opponent to identify the source of the shout.

"Wallace!" Kane shouted, a mistake that provided the Russian with an opening. Medved stepped wide, getting his legs and hips behind Kane's, and powered back into him.

Medved took Kane down and positioned himself on top, pounding Kane's ears and the back of his head. Kane shot out with a John Fritz long sit-out and stood, feeling battered.

Shit, stupid bush-league mistake.

Medved came at him, throwing jabs, overhand rights, and low leg kicks with real power. Kane stepped inside Medved's guard and snapped a short overhand right, followed by a Muay Thai knee to Medved's abdomen. An unexpected spinning back elbow landed flush, breaking Medved's large Russian nose. Everyone in the first twenty rows heard the crack.

Even Angus cringed, but Medved wasn't slowed at all. He charged at Kane, blood running down his face like a raging bull. He had Kane pinned against the cage, pounding him relentlessly until Kane threw a desperation uppercut that knocked the big Russian back.

The crowd went wild. Kane had become something of a fan favorite after refusing to beat a defenseless Polish fighter. Medved had instantly become a villain when he brutalized a fighter in an earlier round.

The two continued fighting through the bell at the end of the first round.

Kane dropped onto his stool for the 30-second break. "I think I made him mad, Angus."

"Mad?" Angus Walsh replied quickly, tending to a cut on Kane's forehead. "I think you broke his fucking nose. He wants to kill you. I'm glad it's you in there, not me."

"You're pretty new to this whole coaching thing. You're no Knute Rockne, Angus. The whole brutal honesty thing needs work," Kane said, spitting a mouthful of blood into the bucket.

"Sorry, laddie, I'm lying to you; I wish I were in there so I could show you how it's done." Kane choked back a laugh as he took a swig. "That's the ticket, Angus."

The second period began with a few cheap shots from Medved. He headbutted Kane in an attempt to open the cut, then grabbed the cage behind him and drove a knee into Kane's groin—a low blow while the ring ref, Big Boris Majich, a former Serbian general generally considered to lack humanity, was obscured by Medved's back.

The ref reserved his greatest disdain for Americans, who, 25 years earlier, had stopped their regional genocide by bombing the hell out of their country's infrastructure, sending it back to the Stone Age.

At one point, Medved took Kane over with a wicked gut wrench. A wave of pain and crushing pressure robbed Kane of oxygen. A vasovagal nerve response threatened to knock him out, and his body slumped for a few seconds.

Medved was certain he had won. He released Kane's limp body and leaped into the air, bounding around the cage with his arms stretched overhead. He continued to salute himself and encouraged the crowd to join in. However, Kane was not down for the count, and before Majich could finish his eight-count, Kane rose from the mat.

He had been playing possum, and Majich turned to Medved, ordering him to fight. In those few seconds, Kane went on the offensive.

Medved, still focused on the crowd, waved his arms even as the referee demanded he reengage.

Kane lunged past the referee and tackled Medved with a powerful shoulder to his lower back. He drove the furious Russian hard into the cage, smashing Medved's already broken nose into the fencing. For the first time in the match, Medved realized he could lose.

The second period ended moments later, and both men staggered back to their corners.

When the Russian Spetsnaz reached the center of the ring, he shoved the referee for not calling the American out. He was pulled away by his corner, but the referee docked the furious Russian a point. The cursing and shouting continued.

Angus jumped into the octagon and pulled Kane back. Kane was practically on his last legs. As they reached the corner, Angus urged Kane to sit. Exhausted and struggling to stay upright, Kane waved off the seat and stood instead.

"I want it, but I don't need it," Kane shouted.

Medved sat directly across the octagon on his stool, where he leaned to one side and glanced past his cornermen at Kane.

"It'll get into Medved's thick skull, Angus."

"With a mouthpiece and all that hubris," Walsh added, "I'm surprised there's room."

"He's strong, Angus, and hits like a fucking Russian mule."

"Yeah, we knew that going in. So what's your strategy?" Angus asked.

Kane spat some blood into the bucket and scanned the front row to his right. He spotted Wallace staring back at him.

"That punk's got some nerve calling out moves to me after ruining my career."

Angus looked around the arena. "Who?"

"That guy over there in the denim shirt is staring at us. Do you see him?"

Angus nodded. "You need to nab him before he squirts. He ruined my career."

"10 SECONDS," shouted the referee. "10 SECONDS."

"I'll try, laddie, but our primary mission is to get you home alive and in one piece. Now, Kyle, remember what I told you."

Kane flashed Walsh a bloody smile, though he hadn't heard a word Angus had said. Angus shoved Kyle's mouthpiece in, trying to revive his battered old body. He shook out his arms and stretched his neck side to side.

"Ground and pound, Kyle. Start with the rope-a-dope."

Kane didn't need to look to know who had shouted at him; he recognized Wallace's voice.

Angus quickly told Kane, "One more round, Kyle, and you're the World Warrior Champion. Strength and honor, boyo."

Kane pointed at Wallace. "Just what he said, Angus. I'm going to take it to the mat if I can. Rasputin's got killer stand-up."

Angus shook his head. "Now we're taking fight tips from the enemy?"

Majich called the two fighters together and signaled for them to begin. Medved walked away from his corner, ignoring instructions to stay put, despite having won the first two rounds. The match was his if he played it smart. Medved turned and spat at them.

Kane started with a dance: left, right, left, left, right, left. He snapped out jabs and moved from side to side, changing planes and angles. However, Medved was always beating him to the spot. The young juggernaut was cutting off the ring and landing heavy punches whenever he found Kane off balance.

"I've *got to find a way to get inside. He's got heavy hands, and his defense is too strong to break through."*

Wallace had left his seat and made his way to the edge of the cage. Several security personnel moved to grab him and push him back into his seat.

"Russian two-on-one, then sweep him!" Wallace called out. "Russian two-on-one, Kane!"

A blow knocked Kane back into the cage, causing him to bounce off into Medved's close-in hook. All Kane could do was keep his defenses up to absorb the worst of the punches and low calf strikes.

Medved was a killing machine, intent on hurting his opponent. With a minute and a half left, Kane decided to revert to the Ali-style rope-a-dope. He was paying the same price he had throughout the fight: blows to the body and strikes against his arms, which began to feel as heavy as sacks of concrete.

It wasn't long before Medved's hands started to drop. He had hit the wall Kane had been working toward all fight. When Medved began throwing punches from the belt, Kane sensed an opening.

Ivan's starting to grab and hold. He's punching himself out. The next time he tries to clinch, I'm going to take him down and finish this on the ground.

Sure enough, Medved unleashed a vicious flurry of hooks followed by a battering ram straight left. He landed blows all over Kane's defenses, but when his energy waned, he reached for a clinch.

Instinctively, Kane pushed hard against Medved's chest. He followed up with a couple of thudding body shots that forced Medved back. That was the moment Kane had been waiting for.

He grasped Medved's left elbow with an underhand grip while simultaneously seizing the Russian's left wrist. Medved's instinctive reaction was to pull back, creating an opening for Kane's leg attack.

Kane pulled Medved's arm into his chest and swept his left leg into the air. He released Medved's wrist and caught his foot and ankle as it rose. At the same time, he lunged forward and hooked Medved's right leg, the only thing keeping him upright.

Medved fell, and Kane landed hard on top of him. The air was knocked out of Medved's lungs for a long second, giving Kane his first real opportunity to hurt the Russian.

Never pass up a kneebar when your opponent's an A-hole.

Kane maintained his grip on Medved's right foot as he stepped over his body, scissoring Medved's upper thigh. The big man desperately tried to pull his leg free from Kane's hold. It was a trap, and the Russian had walked right into it.

Kane laid back on the hooked foot, applying pressure down to the mat while arching his midsection up. Medved's knee joint was caught in the middle. Anger and rage surged through Kane.

Lines, tubes, and drains; IVs; clear fluid pumping in through one and dark malignancies flowing out of another. Arterial blood pressure lines floated in her tiny neck. These split-second images shattered Kane's impulse control.

Without a second thought, he cranked up his submission hold to demolition status.

Medved grunted in pain, and Kane registered the sound of ligaments snapping like uncooked linguini. There was no time for a tap-out. Referee Majich heard the sound and quickly dropped down onto the two men. He pulled Kane's knee bar apart and pushed him off.

Kane released his hold. Medved yelled, clutching his injured knee, cursing Kane as his leg turned red and began to swell. He writhed in agony until his corner reached him and held him down.

Kane tried to apologize, to reach out to Medved, but the injured athlete slapped his hand away, cursing him. “Вы чертовски животных, вы искалечили его.”

Angus led Kane back to his corner. "I didn't mean to," Kane said. "I just lost it."

Kane looked around the arena, surprised at how quiet the crowd had become. Everything seemed to unfold in slow motion. Eyes were fixed on the Jumbotrons, which replayed the final, brutal snap. Medved's ACL, ICL, and every other cruciate ligament had ruptured in his right knee.

Kane turned to his corner, but Angus was gone. He remembered asking him to track down the CIA rat, Wallace. Spinning around, he saw no sign of Wallace.

"Where the hell did that little rat go?" Kane shouted. "Damn it!"

The chaos in the cage engulfed everyone. Kane attempted to return to the center, but the crowd had flooded the octagon, pushing him back to his corner.

He watched Medved's team wrap bags of ice around the injured knee, demanding they bring him to the center of the octagon. Alone and in excruciating pain, he was surrounded by venue security.

The Bruce Buffer wannabe rambled through the closing announcements, and the two fighters faced each other. Medved shook Kane's hand, staring intensely with his dark, bloodshot eyes. Kane felt the unspoken message loud and clear: *Next time we meet, I kill you.*

The Russian turned away and, using his one good leg, hobbled out of the octagon. At the cage door, he collapsed onto the shoulders of his brother Alphas, who had worked his corner. Team Alpha drove the crowd back as they supported Medved down the steps, into the tunnel, and out of sight.

Kyle Kane took a triumphant victory lap. "This is the fucking life!"

The crowd, many of whom were former soldiers, reveled in the moment. Most had grown up hating the USSR, and for them, this felt like justice.

Kane began to think about Wallace, but when a throng of people, including Francesca Renaud, blocked his path to the little rat, he decided to leave it to Angus Walsh.

Bruised, bloodied, and clad only in his fighting pants, Kane struggled to remove his fight gloves. Francesca Renaud offered to cut them off and produced a slender ivory-handled stiletto—long enough to kill yet delicate enough to fit snugly in her silk and lace garter.

"I should have known you'd have one of those," Kane remarked. Francesca smiled as she slid off his gloves, cutting the tape on both hands before returning the blade to its leather sheath.

The announcer pulled Kane aside as a camera crew began filming. “Lieutenant Commander Kyle Kane, congratulations on a fantastic tournament and championship bout. You triumphed over a much bigger and younger opponent. Can you share your strategy and how you managed to pull it off?"

Kane smiled through bloody teeth. "Yevgeny was a formidable opponent. I had one strategy: let him punch himself out."

Kane started to drift mentally. The interviewer noticed and began asking him a series of easy questions. At one point, Francesca Renaud stepped in and signaled to the crew that it was time to cut the interview short.

A crowd of characters closed in on Kane as Renaud took him by the arm. "Kyle Kane, we need to talk. This draft represents a major turning point in your life."

The sea of suits surrounding them began firing off offers. Kyle tried to push his way through. One man standing next to Renaud said over her shoulder, "You don't want to pull down a multimillion-dollar payday and end up in a crazy hostage rescue in Somalia or a Soweto ghetto."

"Those K&R firms will get you killed," another man added.

Yet another man shoved a contract in front of Kane and said, "If we get you in the draft, son, I'll make you richer than anything these folks could offer."

Kane's head was on a swivel as he tried to listen to everyone around him. Finally, he pushed his way through the crowd with the vivacious Ms. Renaud in tow.

They stopped at the octagon cage door. "I just want to look back at this," Kane said. Renaud nodded and placed her hand on his chest. He was dripping with sweat and blood, and she could just about see into his eyes as she stood in her stiletto heels.

"Who are all these people, Francesca?" he asked.

"Agents and lawyers, to be more specific. People who want a piece of you—or the whole thing."

"They want to talk to me?"

"It's a bit more than that, but yes, in a broader sense, they want you to sign with them."

Francesca Renaud, in all her Versace sartorial splendor, tilted her head slightly, which highlighted her long, elegant neck. It captivated Kane. His thoughts drifted to kissing her shoulder and gliding his lips up her porcelain-smooth skin to just below her ear.

He was enchanted by her sophisticated beauty and her scent, a blend of sea anemone pheromones that drew out his inner wildness. He stepped closer to her, and everything came together with an 'Exile' song playing in his head: *I want to kiss you all over and over again.*

She touched his cuts and swollen face, her fingers lingering on his left cheek, which seemed to intrigue her. She gently kissed it.

"My dear Lieutenant Commander Kane," she said, "to quote the esteemed promoter Don King, 'If you cast your bread upon the water and you have faith, you'll get back cash. If you don't have faith, you'll get back soggy bread.'"

"What's the moral?" Kane asked.

"You need professional representation. There's more than a couple million on the table, Lieutenant Commander… and you'll need my kind of faith."

Kane looked deeply into her blue eyes. "Then it will be you, my lady. You can cast my bread upon the water, and you can bring faith to my cause."

She pulled her hand back from his chest. "Oh no, my dear Lieutenant Commander. I'm a woman of means, and as such, legal matters—particularly business negotiations—are far too tedious and pedestrian for me to be involved in."

She smiled and took his hand. "My job is to make the entente cordial, professional, and, of course, personal. I will endeavor to connect you with the right person."

Ms. Renaud left the octagon, leaving Kane to watch her nearly perfect figure sashay away.

Agents closed in around him like the Red Sea swallowing the Pharaoh, desperate to sign the new World Warrior Tournament Champion before the impending draft. In that moment, he understood the prize he had become. He attempted to navigate around the throng but ultimately gave up and listened.

"I'm sorry, guys, but right now I need to take care of a few things," he said, wiping the blood from the gash on his forehead. "Let’s talk after I get cleaned up and stitched."

He moved past the men, down the octagon steps, toward the stadium tunnels.

"You don't want to leave before the draft starts," shouted one man.

Kane called over to Francesca Renaud, who had made her way to the bank of express super-box elevators. She replied, “I go to cast your bread upon the water."

Kane arrived at the contestant’s locker room and found Angus Walsh sitting on a bench with an ice pack on his head.

"Don't tell me, Angus, a head as big as yours can't swell anymore. It'd throw the entire solar system out of balance."

"I'm sorry, mate. I had that guy—Wallace—by the scruff of his neck; he knew I had him dead to rights."

Kane shook his head. "A two hundred fifty-pound Highlander, a caber-tossing madman—what happened?"

"He used an unconscionably underhanded trick."

"What did he do, kick you in the jimmies?"

"Worse, Kyle, far worse. He invoked a force of nature; it was like a tsunami coming onshore. Picture two Scotsmen meeting up—and he asked if I would share a wee dram to ward off disease. To ward off disease!"

Kane turned and sat on a bench across the aisle. "So you had a drink with the jerk who ruined my career?"

"Yes, governor, I did. It caught me off guard too, Kyle dearie. Not a second after we finished the pint."

"He brought a pint—for the two of you—and so the legend of the cheap Scotsman—"

"Easy now, Kyle Kane. That is normally an outlandish slur, but in this moment, it has the ring of truth—just in this moment of singular veracity." Angus shifted the ice pack to the other side of his head.

"So he hit you right on top of your noggin?" Angus nodded. Kane stood up and examined the welt on top of Walsh's head. "Serves you right."

Kane turned to the mirror next to his locker, scrutinizing his own wounds.

"I can stitch that up, Commander dearie," he offered.

"I'll pass. With your steady hands, I'll probably end up with an eye sewn shut." Kane wrapped himself in a towel and headed toward the showers.

"And what part of 'I told you Wallace was bad news' did you not understand?" Kane continued. "Did he say anything —anything that could help me?"

Angus nodded emphatically. "Aye, he did. He said, *'Be careful and trust no one.'*"

"Yet another cryptic warning. Why is he trying to help me now? What could it mean? He could have just vanished into the ether and never been seen again."

Angus raised his hand, still a bit drunk and woozy from the blow. "He told me, 'If you can figure out the code, you can use it to identify the people behind this cabal. Use the numbers and convert them to the initials of the biggest players involved.'"

"That's admirable, Angus—a sincere traitor," said Kane, helping Angus to his feet.

"Maybe he's not the traitor. Maybe he's pointing us to the real traitors."

"Okay, buddy, let's change seats. I need to get to my locker so I can go back out there and be the belle of the ball."

Angus looked confused as he stumbled to the opposite bench. "Aye, laddie, that reminds me—Corrado dropped off your suit; it's in your locker."

"Well, that is something, Angus. I've never owned a suit before. I had a sport coat in high school, but since then, it's been camo or dress uniforms."

"You can put away the ice cream suit; you're now a finely tailored Petrozzi man."

"If you have to wear a suit," said Kane, holding up the jacket, "you might as well make it a Petrozzi bespoke suit."

Chapter 16

MetLife Stadium, Meadowlands, NJ. 22:38

A jumbo cocktail party raged at one end, while a white-glove dinner service took place at fifty tables on the stadium floor. Two Jumbotrons were suspended above the raised dais, adorned with a striking black and silver GGIG banner at the opposite end. The transformation was as impressive as it was swift.

In front of the dais stood men and women from various backgrounds, representing some of the world's wealthiest individuals, all negotiating for the best possible draft choice in the upcoming GGIG World Warrior Draft.

The rows of professionals moved frantically in and out of the area, engaging in deals and offers, secondary trades, and late-round shuffling and bundling of agreements. It was a carnival of covenants, conventions, and contracts, exchanged around the tables, sent over the wire, or transmitted through the internet.

Each member of this tribe wore their ceremonial headdresses proudly; radio communications, headsets, and microphones were the order of the day. Teams faced off in a scramble of buying and selling, negotiating, wheeling, and dealing as they sought to secure the best warriors, the most tactical leaders for their teams, and the best security deals available.

Finding a first-team spec ops leader was as challenging as drafting an NFL-ready quarterback. While many NFL draft picks possessed great physical skills, few could rise to the operational tempo and purposeful chaos created by offensive and defensive masterminds. Similarly, running a spec ops-level private military operation required a unique combination of intelligence and physical capability, along with exceptional tactical thinking in the field, always mindful of the strategic impact. Yet, few could endure the pressure of first-team reps.

***

Sheila, the awesome Aussie card girl, met up with Kane as they enjoyed a diverse collection of scotch. She shared her views on the GGIG Draft from a fight night card girl's perspective.

"Your name is Sheila, you're an Aussie, and your real name is Sheila? Isn't 'Sheila' Aussie slang for, like, young chick?"

"Yes, Mr. Kane, but that doesn't change the facts. My parents were both stand-up comedians from Perth, and for a great gag, they chose my name as part of their shtick."

"First off, call me Kyle, and secondly—"

A familiar voice came from behind Kane. "Kyle, there you are."

He recognized the sultry French voice of the mercurial Ms. Renaud. His interest and focus shifted in an instant. He felt for a moment like Hugh Hefner standing between two beautiful woman on either arm.

***

The event promoters did everything they could to showcase every aspect of the draft on the big screens, just as they had for the combines and the hand-to-hand tournament. They delivered every important moment to the crowd: individual military records, combine action and stats, tournament fight clips, and even some battlefield videos, before displaying projected choices by various teams and, of course, the draft picks.

Kane watched as one of the Jumbotrons replayed his fight with Medved. It was the first time he had watched it closely, and he almost felt some remorse—until they showed his 40-yard dash in slow motion.

"Commander dearie, you look a wee bit sluggish—accurate, but sluggish."

"It's slow motion, ya big galoot," Kane replied. “Where’s my scotch, Gunga Din?”

Angus laughed. "Honestly, Kyle, that 40 could legally be considered loitering. A little slower, and you could be going backward."

"The word is backward, not backwards."

"The King's English is backwards."

"I'll agree with that."

Angus spotted a relatively empty service bar along the back wall and set his drink down. "Aye, Mr. Kane, I'm seeing an opportunity for a pivot."

Kane smiled. "Lead on, Din; single malt can't be far." He stopped to pull out his cell phone and check his text messages. He spotted one from his neighbor, opened it, and closed it quickly. His expression said it all.

Jerry Desoto had asked his wife to break enough laws to at least get her fired and, under the Biden Justice Department, likely face jail time in some DC gulag. There was nothing, no rule—written or unwritten—that the CCP-controlled administration wouldn't break. If a citizen did it, it was a crime; when the government did it, that was national security.

Kane dialed the number just as Angus approached with two tumblers of scotch that splashed about.

"We'll be putting on a clinic, laddie, if they keep giving away 18-year-old Glenfiddich."

Kane raised an index finger as he spoke into the phone, "Hello, Daisha—hi, yeah—ah yes, it's Kyle, Kyle Kane. You know, Lieutenant Commander Kane, FOB Chapman, Khost. How did I get your number? I'm a frogman… I got froggy. You're in New York City, seriously? Can we meet? Sunday, like tomorrow Sunday? Sure. Tavern on the Green… I know where that is. I'll be there." He took a glass from Walsh and smiled. "Yeah, I know it's weird, Daisha. I'll lose the number."

Angus laughed and took a drink, handing Kane a napkin filled with some bizarre hors d'oeuvres.

"What is this, Angus?"

"It's a mini haggis."

Kane set it down on the bar and turned back to Walsh. "I'm not sure I can keep up this torrid pace."

"Aye, Lieutenant Commander, you're at the top of the list of potential draft picks." He pointed to one of the big screens where Kane's name was flashing. "It was at the top of the list a minute ago."

"Yevgeny Medved's name is in the top spot, so we just keep drinking until it changes," Kane said. “It’s the sympathy vote."

"Medved's name is now in the second spot," Angus replied.

"I really messed that Sputnik up, didn't I?"

"Aye, Laddie, that's true, but in my mind, you did humanity a favor."

"That's a bit strong, don't you think?" Kane replied.

Angus swallowed the remainder of his drink and belched. "Pardon me."

He raised a finger, leaned toward Kyle, and said, "He kills for pleasure, Kyle, and you’re at the top of his list."

Kane shook his head. "Stay out of his crosshairs; that’s my motto."

"At least for the time being, Lieutenant Commander, dearie."

Kane turned away from the crowd and said, "Medved is going to have a tough time rocking my world from a wheelchair."

Angus spun around just in time to see Medved being rolled into the room, accompanied by a group of hard-looking Russians.

"Looks like the Spetsnaz boys are spoiling for a fight," Angus remarked.

Kane laughed and replied, "Yeah, you're right. They're after my head."

"Are you strapped?" Angus asked.

"You can’t get in here with a shootin’ iron, Sergeant?" Kane replied, stepping forward and hiking up his pant leg to reveal a .45 magnum derringer in an ankle holster. “A gift from Francesca.”

"Use a large caliber bullet for a large caliber man," Angus said before swallowing the last of his drink and tossing Kane his glass. "And the Russian is a large-caliber hombre."

"You gotta take the bull by the horns, walk into the lion's den, and fight fire with fire."

Kane shook his head as he crossed the front of the stage at the far end of the hall. He walked up the center aisle, with the entire room watching him. After a moment, the noise subsided, and the room grew relatively quiet.

The four thugs who had entered with Medved surrounded Kane. Medved rose from his wheelchair, using a cane for support, and stepped forward with great effort. Standing nose to nose with Kane, he radiated pain and fury but extended his hand.

"I would have done the same to you, cowboy. Be thankful you beat me to it." They shook hands, and as they released their grip, Medved pushed Kane. The room erupted in cheers before returning to the revelry of the party.

Medved half-turned and said, "When I see you again, I will kill you."

Kane laughed. "We'll see how that goes. I wouldn't get too worked up; you haven’t got a leg to stand on."

Medved's thug posse moved in on Kane, and Angus, who had crossed the room in record time, reached Kane just as he took hold of his retractable steel baton. Before he could extend it, the inimitable Francesca Renaud pressed her prodigious chest into Kane's back.

"Some guys just can't take a joke," she said, pulling Kane back from the circle.

Kane left his baton in his pocket and smiled at the four Russians, who were grinding their teeth.

Kane turned toward Francesca Renaud, and she took his arm and led him away.

"Miss Renaud, you have an incredible sense of timing."

"Thank you, Kyle. I didn't want you to miss out on a chance to get flattened."

"What, those lug nuts? They're a bunch of second-raters," said Kane.

"Yes, Mr. Kane, this is not Bollywood. With four-on-one odds, even the World Warrior Champion would have trouble."

Kyle pointed to Angus Walsh, who stood on the perimeter with a broken chair leg he had picked up on the way over. "It's four on two, Francesca, and I have you in my corner."

"Tout à fait, Lieutenant Commander, but I'm really here to repay a friend."

"So you were protecting me, the asset—as it were."

"Why, Mr. Kane, are you accusing me of outright decency?"

"That's not all I was thinking of."

"The night is young, Lieutenant Commander, but I digress; I have someone I want you to meet."

The two walked to the private elevator bank. Kane seized the opportunity to pop in a dip. He wasn't surprised that his new friend made no comment; she didn’t seem like the type of woman who spent much time kissing.

They took the private elevator to the GGIG corporate boxes.

"So this is how the other side lives," Kyle said as they entered a world of wealth and opulence. Kane gazed around the spacious triple box, complete with oak wall panels, marble floors, and crystal fixtures. The array of antiques and obviously expensive artwork gave Kane an idea of who the short man was.

“Why would anyone put all this treasure in a football stadium? The furniture alone is worth a king's ransom.” Kane paused to look into the climate-controlled walk-in humidor stocked with cigars and wine.

Renaud pulled Kane along past a row of Queen Anne sideboards filled with silver chafing dishes. He began to inhale the aromas of the end-to-end delicacies. Every conceivable dish was represented, from steamed cracked lobster claws to Iranian caviar and prime rib bites. A tuxedoed waitress passed by with a silver tray of flutes filled with champagne, and Kane tried to grab one.

He stopped Francesca. "It's been a while since I've been to a sporting event. Do they always serve Cristal and lobster?"

Renaud ignored Kane's sarcasm and continued scanning the crowd. Still holding his hand, she gave it a squeeze when she spotted what she was looking for.

Kane’s earlier conclusion was confirmed when the same short man who had tried to influence Kane's semifinal match stood before him, holding court in the center of a large group that resembled rent-a-guests.

"Come, Lieutenant Commander, your future awaits," she said, unabashedly pushing her way to the front. "Excuse me, pardon me, if you please." She navigated through the five-deep throng of surging sycophants.

"He's believed to be the third richest man in the world," she said excitedly. "And he’s the founder of the multinational conglomerate CCU." She spun around and found herself directly in front of Roland Moreau.

"Rollie, my good man, how's it hanging?" Kane said, thrusting his big, bruised, and calloused hand into Moreau’s.

Moreau's eyes widened, and Francesca let out a low gasp.

"A little to the right, Lieutenant Commander, if you must know," Moreau replied without missing a beat. Kane smiled, surprised by his glib response and firm grip.

"Please come with me," Moreau said. "I have a few things to discuss with you, Mr. Kane, before the draft begins."

The three of them began to navigate through the crowd toward Moreau's private suite in the third of his CCU super box suites. Moreau gestured for Renaud to stay behind.

"Fetch the lieutenant commander whatever he desires."

Kane looked back and forth between the two, somewhat amazed at how casually Moreau had dismissed Francesca.

"Don't worry, Mr. Kane. Serving is Francesca's best possible self."

Kane smiled uneasily. As they walked, he glanced down at the throng of people drinking and shuffling around the stadium floor.

"I guess they're all here to serve you, when you think about it."

Moreau smiled. "They're here to serve us. Face it, Lieutenant Commander Kane, you're an elite among elites."

Inside Moreau's office suite, he gestured for Kane to take a seat across the desk from him. However, Kane remained standing, observing the crowd.

"You scored exceptionally well on the Milstein Tidewell Human Awareness section of the comp test, which is a fantastic predictive tool," Moreau remarked, as if Kane needed an explanation.

"Yeah, and I quit that test early because I was getting bored," Kane replied. "I'm sure I have a touch of ADD or something." He glanced around the room, projecting his boredom onto his host.

Moreau regarded him in disbelief. "The longer you test, the higher your score will be. Once you accumulate enough incorrect answers, the test ends."

"Yeah, I got that. I tossed in a couple of wrong answers at the end. The sun was over the yardarm, and the drinking lamp was lit."

Moreau shook his head in disbelief. "You are an incredible specimen, Mr. Kane. You could have—"

"I haven't felt so special lately, Rollie."

"Please sit," said Moreau, motioning to the cordovan red leather seating. Kane settled into one of the comfortable semicircle groupings around a crackling fire, fueled by actual burning logs.

"That's a fantastic fireplace."

"You have a good eye, Mr. Kane; it's an 18th-century Bossi, hand-carved from statuary marble with Scagliola inlay. It's valued at—well, let's just say twenty years of hazardous duty pay."

"I gotta say, Rollie, I think you overpaid."

"As you'll see, Mr. Kane, acquiring what you want when you want it may cost you more than you ever thought. Take, for instance, Jerry Jones' purchase of the Dallas Cowboys. At the time, people called one hundred and forty million a ridiculous price; today, it's worth several billion."

“That’s due to Crazy Joe’s division champs, Team Hatred. The world may be turned off by entertainers, actors, musicians, and artists, but like the gladiatorial games of Rome, the American people crave the truth of sports, especially football. Players are elevated to demigod status, and NFL merchandise is worth the GDP of Spain. Jerry’s investment doesn’t seem so crazy anymore.”

“Regardless, I didn’t bring you up here to dispense history lessons or discuss current events. My scouts view your physical gifts as a borderline negative, but your mental acuity in tactical matters is at a genius level. You exhibit abstract sequential thinking that is off the charts. Artificial intelligence may be the wave of the future, but it is unlikely to ever replace someone who thinks like you.”

"I'm sure you are aware that I was forced out of the Navy."

"I am, Mr. Kane, and that’s the Navy’s loss. The abstract aspects of your thinking favor imagination, which contributes to the development of new tactics and out-of-the-box problem-solving. My security team will benefit from your mission design concepts. The linear component of your thought processes allows you to follow ordered, logical steps, even though the sum of those steps, the result, may appear to be a radical departure from standard tactical norms."

"This doesn’t mean we're going steady, Rollie." Moreau laughed. “I’ll bet you don’t do that often.”

"That’s true, Mr. Kane. It’s rare for anyone in my presence to gamble their career on a joke. Anyway, I have reviewed all the definable aspects of your elite-level performances, and the only remaining area of concern is your moral—or, more precisely, your ethical—substrate."

Kane scratched his beard. “I've been dealing with that a lot lately, Rollie." He scanned the room for a spit cup. Moreau looked at Kane questioningly, and Kane pointed to his mouth. Moreau nodded. Before Kane could reach for a Baccarat Crystal snifter off the silver tray, with its decanter of Louis XIII cognac, Moreau said, "If you must."

Kane nodded thoughtfully and, with as much restraint as possible, spat out a wad of chew. He wiped his chin with the back of his hand and nodded to Moreau.

"Thank you kindly; it's one of my vices that, unfortunately, isn't going away anytime soon."

Moreau smiled. "That is comforting news; I own several tobacco companies."

"Where I came from," Kane said, “every man's opinion is worth something, and everyone

of my men was the elite of elites."

"And so it shall be under the CCU banner. I have two officers, each commanding a platoon, and each squad has eight world-class operators," Moreau replied.

Kane interrupted Moreau, clearly not accustomed to being cut off. "So you can muster thirty-two tier-one operators? With officers, that’s two platoons’ worth of firepower. Why so much?"

"Lieutenant Commander, the world has become a much more unpredictable and complicated place," Moreau replied.

"And no one knows that better than I do," Kane shot back, spitting into his snifter. "A platoon of highly trained tier-one door kickers, with the right gear and a solid mission plan, could shut down a small city for twenty-four hours."

"I am well aware of what my men are capable of. As for your point about a solid plan, I need someone who can lead them—someone who can act as my surrogate. Someone who can make life-or-death decisions when I’m not there."

"Do you have a high draft choice?" Kane asked. "Shouldn’t Ms. Renaud be here for this part of the discussion?"

Moreau glanced at his platinum Patek and replied, "At this point, no, I don't have a high draft choice. I had the number one pick last year, so this year I'm way down in the order."

Kane leaned back in the leather chair and asked, "Do you have any bourbon in one of those fine-looking k-rafes?"

Moreau nodded to a tuxedoed waitress nearby. She returned with a bottle of Maker's Mark and poured an ounce. Handing Kane a snifter, he drank it down.

“My cornerman is a mad Scotsman, and I’ve been on a steady diet of single malts.”

The waitress repeated this process twice more before Moreau, with a hint of unease, said, "Just leave the bottle in front of the Lieutenant Commander; he'll be fine."

"That's alright, Mr. Moreau, I was just enjoying the scenery," Kane replied with a wry smile.

"Lieutenant Commander Kane, if you sign with my team, part of your compensation—beyond a substantial signing bonus—will include seven days at my villa in Monte Carlo. You’ll have access to my stable of sixty-three sports cars and any club, restaurant, or establishment of your choice."

Kane leaned forward in his chair. “I’m so sorry, Rollie; I forgot to thank you for the fantastic greeting you laid out for me.”

“No need to thank me. I called an acquaintance of mine, a very successful university football coach. He told me the best way to secure a recruit is through blackmail.”

Kane looked like the cat that swallowed the canary but managed to keep it in.

"The same technique the CCP has used on American politicians and elites for decades.”

A PA announcement shifted the mood of the negotiation. "With the first pick in today’s Warrior Draft, Thorn Protective Services chooses ... Yevgeny Medved."

Kane, surprised by the announcement, remained subdued. "Is Thorne one of yours?”

Moreau considered lying but dismissed the idea, knowing it would be a poor way to start an important relationship. "In response to your question about Miss Renaud, she has completed her part of the recruitment effort. We have the third pick in this year's draft, and Miss Renaud has effectively seeded doubts about your combine performance. Most importantly, she’s circulated rumors of a degenerative hip that will limit your operational capacity going forward," Moreau said, wearing a smug expression that Kane wanted to slap off his face.

"Won't that significantly decrease your bargaining position?" Kane said, realizing the lack of insight as soon as he uttered it. "You want to reduce my value."

"Kyle, may I call you Kyle?" Moreau asked. Without waiting for a response, he continued, "I own Thorn, and I'm going to offer Yevgeny Medved a five million dollar signing bonus and nine hundred thousand annually. I'm offering you a ten million dollar signing bonus, which will be in your account as soon as you sign—immediate and irrevocable. You'll receive three million dollars annually in compensation, for which you will take over operational control of my CCU Corporate Security assets."

Kane sat dumbfounded. "Okay, where's the camera?" he said. "Did Angus put you up to this? I have to say, you had me going."

Moreau's demeanor shifted from collegial to dangerously intense. "Lieutenant Commander Kane, I am not to be taken lightly. I moved several pieces around the board to get you into this competition. I brought you here for a purpose, and I can easily cast you back into the pool of undifferentiated grunts if I choose!"

“Were you involved in my court-martial?”

Kane's emotional reactor scrammed. His fuel rods were dry, and his instinctive response was aggression, but in that moment, Kane chose calm. He rose and stood in front of his host, realizing he was projecting his anger from both past and present experiences.

"Mr. Kane, do not walk away. This is an opportunity to command your own team."

Kane stopped and turned back to Moreau. You know something, Rollie, I see tremendous similarities between the military and the NFL, beyond the whole draft hoopla. You look at the offense versus defense, the line of scrimmage, and a ground game that uses armor like linemen to open up holes in the D, and you send your fast movers through. Air attacks that move the action deep down the field, and there’s the QB, the on-field leader who makes the choices that will win or lose a battle.

"Mr. Kane, I value your intelligence and leadership qualities."

Kane thought for a *moment. The money was too good to walk away from. A year maybe two and I could retire and build sailboats.*

"I think real NFL QB money, Rollie, fifteen million in signing bonus, and I'll sign on to your team," Kane said in an even, emotionless tone.

Moreau's expression changed immediately, shifting back to a more pleasant, professional demeanor.

"One thing I must insist on," Kane continued, "is that the safety of my men comes first. No exceptions."

Moreau agreed so quickly that Kane wondered if he had even considered the demand.

The two shook hands swiftly, and Moreau said, "I'll have a contract in front of you within the hour."

A voice came over the speaker system in Moreau's office. "Demigol Industries, you are on the clock for the second pick of the draft."

Moreau quickly texted a message on his phone. Within a minute, the speaker announced,

"And with the second pick, Demigol Industries trades its second pick in the draft to CCU Industries."

Seconds later, the PA system declared, "CCU's choice for the second pick in the World Warrior Draft is Lieutenant Commander Kyle Kane." A handful of people spotted Kane and turned to cheer in Moreau's super box. A group of rowdy former military members began a raucous chant of “Knee bar—knee bar.”

As the recently crowned World Warrior Champion, Kane now had a group of fans and supporters.

Kane walked to the bank of floor-to-ceiling windows that opened onto the stadium.

"So this is how it feels to be a rock star," he thought, raising his hand to wave before heading down to the stadium floor.

***

The crowd of fans, corporate security personnel, and active-duty and retired military members greeted Kane as he exited the private elevators. Everyone within range patted him on the shoulders. He hurried up the center aisle to the podium and leaped onto the stage.

Alexander Timcenko greeted Kane with a bro hug and handed him a green and gold jersey featuring the number one, his name, and the CCU logo embossed on the back.

"I want to thank my cornerman and all-around single malt co-pilot, Angus 'Gunga Din' Walsh, and the beautiful Francesca Renaud, who provided me with incredible support from her friends Anna and Mia. But most of all, I'd like to thank the son of a bitch in the US government who left me without a chair when the music stopped." Kane raised his CCU Industries jersey and waved to the cheering crowd. “Oh yeah, and a big shout-out to my men of Six, the best warriors in this man’s Navy.”

Kane walked through the rows of draft day experts, lawyers, and scouts who were still grinding and would continue to do so through the night.

With his new company colors slung over his shoulder, Kane received applause and handshakes as he headed into the football field-sized party.

He was looking for Francesca and Angus to do some advanced celebrating. He had reached a common area and eventually found himself in the trade show area filled with company banners and dummy ordnance.

It seemed to Kane that every empty space outside the field area was filled with booths, elaborate product simulations, and actual pieces of defense and military hardware.

The grand showcase of weapons and defense technology revolved around the business of war, arguably the most profitable industry worldwide. It was organized by the corporations and marketing firms of the international military-industrial complex.

“Military heavy industry and technology—that’s CCU’s core business,” said Gary Willitz, a top salesman for Aerodyne Industries, which makes missile technology, and both military technology subsidiaries of CCU. He stood in front of a sleek, cylindrical missile with the questionable title of Ulysses Arrow.

“Microlite—that’s part of the CCU Conglomerate?” Kane asked.

“It is,” Willitz replied. “It’s the Defense Aerospace subsidiary of CCU.”

“And part of the military-industrial complex, right?” Kane said.

"It’s really become the drone industrial complex, Mr. Kane. 'Drone' refers to any unmanned weapons or surveillance platform. I’m pretty sure the boss recruited you because he wants to AI-map your intellect. If we can map your warfighting capabilities and download them into just one supercomputer that can control a drone military—we’ll have the greatest weapons system ever created.”

“You’ve heard people in CCU meetings discuss this,” Kane asked, “this whole drone army concept?”

“Not a drone army, but a complete drone military, managed by the Gary Fischer of military planning, capable of relying on warriors—boots on the ground—that can execute your exact orders to perfection, without concern or complaint. The orders generated by a Kyle Kane-mapped AI supercomputer could provide General Gary Fischer with a list of options, complete with the statistical likelihood of success and the potential for collateral damage.”

“You didn’t answer my question.”

“Yes, I did.”

Kane was finishing his bourbon when a PA announcement requested his return to the CCU super box suites. He looked at Gary Willitz and remarked, "You know what Einstein said: 'I know not with what weapons World War III will be fought, but World War IV will be fought with sticks and stones.'"

Whether he realized it or not, Kane was about to sign on as a very deadly instrument of war.

Kane returned to Moreau's stately office. The little Frenchman was gone, so Kane took a moment before signing. He was alone in the room except for a young woman server, the same one who had served him Maker's Mark earlier. She stood at attention twenty feet away.

Kane approached the Louis XIII writing table near Moreau's desk. *Probably worth more than my house.*

He picked up one of the decanters, opened it, and sniffed.

"Single malt; it's a shame Angus isn't here." He filled his glass and took a sip.

There was a tablet on the table, and it was Kane's contract. He attempted to read the twenty-page document but cursed at the absurd legal jargon. *Fucking lawyers. This is the same fucking technique Pelosi uses. She orders a two-thousand-page document filled with the language of obfuscation, misdirection, and what amounts to government theft, then calls for a vote thirty minutes later. That's why the country's twenty trillion in debt, right where the elites want us.*

Kane signed an e-doc. "I'm a fucking millionaire! Fifteen million for signing my name. Holy hell!" he exclaimed.

The young woman who had stood at attention for most of the night laughed.

"Thank you very much for everything," said Kyle as he looked at the pretty college-aged woman with long, curly brown hair. She smiled at him before she looked away nervously.

Kane paused and gazed into her doe-brown eyes. "So, can you speak?"

Her bright white smile lit up, making Kane grin.

"What's your name?"

"Colleen," she replied with a charming Irish brogue, "Mr. Kane."

"Call me Kyle—and you know my name?"

"It's been flashing on the Jumbotron for the last few days. I know your favorite color, along with your vertical leap and the size of your…shoes." Colleen started laughing at Kane's reaction. It brought a warm feeling to Kane, and it showed on his face. "Just joshin' you, Mr. Kane. There was a fair amount of very personal data displayed up there, but nothing about your shoe size."

Kane paused before asking, "How old are you?" He hesitated for a moment. “I ask because you seem so young to be a personal assistant to Moreau."

"You could call it that," replied the young woman. "But 'indentured servant' would be more apropos," she added in a whisper. “I’m sure Mr. Moreau still has his communion money.”

It took a moment for Kane to grasp her meaning, but when he did, he grinned at her.

“You’re from Cork?”

"Cork? Do I look like a Cork woman? I'm a Dubliner, Mr. Kyle Kane, which explains my slave status."

"Oh really?" said Kane. "Where in Dublin?"

"Sheriff Street," she replied, giving him a curious look. “You know where Sheriff Street is?”

Kane invited her to sit, but she politely declined, citing the code of conduct for all employees.

"Pishaw," Kane said with a chuckle and a wave of his hand. "Then you will accompany me to dinner tonight, and we will have a nice time. You didn’t answer my question.”

Her face took on a rosy glow of shyness. “I’ll be twenty-six on the fifth of next month, and I look forward to the day I can return home.”

For the second time in as many minutes, the cover girl was hiding something. She glanced around nervously, then stepped within whispering distance of Kane's ear and said, "After eleven tonight."

It took Kane a moment to calculate civilian time as she passed him a note with her address.

"One last thing," she said nervously, "he never loses! Keep that in mind in any dealings with him."

"Yeah, I think we've seen people like Moreau; Napoleon comes to mind."

Colleen flashed a smirk and quietly added, “When you two got a little heated earlier, you didn't notice the red dots painting the back of your head.” She left the room with a few empty glasses.

Down on the stadium floor, the draft had ended for the day. More draft action would resume in eight hours, after the hospitality team could restock and reset the party. The evening's festivities were dwindling when Kane caught up with Angus Walsh, who was leaning heavily on the bar for support. The big Scotsman was surrounded by his newest friends, all in various states of disarray. Jackets were off, sleeves rolled up, ties wrapped around heads, and shoes—especially the torturous spiked heels—were discarded. The women, with their hair down, danced barefoot, drinks sloshing back and forth before they coated the floor. Thus was the dress code.

The gala event had concluded an hour earlier, taking with it the more refined crowd, who had departed for a cigar bar or a late-night club. Even the nightcrawlers, the diehard partygoers who had led the charge into a bacchanalian state, now only a stone's throw from the frat house circle of Dante's Inferno, began seeking alternative sources of entertainment.

One of the party leaders, the mass consumption specialist, Regimental Master Sergeant Walsh, was spinning grand tales of SAS gallantry and military genius to a few general admission attendees who had somehow slipped into the after-hours show.

Angus was well into the process of replacing his entire blood supply with single malt scotch when he spotted Kyle Kane. A broad smile broke across his face.

"Angus, if you had been born in the tenth century, you'd have been Henry the Eighth's drinking buddy or a Highland warrior for whom many songs would have been written."

Walsh leaned back and tried to focus. "Aye, ladies and gents, it's my good—nay—my great pleasure to introduce my friend and bodyguard, the World Wrestling Champion—"

"Warrior, Angus, World Warrior Champion," interjected the bloke standing next to Angus.

"Right you are, gov. It's my great—I did say great—great pleasure to introduce to you fine folks, Kyle Kane, Lieutenant Colonel, Retired, United States Navy SEAL."

Kyle just shook his head, and the group, unaware of Angus's field promotion, cheered raucously. One drunk young man smashed his crystal tumbler on the floor, causing a cascading effect as a dozen more followed suit.

Kane looked at Angus and rolled his eyes. "Any more toasts you want to raise, old friend?"

"No—no, I think a quick and surreptitious retreat is called for, Kyle, dearie."

"Lead the way, Command Master Sergeant."

Angus started to walk away but quickly turned back. He scuttled over to the bar like an elephant seal performing a sand bath before grabbing a bottle of Glenfiddich.

Kane could have advised him against it, but Angus was already back at the bar and walking away. "The package is secure, Commander darlin'."

Chapter 17

Lincoln Tunnel, Manhattan, 02:00

In the early hours, the Lincoln Tunnel resembled a zombie land. The recessed fluorescent lights flashed past the passengers in a hypnotic display that captivated Angus. As Kane drove, Angus provided a running commentary on the tunnel. It was old—87 years—and situated ninety-seven feet below the surface of one of the widest rivers in the Union, the Hudson River.

Crammed into the passenger seat of his Toyota Tundra, Angus fired off one inane question after another. "Why don't they clean the tile walls of the tunnel? What would we do if the tunnel leaked and the Hudson River came rushing in? Did you know, Kyle dearie, that the Hudson River flows past West Point, where it's almost two hundred feet deep? Uniquely, it's called the *Hudson Fjord.* Do you know how I know?"

Kane waited for Angus to finish, but all he got was a massive snore.

***

Once in Midtown, the Tundra turned right onto Tenth Avenue South and headed to their hotel. Angus Walsh spilled out of the passenger seat while Kane paid the doorman a hundred-dollar bill to ensure his friend got to his room.

Kane quickly jumped back onto Tenth Avenue and headed north to Colleen's apartment on 89th Street.

He found an open parking space surprisingly close to the building entrance. *A free spot late on a Saturday night—how fortuitous. If Colleen is still awake, I'm batting a thousand.*

Kane slipped his pistol into the small of his back and approached the door. He pressed the buzzer for Colleen's apartment, and the door buzzed and popped open. He waited for Colleen's sultry voice on the intercom speaker, but silence was all he got.

With the door open, he walked through the vestibule into an empty lobby. He passed a wall of mailboxes, each with an observation window above the key lock. Colleen's letterbox, number eighty-three, contained a half dozen envelopes still inside.

Kane searched for the security camera and moved out of its view. He drew his Springfield XD and chambered a round, sliding it into his quick-draw spot on the inside of his waistband.

The elevator to the eighth floor dinged, and Kane stepped out slowly. He checked east and west and spotted his secondary exfil, the stairwell *door.*

He walked quietly to number 83, counting his strides. He knocked once, and to his immediate alarm, the door was open.

"Oh shit," he muttered under his breath. Kane held his 9mm to his chest and slowly pushed the door open with his free hand. Peering through the hinged side, he saw the apartment was dark except for a sliver of light at the far end of the hallway.

With his pistol aimed upward, Kane's instincts tingled. He moved into a Weaver stance and methodically checked each room, *aware* that every door could be a potential death trap.

He touched nothing until he accidentally kicked an object on the floor. Crouching down in the darkness, he picked it up and recognized it immediately: *a stiletto.* He examined it for a moment before instinctively pocketing the weapon.

Moving through the apartment room by room felt like a familiar dance he'd performed a thousand times before, only this time he was alone, in a place he never imagined he would be.

I really miss the security of the stack, where I know everyone's moves. This is a real cock-up.

He approached the last door. *It's always the bathroom at the end of the hall.*

The door was ajar, spilling a yellowish light into the hall. The same nerve impulses that prickled the hairs on the back of Kane's neck warned him of what lay beyond the open door.

He pushed the door open slowly, and when he stepped in, he found Colleen's slim, demure figure, with skin as pure as freshly poured cream, sitting quietly on the loo.

The beautiful Dubliner was stripped naked and bound to the plumbing with duct tape.

A stream of fresh blood flowed from her recently slit throat, resembling ruby-red latex paint poured perfectly over her posed body.

Drips fell like a metronomic pulse from the bottom of her leg, pooling on the tile floor. It sickened Kane, igniting a wave of anger that felt dangerously homicidal. Despite the validity of his feelings, Kane realized he had strayed from the steely, unshakable mission focus forged in BUD/S and honed to a fine surgical edge over twenty years in the Teams.

His pause lasted only a second or two, but those were seconds he couldn't afford.

The short loop of death—images of his daughter, his comrades, and now this beautiful woman—played in Kane's mind. He fought to break free. *The stiletto is part of this carnage. The stiletto from the floor? He pulled out the knife. Murder weapon? Purposeful or just clumsiness? Shit, this smells like a setup!*

The blow came from behind. Pure white engulfed everything before the inevitable rush to black. His mind registered the pain, followed by a scattering of neurons. The last thing he heard was the clang of the stiletto as it skittered across the tiles.

***

The singular sound of a sonar ping—Kane's ringtone—registered in his disoriented mind.

He pulled himself out of the gray haze and came face-to-face with the cold tile floor. Shutting his open mouth, he lifted his face from the pool of drool that had accumulated.

Pushing himself up, he reached for his phone and opened the 'unknown' text window: "Get out now; NYPD is on the way." *Who the hell is this?*

Kane grabbed a hand towel off the rack and wiped up his saliva before pocketing it and heading into the hallway. The sounds of a patrolman's radio pierced the silence.

Shit, they're coming up the hall. He left the bathroom door ajar and ducked into the closest room. The living room was dark as he moved silently into the deepest shadow. Crouching next to a recliner, he pulled himself into a tight ball.

"NYPD!" shouted a voice. "NYPD, we have a report of a break-in! We're coming in!" Kane's gut tightened. The two officers who entered were not his enemies, and he prayed they wouldn't spot him.

He watched the flashlights and the shadows of a two-man stack as they cleared the rooms.

He pulled his knees tighter into his chest as the patrolmen quickly searched the living room. He knew the light at the end of the hallway was foremost in their minds. Their tactical lights swept over Kane as he huddled in the shadow of the chair.

The beams moved through the kitchen directly across the hall before leading them down the hallway. The last thing Kane saw as he slipped from the living room to the front door was one of the officers placing his hand on the bathroom door.

"NYPD, identify yourself; we're coming in."

Kane bolted down the hallway. The last thing he heard was, "Call it in; secure the building."

He passed the elevator. *An easy way to get trapped.* Instead, he took the secondary staircase at full speed, descending two or three steps at a time, as fast as, if not faster than, the elevator.

His mind replayed the sound of the stiletto skittering away from him.

Breathing hard, he crossed the street and ducked into a dark alley two blocks away.

The grimy alleyway matched Kane's mood perfectly. He squatted next to a dumpster across from 89th Street, watching Colleen's apartment. The screech of tires followed the sirens of the approaching NYPD cruisers converging from both directions. A minute later, a pair of unmarked cars added to the response.

The sirens blared through the streets as emergency vehicles flooded the scene. At that moment, Kane remembered Angus's truck. *Shit. I parked too close to the apartment entrance; I'm bound to be in the sweep.*

A few hours ago, I couldn't believe my good luck; now I wonder. I got lazy *and let my guard down, and for that, a young girl is dead. I should have recognized the potential for danger. She was just starting her life, so young.*

Anger and remorse churned in his gut as he watched several officers posted outside the apartment lean against the hood of Angus's Tundra.

What's this? A new brand of lawman arriving in a Chevy Suburban with a big block engine, lifted and with tinted windows?

"Oh yeah, navy blue jackets, tall yellow letters—smells like FBI. Why? This is NYPD jurisdiction. Murder is a state crime, and the FBI is here from the jump; it can mean only one thing: prior knowledge. Kane opened his phone and checked the text he had received on the bathroom floor.

Kane's gut twisted. *Poor girl, caught in the middle of God knows what.* "Why would someone do this?" he asked.

"That's quite the question, isn't it, Lieutenant Commander Kane?"

Kane reached for his pistol as he spun around, facing the cave-darkness. He

saw the red glimmer of a laser sight and kept the gun at his side, aware that he was in trouble. Although he was a world-class gunfighter, he knew the odds were not in his favor.

"It's a question for the police, isn't it?"

The voice sounds Middle Eastern.

"Down in the dark of the alley, that's where evil sits and waits," said the shadow.

Kane moved his hand toward the handle of his Springfield but hesitated when the red beam of the laser sight flickered back on. As his eyes adjusted, he saw that the laser was mounted on a silenced machine pistol.

"I wouldn't do that, sailor; it would be a quick end to what could be a very profitable career in corporate security." The voice resonated with Kane, turning the wheels in his head.

"That was you at the cigar bar in Virginia Beach?" Kane said. "Why kill the girl?"

"If you're looking for a confession, choir boy, you won't find one out here," the shadow

began to laugh. "I don't suffer from human foibles such as empathy or guilt."

"No, for sure not. You're a fucking sociopath!"

"I recall that term being used once or twice in my childhood. Like you, I made a

conscious decision that other lives and obstacles would have to end for me to be successful."

"You would have killed me already if that were your purpose."

"Listen closely, Kane. On the battlefield, you may be supercock, but in the urban jungle, I reign supreme. I am the apex predator. If they told me to kill you, you'd be dead right here in the bathroom; it matters not."

"You didn't have to kill Collene. She was just a young girl."

"Okay, Mr. Seal-man, I'm here to tell you that, if need be, you are the prime suspect in the

Colleen Michinard murder." The shadow held out an evidence baggie and let it unroll. In the low light, Kane saw the knife.

"It might be the stiletto, or it might not," said Kane. "Let me see it."

"You'll just have to take my word for it, squid."

"I know you; the Cigar Emporium. I'll see you around."

"Make any waves regarding the death of Mullah Attah Kassem, reopen the military investigation, or become involved in any investigation," said the voice. "You'll spend the rest of your life in prison. Murder one, I believe you call it."

The shadow backed away. "We'll meet again, Mr. Kane, and when that time comes, I will kill you." He vanished into the darkness.

I need to take that bastard down, but here, in the pitch black, it's a fool's errand.

"This is completely fubar," Kane said aloud. He pulled over a produce crate, dumped out the brown romaine lettuce, and turned it over. From his vantage point at the head of the alley, he watched the front of the apartment.

***

NYPD wraps up their investigation in record time; let the Feds take over. Another hour passed, and the FBI concluded their hijacking case. They loaded up their easily recognizable undercover black Suburbans.

Same make, model, color, and tinted windows. Federal government plates and a cab full of high-and-tight haircuts all around; not a whisker between them. They really sold their cover as four overpaid government workers.

Kane gave it one more hour before stepping out of the alley. Sure enough, another black window-tinted Suburban rolled by the apartment. They eyed the building and then drove off.

Criminals do return to the scene of their crime. It's true. He walked to the Tundra half an hour later and started the truck.

He passed through the West Side of Midtown Manhattan, and as he approached the Lincoln Tunnel, he began to think. *How many CCTV security feeds have I passed? They're everywhere in New York.*

***

Kane walked into the hotel at 8 AM, his heart heavy and his anger at a boiling point.

The night crew was wrapping up while the day crew changed out drawers. The smell of breakfast wafted from around the corner, tempting him to sit down and eat.

I need some Starbucks, some Ethiopian super brew, to get me back in the game. He decided to head to the second floor to try to wake Angus Walsh.

This could be an exercise in futility, or I could just drag his big ass down the stairs and

out onto the street. That would be one way to get it done.

The midnight-to-eight staff were passing through the lobby on their way to their cars.

Kane walked past the front desk, showed his key card, and asked the bewildered night manager, “Have you seen a rather large—” But before he could finish with the word *Scotsman*, the woman pointed toward the bar area, wearing an angry expression.

Kane laughed. “You’re kidding,” he said rhetorically.

“Not a chance,” the woman replied, showing no hint of humor.

Kane entered the bar area, expecting to find Angus Walsh passed out on the floor.

Instead, he saw a weary bartender rubbing out the watermarks on some glasses, likely for the third time around.

The bartender looked up at Kane and asked, “You’re Angus’ friend?”

“Yeah. How much does he owe?” Kane replied.

“Nothing. He paid for everything and gave me a three hundred dollar tip to keep the

bar open and the drinks flowing.”

Angus’ booming voice cut through the conversation, completely unaffected by the staggering amount of alcohol he had consumed over the past twelve hours. “Laddie, I won 86,000 dollars! Vegas was carrying the World Warriors Hand-to-Hand Tournament. I put a C-note on you to win. I parlayed it with the Curling World Championships in Reykjavik and the Scotland vs. Zimbabwe cricket match. Scots ran the table.”

“So you’re giving it all back playing cards?” Kane asked.

Across from Angus sat a five-foot-tall Asian man named Quak. Vietnamese by birth, he

had grown up in a Shaolin temple in China.

"He's got a huge stack of chips, Angus, compared to your tiny stack."

"Aye, Commander dearie, I'm about to go on a grand run of cards. I'm counting cards."

"Looks like you forgot how to count, Glasgow Slim. You're dealing from one deck, not a shoe, and the cards are shuffled before every hand—there's nothing to count. Now wrap it up."

Angus glanced at the two players next to Quak, who had folded their hands and rested their heads on the table.

Walsh pushed all his chips, his Concord watch, and his SAS ring into the pot.

"Mr. Quak, are you all in?" he asked.

"I'm all in, Mr. Creosote."

"He calls me Mr. Creosote. That's a bit funny, right? Who is this Creosote chap?"

Kane laughed and said, *"Does eight brown ales and a bucket* mean anything to you?"

"Okay, little man, one card down," said Angus.

Quak flipped over a queen of diamonds, and Angus let out a cheer. He revealed a full house: queens over twos.

"Full house, brother Quak, pay up."

Quak threw down his cards and cursed in Vietnamese.

"Now it seems to me that some fine things have been laid upon your table, but you only want the ones you can't have—desperado."

"Don't sing, Angus; it's bad form, literally. What are you so excited about anyway? He's still walking away with some of your money."

"Yeah, but I had fun," said Walsh. "Quak—I call him the Quakster, the Quakenator. I've enjoyed your company, laddie, you and your fine feathered friends. We'll engage in another game of chance some other time."

"You good man, Angus beef," said Quak. "We see you again." Each of the Asian men smiled broadly, stood up, and bowed at the waist before disappearing into the kitchen.

Angus leaned back in his chair like Diamond Jim Brady and patted his substantial stomach. But the chair couldn't handle it. Under extreme pressure, the back two legs splintered, and the chair literally exploded under the big man, and he crashed to the floor.

Kane laughed, which caused the bartender to laugh, and when the desk manager walked in, she laughed too.

"This is your room, big man. Shower up; we're headed to Tavern on the Green."

Kane said as he turned to head down the hall. Angus Walsh saluted, and as he stumbled backward, he fell onto a bed.

Kane opened the door to his room. A large envelope on the bed made him reach for his pistol. He checked the bathroom, then placed his pistol on the bureau. The large envelope lying on the bed captured his attention.

Lieutenant Commander KYLE KANE, USN Ret., was written on the envelope. He dumped the

contents onto the bed: invitations, documents, a passport, and a stack of Euro bills. Among the items, he found a travel itinerary: departing from Teterboro Airport on a chartered Gulfstream 5 for seven days in Monte Carlo. He continued reading through the list of parties, cruises, and receptions.

It's like I won the fucking Super Bowl.

Kane headed back to Angus's room and knocked on the door. A disheveled Angus Walsh answered, wearing a bath towel stretched to its limits.

"How do you feel about Monte Carlo?"

"It's a wee bit overpriced, but a grand place, no doubt," Walsh replied as he walked back to

the bathroom.

"How about an all-expenses-paid trip to Monte Carlo? Pack your bags; we're going to the show. Don't forget, we're meeting Daisha Willow in an hour at Tavern on the Green."

"You handle that, and pick me up on your way to Teterboro."

"Sounds good, Mr. Creosote.

"Well, Lang, may your lum reek."

"What's that, Scotty?"

"All the best to you, laddie," said Angus as he shut his door.

Chapter 18

Tavern on the Green, Manhattan, NYC. 09:50

Kane stood before one of New York City's historic buildings. Not historic in the sense of the Museum of Modern Art, but more like a gathering place for any New Yorker willing to pay the freight.

The architectural bones of the old girl, despite all the postmodern, Euro-austere plate glass and high-gloss blonde wood makeovers, are still here.

He was standing at the hostess station when he spotted Daisha sitting at the bar. She was sipping a passion fruit mimosa and looking around nervously.

Kane navigated through the brunch crowd, employing the tradecraft he had picked up in some of the deadliest rooms in the world.

"Lady Di, so good to see you." Daisha jumped off the bar stool and hugged him tightly.

Kane took hold of her arms and held her. "Everything okay?" He noticed her lower left arm was bandaged.

She glanced around, then leaned in and whispered, "Things are spinning like a high-speed centrifuge and could get out of control quickly."

"They could," said Kane, "but out of control is an operational tempo I know and well."

"Kyle Kane, man of action," she said with a forced smile.

"Sort of," Kane replied as he dropped a twenty on the bar and motioned for Daisha to follow him. The bartender shook her head. Kane then dropped a fifty, but she shook her head again.

"Sorry, Kyle, I needed a good deal of self-medication—Piper Heidsieck mimosas."

"I understand, but tell me, what prompts an agency gal to spin off-center so dramatically?"

"You saw Admiral Martin Corbett get murdered in front of the Pentagon?"

"I did, and?"

"The agency is moving all kinds of pieces around the chessboard—assets, top case officers—many have been recalled to Langley and then reassigned to South America, Korea, or Malaysia. These reassignments were sudden and geographically unfamiliar to the agents, forcing them to establish a foothold in new postings while chasing God knows what. From an intelligence standpoint, it looks like we just punted on third down."

A waitress seated Daisha and Kane. Kyle scanned the area around them. Kane checked out the tables in front of him, while Daisha surveyed the room before her. Their eyes met in the middle, and they laughed.

"Clear," said Kane, smirking.

Daisha nodded, still laughing. "Clear."

"Okay, I have something to tell you. The last few days have been a whirlwind of chaos."

"Intense?"

"Murder—capital murder."

"You?"

"No, Di, it was—well, let me start by saying I won the World Warrior Championship."

"For real? That's great! What does that have to do with capital murder?"

"I won the tournament and was drafted third in the GGIG warrior draft. That's the Groupe de Guerrier's International Guild's annual selection process for the best mercenaries."

"I know what the GGIG is and what the draft entails," Daisha replied. "Some of our Special Operations Group, the paras, were hired away by the GGIG."

"How come I never heard about the GGIG or the draft?"

Just then, Kane's nova and cream cheese on a toasted egg bagel arrived, while Daisha tucked into her fruit and granola yogurt parfait.

"I got a fifteen million dollar signing bonus."

"Shit. That's incredible, Kyle. What are you going to do with it?"

"Buy you another passionfruit mimosa."

"My boss, Warren Trask, considers GGIG a top-tier producer of paramilitary talent. He's thinking about sole-sourcing our SOG operators from GGIG. He views them as if they're tier one operators, which some are, but DEVGRU's greatness is in their teamwork."

Kane swallowed hard and chased it with some coffee. "He wants to create a separate group of operators… like DEVGRU, using GGIG for their personnel?"

"Yeah, it's like his pet project."

"Have you ever heard of a man named Roland Moreau?"

"Funny you should ask; I have. He visited Langley while I was waiting for an assignment, so they detailed me to his security detachment during his visit."

"What was he there for?"

"High-level meeting with Trask—just after Biden's election. What does this have to do with murder?"

Kane thought for a moment, his expression turning serious. "I met this young woman after I won the tournament. She worked for Moreau, who had just offered me a huge contract with an irrevocable fifteen million dollar signing bonus."

"That's sick money."

"I was in his bloody superbox when I met this young Irish woman, Colleen Michinard. We agreed to meet at her apartment here in the city. When I arrived, she was naked, her throat cut, and taped to the goddamn toilet. They cut her fucking throat, for fuck's sake."

Kane's eyes welled up, and the veins in his neck threatened to burst.

Daisha's eyes widened. "Was it Moreau?"

Kane looked down and wiped his eyes. "I'm pretty sure. I barely escaped—just in the nick of time. I surveilled her apartment from an alley a block away when some character showed up behind me. They must have been watching me. He caught me off guard, staying in the shadows with a laser-sighted Mac 10 or an Uzi aimed at me. He threatened to use planted evidence to pin her murder on me."

"Could you identify the guy?"

"I could. I'm fairly certain he ambushed me with a group of four thugs back in Virginia. Based on our conversation, I'm ninety-nine percent sure it was him, or maybe it's your boy Wallace?"

"He's not my boy, for starters, and he's not—at least I don't think he's a cold-blooded killer."

"Yeah, I kind of got that impression at Chapman," Kane said, pushing his plate aside. "He contacted me at the Warrior games. He said he's trying to help me, and he gave me this."

Kane handed Daisha the program. "It has numbers circled—lots of them—and some letters. I'm hoping it will provide me with some answers."

Daisha had spent a long time in CIA SIGINT evaluation. She understood what the numbers and letters represented, and Kane sensed it.

"We need to get out of here, Kyle," Daisha said, glancing around nervously.

"What's wrong?" Kane asked, noticing the change in her expression. He signaled for the check.

As they walked out of Tavern on the Green, Daisha limped. When Kane mentioned it, she quickly changed the subject. They stepped onto the bricked walkway that wound through the beautiful gardens surrounding the tavern.

"So what the hell happened to you, Di?"

"Hmm, a couple of lug nuts tried to tune me up. It got ugly. I shot one, and the other one hammered my knee before running off with his partner."

"Good for you, girl. Where and when?"

"Coming out of my gym near Langley. They were ex-military, I'm pretty sure."

Kane took Daisha by the arm and turned her to face him. "Why are we here? Who would want to mess you up?"

"More importantly, Kyle, Will Wallace is waiting for us at the Four Seasons on Fifty-Seventh Street."

Kane's jaw dropped. "You're kidding me?"

"I wish I were. He called me a few hours after you did. He's terrified. I set him up in the hotel with an off-the-books company card. What else could I do?"

Kane nodded his understanding but also recognized the company's ability to surveil its own employees.

They drove a few blocks, and Kane kept an eye out for any tails. He asked Daisha directly what was going on, but she tried to evade the question and changed the subject to her upbringing in Manhattan.

"Is that important?" Kane asked.

Daisha took a left and rolled down an alleyway one building over from the Four Seasons Hotel. She parked the car, and Kane got out. From their vantage point, they could see the hotel, and he seized the opportunity to scan it thoroughly.

"How'd you find this place, Di?"

"I'm not sure, but it's a name I've heard. I thought I'd give it a shot."

"Works for me."

The pair walked through the lobby, drawing a few curious glances. Kane recognized several eyes that quickly darted away behind newspapers. He noticed Daisha quickening her pace.

Kane caught up to her and whispered, "I'd say your off-the-books card is no longer off the books."

She turned and leaned into him. "Are you strapped?"

"Seriously, girl, I grew up in a place where it's always danger close."

"Wallace is on the eighth floor; let's grab this elevator and talk," Daisha said. As the elevator doors closed, Kane noticed six or seven people moving around in the lobby from his vantage point.

"What's going on, Di? I counted six players on the move," Kane said. "Who are they?"

"Could be anyone—maybe a CIA SOG team, the FBI, or local cops, but I don't think they're NYPD. Some of them looked Middle Eastern; could be Mossad."

"Mossad? What would Israeli intelligence be doing here?"

Daisha shrugged, and her lack of surprise gave Kane pause. "Lieutenant Commander, you need to start thinking globally. You were the tip of the spear in an operation involving one of the highest-value targets since Bin Laden. Do you really believe his money doesn't have U.S. ties?"

The elevator stopped, and Kane cautiously stepped forward. Daisha pressed the elevator's stop button, causing the car to jolt. They had reached the sixth floor.

"Mullah Atta Kassem's laptop was lost along with his life," Daisha said. "It was potentially the greatest loss of intel in the war on terror." She began pacing the elevator. "Mossad's interested, the Russians are interested, the Saudi Royal Family is interested, and the list goes on." Kane could see the concern etched on Daisha's face. "Many dangerous people within the U.S. government and its intelligence apparatus are very concerned."

Daisha Willow released the hold button. Kane pulled out his Springfield XD, chambered a round, and held it by his side as the car stopped on the eighth floor. He stepped into the hallway and cleared it in both directions.

"How could they get this close? Did you call anyone?" Kane asked.

Daisha shook her head. "I swept my apartment and my car. I picked up Wallace at the Amtrak Station in Iselin, New Jersey." She pulled her Ruger LC9 from her ankle holster, racked the slide, and slipped it into her purse. "No one followed us."

A young couple emerged from a room halfway down the eighth floor, heading toward their destination.

Kane put on a jacket over his pistol and followed Daisha down the hallway. The two couples passed each other, exchanging smiles.

Kane glanced at Daisha, raising his eyebrows. "Can't tell," said Di.

"The best way to handle it is to shoot first and ask questions later," Kane replied.

Daisha grabbed his shooting arm and whispered urgently, "Kyle, no!"

Kyle laughed. "I don't shoot people in the back; that's spy work."

The two watched the couple enter an elevator. "Cheap shot, Kyle."

Daisha stopped in front of one door, feigned a knock, then moved two doors over and knocked once, followed by a quick double tap and a single knock. She looked at Kane first, and he nodded. After a couple of seconds, she pulled out a key card and opened the door.

"Maid service," she said. Kane followed her in, his pistol at his side.

Inside, they found themselves at the business end of a gun. On the other side of the room, silhouetted by the bright midday sun streaming through a plate glass window, stood William Wallace. The Glock 22 he held shook so violently it bounced between Daisha and Kane.

"Put your gun on the bureau, Mr. Kane," Wallace said nervously.

"Finally, someone calls me by my proper name," Kane replied, sliding his pistol onto a chest of drawers.

"Nice choice of lodging, Mr. Wallace."

"I can take no credit. I was thinking more of a safe house on the beach at Deal."

Lady Di held up a wallet with a license for a thirty-year-old. "Tradecraft provided creds, cards, and money, Will. Now lower the weapon. Kane's not here to hurt you."

"Is this a quid pro quo for all this—a meeting with me—before you vanish into the wallpaper of the world?" Kane asked.

Wallace moved away from the window and picked up Kane's pistol. "Yeah, that sounds about right."

"Watch that weapon, CIA man—it's got a hair trigger."

"Don't worry, Kane, I'm familiar with firearms," Wallace replied.

"Yeah, like standing with your back to a big fucking window; real tradecraft."

Wallace motioned for Kane to sit. The tension between them was palpable.

Not long ago, Kyle wanted to kill Wallace for what he had done; he just didn't have enough proof to carry out the deed.

Wallace was scared—terrified, in fact. Every day, someone in the U.S. or Europe finds themselves in the same position as Will Wallace: cut loose, blacklisted, with no friends in the world and an army of full- and part-time killers on the lookout for them.

"Please sit, Mr. Kane; we have a lot to talk about."

Kane spun a desk chair around and sat, watching Wallace closely.

Wallace stepped closer to Daisha and asked, "Are you okay?"

She sank onto one of the two king beds, replying, "Hell no, Will. You pulled me into a real shit show."

Wallace took a seat directly across from Daisha and said, "Listen, Mr. Kane, I was sent to Chapman by Tyler Cox; he's an Associate Deputy Director of Special Ops. Daisha was my contact at the base, nothing more."

"I spoke to Tyler Cox; he told me you were a part of our mission," said Kane, "and his boss is Trask, Warren Trask."

"Hold on there, Will," Daisha interjected. "I was told nothing about your real mission. Cox told me your mission was to interrogate Kassem, not to murder him and steal the intel."

"I didn't murder Kassem!" He paused for a few seconds to calm himself. "I think you know that. I was not informed of any mission objective that included murder. I could never do that."

"Will, you told them you wanted to go operational; what did you think would happen?"

Kane stared hard at the two of them before standing up anxiously. "You're telling me that someone else was on that base working for the CIA in tandem?"

Kane's anger flared at the thought of traitors in the mix. He glanced at Daisha, then back at Wallace.

Kane took his seat again and said, “You set me up.”

Wallace was starting to look irrational, his hand trembling as it gripped the pistol.

“Please, Mr. Kane, stay calm.”

Kane fixed his gaze on Wallace. “Did you try to kill Kassem at Darbart?”

Wallace looked shocked. “No! How could I—”

“Someone took a shot at Kassem and almost hit me!” Kane exclaimed.

Daisha shook her head at Kane when he stood up to reveal the bullet burn. He began to pace, wanting to close the distance between himself and Wallace, still unsure if this was a trap.

Had Wallace conned Daisha into getting me here just to kill us both? Or maybe Daisha’s in on it, and I’m the biggest fool on the planet.

He stopped pacing and shrugged.

“Did you just say that I set you up, Kyle?” Daisha asked, her voice laced with anger.

Kyle shook his head, unsure if he had said it or not. “What? No, not you.”

“Wallace isn’t a killer,” Daisha insisted.

“Like I said, I tend to believe you,” said Kane as he took his seat. Wallace breathed a sigh of relief.

“So the plan was to overpower me with a flashbang, knock me out, and take the laptop. But why?” Kane realized how foolish he sounded. “I mean, I get it; you’re part of the most underhanded American institution since Hoover’s FBI. Honestly, I’m lucky you didn’t cut my throat.”

“That was never on the table,” Wallace replied. “I wouldn’t—” He glanced at Daisha and fell silent. “I just never would.”

“He was killed by someone,” Kane said.

“I don’t know who!” Wallace shouted.

Kane asked tensely, “Was it one of my guys?”

Wallace shook his head.

Kane could see there was so much Wallace knew that he would never share. He recognized the potential for real trouble coming from any direction.

"Are you kidding, Kane? You guys are as tight as a frog's ass. What part of "I *just don't know;* do you not understand?"

"Easy, little man. You're punching above your weight," Kane said.

"If I think about it, maybe they chose me because I was new to operations and wouldn't see the real danger in taking this mission. My ticket was punched the minute I arrived in Khost."

"What's on the laptop that's worth murdering a man for?" Daisha asked anxiously.

"Don't get preachy about murder; hundreds were killed using drones under Obama. It was his own personal hit squad!" Wallace exclaimed.

"Are you serious, Will? Do you think I know Obama personally, or is it just because I'm a person of color?"

"I'm sorry, Di. I'm talking out of my ass. I'm scared."

"Where's the laptop, Wallace?" Kane pressed.

Wallace reached under the bed and pulled out an aluminum briefcase. Kane's jaw dropped as Wallace removed the laptop.

The hardened laptop cover bore a couple of stickers with Farsi lettering.

Kyle couldn't take his eyes off it. "That's it? Open it—open the laptop."

Wallace tried a few passwords. "I've cracked the encryption on the hardware, but some of the data is still protected."

"Those look like ledger entries," said Daisha. "You can see the numbers."

Wallace examined it closely. "Payoffs, maybe—almost a hundred of them."

"How much are we talking about?" asked Kane.

"Upwards of half a billion dollars by my count," Daisha replied, dropping back onto the other bed.

"So why are we here? What or who ordered this mess?" Kane asked.

Wallace stood up from the bed and walked to the window. "We were operational. We had orders to secure the intel."

"Right, but why kill the package? No, don't answer that!" said Kane, looking around nervously. "This smells like some kind of '*Three Days of the Condor*' crazy shit!"

Wallace agreed, "You're more right than you know."

"Clarify that for me, Will. Tell me what's on that laptop," urged Kane.

Wallace peered closely at the street below. "Statistically speaking, there's an abnormally high number of large black SUVs in front of this hotel."

Kane replied, "We saw a small reception committee in the lobby."

Wallace turned to Daisha, whining, "When were you going to tell me that?"

Daisha shrugged. "I didn't want to freak you out, Will. We have a fucking SEAL with us."

"Retired," Wallace corrected. "Who was it, Di?"

Kane considered flattening Wallace but instead said, "They looked like Mossad."

Wallace's jaw dropped. "Mossad… shit, they're ruthless fanatics. Torture is on their business cards."

"So let's blow this pop stand," said Daisha.

"I'm all for that," Kyle replied as he walked to the window and looked over Wallace's shoulder. "Damn, you're right." Kane turned Wallace around. "So tell me, what happened at the I&I Center?"

"I told you, they rolled in a flashbang, and in the chaos, I slipped the laptop into my waistband and stumbled out."

"And?"

"I left Chapman and headed to Kandahar. I was instructed to hand off the intel to an asset."

"A handoff to who?" Kane asked brusquely.

Wallace hesitated, reluctant to reveal the name. He hemmed and hawed before finally saying, "It was a local asset."

"A CIA asset?"

Surprised, Wallace said, "You did say 'Three Days of the Condor.'"

Kane shook his head. "Is this some rogue element in the CIA?"

"Don't stop there, Mr. Kane," Will Wallace replied. "There's room at the top for a substantial rogues' gallery."

A loud knock at the door caused everyone to freeze. Kane moved to the wall next to the door while Wallace approached nervously. The Glock trembled in his hand as he checked the peephole. "It's some scraggly-looking dude. He looks like a roided-out Burl Ives. His neck is as thick as my waist, and he's got a huge bucket head."

Kane smirked and asked, "Looks like a homeless Santa Claus with a handlebar mustache?"

Wallace pointed his pistol at Kane's chest. "How'd you know that?"

Kane snatched the pistol from Wallace and tapped him on the head with it.

Daisha shouted, "No, Kyle, you promised!"

"Enough of this bullshit." Kane grabbed Wallace by the collar and pulled him off the floor. "You ever point a gun at me again, and I'll do what I should have done at Chapman."

Kyle reached for the door slowly, and when he opened it, he pulled Angus Walsh into the room. He checked the hallway to the east and west. "What the hell are you doing here?"

Angus, nearly five stones heavier than Kane, spun him around and shoved him against the wall. Kane chopped at Walsh's arm and pushed him back.

"I told you, Kyle, I'm your second, and I won't be fobbed off," Angus said. "Especially when your life's on the line. And by the way, there are enough bloody spies downstairs to start a UN softball team."

Angus looked at Daisha and Wallace. "And who do we have here?"

Kane smiled. "We don't have time to discuss the details, but the long and short of it is that two CIA operatives, Daisha and your old friend William Wallace, got caught up in a rogue mission.”

“There’s a lot of that rogue shit going on, right, Wallace?” said Walsh. “Nettle, nettle, your ass is in the kettle, little Braveheart!”

“What do you know about it, fat man?” Wallace shot back.

Kane didn’t need to see the crooked smile on Angus's face to know what was coming next. He stepped between them and ushered Angus toward the door.

“I’ll wager you two are on the burn list. That’s a virtual death sentence. I feel for you, Ms. Daisha, but you, Wallace, can fuck off.”

Chapter 19

Midtown Manhattan at 11:10

Kane walked Angus down to the elevators, instructing him to meet them on the street five blocks west of the hotel. He returned to the room and sat down with Daisha and Wallace. His plan was to get them out of the hotel and to a safe house across the George Washington Bridge in Edgewater. Angus had called in a favor from an SIS buddy, outside of their primary intel grid.

"Everyone's best chance of getting out of this situation," Kane said, "is to get the hell outta here."

Daisha raised her hand and then lowered it. "What happens if the agents downstairs come after us?"

"I doubt they'd rush us in the middle of the Four Seasons. They'd probably wait until we reach the street," Wallace replied as he stashed the laptop in the knapsack and slung it over his shoulder.

Kane opened the door and cleared the hallway, scanning both directions.

The three gathered their gear and left the room. Wallace, Daisha, and Kane moved together toward the elevators. Just before they reached them, two CIA agents emerged. It was a tense moment, with all five standing motionless until Wallace smiled and broke the ice.

"Gale, great to see you guys."

Wallace extended his hand, and they shook. Kane stood, eyeing her male partner. The female agent positioned herself between Wallace and the others.

The second agent, a large Latino, attempted to draw his weapon on cue. He didn't manage to get it out of his holster before Kane dropped him with a low Muay Thai kick to the side of his knee, followed by an open-hand chop to his neck that momentarily cut off blood flow to his brain. The man hit the deck, and Kane disarmed him. Daisha took down the agent speaking to Wallace with a swift roundhouse kick.

"Why the hell did you do that? She was telling me we could slip out through the restaurant kitchen on the first floor."

Kane found their handcuffs and secured them both. "How do you know her?"

"We came through the farm together."

Kane took their radios along with their weapons. "Check for backup ammo," he said.

"What the hell for?" Wallace replied angrily.

"It may be true that you know someone, but let me tell you this: giving you a way out just doesn't make sense, agent!"

"How the hell do you know?" Wallace shot back.

"It's got nothing to do with knowing and everything to do with betting our lives on it, you idiot."

Wallace listened to Kane. "You're right—I should have thought it through."

Kane shook his head at Wallace and said, "You're not a SOG operator, are you?" Wallace flinched at Kane's question. "And you're not a case officer, either?"

"No, I'm not. I'm just a damn analyst, a run-of-the-mill analyst!"

"An analyst," Kane replied. "They sent an analyst to retrieve the biggest cache of terrorist intel in the last twenty years? Now that I say it, it doesn't sound so absurd."

Wallace looked confused. "Why do you say that?"

"Because an analyst is much less likely to figure out the who, when, and why of what he was being asked to do."

"Figure out what?"

"At some point, they were going to clean up after themselves. You know, like killing you."

They took the elevator down, and when it stopped at the lobby floor and opened, a group of six or eight people was waiting. Kane realized what was about to happen in less than a second. He hit the close door button and selected the fourth floor simultaneously.

The agents' first reaction was to grab for the door; when that failed, half of them reached for their weapons. Kane pulled Wallace from the center of the elevator just as a dozen silenced rounds ripped through the doors and lodged in the back wall panels.

Daisha looked at Wallace, who was pinned to the wall by Kane’s forearm and terrified. "Why didn't you tell me you were an analyst?"

"You never asked."

The elevator stopped on the fourth floor, and Kane jumped off.

"What are you doing? This is the fourth floor!" shouted Wallace.

Kane didn't bother to answer. The two followed him, shrugging their shoulders.

"Where the hell are you going, Kyle?” asked Daisha.

"Come on, Di, follow me or—follow the analyst?"

"Low blow, Captain America," said Wallace. "Lead on."

The trio bolted down the hallway, away from the hotel's central core. They reached the first corner just as shots rang out behind them. A chorus of bullets fired in rapid succession, tearing up the sheetrock close behind.

"Great, automatic weapons!" shouted Daisha.

They reached the second corner, and Kane stopped two doors down at room 421. He kicked in the door, followed by Daisha and then Wallace.

"This is a fucking kill box, Kane," said Wallace. "It’s a dead end."

Kane pushed the door shut and secured the two locks. He scanned the room and spotted a large five-by-five rolling toolbox. He pushed it in front of the door and locked the wheels down.

"We'll be long gone by the time they get through that," said Kane as he led the others through the suite.

"They're coming, and we gotta move," Wallace urged.

The trio walked across the Visqueen-covered floor, past walls stripped down to the steel studs. On the far side of the bedroom, a pair of windows framed a debris chute set in a wooden buck. It gaped open, dropping four stories into a dumpster in the hotel's back parking lot.

"How did you know?" Wallace asked.

"I've been doing this for twenty years, Wallace. Never enter a structure you don't know how to exit. That’s something they don’t teach analysts over at Langley."

Daisha stood at the chute's opening. "After you, Lieutenant Commander."

"Good copy," Kane replied, climbing into the three-foot-wide flexi-tube as if he’d done it a hundred times before.

He descended a few feet and looked back up at Daisha and Wallace. "Use the steel rings in the tube as footholds; press off against them with your elbows and feet to keep from falling." He then dropped down and disappeared from view.

A minute later, Kane emerged from the bottom of the chute, rising into a shooting stance as he surveyed his surroundings. He scanned 360 degrees and spotted a few kitchen workers smoking on the loading dock to his left. His mind flicked back to the agent who had suggested an escape through the kitchen, and he immediately classified them as potential threats. Looking up into the tube, he called to Daisha and Wallace to come on.

He called quietly into the chute. "Move or die in place!" Kane piled some torn-up pieces of insulation under the tube, just in time to catch Wallace as he fell the last few feet into the dumpster.

"Draw your pistol, Wallace; you're going to need it. Fire discipline!"

Lady Di descended more gracefully. "Watch the loading dock, Di."

Kane pulled the radio he had snatched from the agents and inserted the earpiece. He listened for a moment. "They're coming this way. Give them a reason to stop, Mr. Wallace!" With that, Wallace began firing, demonstrating why he barely qualified with a handgun.

"Di, help him out," Kane said. "His spray and pray is wasting ammo."

"What are you going to do?" she asked.

"Exfil, Lady Di." He started looking for a way out.

Daisha turned away from Kane and smiled broadly. "Fire discipline, Will—one shot, one kill!"

Kane turned back to the hundred feet of open blacktop between the dumpster and the corner of the building, the alleyway, and the street beyond.

He spotted a shotgun-wielding shooter rounding the south corner. “Contact!” he shouted, dropping down behind the dumpster wall. A shotgun blast ripped into the sturdy steel side.

"Shit! That could've hurt!" A second round pounded the dumpster.

Kane rose up and aimed at the shooter. A single gunshot rang out from behind, hitting the shooter just below the chin.

Kyle turned back to see Wallace grinning like the Cheshire Cat. "Fire discipline, right?"

"We gotta go, guys!" shouted Kane. "Check your ammo and get ready for a run and shoot." He popped his head up over the dumpster. "There's a hundred feet of exposed distance to cross."

"It’s a hundred feet?"

"I don't know—plus or minus. Is that important Wallace the analyst?"

Kane hopped out of the six-foot-tall dumpster, hit the ground hard, and ran to the other side before dropping behind the corner of the hotel.

Wallace looked at Daisha and said, "Go, I got this." He popped up and fired four more rounds. Go, Lady Di. I’ve got some unfinished business. Go, before I change my mind.”

Daisha placed her hand on the dumpster rim, ready to leap over it, but fate double-crossed her, and her grip slipped.

"Whoa!" Two rounds snapped just overhead as she dropped hard onto the pavement. Pushing up as quickly as she could, she ran, swaying back and forth toward Kane’s position.

A shooter emerged from behind the lot wall, aiming directly at her. For some reason, he hesitated for a moment, grinning at Daisha with a sick smile before taking aim.

Kane stepped out from his cover and, with one shot, dropped the man.

Daisha stumbled across the blacktop through the gunfire. Kane continued laying down cover fire until she launched herself the last ten feet into his arms.

"Slipping and falling off that dumpster saved your life."

"And put us here now," Daisha replied, "with zero degrees of separation."

She touched her bleeding hairline and examined her fingers. “I’ll put that in my memoirs.”

Wallace fired off a couple of last rounds before bounding out from the far side of the dumpster. With a surprisingly athletic run, he set off across the parking lot toward the loading dock.

To Kyle, it looked like William Wallace was drawing fire away from them. When he ran up the steps to the kitchen loading dock under fire, the die was cast.

“Daisha, keep up the cover fire; I'm going for Will.”

“No, Kyle, he’s not coming.”

Kane fired a few rounds downrange and turned to Daisha. “Why?”

“That ship has sailed.”

“So, you're saying he has a plan, and he’s executing it?”

“If we try to bring him back, we'll be fatally outgunned. We need to get the hell out of here,” said Daisha. Two rounds struck just overhead, sending shards of brick raining down on them.

“We can try to pick him up on the other side of the building.”

Daisha nodded, still scanning for good targets. They were running low on ammo. “If they don’t grab him first.”

Daisha regained her footing, touched the road rash on her hairline, and stood up.

Kane took off his pullover. “Take off your jacket.”

Kyle pulled her tight to his side, and the two made their way up the alleyway toward Fifty-Seventh Street.

"Can you walk on your own? If you can, go ahead."

Daisha nodded and stepped out onto the street, moving away from the Four Seasons.

Kyle followed, five meters behind her. At one point, he quietly instructed her to cross the street. Kane pointed out an alleyway across 57th Street. "Alleyway to the right."

The vintage smell of an overdue dumpster greeted them. The same nauseating stench pulled him back to the night before and the showdown with the Persian. They set up a vantage point amid the cartons, cases, and empty crates of rotten vegetables. Kyle wanted to move another block over and exit onto the street, but Daisha was not ready to leave the Four Seasons.

"Let's wait here. Maybe we can help Will."

"I'm not sure that's a good idea. If we're spotted and we're on foot—"

"I can't just leave him hanging."

"He's made his bed, Di."

"What happened to the SEAL motto: Leave no man behind?"

Kyle glanced at her for a moment before returning to his mini binoculars. "Wallace chose not to run with us. He no longer has the intel, so what's his play?"

In the bustling kitchen of the Four Seasons, William Wallace paused to inhale the aroma of the white truffle risotto being plated on the line.

He straightened his two-day-old button-down shirt and walked past the garnish station, which was piled high with chopped parsley.

A large glass stein filled with Pilsner Urquell ale sat alone on a stainless-steel prep table, awaiting incorporation into a beer batter. Wallace grabbed it and took a hearty swig as he made his way out.

He pushed through one of the swinging doors into a busy lunch seating. More than a few curious diners noticed him as he walked through the dining room. He stopped at the end of the bar, punctuating his arrival by finishing his Pilsner Urquell and letting out a deep belch.

The reaction to Wallace was immediate and predictable, given their profession.

Regardless of their intentions, Wallace paid them no attention. One man charged at him, only to be stopped by a member of his team.

From their vantage point in the alley, Daisha pointed anxiously at the hotel entrance. “There he is, Kyle!”

“I see him; he’s coming out of the main entrance.”

Wallace pushed through the bronze plate glass doors, stopping before the wide expanse of sidewalk with a carefree smile. He pulled out a crumpled pack of Lucky Strike cigarettes, and as a cool breeze brushed his face, he struck a match, hoping the name on the cigarette pack was a sign. He took a long, deep drag.

“What is he doing?” Daisha asked.

Kane handed her the binoculars. “I don’t know.”

“No, no way! I’m going up there, Kyle.”

He grabbed Daisha around the waist. “That would be a big mistake, girl.”

Wallace finished his cigarette and flicked it onto the sidewalk in an arrogant arc. He glanced up and down the street, clearly aware of the afternoon's portent.

As he took a step, a pair of tiny red spots glistened on his forehead. One more step, and two low-velocity rounds entered his brain, mushrooming against the other side of his skull. The small-caliber bullets eviscerated his brain. He was dead before he hit the granite.

“Oh my God!” shouted Daisha Willow, her reaction muffled by her hands. “They killed him, Kyle—they fucking killed him.”

Kane pulled her back deeper into the alleyway, wrapping his arms around her as she cried.

“I’m sorry, Di. Was that the first person you’ve seen killed?”

She lifted her head and nodded. “I’m going to make them pay.”

“Not if we don’t get out of here.”

“I grew up here; we’re not going anywhere.”

***

Through the alleyway, they crossed 58th Street. “I need to stop,” said Di.

Kane walked Daisha a few hundred feet to a small bodega with a street-side café. They sat at a table just inside the front door.

He eased Di into a plastic chair. She was still shaky from her fall. As he pulled out his cell to make a call, the screeching of tires interrupted him.

Down the block, in front of the alley they had just exited, two all-black Suburbans skidded to a halt, blocking traffic.

Eight operators in full black tactical body armor and armed with silenced Colt M4s jumped out of the vehicles.

“Damn, government operators,” Kane said. “They’re hunting us.” He checked his pistol. “We need to go, Di. Those guys are probably CIA SACSOG operators. We leave now, or we die.”

Summoning her strength, she began to walk toward the back of the store.

The barista, preparing a macchiato, smiled at them. “I'll be with you folks in a second.”

Kane nodded and continued through the aisles stacked high with cans, boxes, bottles, and bags of Goya sundry goods.

They reached the back of the bodega and considered making a run across the alley. Di pointed to an accessway that ran behind all the buildings on that block. She looked both ways and took a step forward, but Kane grabbed her and pulled her back. He pointed to the cross street that bisected their escape route. A third Suburban had pulled into the alley, blocking their path.

“How many rounds do you have?”

Di pulled back the slide and dropped the magazine. “Three rounds.”

Kyle drew the .40 caliber Smith & Wesson he had taken from one of the agents. “This is a double stack, fully loaded —probably twenty-one rounds.” He glanced at the Suburban. “There are at least two of them covering the alleyway.”

“Is that our best option?”

"It's either that, or we make a break across 58th Street."

Daisha nodded toward the front of the store. The two of them hid the weapons and walked slowly toward the storefront. They stopped, and Kane used the store owner, who had stepped outside to watch, as cover to assess their next five minutes. Without a good exfiltration plan he knew they'd be lucky to make five.

"They have two four-man search teams and two covering the street."

Di looked at the ground and sighed. "They've got us boxed in."

A loud screeching of wheels was followed by the sound of a crash. All six SOG operators converged on the green Toyota Tundra, pulling a big, scruffy fellow out of the truck and throwing him onto the hood of one of their Suburbans.

Kane motioned with his head for Di to head down 58th, away from the wreck.

"Was that—"

"Yeah, our SAS angel."

They doubled back past the Four Seasons, two blocks north, trying to walk as casually as possible. They were out in the open, and the threat level was high.

Kane was sure they had drones in the air. Di directed him to a subway stop. They hurried down the bluestone steps, worn in the center from centuries of foot traffic. It didn't take long to drop sixty feet into the underground of the city. After a few left turns, they reached the turnstiles.

"Not smart, Di, disappearing underground into the subway system?"

"Not as dumb as it sounds, Kyle Kane. The Manhattan subway system is covered by a massive CCTV surveillance network. The agencies will likely be monitoring it in real time."

"Okay homegirl, we walked into a surveillance trap. Why, and what are our options?"

"Follow me, sensei." She led Kane to the end of the platform.

When they reached the end, Kane turned to Di. "Where to now?"

An A train pulled into the station, and Daisha made her way down the grimy access space and around the far end of the train. She led Kane into the dark. “We’re going into a dead zone—zero cameras.”

Feeling still woozy, Daisha quickly took a seat on one of the switching boxes. “We need to catch the 4-5-6 train that goes uptown. 125th and Lex is our stop.”

“We're headed uptown, to Harlem?”

“Harlem was my home, Kyle. I need a burner if you see someone selling one.”

Kane laughed. “Yeah, and I need my MK12, but that's not happening.”

Daisha shook her head.

"What?" Kane said. "It's my security blanket."

Daisha started to laugh. "That's really funny optics, you clutching your little assault rifle. I meant a phone—a burner phone."

"Right, I knew that. If you're from here, you have got to have assets in place—right?"

Daisha smiled and replied, "They're not assets in the truest sense of the word." She paused for a moment. "You're sworn to silence about this, Kane. I’ll have to kill you if you say a word about what I’m going to tell you to anyone. Understood?”

Kane sat next to Daisha, smiling. “I can’t wait to hear this one.”

“Before Langley, really before I got into Columbia, I ran with the Kings."

"The Kings—the street gang?"

"These are their streets, and they are a gang."

"I guess that makes you a Latin queen? That's so—"

"Stow it, sailor boy."

"Whoa, touchy. You do realize 'diva' is another name for a queen?"

"Yes, but the Kings may be our only way out."

"You’re sure they'll help us?"

"Once a Reina Latina, always a Reina Latina, carnal."

"Good copy, Lady Di."

Daisha led Kane to the far end of the train. For Kane, it was the very back of the train; for Daisha, it was a ride on the wings of eagles. They climbed into the doorway of the 6 Train, headed due north. It had been a long time since Kane had even seen an underground train, let alone surfed on one.

The 6 train sped through a couple of stations, its hot air venting from the huge electric motors, mingling with the unmistakable scent of old subterranean New York. Kyle and Daisha rode through the tunnels until the Uptown Limited began making its stops. Kyle glanced inside at the riders. To his amazement, they either couldn't see him or simply didn't care. Their heads were uniformly pointed straight, and their faces had a blank, expressionless bearing that was the unmistakable look of a commuter zombie, someone who was locked inside their personal space, unwilling or unable to engage the world around them, or even offer a smile.

The train slowed to a stop at a crowded platform that Daisha recognized as 125th Street & Lexington Ave. She pulled Kane off the train. He pulled his hoodie down over his eyes and joined the steady climb to the surface.

Greeted by sunshine and fresh air—or what passed for fresh air in the granite canyons. The pair stepped onto the concrete that stretched in all directions, from wall to wall, uptown to downtown.

Chapter 20

Harlem, NYC. 13:13

"We need to stop and get a lock on our location," said Kane.

"Always the Seal," Daisha replied, pointing to a bodega on the opposite corner. "I had breakfast there almost every morning when I was young. We can grab a couple of burners in there."

"Roger that. Do they have coffee?"

"Oh yeah, they've got coffee. It's as good as it gets."

"How so?"

"This is Spanish Harlem, baby. Café Cubano is on every corner."

Kane and Daisha crossed the street, then the avenue, and entered Alvarado's Corner. On either side of the front door, terraced fruit stands displayed mangoes, guavas, avocados, plantains, and yucca.

Inside, the shop was well-organized, with an abundance of sundry goods stacked to the ceiling. A steaming line of coffee pots sat on electric burners at a brewing station next to a row of deli cases.

"The only true way to make Café Cubano," said Daisha as she walked past Kyle, "is with espumita."

Two cups from a fresh pot of coffee were poured, and a sugary dark syrup followed the dark roast into the demitasse cups. Daisha looked at Kane. "Espumita, senior?"

"Espumita… Yeah, sure, espumita-me."

"It's whipped raw sugar. You'll love it."

"I already do," Kane replied. He took a sip, and his eyes widened. "That's some high test rocket fuel."

"Can find this all over Manhattan? I'll take another one, Di; no, make it a double."

The two sat and enjoyed their coffee while devouring a plate of churros.

Daisha grabbed a couple of burner phones and fumbled with the difficult plastic packaging.

"Let me give it a go," said Kane, opening his folding knife. She extended her hand. "This blade is very sharp."

"I did graduate from the farm, Kyle. I could kill you with a plastic straw—if our lunatic mayor didn't outlaw them."

"Speaking of old friends, who are we calling here at 125th and Lex?" Kane took another sip. "This brew should be a mission load-out item!"

"I should have warned you," Di said, taking a big sip. "It's not for the weak of heart, literally."

"There'll be no sleeping tonight."

"Good copy, Lieutenant Commander."

"Who are you calling?"

"My sister and I both ran numbers for the Kings."

"Shut up," he said, looking amazed. "How'd you get past the Agency's extensive background checks?"

I come from a different kind of place, Kyle. The people I knew fell into two categories: old school Harlem or St. Catherine's High School alumni.

I had straight A's and portrayed myself as a model student. The old neighborhood in

Harlem was tough, but Octavio Javier Lena, OJ, Lord of the Kings in East Harlem

Chapter was my godfather. Not my actual godfather. I didn't come from a place that had luxuries like that. He befriended my family. He controls the streets of East Harlem, and when he put out the word, there was nothing anyone was going to say about me."

"No police record, no run-ins at all?"

"Nada. Remember, I was an honor student at St. Catherine's while running a numbers crew for the Kings; at Columbia, I ran a very small, very close-to-the-vest sportsbook. Trust fund babies only. My sister was the face of the operation, and we ran the book through a remote Paris server. We put the word out that it was run by the Corsican mob. I graduated cum laude. Now, let me call OJ."

***

Daisha put down her cell. "Let's go talk to the man."

Kane nodded. "We need a safe spot to hold up. Who were you talking to?"

"Chill, Kyle. These are hard people, but they're fair."

"We need to get off the streets. Everywhere I look, I see CCTV feeds. The more we walk around, the greater the chance they'll pick us up on camera and run us through a facial recognition app. and bingo, Bob's your uncle."

"I lost my teleportation skills, and it's doubtful any Uber driver's gonna take us to where we gotta go."

Kane swallowed the last of his coffee and shook his head. He followed Daisha Willow out the door, pulled on his hoodie, and the two headed east towards the Latin King's territory.

***

Daisha led Kane across 3rd Avenue. As they passed a store window, Kane instinctively checked his six. "We picked up a tail. A pair of walkers."

Daisha turned and waved.

"What are you doing? They've been on our six for half a block."

"Seriously, you didn't notice the yellow and black bandanas or the baseball caps?"

"No, should I have?" Kane replied as Daisha guided him down another block of old brownstones, each in varying stages of decay or restoration, depending on perspective.

They reached 149th Street, and suddenly, six hard-looking hombres appeared. They formed a phalanx, three on each side, escorting Daisha and Kane down the street. It seemed, at first glance, to be an ordinary neighborhood, but beneath the surface lay a society—a micro-economy—operating under the watchful eye of the Latin Kings.

The soldiers led the group into a three-story brownstone. They had to navigate through purpose-built construction debris roadblocks; rival gangs and allies alike would have to zigzag through the piles of debris, equipment, and materials stacked so as to allow the defenders of the King's headquarters to lay down defilading gun fire. obstruct a straight path to the front door. The two ascended the granite steps and entered.

A quick punch from Kane's right glanced off his jaw. Instinctively, he threw a side kick followed by a palm strike, which landed on the nose of a big, nasty-looking doorman.

"That won't do much for your face," Kane said, backpedaling to create space.

The bloodied man rushed at him, shouting, "Pendejo!" He grabbed Kane with powerful, tattoo-covered forearms.

"Orillio," shouted one of the other gangsters. The big man drew back a fist, and Kane instinctively raised his left hand to block while shooting out a hard right. He matched Orillio's grip with his own and leaned in. The pressure on Orillio's hand and wrist brought him to the floor.

"This is gonna hurt, asshole." He almost snapped the metacarpals, and when Orillio cried out from his knees, Kane looked over at Daisha.

She frowned at him and shouted, "No, Kyle, don't."

Kane looked around at the other thugs that had encircled him, released the hand lock, and waited a second before he dropped Orillio with a hard left hook.

It was a loud, sharp crack, and the big man fell to the deck. Kane was immediately gang tackled by four other Latin Kings that came at him from every angle.

A big scuffle ensued, four against one, and Kane was taking some shots until a powerful, bellowing voice came from another room.

"¡Qué mierda, idiotas!" An older, imposing-looking man, resembling a slightly younger Danny Trejo, pushed back his gray dreads and shoved his way through the crowd. His soldiers parted, and Orillio climbed to his feet. His face was a bloody mess.

Daisha shook her head at Kane, who, despite a few new cuts on his face, looked like he was enjoying himself.

"Lady Di, girl, what's up?" said the big man, with open arms. He wrapped Daisha in a hug and lifted her off the ground.

They exchanged huge smiles.

"Enough!" he shouted. Kane shoved a few bodies aside as he stood up in the middle of the dogpile, wiping a bloody cut on his cheek with his bloodied knuckles.

"Di, come inside and bring your luchador. Tell me what, in all that is holy, brought you back here," said OJ.

"Candita didn't tell you we were coming?"

"Does that surprise you, Lady Di?"

"She's a savant, Di, a stone-cold genius who can't tie her own shoes."

Daisha and Kane followed OJ into a beautifully finished library, complete with a large conference table where they took their seats. Kane glanced at the floor-to-ceiling bookcases surrounding them, filled with books from a different era.

OJ leaned into Daisha and whispered something. They both laughed as they looked at Kane.

"Octavio Javier Lena, this is Lieutenant Commander, Retired, Kyle Kane. Kyle and I are caught up in some sticky shit."

"Sticky shit is something I can relate to," Lena said. "Daisha here was the best runner in Harlem. From the age of twelve, she held the record, never getting caught, right up until she received a scholarship from Columbia at seventeen."

Even at Columbia, she worked a side hustle. "A sports book for those rich little trust-fund babies," Octavio added, "right up until she graduated cum laude with a degree in political science."

Lena sat down and motioned for Daisha and Kane to speak. "That's when the folks in dark suits came around, prying up every manhole and looking in every dumpster."

Kane looked around the room. "A testament to your organization that she passed an FBI background check and CIA vetting."

Lena smiled. "She never once scammed a nickel, and that too is a record that will never be broken."

Kane looked surprised. "You tolerate people scamming cash?"

"A little cash," Octavio replied, "when it's used for an extra pack of Pampers or a kid's birthday present, I get it."

Kane said, “That’s not what I would have imagined you’d say.”

“Don’t get me wrong, Mr. Kyle, we don’t tolerate thieving from the Nation. That’s dealt with harshly,” said Lena. “Tell me how I can help you.”

Daisha leaned in and said quietly, “We need some help cracking some encrypted data.”

“And a place to cool our heels,” said Kane, “for a few days.”

“I have a few exceptional computer folks if that helps. I think you know one of them, Daisha.”

“Was she formerly an Air Force drone pilot who got bounced for speaking her mind? I think I know who that is.” She turned to Kane. “It’s my sister, Candita.”

“Speaking your mind—that’s something the brass can’t take kindly to,” said Kane. “Especially when you're involved in publicly sensitive work.”

Octavio nodded. “I remember back in the seventies when they were handing out life sentences for a pound of Michoacán.”

“Times, they are a-changin’,” said Daisha.

“So,” said OJ, “you two need our help, if possible?”

“We do, Octavio,” said Kane. “This could be a big deal.”

Lena smiled. “We’ll gladly take a cut of the spoils or a get-out-of-jail-free card from the Feds. That would be much appreciated.”

“I’ll see what I can do,” Daisha replied.

“Make no mistake, OJ, helping us will put you and anyone who assists us in the crosshairs of some very bad people.”

“I appreciate the heads-up, but I’ve lived most of my life at the sharp end of the stick. Five-O, Bloods, Aryans, Crips, and a hundred other smaller players are out there. Someone has always had a beef with the Kings.”

Octavio motioned for one of his security team members to accompany Kane and Daisha.

“Mr. Kane, you'll be going with Tico to our tech site.”

Kane shook hands with OJ while Lena hugged Daisha.

Outside, Kane climbed into a van along with Daisha. A man in the front seat handed them a pair of blacked-out ski goggles.

"I guess it's necessary," Kane said.

"If not, I'd have to kill you," Tico replied, flashing a smile that revealed a half dozen gold teeth. Daisha looked at Kane nervously. "He's kidding, Kyle! He's just kidding."

"Good copy," Kane responded.

The van drove a few blocks, turned down an alleyway, and stopped. Tico and his buddy exited the van, helping Daisha out on one side and Kane out the other. The two men escorted their charges into a refrigeration warehouse along the East River.

"Smells like Peking duck," Kane remarked.

"Beijing Duck now, Mr. Seal Guy," said Tico. "Watch your step." Inside, a four-man gun crew covered the entrance with Uzis and Tech 9s. Tico removed Kane's glasses, then Daisha's. They hurried through a large refrigerated area filled with pallets of perishables. The security detail rushed the two across. On the other side they passed through a heavy steel security door.

"Can you feel that, Kyle?"

"Yeah, it's a real temperature drop—at least forty degrees."

Behind the next heavy steel door was a completely different environment. Still very cold, it housed a couple of thousand square feet of raised-floor IT space.

Kane checked out the walls and ceiling. *The entire room is completely encased in copper chain link.*

"It's a Faraday cage," said Daisha as she watched Kyle's reaction.

"I see that; it's a nice touch."

"You know about Faraday?" asked Di, a little surprised.

"Yeah, I've seen it. We shut down an Al Qaeda hacking operation in Ethiopia—similar setup. Half of a warehouse lined with copper wire," Kane said. "I think they call it prima facie evidence."

Di shushed Kane as they walked through a room filled with a dozen people typing away at workstations, most of whom were fresh out of high school.

"This is an advanced operation," Kane remarked.

Everyone turned toward the sound of an unfamiliar voice. He waved his hand awkwardly, but no one responded. They returned to their work, whispering among themselves. A low murmur, a mix of Spanish and Brooklynese, filled the room.

Daisha looked around at the tangle of Ethernet cables, power conduits, and phone lines strung through the crisscross of copper chain link. Almost all of it connected to an impressive server room.

In the background, RF comms played over the speaker system. It was a blend of chatter from domino players at the corner café, grandmothers sitting in the windows, and newly minted mamacitas pushing their infants up and down the block.

The neighborhood had their eyes and ears focused on the streets. They watched everything and everyone that came and went in the ten-block no-fly zone that was Latin King territory. Beyond those ten blocks was a border area of streets, unsettled turf that was prone to the types of insane violence that left gangsters and the unlucky civilians equally dead.

In the center of all the tech-savvy brilliance sat a lanky young woman with orange-red hair, reminiscent of Daisha's. She had the same long, angular features. When she stood, it was clear she possessed the same enviable figure—all very J-Lo-esque.

When Kane looked a little closer, he said, "That's gotta be your—"

"Yes, Signore Kane, we are sisters." Beautiful green eyes stopped Kane in his tracks.

"I see it," said Kane. "I really see it."

"Sister mine! It's so good to see you," said Candita as she hugged Daisha.

"La hermanita," said Daisha, "you look great." She turned to Kane. "And this is—"

"The tall, not-so-dark, and handsome one you were spotted walking with," Candita said, instantly attracted to his rugged good looks. "We heard about him on the radio." She took Kane by the arms. "So where did you two meet? You must tell me everything."

Kane hesitated for a moment, unsure of what to say.

Candita pulled the two over to her workstation. "Come on over here. I've got my own thing going on." She grabbed Daisha by the arm. "You never thought I'd end up here, from being a hotshot Air Force drone pilot to an anti-terrorism specialist, and now the mad key jammer for the Harlem Chapter of Los Reyes Latino," she shouted. "Hoorah."

"That's it?" Daisha asked.

"I'm also writing a book."

"That's great?" Daisha replied. "You were always a good writer; what kind?"

"A government conspiracy, what else?" Candita said. She then turned to Kane and began asking him probing questions about his life in the Seals and his training.

"Tell me about your book, Candy."

"I just did. It reads like a novel… like a government conspiracy."

"Surprise, surprise," said Daisha. "Growing up, she carried that JFK assassination book like it was her Bible."

"Why so many questions, Candy?"

"Just a little background material, Lieutenant Commander."

"Give me your background, little sister," Kane asked.

Daisha shot him a look.

"I joined the Air Force after my big sister left. I ended up as a drone pilot in Nevada. I lost my commission for insubordination. I admit, I smoked a little weed, but they discharged me because I refused to engage a supposed HVT target. It was a bazaar, a small marketplace," she said blankly. "It was filled with women and children. The CIA case officer making the call was one of those Biden zombies. They're doing all kinds of crazy things.

"Did they kick you out?" Kane asked.

"Can't keep a good girl down; the brass transferred me to the 16th Air Force Group. It's the intel arm of the Air Force, providing global intelligence, surveillance and reconnaissance, cyber and electronic warfare, and information operations. It also serves as the cryptologic component responsible to the NSA and CSS. In two years, I repaired my standing with the brass. I worked my way up to a crypto analyst. I saw some things, Lodge."

"I'll bet you did," said Kane. "You were a cryptography analyst?"

"Candy, we really need your skills," Daisha replied.

"For what, a credit card bill?"

"We have a laptop with some encrypted, security-critical data."

"Oooh yeah, Di, I'm getting all juicy; tell me more."

Daisha frowned as she handed her sister the knapsack. "I carried that thing through hell and high water." The three of them sat down, and Candy opened Kassem's laptop.

"Ah yes, military-grade hardware—encryption is sure to follow. I can smell it. Former Lieutenant Commander Kane, what should I call you?" asked Candy.

"Just call me Kyle, fly girl."

Her fingers danced across the keyboard. "You can call me anything you want—Kyle."

Kane looked around the room. "What are you guys doing in here?"

OJ Lena walked in, and the chatter stopped. He took a seat next to Daisha.

Candy looked at OJ, who nodded his okay. "We're into credit card data repurposing, mostly."

Candy pointed to a large, mainframe-looking device behind a glass wall.

"That's a mighty bank of servers you've got there," said Kane.

"Actually, it's not a server," OJ corrected.

"What is it then?"

"It's a CDC 7600, a second-generation supercomputer."

Kyle shook his head. "How does a street gang get its hands on such a valuable piece of hardware?"

OJ pointed to Candy, who bowed with steepled hands. "One problem, Kyle, it runs hot—like me."

"I get it, wire fraud with a supercomputer. Quite ingenious."

"Don't feel bad, Captain America," said Candy. "Credit card companies are anything but honest. They write it off on their taxes as a business loss. It's part and parcel of the cycle of life. Americans' ability to escape credit card debt has been greatly limited. Credit card companies steal from the public, and we steal it back—like Robin Hood."

Kane raised his hands. "Guys, I'm not here to judge."

"That's good, Mr. Kane," OJ said. "This is not the place for that."

Kane got up and pointed to the little break room. "I smell coffee."

"Feel free," said Lena. "That's our break room. We can't have these kids walking in and out all day, so I filled it with food and drinks. There's even a smoking lounge."

"That's some advanced, out-of-the-box thinking, OJ."

Kane headed to the small break room, which was stacked with cardboard cases filled with every imaginable flavor of Hot Pocket, honey buns, and Doritos.

He poured a tall cup of dark coffee and closed his eyes.

Candy nudged Kane, causing him to jump awake with a start. He worked the evil jinn back into the bottle and said, "Sorry, I just got off the line, and my survival skills that kept me alive don't translate well to stateside living."

Candy stepped close to Kane and put a hand on his shoulder, saying with a randy smile, "You must be a handful in bed."

Daisha walked in a minute later. Her sister let her hand slip down to Kane's chest and winked at him.

"Be careful, sailor," said Daisha, "she rides bareback. You don't want any unauthorized little Kyles running around."

Candy returned to the break room with Kassem's Toughbook. She sat down as close to Kane as possible, smiling and batting her eyes playfully.

"This is very cutting-edge stuff, Commander."

"Is this a DoD laptop?" Kane asked curiously.

"Not the actual laptop, but the internals—the real guts, processor chips, RAM, even the motherboard—almost all of it is of a type I believe is closely controlled in the U.S. and sold only to the U.S. military."

"That opens a whole new line of what the hell," said Kane. "Did you crack the code?"

"Yes and no. I found encoded messages from six different security agencies."

"Security agencies, you mean American?"

"All the three-letter agencies, the State Department, and my old employer, the 16th AF Group, are involved... along with the FBI, one Karen Lavette."

"What the hell would the 16th AF be contacting a terrorist financier for?"

"Remember this, Kyle: the 16th Air Force Group is one of our government's most advanced cyber intelligence units. I worked out of a base in San Jose, and between that and my time at Creech AFB flying Predator drones, I witnessed an incredible amount of crazy stuff—real counterintuitive, unconstitutional activities."

"Good copy; that's woke leadership at work," said Kane. He tried to refocus on Candy. "You said the FBI was involved in the encoded emails?"

"Oh yeah."

Kane leaned over Candy, making her squirm a little in her seat. He recognized a few of the names and all of the agencies.

"Warren Trask, Tyler Cox, and Wallace's bosses at the CIA," Kyle said, "Karen Lavette and Cole James."

Daisha sat on the other side of Kane. "The FBI Director is on Kassem's laptop?"

Kane saw a name that shocked him. "No way, no freaking way, not Admiral Martin Corbett."

"Isn't that the guy who got whacked at the Pentagon?" Lena asked.

Kane nodded and said, "How are you coming up with these names, Candy?"

She was surprised by Kane's attitude. "I decrypted the code key and applied it to this encryption soup." She handed Kane the laptop. "See for yourself."

"I'm sorry, Candy. I'm just shocked to see my boss, a man who authorized our missions, someone I trusted with the lives of my men. He was murdered last week in front of the Pentagon, and now appearing in an email to the Chief Financial Officer of the Taliban."

"It's okay, Kyle," said Candy, batting her eyes. "You can make it up to me later."

"Gladly," Kane responded. Daisha stepped on Kane's foot. "Ouch."

Kane refocused. "Most of these communications reference a date. If you match that file with the financial disbursements, you'll be able to infer some information not yet decrypted."

"You think we could infer the possibility of a mission, n'est-ce pas?" Candita asked. "That means isn't it so."

"I can't tell you exactly what their objective is, but I can use the final locations of these significant cash disbursements to paint a clearer picture. For these recipients to receive the money transfers, there must be a location."

Candy brought a long computer printout sheet and placed it on the table between the coffee mugs and the half-eaten pizza pockets.

"Okay, the number of entities that received over ten million dollars in funds is seventy-four. Smaller tranches were released to fifteen locations. Each of these data points corresponds to a location in a Middle Eastern city: Al Aqubah, Ash Shawbak, As Safi, Al Mazraha'ah, Ma'daba, Tibris, and Irbid—all cities on Israel's border with Jordan.

In Lebanon, we have An Naqurah and Bint Jubayl, and in Gaza, cities like Kahn Yunis, Kissufim, Abasan, Nahal Oz, Dier Al-Balah, Beit Hanoun, and Rafah. These are all cities or areas with a high concentration of recipients."

"I'll bet all of it was funneled through the Hawala system," said Kane. "Hawala operates through a network of quickie marts, produce stores, jewelers, and pawnshops. These locations act as branch offices, transferring undocumented and untraceable cash, jewels, and precious metals from country to country."

"The Egyptian Eastern Command Headquarters, Hezbollah's military HQ in Beirut, and the Mukhabarat, the secret police building in Damascus, are all receiving large sums."

Kane stood up and motioned for Daisha to follow him. She looked at him quizzically. "What's up, Kyle?"

Kane replied quietly, "I don't want to involve the people here anymore than they already are."

"What's there to fear?" OJ Lena said as he walked into the break room.

"This could rain down hell on anyone who possesses this information," Kane warned.

"These individuals, identified by Candy, are powerful figures within our government. They will stop at nothing to remain in the shadows," Daisha said.

"They operate under the guise of law and possess near-limitless resources. They label themselves as woke, but their actions are a result of being captured by the CCP's Ministry of State Security. The MSS uses blackmail of one sort or another to force elites in the US to do their bidding. They control operations both inside and outside our borders," Candy explained. "Look at the January 6th commission and their enforcers, the FBI, who targeted grandmothers, fathers, mothers, and scoutmasters, while terrorists crossed our border unchecked, carried off by these criminal NGOs that transport them deep into the country. I've witnessed firsthand how these captured bureaucrats leverage their agencies to ruin lives."

"How are they going to find us here?" OJ asked.

"We used internet searches to identify locations and looked up the coordinates using Google Earth or similar apps," replied Kane.

"Yeah, I know," Candy said. "You saw me pull them up?"

"The NSA, among all the three-letter agencies, has access to your internet queries and anyone else's. They will conduct a targeted search using state-of-the-art supercomputers, filtering it down to a very small group of searches."

Daisha interrupted Kane, "Not all agents in our tri-letter agencies are bad—far from it."

"You're right, Di. I should have clarified that. Anyway, it's highly unlikely there will be many searches that fall within those parameters," Kane said, "aside from ours."

"The proxy servers will give us some cover, but it's not indefinite," Di replied.

"Google won't give up our data," Candy asserted.

Kane looked at her in disbelief. "You're kidding; they'll hand it over as fast as you can type. In the end, Google—like Facebook and Twitter—sold out Americans in the 2020 election. They ran cover for the Hunter Biden laptop. They will play ball with Biden's fascist flunkies.

The forces arrayed against them are too great," OJ remarked. "How long do you think we have?" Lena asked.

"Until they find this exact spot? Two months," Candy replied. "It'll take that long for Google to cave or for them to need something from the government."

"Okay. What I'm about to tell you is almost certainly going to get you all in trouble, missing, or even killed."

"The Latin Kings Nation loses members every week, somewhere in the world. Every time we put on our colors, they're out there looking for us."

"If we play it right, OJ, we may be able to use this data, if necessary, to get out from under."

"This could be a conspiracy involving individuals at the highest levels of our government." Kane stood up and began pacing, stopping in front of Daisha. "These conspirators are looking to change the dynamics of the Middle East."

"For what, Kyle?" OJ asked. "What possible purpose?"

"They could be using it to fuel another agenda; I just don't know—yet."

OJ cocked his head. "How will this all play out?"

"There's going to be some operation involving Israel," Kane replied.

"Israel is our ally!" Candy exclaimed.

"The CCP has been using Islamist extremists to attack the US since the Iranian revolution. The globalists support this, and open borders are their way to control the census and give body to their endemic voter fraud machine. They have flooded western democracies with an Islamic invasion. All of Europe is being destroyed by this insane wave of nonconformist emigrants. In the UK the government has outlawed free speech. The puppet Biden wants to weaken the State of Israel and the United States." said Di.

"For those of you who consider me a huge conspiracy nut," said Candy, glancing at her sister, "I'm writing a book—a treatise on the selling off of America, which began with the election of Mr. Peanut, who gave away the Panama Canal, the greatest engineering feat in modern times."

Daisha looked at the ceiling. "Here we go."

"If the foo shits, big sister, wear it!"

"The CIA is deep state central. It's pretty clear: cocaine was flown into an Arkansas airport, where the government used it to fund its private Contra war. Didn't Clinton get elected despite being outed by his on-the-payroll mistress, Jennifer Flowers? How did that happen? The World Trade Organization looked the other way when the CCP killed five thousand Chinese citizens at Tiananmen Square. The Clintons orchestrated a deal to sell a significant portion of our uranium to Russia. Obama gave Iran, a terrorist state, one hundred and fifty billion dollars, which you can imagine was used to further their proxy attacks on Israel and to kill Americans. Look at the woke agenda—DEI, defund the police; it's all about damaging the US. We'll never stop the fucking Chinese Communist Party unless we publicly name both Democrat and Republican politicians in Washington who are under the control of the CCP, with payoffs and blackmail files a mile long. From the Kennedy assassination to the Biden regime, the entire worldwide mess of the past 80 years starts and ends with the deep state."

Kane was in awe. "Damn, girl, you're good. You broke it all down in just thirty seconds."

Candy smiled at the encouragement. "Here's another ten seconds' worth of democratic damnation: Chinese missile technology, which they threaten us with today, and the Uranium One deal with Russia provided the fissionable material they threaten us with today. Do you smell a rat?"

Kane looked at OJ and said, "Let's lay out our current data on a whiteboard."

"This isn't a classroom," OJ replied. "There are no white or blackboards available, but I can see what we have lying around."

Lena returned with a sheet of gypsum board, propping it up on the table, while Candy produced a box of colored Sharpies.

"This will serve as our blackboard until a real one arrives," said Kane.

Kane drew a rough map of the Middle East as Candy read the list of destination cities from Kassem's laptop. They transferred the information from the spreadsheet to the map.

Kane had a general idea of where most of the cities receiving cash were located. He drew a line connecting all the points.

"I'll be damned," OJ exclaimed. "If those locations are accurate, Mr. Kane, you just drew a perimeter line around the state of Israel."

"At this point, we can only speculate about the operation, but whatever it entails will impact a significant portion of the Israeli border, at a minimum."

Candy raised her hand again, then lowered it. "We could find someone in the U.S. Attorney's office or The New York Times… well, maybe not the Times; how about—"

"The Times is a propaganda rag," OJ interjected. "It's nothing but well-written birdcage liner."

"OJ's right," Daisha agreed. "The Times could easily kill a story, and that would put us in the barrel."

They discussed Admiral Corbett and how the plotters had silenced him. "If we try to bring this to the U.S. intelligence services or any part of the government, we risk exposure," Kane warned. "The people behind this will ensure we're dead before a word from us goes on record."

Based on the data from the laptop and their personal experiences, it became clear they were up against very powerful individuals—unelected bureaucrats deeply embedded within the U.S. government. Every choice they made had to be the right one.

"We'll get one shot at this. If we fail, we'll never see the inside of a courtroom," Di said. "OJ, are you set up for this kind of heat?"

He responded thoughtfully, "To the extent it doesn't bring blowback on the nation, I can close the watertight doors and rig for impact."

Kane looked at OJ curiously and asked, "You're a former Navy man, a submariner?"

"USS Olympia, SSN 717," OJ replied.

Kane smiled. "Los Angeles-class attack sub."

"I was a TMC, a torpedoman's mate chief, on board the Olympia when she was the oldest attack sub in the fleet. I meant it when I said we're red-blooded Americans. I can't speak for everyone, but if the Chinese sailed into New York Harbor, we'd be fighting side by side with the good guys."

"That's not far from possible," said Candy. "The Canadian communist-in-chief, Castro's illegitimate son, has talked about inviting the CCP's People's Liberation Army to conduct war games on Canadian soil."

"Let's get back on track, boys," Daisha said. "We need a plan moving forward."

Kane interrupted, "I speak Farsi, Di; you speak Farsi. Let's do what you do best."

"You really want to go to the Middle East?" Daisha asked, surprised by the idea. "Where and how? We'd need money and documentation, plus support to navigate the chessboard."

"Well," Kane said, looking at the rudimentary map, "how about Gaza? There are a lot of foreign aid workers in the refugee camps. That would provide good cover."

The four of them discussed what they would need to move forward. They talked about obtaining good passports, aid worker IDs, and work visas. The next question posed by Lena was about cash.

"We'll need Jordanian dinars and Israeli shekels," Di said. "It's one less reason for Hamas to think we're spies."

"How did things get so messed up?" OJ asked. "I mean, this looks like outright treason."

Kane stood up and poured another cup of coffee. "It is treason. That's my point of view. Sowing the seeds of dissent and division in America is their cover. They loop in every disparate group and try to form a coalition, a consensus of the eternally unhappy. They pay agitators to incite them and ultimately turn this coalition against the middle class."

Candy clapped. "Very good, Mr. Kane. I've always heard that SEALs, to a man, are very intelligent. Do you know how and why we got here? I know why, and I know how they are doing it." Everyone turned to Candy, who was sitting on the break room counter.

"Okay, conspiracy girl," OJ said, "tell us how."

"This is the short version, but it still spans over thirty years. If this were my book, and you're uninterested in the greatest Trojan horse attack in history, I suggest you skip to the next chapter or go grab a slice."

"The power of the federal government has grown with every iteration of power-mad megalomaniacs." Candy hopped off the counter. "During World War II, two very powerful forces were born, like twin Krakens: the military-industrial complex and the Office of Strategic Services, the mother of the CIA. These two juggernauts have fed off each other, interacting throughout American society but most notoriously in American politics."

Consider the Kennedy assassination and the absurd Warren Report issued by the Chief Justice of our Supreme Court. This level of obvious disinformation suggests that a group within our government may have facilitated the killers, if not outright supplied them. JFK was determined to shut down the CIA. Could there be a more dangerous adversary?

Recall a certain Republican president who, before rising to the most powerful position in the world, served as the director of the CIA. Funding a proxy war by selling cocaine within the United States was unprecedented. It was a cataclysmic moment, yet they emerged relatively unscathed. From that turmoil, we got a certain Democratic politician—

OJ waved his arm. "Why aren't you using names?"

"Seriously, boss? When a dishwasher can act as a bug and transmit your conversation, that nice new microwave you installed in our break room, OJ, could be setting us up for an FBI raid."

"If what we have seen in the US since Kennedy is accurate, the US has had only one fair election since 1960: Trump's 2016 election. Every other election has been merely a pro forma dance followed by a coronation. The uniblob party—with its permanent Washington bureaucrats and crooked Democrats, not to mention the RINO Republicans, all of whom follow the orders of their CCP captors. They've been on the take for decades. The situation began to unravel when the Democrats, heavily reliant on CCP money that came to them from compliant Wall Street banks and private equity firms sending American businesses to China wholesale, coupled with massive congressional and State Department NGO fraud, were threatened when Trump pulled out the greatest come-from-behind victory, greater even than Rich Strike's Derby victory at 80 to 1."

Daisha turned to Kane and said, "She takes action on the ponies too."

Candy smiled at her sister and continued, "The intellectually lazy Obamites that populated DC decided they weren't going to put their kleptocracy on ice, slow-roll the terminally red-tape-strangled federal government with Pelosi, the wicked witch of the west, at the helm, and wait out a four-year term. No, instead they went at Trump full steam ahead with fraudulent attacks from all sides, chief among them the FBI.

"Political movements have a shelf life, little sister. The political and financial grip on the core elements of the globalist movement could vanish in the shifting sands of the Beltway desert, but the CCP's hold over our society's elites is ironclad. Didn't you ever wonder why our politicians refuse to retire? Their Ministry of State Security handlers won't allow it. I'm sure the actual Epstein files, the full collection, have been handed over to the CCP. I have no doubt that someone in the crooked Biden regime made copies and sold them to their MSS handler. The invasive financial corruption that has metastasized throughout Washington's elites means we may never get out from under the evil red hand of CCP corruption. I believe we need martial law, suspend due process, and the release of all the evidence, and let the trees fall where they may. This is what you're up against."

"Are we done with your book synopsis?" said Kane, winking. Candy was captivated, while her sister rolled her eyes.

"So now what, Captain America?" Daisha asked.

"We fly to Egypt," he replied.

Candy jumped off the table and pushed past her sister. "Sounds so romantic."

"As unfair and unpredictable as our country can be," OJ Lena said, "it's our goddamn country, and nobody's going to give it to the fucking Chinese. What's your plan, Seal Man?"

"I'm just an old door kicker. I'd have to defer to Daisha on this matter."

"Looking at the locations we have to choose from," Di said, "we need a copy of the mission plan—proof that an attack is imminent and real."

Candy asked, "Where do we find that?"

Daisha looked at Kyle, nodded, and said, "Gaza's our best bet."

OJ looked up at Di and said, "Lady Di? Gaza's a war zone!"

"Good copy. It's a powder keg, but it's also an intelligence-gathering hotspot," said Di. You can't swing a stick in Gaza without hitting a spook from some government," Daisha replied.

Sarcastically, Kane said, "Yeah, my favorite kind of people."

"I'm sure I know some of them, Kyle: Iran, the CCP proxy, CIA, Egypt's GID, Russia's FSB, Jordanian GID, the CIA, and of course Mossad—they're all there."

"And they're more than willing to help… if you have the money."

"We can do that," said Kane.

"Where are you going to get that kind of money? You're a retired naval officer," OJ replied. "Not exactly a Goldman Sachs partner."

"I'm the World Warrior Hand-to-Hand Champion," Kane said, laughing.

Candy slapped him on the rear. “Congrats! Is that like the WWE?”

He looked at Candy. "Sort of. I can cover whatever we need for the short run."

Kane turned to Daisha. "What about weapons?"

"I have a weapons guy in Gaza City."

"Lawyers, guns, and money," OJ said as he pulled out a case of Carta Blanca, and the four of them started drinking.

Kane pulled Daisha aside and asked, "Do you know anything about how my mission kicked off? I'm trying to track down an email from Langley and Admiral Corbett's office. Am I on the right track?"

"All I know, Kyle, is that if the Agency went to the trouble of ghosting an encrypted email on a secured network, it’s definitely gone. A woman from MI6, a key player connected by blood to the royals, came to the US to brief representatives from some of the administration's major departments in a confidential meeting in the Capitol basement SCIF. The subject was your high-value target, and I would bet dollars to donuts that your mission originated in that meeting. Her name was Lady Mary Carrier, and she may be able to shed some light on your missing orders."

Chapter 21

Harlem, NYC. 04:30

Kane stood in front of the floor-length mirror in the 19th-century brownstone, having just shaved off his perennial full-face beard. He was dressed in the rugged, casual attire of an in-country foreign aid worker.

He made his way down the grand staircase in the center hall, checking the space before entering the front sitting room.

Lady Di called from her seat on a dilapidated leather Chesterfield. "Wow, what a difference a shave makes!"

"Come sit, Kyle. This entire furniture set was once owned by old John Jacob Astor. He probably sat right there before he left on his fateful ride aboard the Titanic. Did you and Candy enjoy catching up last night?"

Kane cleared the expansive room and the servants' hallway beyond. “I spent the night alone."

"As it should be, the night before a big operation, Lieutenant Commander."

"Indeed, Lady Di, indeed. Do we have time to eat?"

"On the way."

***

The two arrived curbside at the JFK terminal. It took an hour to get through security and customs. Kane ate a fifteen-dollar breakfast burrito and had a coffee on the way to board.

Kane, used to flying direct to his destination, asked, "Tell me again why we are flying to South Africa and then on to the Middle East?" Kane asked as he opened his laptop.

"Why, Kyle, did I mention how handsome you look without that beard?"

"Don't dodge the question, Lady Di. Why South Africa?"

Kane dropped into the seat next to Di, and she said quietly, "Our cover story needed some depth. Flying direct from the U.S. could raise a red flag. Speaking of cover stories, what's yours, Kyle, the aid worker?"

"I gave that some thought last night. I've been cross-trained as a medic, and my training in trauma medicine will hold up."

"Could you pass for a trauma doc?"

"Good question; trauma doctors have the toughest job in the entire hospital."

"No, I think the toughest job is the trauma nurse working for the trauma doc in the ED."

"I could pass for a nonspecialist medical professional."

Di jumped off the couch and took Kyle by the arm. “Come on, skin-chin, we need to take some Polaroids to use in our new documents.”

***

Daisha handed Kane a file with his cover data and CFH International badges and credentials.

"Your new documents list you as a general practitioner. Here’s a multi-entry visa—an absolute must to move around the Middle East. The NGO we're working for in Gaza is CFH."

"Everything matches: Dr. Kyle Lewis, your passport, doctor's license, driver's license, and a working visa."

"OJ put all this together? I must admit I prejudged him. With the dreads and his funky Hawaiian shirt, I pegged him for a street hustler."

"And he's Navy, right?" Di said.

"He's the genuine article. Tell me, what's your cover going to be?"

"I'm a logistics specialist, also from CFH International," Di replied. "Our cover story is that we are the advance team, scouting suitable locations for a large-scale vaccine program."

"What vaccine will we be setting up for?"

"Measles, Dr. Lewis. It's a hot disease, on the rise, and there's potential for worldwide spread."

"Don't you mean outbreak?"

"There's already been an outbreak, and the adults in the room are trying to control it," said Daisha. "It can lead to encephalitis, a rapid swelling of the brain, which may result in a terrible death."

“That’s a cheerful prognosis,” said Kyle as he followed Di out the door to their cab. ”

***

"Thai chicken or a green burrito?" asked a flight attendant in the aisle next to Kane's seat.

"Another beer for me," Kane replied. "Where I come from, a green burrito is never a good thing... so chicken for me, please."

"Good choice," said the attendant. "It could be the last decent meal until we reach Cairo."

"A green burrito... on a flight to Egypt," Di remarked. "That's potentially hazardous."

"You mean a gas leak?"

"No, not directly. More like spending the trip in the cramped onboard bathrooms.”

The cabin was fairly bright, even though most passengers had switched off their lights and closed their eyes. Kane and Daisha worked through the flight, drafting alternative action plans. The journey to Johannesburg included a couple of movies, a snooze, a few more snacks, and a whole lot of drinks.

The flight to Cairo touched down in Liberia for a quick stop. Upon arrival, Kane decided to deplane and check out the duty-free shops.

"Come on, Di, let's stretch our legs."

"Sure, we can grab some snacks."

"Snacks? For me, mini bottles are snacks. I was thinking more along the lines of tequila—a bit of old Jose."

Roberts International Airport was a blend of concrete and glass, featuring a spacious lobby with shops and vendors who paid an entry fee. These vendors offered a mix of twentieth-century necessities and time-honored novelties, showcasing trinkets from their culture.

Kane found a less-than-reputable duty-free agent who eagerly sold him a bottle of cash-and-carry tequila for triple the price.

They reboarded their 737 to Cairo. Once back on the plane, the two discussed potential mission issues and their solutions.

At one point, Kane turned to Daisha. "Tequila shots?"

"You want to crack open that bottle of tequila? We'll be flying over a Muslim country."

Kane grinned and pulled out the liter of Two Fingers Gold. They began the flight by discussing the mission in code and spiking their grapefruit juice with tequila. Before long, they abandoned the grapefruit juice and switched to shots.

They quickly made a serious dent in the bottle. Daisha leaned into Kane and said playfully, "Let's move to the back; there's nobody in the rear half of the plane."

She motioned with her head, and Kane grinned from ear to ear.

Daisha winked at him. "We've definitely reached a new level of inhibition."

They moved into the darkness. On the way, Kane grabbed a blanket from one of the overhead compartments and covered the tequila before following Daisha into the aft section.

"What's that for?" Daisha asked.

Kane held it up and shook it out. "Camo, cover girl." They slipped into the seat next to the window and downed another round of shots.

Daisha smiled and proposed a toast. "Here's to a spot in the mile-high club."

Kane placed the bottle of tequila next to his leg. He reclined his seat, and Daisha leaned over to kiss him.

Kane pulled Daisha's voluptuous body closer, grabbing her curvy waist and squeezing. His hands dropped to her long, strong thighs as she rubbed her chest and abs against his face. It was on like Donkey Kong.

He kissed her full, glossy lips that beckoned to him. They kissed so deeply that they lost themselves in the longing, a grinding yearning to find that perfect spot.

Kane made her jump.

Her body was flushed with sexual excitement, and before Kane could pop all her buttons, Daisha ripped open her shirt and pulled him closer. He hiked up her skirt and was thrilled to discover that she had removed her panties in the Liberian airport.

"And I thought I was running this op," Kane said.

Daisha watched as Kyle struggled to get his pants off over his boots.

"Rookie mistake, Kane. BUD/S training 101—shoes off first."

"Right, right, shoes off first."

"Come to attention and join the mile-high club, rookie," Daisha said as she pushed down on his shoulders and effectively pinned him in place. Kane's eyes widened, and his muscles tightened across his torso. He rose to the occasion and kissed the beautiful mocha skin of her neck.

Daisha started gently, but soon she unleashed the full force of her powerful hips. Kane tried to gain control of the situation, but Daisha pushed him back into his seat. He lifted Daisha higher, and she writhed with pleasure. Waves of primal ecstasy surged through her body. She began to rock, grinding her hips in perfect rhythm. Their body heat drew them closer, as if they were one.

At some point, Daisha raised her arms, and her firm fullness bounced enticingly in front of Kane's mesmerized gaze. Both had lost track of their surroundings.

The frantic motion escalated to the point where their seats, along with those around them, slammed back and forth.

In a moment of sheer bliss, Daisha experienced a fugue moment before she let out a scream, followed by a deep, unmistakable moan.

It was a moment like so many in a person's life when unintended words and sounds didn't just fall away in the din or get absorbed by the constant roar of a jet engine, no, instead it seemed to take on a life of their own, like the word “moan” in foot-tall letters, drifting forward on a collision course with the sleeping passengers in the front of the plane. Kane tried to muffle Daisha, but she was too far gone. He watched the heads of the passengers turn from side to side and bob up and down in an attempt to identify the source of the salaciously sensual sounds, the ribald utterances that had invaded their air space.

He knew they were in trouble when disgruntled heads began to turn, followed a few seconds later by the illumination of the cabin lights. Kane had to shake Daisha back into reality.

"Evasive action, Agent Willow," he said. He lifted her off of him and dropped her into the seat next to him. “Sorry.” He reached for his clothes just as the stewardesses appeared in the bulkhead doorway. Fingers were pointed, and discussions quickly ensued, followed by the approach of a pair of evidently annoyed attendants.

Daisha pulled down her skirt, buttoned her shirt, and straightened her hair.

"Tradecraft?" Kane asked.

"Ohhhh yeah," she replied, fanning her flushed face.

Kane pulled up his briefs and struggled to get his pants on. Frustrated, he let them drop and covered himself with the pathetic little airport blanket. He watched nervously as the two flight attendants approached their outpost in the dark.

"Two inbound bogies, 12 o'clock," Daisha whispered. Kane looked down at his pants, still bunched around his boots. He tried desperately, but the pants, now stuck mid-boot, refused to budge.

He struggled to stretch the painfully thin blanket over himself. "This is going to be interesting."

Seeing the attendants approach, Daisha jumped up to block their view as they drew closer, with concerned expressions.

"What was that sound?" asked passenger Willows, searching around with a questioning look, attempting to deflect their pointed inquiries.

One of the attendants tried to peer at Kane over and around Daisha. Kane adopted a fake snooze pose while

Daisha, in a coordinated effort, moved her curvy hips from side to side to obstruct their view.

"The sound came from the back of the cabin. Why are you two back here, so isolated? And in the dark!" said the tall one, attempting to peer over Passenger Willows.

Daisha thought quickly. *Next to a plane crash, what is an attendant's worst fear?*

"My friend is feeling unwell—airsick," she said dramatically, glancing at the other gawking passengers. "Air sickness can trigger a rolling sympathetic reaction, leading to dozens of passengers vomiting all over the plane. We separated ourselves because air sickness can cause contagious vomiting."

One of the attendants exchanged a glance with the other and whispered something before they both nodded in agreement.

Daisha smiled. *Chalk one up for basic tradecraft.* She looked down at Kane and winked.

One of the attendants waved over a very constipated-looking co-pilot who had just entered the cabin. Daisha was intrigued by his peculiar appearance.

She leaned down to Kane and whispered, "Check out this guy's face; it looks like it got caught in a powerful vacuum cleaner."

"You mean the mummified-looking guy? He looks like he just stepped out of the Valley of the Kings."

The serious co-pilot stepped between the two attendants and leaned in close to Daisha. He sniffed deeply with his enormous nose, and Daisha felt as if she were being pulled toward him.

"You smell remarkably like alcohol. You do realize we are flying over an Islamic country where alcohol consumption is prohibited?"

"We had drinks at Tambo Airport; it's not a crime."

The co-pilot and attendants scowled at Daisha's excuse, shaking their heads in disbelief.

The situation was close to resolution when the jet banked hard for its final approach to Cairo Airport. The maneuver caused the jet to pull a few G's, forcing Daisha, the attendants, and the tense co-pilot to grip their seats.

This shift in gravity, combined with a stroke of fortuna mala, caused Kane's foot to shift. The unfortunate circumstances led to the bottle of Two Finger's Tequila to slip from under his foot. The cylindrical vessel rolled free for a few seconds before it clanged against the steel legs of the passenger seats on its way toward the cockpit.

"Oh shit," Daisha muttered under her breath. She turned to look at Kane, who cracked one eye open and smirked.

Kane sat up, realizing the tequila bottle was loose and on its way somewhere. With attention diverted, he discreetly attempted to pull on his pants.

The bottle rolled forward rapidly into the front of the cabin.

Kane glanced at Daisha and asked, "What the heck is that?"

The bottle changed course and rolled across the aisle, weaving around the seats like a hapless slalom skier hitting every gate all the way to first class.

Daisha observed the expressions on the flight attendants' faces and asked seriously, "Is the jet falling apart?"

"The jet is not falling apart, madame," the co-pilot shouted angrily. "Please take your seats!"

One of the stewardesses hurriedly followed the path of the bottle as it zigzagged away. Kane seized the opportunity to buckle his pants, which were cinched up just in time for the inquisition to return with the nearly empty tequila bottle.

"Excuse me," said the co-pilot, "does this bottle belong to either of you?"

"What is it?" Kane asked.

"It looks like alcohol," replied the officious-looking stewardess.

Kane gestured for the co-pilot to hand him the bottle. The man was surprised but complied.

Kane opened it and took a whiff. Then he took a big swig, shocking everyone except Di. The co-pilot reached for the bottle, speechless. Kane pulled it back and handed it to Daisha.

"Hold on, Captain, I need a second opinion, and since my traveling companion is an expert on alcohol and its consumption."

Di finished with one last big swallow.

"It's tequila," she said, letting out a semi-raucous burp.

The co-pilot and the stewardess were taken aback by the potent airborne vapors blown their way by Daisha.

"It's definitely tequila," she said, examining the bottle, turning it upside down, then handing it back to the crew. The co-pilot shook his head and walked away, muttering something in a Farsi dialect that Kane didn't understand.

"What did he say?" asked Kyle.

"I think he called you a dog of a thousand pigs."

"Ouch, that's hurtful."

Kane led Daisha back to their seats in the economy section of the cabin. The other travelers seemed to shun them, except for a little old lady who smiled and gave them a thumbs-up.

They returned to formulating an action plan as best they could.

"How should we approach the problem of getting our hands on an actual copy of the plan?" asked Daisha.

"I think we'll have to tackle that problem on the ground," Kane replied. "I believe copies of the mission will end up in the hands of the relatively unsophisticated. That's where we must strike."

"You mean we're going to wing it?" said Di.

"Yeah, that part gives me pause too. Missions that run without a defined objective have a much greater chance of failure."

The two knew they were flying by the seat of their pants. Lacking the necessary intel to formulate a specific plan was, at best, dangerous and, at worst, fatal.

"Speaking of pants," Di said, "I'm going to head to the bathroom and change into slacks and a button-down."

"Don't forget your panties."

"Right."

When she returned, Kane was watching the sun rise over the city of Cairo below. He asked her, "Did you bring your hijab?"

"As a fan of the 1960s Jackie O look, I bought big sunglasses and a couple of cool British Beat chick scarves. Not as a fashion statement; I just don’t want to stand out."

"So, you have one?"

"Multiple colors and styles."

Chapter 22

Cairo, Egypt, 06:00

The jet touched down at Cairo International Airport. Daisha walked out onto the walkway near the cab stand. She found a quiet corner and made a call.

Kane immediately moved into threat assessment. He scanned the area relentlessly. “Everyone looks like a tango,” said Kane quietly.

Daisha put her hand over the phone. “That’s a problem, Dr. Lewis; ninety-nine percent of these people are just everyday folks. We flew to Johannesburg and then to Cairo to throw off suspicion, and your first reaction is to scrutinize everyone like it’s a tier one operation.”

“Good point,” Kane admitted. "Decades of training as an operator are hard to change."

“It's tradecraft, my dear Dr. Lewis,” said Daisha. “You need to get into character. At the agency, we used The Method. We trained in the Stanislavski system to encourage sincere and expressive performances in our deep cover roles. We identified with our characters using compassion to understand them. You look at your characters’ life experiences and how that created their inner motivation and resulted in their outer emotions.”

“You do realize I’m a special forces operator.”

Daisha went back to speaking into her cell phone, “That’s perfect, Sami. See you soon.” She ended the call and turned to Kyle. “Come on, Kyle, some of the best actors came from the military: Clint Eastwood, Morgan Freeman, Gene Hackman, James Earl Jones, Steve McQueen, and Paul Newman, to name a few. We’re traveling as aid workers in

Cairo, not a Secret Service advance team. Wrap your mind around your role and act accordingly."

"I'm competing for a taxi in Cairo right now. I'm sure my motivation is to ride to our destination, and I'll show joy if I find one," said Kane sarcastically as he walked to the end of the platform and jumped in front of a dusty green, late-model Mercedes.

"Excellent choice," shouted an annoyed Daisha.

The driver locked up, and the hunter green sedan swerved before screeching to a halt. An angry Egyptian man jumped out and yelled at Kane in florid local slang, but with a surprisingly refined British accent.

"You bloody idiot!" he shouted. "I could have killed you!"

With his unusual sense of humor, Kane approached the lanky, bearded cabbie and replied, "Well, it's a good thing you didn't; you'd have lost a fare, and then I'd have to kill ya."

"You'd be killing a national treasure, my rambunctious American fare. I may be the only cabbie in all of Sinai who understands Cockney slang and can get you to Gaza without you getting killed."

Kane's eyes widened in surprise. "That would be a true loss," he said. "Who are you?"

"Ask Di if I can drive," the man said. "A Cockney accent is an aesthetic that will cost you extra, Mr. Kyle."

"It's Dr. Lewis to you! And how the hell do you know me?" Kane asked, turning to Daisha.

Kane instinctively reached behind his back, but the burner wasn't there. "How does he know my name?"

Daisha held up her phone and jiggled it. "I just called him."

The lanky Egyptian offered his hand to take Daisha's luggage. "You can call me Samir, or if you prefer, Sami."

Kane nodded. "I'm okay with Sami—Samir. We're American aid workers."

"Sure you are," the cabbie said, smirking as he took the bags.

“As aid workers, we’re used to getting ripped off by locals and the occasional out-of-work thespian.”

“Nice, Kyle. We’ve stumbled upon the only cabbie who will drive you to Gaza and knows what the hell 'thespian' means.”

“As a rule, Dr. Lewis,” said the cabbie, “I don’t use terms like 'thespian' with anyone from the Tribals; they might misunderstand the word and kill you.”

“So what you're saying is, watch what you say—it could get you killed.”

“Samir Khamundi,” said the cabbie, extending his hand. "And yes, to answer your question: imagine Cairo is like New York City; then the Tribals would be hillbilly country in the heart of Appalachia, and Gaza is South Central."

They shook hands, and Kane asked, “Do you have a secure spot in the car?”

Samir took the knapsack from Kane, weighing it in his hands as he leaned into the back seat. He pressed several buttons on his key fob, and the back seat split apart, revealing a secret compartment into which he dropped the heavy rucksack.

Daisha was looking at a travel map she’d picked up from the poorly stocked information kiosk inside Cairo airport. She walked over to the car and nodded her approval of Samir's ingenuity.

Samir's mustache and beard, along with his index and middle fingers, were yellowed from his nonstop, unfiltered Camel cigarette smoking. When he hugged Daisha, he almost poked her cheek with the brightly burning end of his cigarette.

"Sami, you old codger," she said, "you almost got me. It’s so good to see you’re still alive.”

Samir, momentarily forgetting his religious tenets, held Daisha and smiled broadly. “Lady Di, the pleasure is all mine, and look, I still have all ten fingers.”

“It’s hard to believe. The last I heard, you were in a tight spot in the Panjshir. Your future looked bleak—a stoning or a beheading.”

"Oh yes," said Samir, "that was quite unfortunate—a misunderstanding with General Dostum and his Northern Alliance. I call him General Dustup. Those Pashtuns, such jokers."

"I've met quite a few," Kane replied, "and 'jokers' is not an adjective I would apply to them." Kane scanned the immediate surroundings. "You know where we're headed, right? Gaza City?"

"That's one hot location," Samir said.

"Like twenty-six million Jordanian dinars hot?" Daisha asked. "Gotta love those Hawalas."

Kane shot Daisha a hard look before leaning in and whispering, "How much have you told him?"

"Nothing could ever make him give us up."

The bespectacled cabbie looked at Kane. "Two things to remember about Gaza: there are no straight lines, and nothing is as it seems."

Kane stared out the passenger-side window at early morning Cairo, watching the crowd on the streets as they headed to their jobs and the vendors who were rolling up their steel gates and opening their shops. "People keep telling me that, Sami."

"Telling you what, Dr. Lewis?" asked Samir Khamundi.

"Things are not as they seem. When we get to Gaza, you need to point those things out to me."

"We can start by staying close to the shoreline; if possible, the nicer areas are easier to travel through," Kane suggested.

Samir adjusted his rearview mirror to watch Kane as the three of them drove through Cairo.

"Considering checkpoint Erez and the random stops and searches by Hamas or whichever militia group, we can be in Gaza City by two in the afternoon," Samir said. "We can have lunch in Gaza Beach."

Daisha looked at her map and, with a questioning tone, asked, "Why Gazah Beach? It's a mile or two south of Gaza City, and my cousin owns a restaurant there."

"There's also less chance of being robbed by moonlighting Hamas thugs," Samir replied. "You will find the occasional tourist in the country, but they are extreme travelers who oftentimes will find themselves in a sticky wicket and end up phoning home for some ransom money."

"I'm getting the feeling, Samir, that you don't like Hamas," Kane observed.

Samir stopped the car in the middle of an intersection; horns were honking, and some people were yelling at them.

He turned to Kane and said, "Imagine, my aid worker friend, that one day Iranian-backed thugs marched into your town in the middle of your Revolutionary War and killed your George Washington or your Thomas Adams—"

Kane shook his head. "Jefferson, you mean Thomas Jefferson."

"Okay, Thomas Jefferson. These invaders have turned your fight for freedom into a distorted, money-making Iranian power grab—a pseudo-religious fatwa jihad circus. Yasser Arafat was Palestine's George Washington; he was corrupt, unprincipled, and at times evil. But for all his faults and that nasty stubble he called a beard, he fought for the Palestinian people—not for the Iranian mullahs, the Muslim Brotherhood, or the amoral optometrist, and certainly not for the West. They took his life, and then they took Gaza."

Samir drove the two hundred twenty miles to the Israeli border in silence, feeling he had treated his guests poorly. He regretted leveling such a polemic at a guest in his cab. His quiet reflection during the drive through the Sinai, as it transformed into the Negev, served as penance and a form of apology that he and Daisha understood, but Kyle did not. Such was the difference in their cultures.

The border patrol checked their credentials, and thanks to the skill of OJ Lena's forger, the three were quickly on their way.

The personal interviews at the border went just as smoothly, and all three passed. The big sedan pulled out into the Negev desert, and the trio continued their journey.

Kane broke the self-imposed silence. "So we're inside Israel? Tell me, Samir, you mentioned that Hamas was making money by controlling Gaza, which I understand, but can you explain how?"

Samir could not remain silent on such a painful subject. “Gaza is a besieged land. Egypt, Iran, and Hezbollah all have a grip on Gaza, and surprisingly, Israel has the lightest hold. Hamas’ black market pirates operate tunnels beneath the border with Egypt, smuggling in everything sold on Gaza’s black market—from washing machines to watermelons, fuel to flour. Guns and butter, and the greatest travesty of all, Dr. Lewis, the billions in financial aid that is stolen right off the top gets funneled to Iran and to the US.”

“I had no idea the Gaza economy was run by black market goods, Samir,” Kane said, glancing at Daisha. “Did you know that?”

Daisha nodded, staring out the passenger-side window with a blank expression.

“Watch as we drive through these towns,” she said. “You’ll see mansions owned by multimillionaires. In Gaza, almost every one of them is a Hamas leader.”

“Some say there are twenty thousand millionaires in Gaza—tiny Gaza—poverty-stricken Gaza,” Samir replied. “I’ve also heard the number is closer to two thousand.”

Samir was speeding, moving at double the limit, and had to swerve to avoid an elderly man with his goat cart.

“Two thousand Hamas millionaires in Gaza, according to some Fatah spokesman in the West Bank, and their wealth is fueled by greed and the skyrocketing prices of black market goods. Their mansions, those lavish villas on the Mediterranean,” he said as he slammed on the brakes, “are an outrage. How can the world stand by and let these brigands destroy an entire country? It’s worse than medieval times."

Samir wove in and out of a line of Bedouin tribesmen seated atop camels and in carts, making their way across the Negev.

“Even one millionaire is one too many in a place like this—a place where disease, starvation, poverty, violence, and never ending despair claim innocent lives every day.”

“Could you just drive the car, Sami,” Daisha said, “before we add to that number?”

Forty-five minutes later, Samir glanced at his watch. “We’ll arrive at Erez in five minutes. Having your credentials ready is a good sign for the IDF profile screeners. If we pass muster at the Erez checkpoint, we can eat at my cousin Mahmoud's café on Gazah Beach. He makes a bitchin' falafel."

Daisha started to laugh, and Samir looked at her with a quizzical smile. "Falafel—it's no good?"

"No, no, Samir, I love falafel, and I'm sure your cousin's falafel is great. I've never heard anyone refer to falafel as bitchin'."

"My language can get a little, how do you say, fubar."

"At times, yes."

They approached the huge gates of the Gaza border checkpoint at Erez. The modern steel structure, with its security walls, interview facilities, and offices, stood in stark contrast in a land that time had forgotten.

Israeli military personnel moved in and out of the lines of vehicles with dogs and undercar mirrors equipped with micro cameras relaying HD images to the command center. Palestinians were generally not allowed to use the Erez checkpoint, except for certain individuals.

After passing the vehicle inspection, the three parked and entered the long walking bridge to the customs area. They were questioned by Israeli border specialists trained to spot even the slightest signs of unease or deceit.

Samir sailed through the process. Outside the checkpoint offices, he found a seat and lit up. There was no shortage of IDF personnel and hardware standing guard at the border. When Kane emerged, he joined Samir as he chain-lit his tenth stubby cigarette.

"You got through quickly?" Kane asked.

"Frequent flyer miles, gov. Besides, I have no tells. My game is clean. I travel through Erez at least twice a month. Some documents never change."

"I wonder why Daisha's interview is taking so long."

"Her childhood, I imagine," replied Sami as he blew out a cloud of smoke into the hot, dry, desert air.

Kane wanted to pursue that line of discussion. Samir's comment didn't make sense, but before he could ask, Daisha pushed through the double glass doors marked "exit" in bold Hebrew letters.

"Hey, guys," she said. "What say we get the hell out of here?" Without much discussion, they climbed into Samir's sedan and headed out.

A short distance away, they encountered a local Hamas checkpoint. It was a very different affair. Samir slipped them a baksheesh, a bribe to expedite their passage. The three drove away without any problems. Their discussion about the U.S. and its policies in the Middle East took a strange turn.

"Hamas indoctrination starts in the first years of school," said Kane. "I believe the CCP sees it as a very effective tool to destabilize the West. They are using the same model in blue states across the US."

"I cannot argue, Dr. Lewis. Here in Gaza, nothing matters more to the people than the destruction of Israel and her people. The business of war involves invasive, multi-generational marketing. When a country becomes involved in a war, it invades like a parasite, pushing its way into every aspect of life."

***

They drove through neighborhoods, towns, and small cities, some of which were quite close to the refugee camps.

"Can you feel it?" Daisha asked, gazing out her backseat window at the people on the street. "They can sense it—the pull of negative energy emanating from the refugee camps. These places of catastrophic despair, filled with the horrors of Gaza, are not unlike the neighborhoods in Baltimore, Belmont in Detroit, or Riverdale in Chicago—all products of external control. In the U.S., before the Democrats began their foreign aid kickback hustle, they sourced their dirty money from inner-city corruption scams. For nearly a century, they have controlled almost all the major cities across the U.S., using corrupt city and state-level politicians to defraud elections and ultimately steal federal taxpayer money earmarked for education and civic improvement projects."

Kyle nodded. "You're right, Di. You can't point to a single Democrat-controlled city—or state, for that matter—

where conditions have ever improved. They maintain control over the poor by buying off ministers, reverends, and community organizers."

"This is no different from Gaza. The same evil that drives Hamas resides in the souls of American politicians," Samir said as he lit up another cigarette. "They do the dirty work for the powerful."

Samir drove his dust-covered Mercedes C-350 sedan through a few small towns, filled with rubble and the occasional intact structure—some homes and other businesses—that had survived the life-or-death game of chance called IEDs, random violence, and the ultimate game ender, 155mm artillery shells. These structures blasted into rubble reflected the hopes and dreams of the people. Their faces were blank, a universal expression of oppressed individuals whose lives were tortured by countries and cultures that had no right to take control of their land. They seemed like dysphoric zombies, unable to rise to the moment and feel peace or joy long enough to grasp who they were and who they could be without the constant madness—the twin harpies of hunger and fear that tore at their souls.

"It's a good thing you're a doctor, Dr. Lewis," said Samir sarcastically. "They wanted to reroute us through another roadblock. It's a common trick used on visitors to elicit additional baksheesh. I convinced them you were desperately needed at the hospital."

"Are you sure it wasn't Daisha's childhood?" asked Kane provocatively.

Daisha turned in her seat, shooting Kane an angry look without responding.

"If looks could kill, they probably will," said Kane.

Samir quickly changed the subject. "The difference between rich and poor in America—is it a big deal? Here in Gaza, those in power look at the average Palestinian as if they were sheep; keep them fed, watered, and controlled, and, most of all, fleeced."

"They continue to punish the poor in Gaza," Daisha said, "and when the American NGOs lobby their crooked politicians in the US, they push for hundreds of millions in aid through USAID or some other corruption-riddled agency. That's how the globalists have been fleecing the US taxpayer for fifty years."

"This land is bleak," said Kane, as he watched people of Gaza, "it's stark dehumanization! No one but a true sociopath could travel this land and remain unaffected by its sights."

"I am an Arab, Mr. Kane, and I see America's mainstream propagandists attributing the entire cause of Gaza's misery to Israel, but that's simply not correct, is it?"

"You don't see Israel as the little Satan, Sami?"

Samir shook his head. "No, I do not. They are not free of guilt, but Hamas controls Gaza; they are Iran's proxy and their war with Israel prevents Palestinians from escaping this awful situation. All commerce is heavily taxed by the paramilitary autocracy that controls the tunnels. They are controlled by Iran, which allows them to do what they want to the people as long as they continue their assaults on Israel."

Kane agreed with Samir. "Iran wants a deep-water port on the Mediterranean."

"Egypt is also trying to pry it loose," said Daisha.

"All parties," Samir added, "except for Israel, have profited from the horrors and misery of Gaza's people."

Daisha shook her head. "Israel exacerbates the situation by retaliating against Hamas, but what else could they do. They either strike back or the attacks will escalate and thousands will die.

Sami lit up a Camel. "And Biden hides behind his choice of ice cream."

"Controlling the flow of goods—fuel, food, and medicine that comes through the hundreds of smuggler tunnels in Rafah, on the border with Egypt, is the key," Daisha explained. "Those tunnels have become a part of Egypt's economy, and they don't want that to change.

Sami said, "The physical ownership of these tunnels goes back decades; it's hard to say for sure who owns them. However, Hamas and its associates took control when they drove all of Arafat's Palestinian Authority, Fatah, out of Gaza through the Erez checkpoint during a very violent period."

Samir looked back to the road, weaving through streets barely wide enough for one car. As they approached the outskirts of Gaza City, the roads widened, and houses, shops, and apartments began to pop up.

"Israel, the West Bank, and Gaza were all under Turkish control, collectively referred to as Palestine. Under the League of Nations mandate in the early 20th century, it fell to the British," Daisha continued.

Samir pulled into a spot along the oceanfront and pointed across the busy boulevard. "Enough with solving the world's problems; we need to eat. Over there is my cousin's café."

"Very nice," said Kane. "Is it close to our objective?"

"You haven't given me the location, Dr. Lewis." Kane handed Samir a sheet of paper.

"It's close enough. I'll take you by the location, but first, we need to eat, and this is the place."

"So tell me, Dr. Lewis, who are you really?" Daisha's heart rate jumped fifty beats, and Kane's hand dropped to his belt, where his gun rested.

"Not sure what you mean, Sami," said Kane. "Do you think I lied to you?"

"Oh no, Dr. Lewis, I'm just trying to clarify how capable you are."

"I have skills, Samir."

"Can you handle this mission you're proposing? Daisha is like a daughter to me, and I worry about her."

"It's Kane; just call me Kane."

"Alright, Mr. Kane, I need to know: can you protect Daisha?"

That was a question Kane couldn't answer honestly. He had never considered protecting anyone beyond the mission package. Operators were always fully self-sufficient. This was a full-scale special forces operation, fraught with dangers and potential catastrophes that could derail any mission, but lacking the planning, logistics, oversight, and quick reaction force that usually accompanied such operations. There would be no big brother to rely on if things went wrong. Daisha and

Kyle would have to survive on their wits, guile, and Samir, the unknown factor.

Sami parked the car across the street from an eatery that Di found intriguing. The facade featured a mix of blue and stainless steel tiles above a wall of sliding panels that opened across the entire front.

“This place is really something, Sami,” Daisha said. “I figured we’d be eating from a sidewalk cart.”

Kane, scanning the area, replied, “I’ve always been a big fan of the beach, and this place has incredible views of the Med.”

Inside the restaurant, Kane tried to guide them to a table against the back wall, but Samir insisted on a four-top in the front, facing the ocean.

As Kane was asking Daisha a question, Samir leaned in. “I’ll tell you this: before Hamas took over in 2007, Gaza wasn’t a terrible place. I operated my family's business, selling construction materials throughout the region. After 2007, I had to shift gears and partner with a Russian chap.”

Daisha excused herself from the table. “I need to call my sister.”

“Use your burner phone,” Kane advised. He turned back to Samir. “You did business with the Russians?”

“Yes, he was a quiet, pleasant fellow. He connected me with the Chinese, who made very reasonable AK-47s and RPG-7s to order. It was lucrative.”

“So you were selling to the Taliban and the Haqqani Network?”

“No, during that time, they had no money to speak of. What they did have came from Syria and the ISI. I worked on the other side, with the Pashtuns, the Northern Alliance, and a few tinpot dictators in Africa. The one time I sold to the Taliban was a shipment of factory refurbishments. My partner conveniently withheld the refurb part from me. I ended up shipping a dozen crates of non-functioning RPG-7s. An unappreciative Imam put me on the receiving end of a religious fatwa.”

“Oh, that’s never a good place to be,” said Kane. “Unless it’s Cat Stevens who’s after you; then it’s a kind of

Fisher-Price fatwa, or like Andy Warhol wants to kick your ass."

Samir laughed. "I narrowly escaped the tribals. I went from the relatively lawless to the profoundly lawless here in Gaza."

Daisha returned from around the corner, and Kane noted her quick nod as he continued his conversation with Samir. "You drive a nice car, your clothes are sharp, and you're wearing a Tudor, so I'm guessing you live in a nice area as well," Kane remarked.

"I do, but nowhere—not even in Cairo—is life easy. I have three children, and at times, with the world as it is, I worry. People starve in our world, and in Gaza, it's easier to die here than almost anywhere else in the world," said Samir.

Kane wasn't sure how much Samir knew. He wished he had remained in character for the sake of continuity. Samir got up from the table to fetch his cousin, Mahmoud.

Kane leaned toward Daisha. "I think he's solid. How well do you know him?"

"What do you mean?" Daisha asked.

"Instead of boosting a car for the mission, we could use Samir."

"If you think so, Kyle. I know he can drive, and he knows the area. We'll need some time to come up with a working plan."

"I agree; I'm not used to flying by the seat of my pants," said Kane. "I saw a motel on the way in. Can we use Samir to get weapons?"

"No, I've got that worked out."

Samir returned with his cousin, whom he introduced to the two aid workers. He smiled whenever Kane and Daisha talked about their jobs.

Mahmoud was a tall, broad man with a thick build and a long black beard that could rival Moses. He motioned for one of his servers to bring out a large platter of baba ghanoush and falafel, flashing a broad smile as he looked between Kane, Daisha, and his cousin Samir.

Kane took a bite and said, "I'm trying to keep things separate. Samir's our driver. He can get us out of Gaza if we get that far. Weapons are traceable, and I don’t want Hamas going after Sami's family.”

“It’s clear you two are related in some way,” said Kyle. “Maybe in a past life?”

Daisha shot him a look before changing the subject. “Once we get back to civilization—”

***

The three checked into a fairly modern motel. It had two floors and two dozen rooms that opened onto an exterior porch that ran the length of the building. Kane checked out the room before Daisha and Samir brought up their gear.

“So who’s our weapons connection?”

“Taz," said Daisha with a smile, "he’s part of the Jordanian General Intelligence Directorate.”

“How do you know him?” asked Kane, watching the street below.

“I was attached to our embassy in Amman, and he was my contact with the J-GID.”

“People are moving around like it’s a normal Saturday night. If there’s a big operation coming, nobody’s talking about it,” Kane said. “Something that significant always filters down to the street.”

Daisha got off the bed and walked to Kane’s side to check the foot traffic below.

“Whatever it is, they’re keeping a tight lid on it.”

“It’s not like Hamas is a friend of the people.” A knock sounded at the door, and Kane was there in a flash. His folding tanto blade was drawn and ready. He checked the peephole.

“One male, twenty-five to thirty, tough-looking, with a beard, Arabic.”

“Can you see his left ear?”

“He doesn’t have one.”

“That’s Taz; let him in,” Daisha said. She walked to the window and closed the blinds. Kane opened the door, positioning himself behind it.

Daisha greeted tall, dark, and handsome with a hug and a kiss. Kane shut the door and nodded at him.

The man extended his hand, and Kane shook it. "Taz," he said.

Kane nodded. "I got the download. I'm—"

"That's okay, Dr. Lewis," he said as he read the name embroidered name on his CFH collared shirt. "No need for formal introductions." Taz understood the need for discretion and dropped his shoulder bag on the bed.

The familiar sounds of weapons, metal clanging, and the jangle of ammo boxes brought a smile to Kane's face. Taz unzipped the bag and stepped aside.

Kane pulled out two Beretta 92X pistols and rummaged around until he found a couple of boxes of Underwood 147-grain 9mm JHP rounds. He held up one of the bullets. "Quite amazing what these beauties are capable of."

"They'll shred your target. On impact, they separate into ten razor-sharp flechettes and cause massive internal damage. Up close they create a real mess," Taz explained.

"I like this guy," Kane said. "He knows his weapons."

"Taz here is on deep cover inside the Palestinian Authority. Officially, he works for the Jordanian GID, but on the side, he serves as a CIA covert asset," Daisha added, smiling.

"So, you're a Jordanian intelligence officer in deep cover with the Palestinian Authority, while deceiving the CIA into thinking you're working for them, and you have a side hustle selling weapons. That's quite a gig," Kane remarked.

"A man's gotta do what a man's gotta do," Di replied.

"Just to be clear, Taz, if anything happens to Di or me—things that can't be explained—there'll be no place for you to hide."

"Whoa, Kyle," Daisha interjected. "That's not necessary. Taz is one of us."

Taz raised his hand. "It's cool, Di. I read the doctor five by five."

Kane racked one of the Beretta pistols and tested the Crimson Trace laser sight.

"I know; everyone pays me," Taz replied. "My side hustle involves all sorts of people."

"That's cool, but you're on our team until we leave Gaza—capisce?"

"Capisco, Dr. Lewis; that's ten grand."

"The price?" Kane asked. "That's cool, per unit?"

"For Di, ten grand—total."

"For real?" Kane said, examining the weapons. "They are the real deal, right?"

Taz nodded and reached into his bag, pulling out two long, matte black cylinders. "I'll throw these in and call it twelve."

"Suppressors too, all in? Deal," Kane said.

"Keep this to yourself. I can't have people expecting wholesale prices when retail is where I make my money."

"In my day job, I obtain and pass on information, but as you said, my side hustle—selling means of protection to those in need—involves discretion. Besides, who'd want to mess with an agent of the Central Intelligence Agency? Your friends have a very long reach and even longer memories."

"Mutually assured annihilation, Taz," Daisha added.

"Agreed." Taz looked at Di and said, "Be aware, little sister, running with the SEALs is hard company. There's no quit in these guys."

Kane looked up from his new weapon and twisted on one of the suppressors at the same time.

"How'd you know that, pal?"

"Several reasons: I caught a glimpse of that faded AB+ tattoo where your watch should be. Some SEALs get blood type tattoos."

"Some," said Kane as he removed his belt and pulled out ten gold Krugerrands.

"You have a trident tattooed on your forearm. It's not the SEAL insignia, but it means something to those of us in the business."

Kane dropped the ten one-ounce gold coins on the bed. "That more than covers it."

"That's more than sufficient. You and I have met before, Lieutenant Commander," said Taz.

Kane slapped in a clip and pulled back the slide. "Really, Jordan?"

Taz nodded. "Yes, as a matter of fact, you and your team took out four ISIS commanders—HVTs all. It was a meeting in Al-Karak. I believe they called the mission *Grand Slam*: four terrorists in one cell."

"I remember the mission," said Kane. "You were part of the Al-Khassa guys, the Red Berets; you provided support."

"We did," said Taz. "The generals wanted Al-Khassa to take down Anwar Hadat and his commanders—but the big dogs gotta eat."

Taz counted the coins again before pulling a file from his canvas duffle.

"Don't put your belt on just yet," said Taz. "The address you texted me, Di, is a large compound in Gaza City, just a ten-minute drive from here. I obtained a plot plan and the last known building plans, courtesy of Gaza City Works. Didn't think they had one of those, did you?"

"Given the state of things around here, I'd say they need a couple," replied Kane.

"Do we have any idea who the owner is?" Daisha interrupted.

"Yeah," Taz said as he leafed through the file. "It's Sheik Ali Ben Mazeri. He sells guns to the militia."

"Makes sense," Kane remarked. "It could only be controlled by a player."

"All gunrunners live comfortably—and in this case, very comfortably," Taz added, "especially with his three wives."

"Three wives? I struck out with just one. How do they manage it?"

"Governments everywhere are corrupt," said the Jordanian. "Look at your own people, Mr. Kane—criminals protecting criminals throughout history. Look at your Senator McConnell; the CCP gives him a wife, and her family, scions of the Chinese Communist Party, gives him a thirty million dollar stake in her family's Chinese shipping company as a dowry, which has grown tenfold. How can he hold a security clearance? The CCP controls his financial wealth."

"Yeah, Taz, but you live in a vastly different world," said Di.

“That’s true. In the American tradition, a politician's mission, beyond making themselves criminally rich, is to conceal America’s wrongdoings around the globe. Exploitation causes great harm.”

“Give me an example,” said Kane, with a hint of indignation.

“Do you remember America’s covert war in El Salvador and Nicaragua?”

"I do," Kane replied.

“MS-13 is the largest, most violent, and most well-armed street gang in the world. This phenomenon is a direct result of a U.S.-backed CIA destabilization operation and the subsequent breakdown of El Salvador's social structure—all thanks to America’s intelligence agencies and the DoD flooding the countries with military-grade weapons.”

Kane turned to Daisha. “Why does everyone feel the need to lecture me on U.S. politics?”

She held up the folder Taz had brought her. “I know this guy. He was a CIA asset in Qatar in 2008 or 2010. He disappeared fifteen years ago with three million dollars earmarked for an operation, and now he resurfaces in Gaza, selling weapons.”

Taz shrugged. “Power and money can make you anything you want to be in Gaza. Now he’s a sheik.”

“That’s true everywhere,” Daisha replied.

“Do you have any intel on his security detail?” Kane asked. Taz waited for Kane to cough up another Krugerrand.

“They run three five-man teams around the clock,” Taz replied. “Two men are with the sheik at all times. Tonight, Saturday, is date night—I should have said dates. Along with the two bodyguards that accompany the sheik are his *three* wives. They’re either going to a comedy club or a karaoke bar, both of which are located in Gaza City. Three men remain in the compound at all times: two guards patrol the grounds, while one monitors all the security feeds from an outbuilding guard shack. All the buildings, including the garage, are integrated into a fifteen-foot-high wall that encircles the entire property, topped with broken bottles mortared into place.”

"Are you available for a mission?" Kane asked.

Taz pulled up the pant leg on his right side, revealing a prosthetic leg from the knee down. "Oh, ouch. How'd that happen?"

"A well-placed OSV-96 round. It's a Russian heavy machine gun round, 12.7x108mm, chambered in a semi-automatic sniper rifle."

"Yeah, I've seen a round or two."

"It took my leg clean off at the knee. I was at a bazaar in the tribals when I got hit. If it weren't for a local gunmaker operating his forge, I would have bled out."

"Slapped hot iron to it?" asked Kane. Taz nodded and tossed Kyle a small rolled-up length of det-chord. "Thanks, brother. I'll find a use for this."

Daisha gave Taz a hug. "We're thankful for your help, Taz."

Taz bowed and shouldered his duffle.

"We'll see you around the pitch, brother," said Kane with a smirk.

Daisha frowned. "Kane!"

"No worries, Di. I like this guy; he's got my sense of humor," Taz replied as he walked out.

The door closed, and Kane checked the peephole. "Call Samir. He can drive us to the Nazeri compound."

"It's Mazeri, Kyle—Ma-zer-ri. Do we have a plan?"

"Looking over the compound drawings and building design sketches," he said, pointing to the building plan, "there's a small HVAC service port behind a bank of air-conditioning units."

"I'm sure it's secured, but there are several ways to defeat static security," Daisha said. "Breaching would be ill-advised, wouldn't you agree?"

"Hamas, like all authoritarian regimes, places foot patrols in the wealthier areas where their leadership and elite reside. That adds a dangerous variable."

Daisha clapped her hands. "Agreed, we'll make a silent entry."

"Right you are, Lady Di. Call Sami, and let's get this show on the road."

"He's smoking with his cousin at Mahmoud's hookah lounge." She dialed his cell and said, "Sami, pick us up in front of the hotel in twenty minutes."

"Listen, Di, our operation has absolutely zero room for error. If the family is at home and we can't subdue them, we kill them all. It's almost easier if we go in with that as our plan."

Daisha furrowed her brows. "You mean go in and kill everyone?"

"Yes, everyone. As soon as we lay eyes on them, we shoot to kill."

"Let's rethink our rules of engagement."

"Okay, we'll go with weapons only. Meaning, if they have a weapon, we shoot them—no questions asked."

"That sounds a little more reasonable."

Kane tucked the long Beretta into his waistband and stood up. Daisha started to laugh.

"What?"

"Is that your Long Dong Silver imitation?"

"Yeah—it is a rather tight fit down there." Kane pulled out the Beretta and unscrewed the suppressor. "Old habits die hard."

"What do you mean?" asked Daisha.

"If I used a suppressor during an op—and I used them a lot—it stayed on."

Daisha nodded and slid the suppressor into her pack.

"Yes, but you're not in a war zone. Carrying a long pistol tucked into your pants... not a good look."

"Good copy, Willow."

"Are you ready for this?" Daisha asked.

"Yeah. Why do you ask?"

"I don't know; sometimes you seem a little out of it."

Kane's eyes narrowed for a moment, then he relaxed. "You might be right. I suffer from some sort of traumatic stress."

"From combat?"

"No, although that could be part of it. I can't pinpoint anything specific. I did watch my two-year-old die of cancer."

Before Daisha could respond, Kane slung the pack over his shoulder and walked toward the door. “Whenever you’re ready, Red.”

Kane watched the parking lot, and when Samir’s green Mercedes pulled in, he signaled with a single flash of his high beams. Kyle turned to Daisha, still studying the house plans. “It’s go time.”

***

“You take shotgun, Di; I’ll cover from the back.”

Kane slipped behind Samir in the back and moved his Beretta to his thigh.

“Sami, I’m glad you came,” said Daisha. Kane stayed silent, waiting for Samir to respond.

“Why are you sitting behind me, Dr. Lewis?”

Daisha placed her hand on Samir’s shoulder. “This could turn into a wild adventure. Are you sure you’re up for it?”

Samir glanced at Daisha in the mirror, then back at Kane. “I knew it; you’re going ahead with this.”

“Yes, we are,” Kane replied. “We need a getaway driver. Do you understand the term?”

“Vin Diesel in ‘Fast and Furious.’”

Daisha agreed. “Yeah, kinda like him.”

“I’m going to go out on a limb and say your mission here is not sanctioned.”

“For the sake of any future conflicts,” Kane said, “let’s just say it’s not a sanctioned mission, unless otherwise indicated. How copy?”

“Inshallah, Kyle Kane, inshallah.”

“Why do you need to break into this gunrunning sheikh? I'm not big on bullshit titles,” said Kane.

“He’s more than just a merchant of military hardware; he’s the money man for the Iranians here in Gaza. His boss is Ismail Haniyeh.”

“The job,” Kane said, “is worth 100 Krugerrands: 10 now and 90 when you get us the hell outta here. Can I send them to you?”

Samir looked at Kane, his head cocked. “Did you not hear me? We’re talking about a real sticky wicket here, Mr.

Doctor Kyle. Whoever you are today, Sheikh Ali Ben Mazeri is a WMD psychopath, a true agent of the Dark Ages. He will turn Gaza upside down and shake it until you two fall out. He has the resources to do that."

"Money's a great motivator and clarifier of intentions," Daisha said. "You know, Sami, just having us as customers in your taxi will be a crime you won't be able to outrun if Hamas gets a lock on us."

Samir pulled the big sedan into an alleyway a few hundred meters down from the southern edge of the Mazeri compound. Daisha put on her hijab and checked it in her side-view mirror.

"The walls are every bit of fifteen feet," said Samir, "and they're topped with jagged glass shards!" Kane showed no signs of concern for Samir's warnings.

"Drop us off a block away from the Mazeri compound," Kane instructed. He tossed his belt onto the dashboard, and ten gold coins clattered with the unmistakable sound of pure gold. "Ten Krugerrands, Sami."

"If you're in for the other ninety pieces of gold, we'll meet up in half an hour."

Samir shook his head, and the three drove the short distance in silence. Kane studied Samir's face in the mirror; it was clear he was struggling with their decision to proceed.

Kane jumped out before Samir could voice any further objections. Daisha was right behind him.

"Okay," Kane said, "we'll see you in thirty. If not, circle the block once, then head home. You can read about us in the funny papers."

Daisha smiled at Samir and then moved off into the night.

"I have hundreds of sacks of gold like these at home," he said, gazing out the window. "I don't live for the accumulation of money! I live for the love and admiration of my family and my friends." His words faded into the darkness.

Samir watched Daisha and Kane disappear, certain he would never see them again. He got out and opened the hidden compartment in the back seat, pulling out Kane's knapsack and opening it.

His eyes widened as he stared at the laptop adorned with a half dozen decals from various Farsi software apps. "The strange has now become the bizarre, the bizarre the impossible, and the impossible has become the norm."

He tossed the belt holding the pieces of gold into the secret compartment along with the laptop, shut it, and drove off.

Chapter 23

Gaza City, 19:00

Daisha and Kane walked down the dark street. They passed quiet houses and several couples enjoying the cool evening air. Up ahead, across the street, was the compound.

"Do we take the guards by force or pick them off one by one?" Daisha asked.

"The gate is just around the corner. I think you need to draw out one or both of the guards patrolling the property," Kane replied.

"I can do that?" Daisha said.

"Leave me your belt, Di. I gave mine to Samir." Daisha looked at him oddly but handed it over anyway. "I'll see you on the inside."

Daisha nodded, feeling a bit concerned about the part of the mission Kane had omitted. Like, the whole thing.

She approached the gate and peered through the bars. On the opposite side of the courtyard, two guards stood smoking.

"Excuse me!" Daisha called out, purposefully using English to provoke them. The guards approached with their AK-47s slung in front of them, their hard, glaring stares revealing they were from the ranks of Hamas.

"Hi there, boys. My name is—"

Before she could finish, both men raised their weapons and shouted, "Shut up, bitch, and raise your hands."

"Put your hands in the air, slut!" one man yelled. Daisha felt an icy finger of fear run down her back.

I'm putting my life in your hands, Kyle; don't be late.

One of the guards unlocked the gate. Daisha considered pulling her Beretta from her ankle holster but stopped short, unsure of Kane's location.

“Big mistake coming into our snake pit, pretty lady,” one man said, pulling her inside and pushing her down onto the ground. “You are a whore.”

“Please, I’m lost and looking for my hotel. I’m an aid worker.” The thought crossed her mind that if it came down to it, she’d draw her weapon and die before allowing these disgusting men to rape her.

One of the guards signaled to the other in what seemed like a well-practiced routine. The barrel of an AK-47 was forced into Daisha’s mouth, and her arms were pulled behind her back and bound with a belt. She was yanked roughly to her feet and bent over a stone bench. The same man violently ripped down her khakis.

Daisha’s face was pressed down onto the middle of the bench, in the center of the courtyard.

“God damn it, Kane!” Daisha shouted, “Where the fuck are you?” The men laughed sadistically. One dropped his pants and pressed himself against her bare ass.

“I’m going to kill you, you fucking pigs!” she shouted.

“Welcome to Gaza, bitch,” said the man attempting to violate her. Daisha squirmed and fought, struggling fiercely, which only angered him. He cuffed the back of her head, nearly popping her eardrum.

Her head spun, and she screamed. The bastard laughed, ready to hit her again, when a silenced pop came from behind them and a 9mm JHP round tore through the man's forehead, ripping open the top of his head. It obliterated his gray matter, eyes, and nose. The buildup of neurostatic pressure sent the entire top half of his head flying across the stone courtyard in a bloody splash of viscera. He toppled over Daisha as his body convulsed and spasmed.

The other guard was only ten feet away when he spun around, his eyes wild with fear. He raised his weapon only to realize he hadn’t chambered a round. He reached for the bolt, but before he could pull it back, a triple tap left three tightly grouped red spots on his chest, and where the rounds exited, a one-foot-diameter chunk was followed by a second bloody splash of viscera.

Daisha rose from the bench and stared down at the carnage across the stone courtyard. The hate in her eyes could have melted steel.

Kane walked slowly out of the shadows, his face perfectly calm as he remarked, “These rounds really are the shit, aye. His head literally exploded.”

Daisha spun around, her hands still tied. “You fuck! I could’ve been killed, you bloody bastard.”

Kane quickly untied her hands, and she pulled up her pants. She shoved him hard and yelled, “Where the fuck were you?”

“I’m sorry, Di,” Kane replied as he checked outside the gates. He dragged what remained of one of the bodies back into the shadows. “I had trouble with the guard on the monitors. He was a big, angry man who refused to go down.”

“So you duked it out with him?”

“I didn’t know where the other two were; I couldn’t take the chance.”

Daisha was starting to feel better about his slow appearance. “So you went hand to hand while I was about to get raped!”

“No, I shot him in the face. Listen, I’m sorry, Di. I didn’t think they would attack you so quickly.”

“Fuck!” she exclaimed. “They’re just fucking animals. It took them only a few seconds to decide to rape me.” She paced around the courtyard, and within a minute, she was back in the game. “Fair enough,” Daisha said. “I’m fine with wasting these scumbags. I know taking prisoners isn’t your strong suit.”

“Rarely an option in my line of work.”

“Did you secure any data on the plan?”

“Not yet,” said Kane. “We need to go back to the shed and try to access the sheik’s network; otherwise, we’ll have to breach the house.”

“Let’s just go straight to breaching the main house. There’s little chance the sheik left any plans out for these assholes to steal,” said Daisha, still shaking from the attack.

She pulled the Beretta from her ankle holster and chambered a round.

The small access door behind the over-spec ten-ton AC units was bolted. Inside the mansion, the door blew open with a controlled, low-intensity det-cord pop. Kane climbed inside, followed by Daisha, with their pistols drawn.

"Tac lights," whispered Kane. The two moved through the expansive kitchen.

"Impressive Viking stoves and Sub-Zero refrigerators—the Sheik knows his major appliances. How did they get this stuff through the tunnels?"

Kane ran his gloved hand over the granite and marble countertops, floors, and walls.

"Look at this place," said Kane. "It's the Taj fucking Mahal."

"This place could give Bloomberg's Bermuda mansion a run for its money," Daisha replied.

"How does it compare to one of Saddam's palaces?" she asked.

"Wouldn't know, Di; I never got near one of those. My war was more about Kukhs and hunting down HVTs."

"I take it Kukhs are houses?"

"Handmade mud huts—some real frontier architecture. Afghans are gritty, soulful, and tough. Pashtunwali is a custom where a guest in an Afghan's home will be protected to the death by the entire village, if necessary."

"Sounds like the Latin Kings ethos."

Kane shrugged as Daisha led the way through a formal dining room into the main hall. "I'm just spitballing, Kyle, but from the floor plans I studied, I'd say there's a library up ahead on the right."

Daisha tried the door while Kane covered her. Once inside, she stopped.

"Whoa, this is quite a library."

"You think the Sheik's got a copy of the Arabian Nights?" Kane asked, smirking.

"Probably a first edition," she replied. "I found a desk and a laptop." She moved to the desk and took a seat, opening the laptop. “We've got a problem, Kyle: it’s password protected!”

“Check the blotter and the drawers. There might be a book of passwords or a sheet among the papers.”

She pulled open a few desk drawers and stopped. “Oh wow, shekels! We’ve got shekels and dinars, Kyle—stacks and stacks of 200-shekel notes.” She began placing the banded bills on top of the desk while Kane continued to look around the room. She paused at the bottom of one drawer.

“Password!” she exclaimed. “He’s a Joseph Heller fan; who would have thought?”

Kane came around the desk. “What have you got?”

“A small piece of paper taped to the bottom of the drawer. It says 'Catch 22.'”

Daisha typed it in. "Bingo." She worked through the files while Kane loaded as much cash as would fit into Di's kit bag.

“Jackpot,” Daisha said, spinning the computer around to show Kane the screen. “We’ve got plans, locations, militia strength, and timetables.”

“Does it discuss the overall plan and the key players?” Kane asked.

“Pretty much. I have the militia timetables for attacks on all the major crossings. It also outlines sabotage missions targeting airports, railways, and electrical plants. There’s a second wave of foreign fighters set to launch twelve hours after the first. Why use foreign fighters when they have boatloads of local militia? This second wave has orders to blend in with the local militia.”

“This is a full-on invasion,” Kane said.

“There’s more: the second wave of foreign fighters, dressed in IDF uniforms, will establish firing positions inside Israel and target cities and towns in Gaza, as well as some highly sensitive targets in the Bekaa Valley.”

Kane began to read the file. “Foreign fighters will focus on Gaza, specifically targeting refugee camps, cities, and their own infrastructure. They are aiming at schools and hospitals. Listen to this, Di: these specially trained foreign fighters will use captured or black market IDF mortars, artillery shells, and rockets to disguise their attacks."

"Iran's Revolutionary Guard, Quds Force, and Syria's military are pledging their support in response. They have prepared press releases accusing Israel of genocide and crimes against humanity."

"That takes some serious audacity," Kane said. "I bet they're counting on the captured media propaganda machine worldwide to line up behind them and spread their disinformation campaign."

"Israel will repel the attacks," Di replied. "This assault won't get far before the IDF halts it, but the damage will be done, and the global community will start blaming Israel." Daisha opened the center desk drawer, searching for a memory stick. "Look, a blue and white UN memory stick. I wonder how he got this."

"What?" Kane asked.

She looked at him and said, "At Langley, we had a supercomputer dedicated to running conflict scenarios for every potential combination of combatants and every possible location in the world. The Middle Eastern war scenarios have been analyzed since the 1950s—run and run again, over and over. Every conceivable variable was considered: weather, terrain, weapons stocks, even the price of gas. Each new administration comes in with its own plan to change the Middle East. Chief among them are those idiots at the State Department."

"I take it you don't like the State Department?"

Daisha rolled her eyes. "The only consistency in the scenarios showed that a major war involving Israel would spark World War III."

"Jerusalem being ground zero?" said Kane.

"Yes and no; more often than not, Gaza was ground zero. But many consider Gaza an outlaw territory of Israel, like the Barbary Coast or the Pakistani Tribal Areas."

"So we've flown into ground zero," Kane said.

"More or less," Di replied as she pushed back from the desk. "Front row seats for the destruction of the Middle East, at a bare minimum."

"We have to warn Israel," Kane insisted. "If they receive no advanced warning and the foreign fighters are able to fire on the refugee camps with Israeli ordnance, the fog of war will control the narrative. The US will do nothing to stop Iran's attack. Biden will cite Israeli atrocities."

"Israel would be in real trouble."

"What would be their fallback?" Kane asked. "And what would be their endgame?"

"As I remember, more than 70 percent of the time, total conflicts ended with nuclear war as the result."

"Oh shit, we've got company," Daisha said. Kane turned to Di. "Look, look at the box in the upper right corner. It's a security split screen. Someone must be trying to get in."

"What am I looking at, Di?"

"Looks like the garage."

"Was there a garage in the plans?"

"I saw a three-car garage built into the rear of this structure."

Kane focused on the screen. "Wow, that's a nice up-armored Toyota Land Cruiser."

A dark blue, late-model Land Cruiser was waiting outside the garage. The steel door engaged and began to rise. Inside, there was a Mercedes AMG 500 SL and a Ferrari Testarossa.

One of the bodyguards jumped out of the front seat. "He's covering their transfer from the Land Cruiser to the house," said Kane. The other bodyguard parked the Land Cruiser, jumped out, and rushed to open the rear door. A short, tubby man dressed in a flowing green and gold bisht waddled in ahead of everyone. "Time for us to exfil, Lady Di!"

"Correct me if I'm wrong," said Daisha, "but they are entering the house through the garage into the—"

"The kitchen," said Kane. "Our exfil is on the opposite wall of the kitchen."

"We're going out through the same kitchen they're coming in?" Daisha asked incredulously. "Are you serious?"

"Do the bodyguards look dangerous?"

"Yeah, they're military-age combatants," Kyle replied. "I'm sure they're trained."

"Can we do this quietly?" Daisha asked.

"Keep your weapon silenced and ready," Kane instructed. "We stay close, and if challenged, don't hesitate to shoot them center mass. If you see body armor, target the head and neck."

The two walked out into the main hallway. A thud reverberated through the house. Kane turned to Daisha and whispered, "Heavy steel garage door."

He motioned for Daisha to move in a crouch as they slid across the blue and gold-streaked white marble floor of the dining room.

They navigated through the shadows and dappled moonlight streaming in from a bank of floor-to-ceiling windows.

As they approached a two-way swinging door, Kane raised a clenched fist. The sound of the kitchen door opening from the garage froze them.

"They're in; we can take them all in the kitchen. Option two: try to slip out undetected," Daisha said, raising two fingers. "Two it is."

They held just inside the dining room door, listening closely to the sounds of the six people who had entered the kitchen.

Light shone under the door just before the sheik's group passed by the dining room. They laughed and joked about the night before, stopping to gather around the marble-topped island at the front of the enormous kitchen.

Someone opened one of the massive double doors of the Sub-Zero fridge, followed by the unmistakable clanking of a six-pack of bottles.

Kane raised his eyebrows. "Bud long necks?"

Daisha whispered, "God, I'd love an ice-cold beer right about now."

Kane smiled as he brought up the suppressed nine. "I can make that happen."

Daisha looked at Kane and frowned. "No, no illegal killing."

He pushed the swinging door open a crack and whispered, “I was just kidding.”

The sheik passed out the sweaty beers to his wives and, surprisingly, to his two bodyguards.

The six of them began to drink, laughing and joking about the comedy show from

earlier that night.

Kane pushed the kitchen door open a crack. He could see that the six people on the opposite end were engaged. With enough darkness to conceal them, Kane motioned for Daisha to walk toward the door that led into the garage.

One of the sheik’s wives, the youngest and prettiest—probably half the sheik’s age—felt emboldened and spoke up. “Husband, the best part of the comedy show was your karaoke. Watching you sing ‘Born in the USA,’ a song glorifying the great Satan, was quite a choice.”

The other two women nearly choked on their beer. They understood how perilous the boundary their inexperienced sister-wife had not only crossed but leaped over. The older women braced themselves for what was coming.

The sheik fixed his young wife with a cold, emotionless stare that quickly transformed into a Hannibal Lecter-esque smile. It was a smile the other two wives had seen before, and they were horrified to see it again.

Everyone froze in anticipation of the sheik’s volatile mental state.

He began with subtle comments, attacking her immodesty. When he turned to her inability to bear him a child—a fault clearly his own, being zero for three—the older woman tried to divert his attention.

Even the guards attempted to calm their boss, but their efforts failed when he lashed out at them. He began to scream at the delicate nineteen-year-old, who cowered in a corner, looking around in terror like a small animal trying to escape a predator.

Daisha watched over Kane’s shoulder, feeling the girl’s fear. Memories of an abusive relationship in her past sent shivers down her spine. She saw the oldest of the wives step between the sheik and the target of his rage. He backhanded her with a handful of gold rings, knocking her to the floor. The other wife shielded the fallen woman as the sheik continued to unleash his fury, swing after swing.

Kane took advantage of the moment. He pushed Daisha to move through the shadows to the back wall of the kitchen. Daisha let the door close gently behind her. They could hear the vicious blows over the horrified screams and broken cries for mercy.

High-pitched voices begged for forgiveness as the two slipped away through the door into the garage.

“I’ll raise the doors quietly,” said Kane. “Slide that rolling jack under the door when I lift it.”

Kane raised the door and strained to hold it up. “Any time, Daisha!” But when he glanced back and saw her expression, he realized the plans had changed.

“Fuck this bullshit, Kyle,” Daisha said in a low growl through gritted teeth.

"We're not walking away from this one, are we?” Kane replied, struggling with the door.

Another horrifying, guttural scream pierced Daisha to the core. Tears streamed down her face as she shook her head.

Kane looked at his partner. *Those are tears of pure rage.* “I got your back, Di. Let’s make it quick and clean.”

Daisha nodded her head as she checked her clip. She slapped it back in and turned toward the kitchen door. She marched back like a vengeful angel, sword in hand, resolute in her determination to set things right.

“I’m not leaving them to this fate.”

She said it with such calm resolve it surprised Kane. She was not an operator, but in the moment she displayed the steely nerves of one.

“What about World War III?” whispered Kane.

“It can wait!”

Kane looked puzzled. “It can?”

“It’s ass-kicking time, Kane; you got my back?”

“You need to ask?”

There was no plan, but Kane could already see his role in this.

Kane followed Daisha through the kitchen door. *Oh shit, this is gonna be a reckoning.*

Daisha's shadow raised her gun. The madness that greeted her shocked even her; it steeled her spine and sharpened her resolve like a samurai's katana.

The next thirty seconds were a blur as Daisha approached the scene. Two wives, beaten and bloodied, were protecting the young girl who lay on the cold stone floor, battered and broken, blood flowing from her face.

The girl was in and out of consciousness, and still, the bastard continued. The sheik pulled the older woman back, who bravely reached for him. They threw themselves in front of the child bride, taking the blows of his rage again and again until the sheik drew his jewel-encrusted knife. He began swinging at them with violent hatred, intent on maiming and killing.

Daisha found herself in a place beyond reason, where her own personal tragedy melded with that of the women in front of her. As she reached the edge of the shadows, where the guards holding the youngest woman up for the foul-breathed pig noticed Daisha standing in the light. Two suppressed pops came from the shadows, and the destructive rounds ripped into the bodyguards. The spray turned the cabinets behind them red; they were dead before they hit the floor. Daisha turned her weapon on the angry little man. She checked her fire, not wanting to hit one of the women.

His ugly, blood-streaked face never looked up. He was so enthralled in his sadistic attack he failed to notice the angel of death that had come for him.

He raised the curved blade to finish the job, and Daisha shouted, "Time to die, you fucking piece of shit! " The sheik turned, and Daisha saw the mind behind his wild eyes, that he was fully consumed by sadistic pleasure, that he considered rushing her with his jambia, but instead, he smiled and motioned for her to come close, to seduce her. He stepped towards Daisha, and she smiled.

Unfortunately for this sheik, it was a venomous, vengeful smile that played across Daisha's face. She was so far beyond rational thought, her next words just tumbled out:

"You have come face to face with a woman ready to do the job at hand, a job left undone for far too long."

The sheik's expression shifted from placid calm back to full-blown madman filled with psychopathy. Daisha purposefully lowered her pistol, and the same sick, manipulative smirk returned to the bastard king's face.

The man's purposeful weight shift triggered Daisha's response. When she squeezed the trigger, the powerful round, with the suppressed little pop, disintegrated the little pretender's right kneecap. Like neutrinos through warm butter, the jacketed hollow point rocketed through flesh and bones and took with it everything between it and the fine marble floor. The tough guy crumpled like the pile of shit he was.

She stood over him, the literal embodiment of misogyny, and thought: *Empty the clip; leave nothing!"*

Daisha pointed the gun at center mass, fully willing to end him.

Strange got even stranger when the oldest of the women, beaten and barely able to stand, forced herself to rise from the pile of battered bodies. A r

The redhead raised a bloody hand and stopped Daisha. So battered was she that she struggled to find her voice to beg Daisha not to kill her lord and master.

Older than the other two, she still carried remnants of her youthful beauty. She stepped closer, and Daisha saw the toll the sheik's rage had taken. Years of violence had left her cheekbones broken and her jaw dislocated. She too had once been a beautiful woman. She pulled herself up with the help of the counter and tried to reach out with a trembling hand.

"Don't, please don't kill him," said in quaking, broken English. It took a moment, but Daisha finally understood.

This is their chance to settle the score, to make things right. Let them have him.

The woman pushed back her red hair and glowered at the coward as he screamed and cursed them. "He's killed four wives; if we die," she said in shaky, broken words, "it will be in service of women that are locked in misery and violence everywhere."

Daisha nodded her head slowly. She spun the Beretta around in her hand and offered her the weapon. She heard Kyle from behind caution her. She raised her fist as if to say, "Hold!"

She understood it was reckless, but without sharing more than a couple of words between them, she understood their plight. Their anger was her anger, as she held the weapon out to them. The two women looked at each other for a long second before they shook their heads and refused the gun. Regardless of how beaten and cut up they were, the two women grabbed knives from the butcher block and turned on the sheik and started to circle.

Mazeri tried to escape, shuffling between screams and curses. Even the young girl, who caught the worst of the beating, climbed to her feet and, with pure hatred in her eyes, grabbed from the block the twelve-inch razor-sharp boning knife. All three women held long, mirror-finish blades that more than anything resembled the fangs of a great snake as they advanced toward the cowering man.

He attempted to push off with his good leg only to spin himself in a bloody circle across the beautiful marble floor.

Each woman stepped forward, inflicting the same terror he had imposed on them for so many years. A wave of razors fell upon him, and they slashed and stabbed mercilessly. Arterial spray filled the air, and when the cowering man stopped crying, it signaled the end.

Daisha watched the carnage until Kane grabbed her by the shoulder.

He pointed toward the garage. “Daisha! They’ve got this under control—the exfil window’s closing!”

She pulled five stacks of ten thousand shekels each and placed them on the counter. She backed away as they stabbed, sliced, kicked, and punched his body.

Daisha told the women in Farsi, “Give us one hour and tell them you were robbed by bandits.”

The women dropped their knives. They stood for a moment out of breath. One by one they went to Daisha and took her hand and brought it to their foreheads, then hugged her. It was obvious they were experiencing a freedom they hadn't felt in forever. Di forced them to listen, to hide the money, and to create a simple story they would have to stick to.

Kane walked up beside her and said, "I hate to break up the sisterhood of the traveling pants, but we've got to go."

The two ran out the door and slid through the two-foot gap in the garage door. Daisha rolled under it while Kane yanked it up and kicked out the jack and said, "I thought you were going to dive right in."

"I totally understand their rage. What you saw there was cosmic justice."

"Yeah, and you brought it to a close with only three rounds. Solid fire discipline."

Rolling blackouts were a *current* reality in Gaza; Gazans lived and died with them, which is why midday was the most sought-after time for surgical procedures at Gaza's terminally overstretched hospitals. In too many cases sunlight provided the most reliable form of light for such operations.

They slipped away into an inky dark alley.

Daisha slipped her 9mm into the waistband at the small of her back.

"Oooh, happiness is a warm gun," said Daisha as she squinted and motioned for Kane to move into the shadows. "I see a car."

"Good copy, agent," Kane said as the headlights moved toward them. He noticed the Mercedes hood ornament and started to push out into the street, but Daisha held him back.

"Remember, one if by land, two if by sea."

The car flashed its lights once, and Samir stopped, jumping out and waving from across the hood.

"What is he doing?" Daisha asked.

"Semaphore," said Kane. "I think."

The two walked around the big Mercedes. "This is becoming a habit, Dr. Lewis," said Samir.

"We're 2 for 2; let's not change that, Sami," Daisha said as she took the front passenger seat, and Kane slammed into the back behind Samir.

"I thought you were going to light a signal fire, Sami," said Kane as he stared at him in the rearview mirror.

Daisha turned in her seat and scolded Kane, "Lighten-up, Kyle,"

"Across the street, Mr. Kane," said Samir, "do you see the three Hamas militiamen seated around that outdoor café table? They're smoking and drinking tea." He added, "Don't look!" as he backed into the alley and slipped deeper into the shadows.

"Oh yeah," Kane replied, "I see them."

"I was waiting here for you two when they sat down next to me," Samir explained. "I told them I was picking up a couple of aid workers and taking them to the Jabalia Camp."

"And they believed you?" Daisha asked.

"It helped that I bought them a couple of bowls of Serbetli Premium," Samir replied.

He waved to the three Hamas soldiers, while Kane forced himself to remain silent.

"My bad, Sami, I misjudged you," Kane said. "Just when I thought you'd blown our cover, you pull this off buying tobacco and rounds of tea for the militia."

"Just so, Rafik, just so," Samir said as he drove away.

"Can you get us to the border?" Kane asked.

"That's your exit plan, Dr. Lewis?" Samir shook his head while driving past the Hamas security guards.

"Do you know why they tried to assault you? They saw you walking around unescorted, judged you instantly, and completely disregarded the written laws of the Koran to violate you. That's the kind of misogynistic animals you encountered back there."

Samir looked at Daisha and touched her forearm. "Did something happen?"

Daisha smiled at her friend. "It's okay." Her eyes grew wet. "We took care of business."

"We should be able to get through the Israeli border checkpoint," said Kane.

Samir nodded at Daisha, then looked back at Kane in the back seat. He laughed momentarily. "You won't get within five hundred meters of the border. Sit tight, and I will show you, Dr. Lewis, how we're going to get out of here."

Samir drove them back toward their hotel.

Kane pressed the barrel of his weapon against the back of Samir's seat. "Why are you taking us back toward the hotel?"

"You paid for my skills," said Samir. "Keeping you alive and out of Hamas' hands is my only concern. If Hamas catches you, they will assault Miss Daisha and torture you until you give up everything, including your Blockbuster Video passcode."

"DVDs are passé, amigo."

"What are we doing here?" said Daisha.

"You're on tape somewhere—in the mansion, the compound, or on the street. They will know what you look like. You'll never escape using traditional crossings or the contraband tunnels, all of which are controlled by Hamas. We must stay mobile. Gaza is the most crowded place in the world."

"No kidding!" said Kane. "Like that crazy episode of Star Trek?"

Samir, watching the streets nervously, replied, "You're referring to the episode where there's no way to be alone—anywhere. That's Gaza."

"That's the one," said Kane.

Samir held up his hand. "Give me your room key."

Kane looked at him. "What for?"

"We need to make sure your room is clear, and I want my money."

He handed Samir the key, and he jumped out of the car.

Kane tapped Daisha on the shoulder, and she turned to see the concern on his face.

"I'm okay, Kyle. I'm just a little shaken."

"It's PTSD, girl. You can suppress it for a while, but it's gonna surface. Tell me again how is Samir our guy."

"He's solid, Kyle. He won't throw us to the wolves."

"How do you know that?" Kane asked, staring out at the burned-out buildings lining the street.

Daisha remained silent, and Kane understood her hesitation.

"Just beyond those buildings," he said, "those bombed-out hovels, are some of the most beautiful views in the world.

If these people could just get rid of the militia, they'd have it all."

"Well, that's just not true. If it wasn't Hamas, some other CCP-backed entity would move in. There's so much beauty in Gaza surrounded by so much evil," said Di. "There are mothers and fathers who would do anything to get their families out of here, to give their kids a fighting chance at life, but that chance is smothered by Iran and its proxies."

"There's just too much wickedness," replied Kane. "Too many truly evil people."

She looked around. "What kind of person can profit off the misery of those around them?"

Kyle started to get out of the car. "We've spent too much time here."

"I grew up here," she responded under her breath.

Kane stopped and closed the car door. "What?" Kane was genuinely surprised. "You grew up a Reina Latina in Spanish Harlem, no?"

"For all intents and purposes, I did, but the earliest days of my life began in a mythically crazy place called Bureij."

"That's a town, or what?"

"A refugee camp," Daisha said, her tone sad. "My father died from typhus. My mother decided that death was hounding our footsteps and that we had to run. We fled through one of the tunnels in Rafah and began walking through the Sinai to Cairo."

Totally stunned, Kane asked, "How did you survive that? The Sinai is home to snakes, scorpions, killer spiders, and nothing else."

"Don't forget the nomads."

"They're just visitors too, Di."

"We almost didn't survive. We were dying on a roadside in the desert when a man, a truly good Samaritan, stopped his truck. I remember his big, beautiful, shiny truck pulling over on that deserted road. He took us in. His air-conditioned cab and cold bottles of water were manna from heaven, literally. For the first time, I saw a world outside the living hell I grew up in. He gave us every bit of food and water he had. He sang, and we sang all the way to Cairo."

"Samir?"

She was quiet for a long minute, small rivulets of tears running down her cheeks. "We were living corpses, huddled on the roadside under my mother's chador, her cape shielding us from the sun.

Samir saved our lives. He took us to Cairo and introduced us to another refugee family. They gave us a home and nursed us back to health. He never asked for anything."

"He got you into the States?"

"After we regained our health, he got us aboard a cargo ship bound for New York."

"I have a renewed sense of who our driver is. What was your name?"

"I was born Layla Minhas. For all intents and purposes, I was born Daisha Willow at Montefiore Medical Center in New York City."

Samir passed by the front of the car with a quizzical look on his face. He jumped into the driver's seat and said, "I don't know what you did, but Hamas is running around with their hair on fire." He looked at Daisha and the tears on her face. "You told him?"

Daisha nodded.

Samir glanced at Kyle and said, "It wasn't really us." He coolly pulled onto the street and drove away. As he did, a dozen Hamas militiamen walked into the motel office.

Daisha turned to Samir. "How do we stay ahead of those guys?"

"With guile and a fundamentally crooked driver," he replied with a toothy grin.

Not far down the road, Di received a call on her cell. Kane read the screen over her shoulder.

"That's a tiny phone," Kane remarked as he looked closer. "DC, do they know you're here?"

"They do now! Let's face it: US intelligence has had its arms wrapped around the entire world for decades. They can GPS-locate any of us. It's that simple."

Kane shook his head and asked, "Who are they? Your agency bosses? Our friendly NSA would be looking for you, Di."

"They've tracked my phone," she said, pulling out the phone's SIM card. "If they don't know exactly where I am, they know the closest tower to my location right now."

"If it's the people behind this rogue coup, then we're screwed," Kane said. "They may use Hamas to take us out."

"You believe there is a coup in America?"

Kane nodded. "There are a few things you need to understand, Sami. A significant number of American bureaucrats and politicians have taken bribes from the Chinese. They're being blackmailed to act in China's favor."

"Let's get out of town, Samir!" Daisha urged.

Samir looked around nervously. "I know the best way out of town."

"Roll the dice and go, Sami; they'll come at us from every direction," Daisha said. "The coup will strike from an unexpected angle. We have at best a few hours."

she added, continuing to try to remove her SIM card.

"Wait, don't destroy it. I'll disable it." Daisha handed Kane her phone; he pulled the SIM card halfway out and slid the entire phone into his shirt pocket. "Save that for later."

Samir checked his rearview mirror. "You mentioned the word 'coup."

"These people," said Kane, "aren't playing for table stakes. This is about nullifying America in any way possible. They want to continue the theft of billions from American taxpayers."

"If you don't mind me asking, what did you do, Mr. Kane?" asked Samir.

Kane looked at Di, Di looked at Samir, then back to Kane.

"You're retired from the Navy, so what's your new job? I know you're an associate of Daisha's, and that's incriminating enough," Samir said jokingly.

"That's for me to know and for you not to find out, Sami," Kane replied, tapping him on the shoulder.

Samir shook his head. "I should at least know who's coming after us… aside

from Hamas."

"Treat it as if everyone, including Spectre, is in on this," Di suggested.

"Okay," Samir said. "Let's consider our options. We could attempt a desert crossing, which I cannot recommend, or—"

Kane smiled. "A desert crossing… like the Anvil of the Sun?"

"The Anvil of the Sun?" asked Samir.

"TE Lawrence, the British officer who united the tribes of the Arabian Peninsula, led a small group of Arabs across the Anvil of the Sun to prove to Sherif Nasir it could be done. Nasir led his Howeitat army across the Anvil and attacked from the undefended desert side of the Red Sea port of Aqaba and drove the Turks out during the Arab Revolt of World War I."

Samir laughed. "The Anvil of the Sun is an impassable section of the Nefud; this is true."

"Not for Hollywood. Richard Harris did it, and when he and his young companion crossed it, the first thing he did was to stop at a British officer's club, dressed in dirty, dusty Arab garb, and demand two glasses of lemonade, one for himself and one for his young Arab friend.

Samir smiled. "You speak of Al Auruns. He is still a hero in the Arab world. For lemonade, he crossed the Nefud."

"Kane, you're off mission; bring it back in, Lieutenant Commander," Daisha said.

"Right, I think the desert is the plan of last resort."

"Then we must rely on the greed and avarice of the truly depraved," Samir said, weaving through traffic and breaking only long enough to maneuver around the occasional donkey-drawn cart, scooter, and throng of pedestrians. Samir was a classic Arab driver, unconcerned about the potential dangers of speeding in heavy traffic. "It's the tunnel for us and the tunnel operators. Can you cover the cost?"

"The good news, Sami, is that we just robbed a very wealthy man."

Samir laughed. "Off to the city of tunnels, then. Pray to Allah to get us through the roadblocks along the way."

"If it helps." Kane winked at Daisha when she turned around.

Kane sat in the back while Daisha rode shotgun, with Samir in the driver's seat. They drove through the desert toward Rafah, each lost in thought.

A few miles outside the city, a line of four cars signaled the first roadblock to their escape.

Samir gripped the steering wheel. "Bloody hell."

"Everyone stay calm," Daisha said. "Stick to the cover story and don't—" She paused and turned to Kane. "Don't get twitchy."

Kane pulled back the slide on his Beretta. "Me... never." He looked up from his pistol to see a black Citroën Pallas, arguably the finest of French luxury cars, coated in fine desert dust, alongside a white Hilux technical. The modified Toyota pickup featured a DShK 12.7 mm heavy machine gun mounted in the bed and welded to the frame. The weapon was manned and aimed at the cars waiting to pass through the checkpoint.

Kane glanced at Daisha, who nodded and pulled the slide on her Beretta. She set the weapon down between the seats, ready to fire.

Samir pulled in behind the other vehicles: a box truck, another Hilux, and the dusty Citroën, all waiting to get through. An old Japanese minivan loaded with a children's soccer team was waved through by one of the AK-toting militia members. Kane pushed his aviator shades up on his nose and pulled his CFH company baseball cap down over his eyes.

Samir looked back at Kane. "Any ideas, Mr. Kyle?"

"Get on the other side of that truck. If we make a move and don't clear that DShK heavy machine gun, we're all dead."

Samir edged into the open lane, attempting to drive through the roadblock. He was surprised when no one ordered them to stop until an angry-looking man jumped in front of his Mercedes. The man aimed his AK-47 casually at Samir's head, his traditional black and white keffiyeh flapping in the wind and obscuring his wraparound shades.

"This guy's not pleased with your driving, Sami," Daisha remarked.

The man gestured for Samir to lower the window. Samir noticed the well-maintained short-barreled AK-47 in the man's hands.

Kane raised his pistol to just below window level. A gust of wind kicked up dust and sand, obscuring Kane's face to the point where the man removed his sunglasses to focus on him.

Kane recognized the look—it was one he had seen more than a few times in places like Fallujah, Rabat, Mogadishu, Caracas, and Damascus. As the man closed in, Kane could sense that his cover was about to fail.

The Palestinian shifted his weapon toward the back seat, and both sides hesitated for a split second. In the blink of an eye, Samir was out of the car, babbling in rapid-fire Hebrew. "Why are you holding us? I have contracts to fulfill. I must get these relief doctors to the Rafah camp within the hour."

Before the confused man could respond, Samir shifted the conversation. "Is that a short-barreled AK?"

The man, clearly proud of his unique weapon, nodded.

Kane glanced at Daisha. His eyes sparked with the instinct to take out the machine gunner, but something urged him to wait.

"Let Sami do his thing," Daisha said quietly.

"Three shots, three kills," Kane muttered under his breath, his trigger finger twitching as he watched Samir.

"Go, go, gooooo!" Kane urged. "Get out of my line of fire."

Things were escalating, and the only thing keeping the jinn in the bottle was an Egyptian weapons dealer with a good soul.

Samir led the man around the Mercedes to the trunk. He popped it open, and Kane lost sight of them in the rearview mirror.

"Be ready, Di. I'm going to take down the DShK gunner, and you need to drop the rover next to the technical."

Daisha shook her head. “Samir knows what he’s doing. Give him a chance. If we get into a gunfight this far outside Rafah, they'll be waiting for us at the gates.”

Daisha could see that Kane was eager to move. He thrived on being fast on the draw. Her heart raced as she pulled her pistol up from between the seats. It was go time when Samir slammed the trunk lid down.

The sight of Samir shaking hands with a Hamas militiaman, both smiling, slowed the roll. Their discussion continued. Kane took a deep breath, leaned back in his seat, and shifted from maximum readiness, DEFCON one, to his normal in-country military readiness, DEFCON two.

Two men approached the car, chatting happily. One of them held up his AK-47 and proudly showcased his new Leupold quick-sight scope to the others at the checkpoint. They all gathered around; even the DShK gunner climbed down to admire the impressive optics.

Samir slipped into the car and started it up. He waved and drove away from his new friends.

“Sami, that was brilliant,” said Daisha.

Kane shook his head, wiping sweat from his brow. “Follow the yellow brick road,” he said. “Follow the yellow brick road.”

The desert opened up around them as they sped along. Kane poked his head out the window and looked at the skies. “We’re picking up some serious clouds from the west, and that can mean only one of two things: nothing or a sandstorm.” He stuck his head even farther out the window. “Shit, we’ve got a bird on our six.”

“How do you know?” Daisha asked.

“Twenty years of watching the skies for those little water bugs,” Kane replied.

“Have they spotted us?” a nervous Samir asked.

“Worry not, my friend; if they knew we were in this car and wanted us dead, they’d have flown a hellfire up our tailpipe from beyond the horizon.”

“Damn those drones,” Samir said. “Just not cricket.”

The profile of Rafah City rose from the dunes. They were just a couple of miles away. The battering Rafah had taken over the past twenty years made it look like a Hollywood backlot set from a zombie apocalypse film.

"There's something up ahead," Daisha said.

“Is it too much to ask for a nice, quiet ride into town?” Samir replied, pulling out a pair of Soviet-era binoculars from under his seat and handing them to Daisha. “Another roadblock?”

“Yeah, it’s a roadblock. Things just keep getting better. Oh, and they have a DShK… and a truck-mounted cannon. Possibly a recoilless rifle.”

“Probably an SPG-9; they’re as old as dirt,” Samir said. “Every crackpot has a few dozen in their arsenal.”

“They’re both real problems,” Kane said, still glancing over his shoulder.

The big Mercedes approached the queue of vehicles waiting to pass.

Kane looked at the vehicles. “Does everything out here have a layer of dust on it?”

“You're referring to the uniquely ubiquitous desert patina, common to anything that crosses the desert?” Samir replied.

“This won’t be easy,” Kane said. They coasted up to the bumper of the last vehicle in line. “Di, if we can get close enough to take those guns out, we’ll have a chance.”

"If you look at the far horizon, Dr. Kyle, beyond Rafah, you will see the darkening skies of a thunderstorm. If the thunderstorm collapses, as so many do, we will have a haboob."

Daisha agreed with Samir. "A sandstorm."

"That is a misnomer, Dr. Kyle; these storms are more dust than sand."

"Thank you, Professor Samir. Now let’s focus on the roadblock."

“I’ll take the DShK first; when I shoot, that will create a distraction, and you can take out the recoilless rifle. Cover me; I’ll cover you—and Di, use your silencer.”

"Let me try talking to them," Samir said.

Kane pointed to the front of the line, where two militiamen were pulling a vehicle apart while the occupants stood at gunpoint.

Daisha counted four militiamen manning the roadblock. The queue dwindled to five vehicles ahead of Samir's Mercedes, then four, and finally three.

Kane leaned in between the front seats. "We need to get clean shots to take out the big guns."

"If we wait until our car is first in line, they'll have a clear line of fire," said Daisha. "They'll cut us to ribbons."

"Roger that. We'll slip out of our vehicle and use the cars ahead of us as cover. We'll crawl forward until we reach optimal shooting angles. I'll go left, and Di, you go right."

Daisha nodded and then checked ahead before fearlessly slipping out the door.

Kane tapped Samir and said, "That's one tough woman." He slapped him on the shoulder. Samir opened his door to block the view of the militiamen while Kane slipped out his door and crouched under the Mercedes.

"This is a bloody bandbox," Samir muttered to himself. He watched the militiamen checking the vehicles ahead. First was a lorry carrying crates of chickens. Next was a short bus, empty of passengers, followed by a cargo van, a large Mercedes Metris filled with canned food.

Kane froze under the truck bed when he noticed one of the militiamen conducting a sweep on his side. He rolled further back under the lorry.

The ground began to shake beneath Daisha's body. She looked back and, from her position under the truck, saw her worst nightmare.

Samir exclaimed, "Oh shit," as he checked his rearview mirror.

"Oh no," Kane muttered to himself. "It's a fucking APC."

Samir watched closely as the twenty-ton BMP-3, one of the latest pieces of Russian-made armor, stopped about twenty meters behind his car.

"Standoff range, smart. I'm sure I could have negotiated them a better deal."

Samir turned back, his heart rate spiking even higher. One of the militiamen walking up the line toward Kane's position had stopped.

Samir jumped out of his car, raving and waving. The militiaman, who was standing just above Kane's position, pointed his weapon at Samir and ran toward him, yelling to get back in his car.

Kane was ready to take the man out from under the truck but held his position. He recognized Samir's plan. "You crazy son of a gun."

Kane continued forward as the dust began to kick up.

He crawled up the line, trying to close the gap between himself and the Dushka. He could see the legs of the militiaman walking toward the BMP-3.

The recoilless rifle—it's our only chance. He continued his crawl toward the heavy machine gun.

Kane reached the short van just as the entire line began to move forward. With a sudden jerk, the driveshaft of the old bus began to spin.

In a split second, Kane grabbed the frame of the four-ton bus and was pulled forward until it stopped, now forty feet closer to the two Hilux pick-ups.

The bus halted behind the van, which was at the head of the line, five meters from the heavy machine gun.

The other roving Hamas man had decided to inspect the van in front of Kane. He cracked open the double doors and climbed inside. He was halfway in when Kane decided to make his move.

Ten steps from this point, I can thread a shot between the armor plates. A four-inch-wide gap from fifty feet—good odds for a frogman..

Kane saw the man behind the Dushka grab his cellphone and start to dial. The man's gaze was momentarily away from the roadblock when Kane rolled out and sprinted directly at the barrel of the death-dealing Dushka. It was the longest ten yards he'd ever run. In slow motion, he felt every muscle in his legs fire and every footfall in his stride.

His silenced Beretta X92 was raised as he approached the shooting point. The machine gunner casually looked up.

The recognition was all over his face. He dropped his cellphone and reached for the butterfly trigger. It became a battle of the reflexes, a race to survival.

With his hands on the trigger, Kane fired two 9mm taps —one round struck the inch-thick steel plate armor in front of the gunner, while the other found its mark square in the forehead. The man dropped straight back onto the Hilux's deck.

Instinctively, Kane changed elevation, dropped, and turned, all the while. It was a move he practiced along with clearing his weapon almost every day during what he called his gun kata, and when a burst of AK fire tore up the technical's hood behind him, just an inch over his head, it had saved his life again.

Kane retrained his Beretta, but before he could pull the trigger, a silenced round struck the trigger man behind the SPG-9. Daisha stood uncovered, holding her pistol. She nodded to Kane, blowing the smoke from the barrel. The antitank gunner slumped over, dead.

A few seconds later, all hell broke loose as the eight-wheeled, heavily armed Russian-made armored vehicle opened fire with its autocannons, machine guns, and chain gun. The concussion from the fusillade rocked everything; the entire roadblock shook.

Hezbollah soldiers had smuggled the APC over the border and handed it off to the foreign fighters who were training with the militia, learning how to operate the complex war machine on the fly. This and several other up-armored vehicles had been disassembled, and the parts smuggled into Gaza from Syria.

The inexperienced crew managed to fire the AGS-30 grenade launcher, chaff, and the remote-operated pair of PKMT machine guns before they got to the BM-57, an autocannon that literally shredded the vehicles in front of them.

When the PKMT machine guns cycled through their ammunition, two of the men opened hatches and began flinging grenades while firing the two topside 7.62 mm PKT machine guns.

The roof of Samir's C-350 sedan was disintegrated by the chaingun, then the flatbed lorry, and the short bus, followed by the cargo van, all of them reduced to scrap by the fusillade.

The weapons had vaporized the 200 chickens along with their crates on top of the flatbed lorry. It created a cloud of blood and viscera that filled the air, and when the firing ceased momentarily, it revealed the delivery van shredded down to its deck plates, and the cases of cans that filled its hold were blown skyward along with the remains of the militiaman. The van was reduced to a burning pile of jagged steel, glass, and wires. It was a scene from hell. Human and animal remains mixed in the curtain of red, while cans of beans, chickpeas, and mangoes rained down in a surreal storm across the roadblock.

The blood spray mixed with tiny fragments of tissue, mingled with smoke from the burning vehicles and windblown sand, formed a gruesome slurry that covered everything.

The gang who couldn't shoot straight was underscored by their persistent misreading of the Cyrillic instrumentation. This resulted in erratic gunfire, with large-caliber ordnance fired in all directions. Tracers, rockets, and antiaircraft rounds ripped through the thick, acrid smoke that swirled around the hellish scene.

At the head of the demolished column, buried deep in the sand at the end of the line of destroyed vehicles, were Daisha Willows and Kyle Kane. They huddled together, shielded from the fusillade by the cast iron engine block of the older Metris cargo van. Though torn down to its frame, the van was spared from total destruction by its German engineering.

Wicked concussions from the heavy weapons kept their heads down. The sounds of the autocannon cycling without firing signaled that all the guns were out of ammunition. The barrage had ceased.

Kane understood that this was only temporary. "They're letting the barrels cool, and the operators are reloading."

He looked to see if the SPG-9 was still mounted on the Hilux.

“The recoilless rifle is still operational,” Kane said. “I’m going to blow that armor to hell!”

Daisha and Kane were on their knees behind the engine block. She glanced at the anti-tank gun and then at Kane, shaking her head vehemently.

“That’s crazy, Kyle. There are twenty yards of open ground between you and that gun, and it's all exposed.”

“I know—I don't have a better idea. I could use a diversion,” Kane replied. He smiled and handed Daisha his last clip. “It’s our only chance, Lady Di. Beyond this roadblock is open desert. They’d gun us down in a second.”

“Roger that, big dog,” she said. Holding her Beretta up, she dropped one clip and slapped in another. "It's time to rock 'n' roll, baby."

Kane grabbed an AK-47 off a dead militiaman and handed it to Daisha. She pulled the bolt, then dropped the clip. “It’s full.”

“Perfect. If I can reach that heavy machine gun, I’ll put a dozen rounds on their viewports; that’ll draw their attention to the DShK.”

Daisha grabbed Kane's arm, and their eyes met. He could see the fear in her soot-covered face. He pushed her auburn hair away from her face and smiled. He forced himself to go.

They both knew failure meant death. She pulled him back and hugged him. He pushed himself away. Another second, and he’d have stayed. He sat back on his haunches and took a deep breath.

Kane handed the AK-47 to Daisha. “We should take the silencers off the Berettas for effect,” he suggested.

“Didn’t you say silencers always stay on?”

“This is a hell of a time to start listening to me, warrior princess.”

Kane checked the APC, then looked at the distance to the antitank gun. The open space between the burning van and the Hilux had created a wavering, unpredictable smokescreen that was there and a second later it wasn't. The coming sandstorm was blowing the black smoke everywhere.

He looked to the heavens. "Lord, if you're ever gonna weigh in on the side of the underdogs, let it be now." Kane dove out six or seven feet and kept rolling. To his absolute amazement the heavy black smoke kept its position, and Kane made it to the other side without a shot being fired.

That just boosted the odds from totally impossible to highly unlikely.

He waited behind the Hilux's rear wheel, hoping that its iron engine block would protect him if the autocannon decided to vaporize the truck, but no fire came.

He looked across the no-man's land at Daisha. She smiled and gave him a thumbs-up.

Essentially, the DShK was a five-foot-long steel pipe with a big, boxy receiver at one end, seated atop a four-foot-tall mounting bracket.

It's in a perfect line of fire, fifty yards away. He slid onto the bed of the truck, hugging the diamond plate bed. He prayed they were too busy screwing things up to see him. When he raised up and peeked through the cab, he saw Samir's Mercedes at the back of the line, 25 meters ahead of the Armored Personnel Carrier. He saw Sami's Mercedes with only the car's steel headrest posts left standing above the sedan's body and the rest of it perforated like an old-school Kuder Preference Test; he was sure Sami was dead.

He focused on the APC 25 meters beyond the sedan. The Lexan viewports were dark, and Kane couldn't see a thing inside the APC. They could be zoned in on the Hilux, waiting for him to make his move. Then something happened: someone, in a total rookie move, opened one of the topside hatches during a gunfight. The interior of the cab was lit up, and Kane saw the crew was reloading the belt-fed heavy machine guns, while the other members of the crew were off gun searching the burning roadblock for targets, them.

Go time. Triggerman is off gun. Kane grabbed the top of the truck bed and positioned himself to reach. *This has to be at the top of the ten stupidest fucking things I've ever done.*

He swallowed hard. The APC turned its engines over. *They're gonna flank the roadblock and finish us with a missile.*

"Now or never!" He reached up and took hold of the twin handles of the Dushka. A million things fired at light speed through his mind as he pulled himself up using the gun as a counterweight, and to his amazement the barrel was perfectly aligned with the APC's forward viewports. Kane placed the dot on the glass and squeezed.

A huge fireball erupted from the barrel along with fifty rounds of brass-jacketed lead in a five-second burst that felt like an eternity. Powerful projectiles pounded the windows. They chipped and fractured the viewports. Inside the APC, panic reigned.

Kane fought the urge to keep squeezing, knowing the Russians built their armored machines to withstand 12.7 mm rounds.

Daisha leaned out from the opposite side of the Metris frame and drew fire with her AK-47. She shielded him with the single second of indecision created inside the APC. He dove out into no-man's-land as the high cyclic rate whine of the PKMT filled the air, and its 7.62 mm armor-piercing rounds ripped up everything around Di. When the 57mm auto cannons spun up, it locked on and shredded the Hilux. A hot second later the gas tank exploded. Shrapnel flew around the roadblock like a nest of angry hornets. The 57mm HE shells forced the pair down into the sand. The Kornet missile fired and ripped over the entire roadblock before it exploded 100 yards out and showered debris back over the roadblock.

Kane immediately pushed himself up. "You okay?"

Daisha nodded. "How did we not get hit by that explosion? Why haven't they driven into us and chewed us up?"

"Too close and too low; the shrapnel flew right over us. I think they're staying back because they don't know if we have an RPG."

"Which begs the question: "Is there an RPG lying around here, Kyle?"

“If it was reachable we would have seen it. We’ve poked them in the eye; now we finish the job!" he shouted, nodding toward the recoilless rifle. “One shot, one kill, agent.”

Daisha shook her head and said, “That’s desperate.”

Kane looked at the Hilux and its recoilless rifle before he turned to Daisha and nodded. “It’s our best shot. They’ve turned over the engines. Might be to charge the batteries, might not. Either way, there’s only desert around us.” He slid out into the wavering smoke screen on the opposite-side no-man’s-land.

Ten yards of direct line of fire—heavy armor—shitty old gun—ordinance that may not penetrate armor—what’s not to like? The only thing between me and disintegration is an unpredictable cloud of smoke. Please don't go.

He belly-crawled toward the anti-tank gun, so low that he was driving sand up with his nose. Halfway across, the wind from the coming sandstorm blew hard. The smoke hung for a moment, as if the gods were buying Kane time, but before he could make use of that fortuitous moment, the hand of Set descended upon the roadblock and whisked the smoke away, and with it Kane’s cover.

I’m too far out to turn around and not close enough to dive. If I move either way, the auto-targeting system will lock onto me and have my ass. He prayed the crew was struggling with the controls. *If these guys had even a week with a Stryker Brigade, we’d be toast. God help us if they figure out how to override their targeting system!*

Kane wanted to look back at Daisha, but he knew the specter of death would be lurking. A second later, his warrior princess switched sides, rose up, and started laying rounds downrange.

“Bloody hell,” shouted Kane as the automatic weapon system locked onto Daisha and fired. He exploded off the ground and never raised more than a foot off the sand before he dove behind the Hilux. He rolled onto his back and looked back to Daisha. *Please be alive!* The smoke parted, and he saw the Latin queen with her AK pushed out around the corner of the Metris frame. She was firing gangster style right up until the PKT rounds struck her hand and took off the tip of her trigger finger. She let out a yell and fell back.

Kane got to a crouch behind the Hilux.

Daisha glanced over at Kane with wild eyes. He was hiding behind the engine block of the Hilux, grateful to put as much steel as possible between himself and the big guns of the APC. He moved to the back of the truck and slid onto the truck bed.

As soon as they see me, they'll blow this whole rig to hell. Again, another insane dumbass move.

Daisha had half a clip left, fifteen shots to draw their fire. She tore off a strip of her shirt. The finger was a bloody mess when she wrapped her finger as tightly as she could. She knew Kane's life hung in the balance, and she knew exactly what she needed to do.

She rose up with the AK pointed downrange. Kane reached up and spun the recoilless rifle toward the armored personnel carrier as Daisha started firing into the armored weapon platform with its half dozen heavy weapons trained on their position.

Daisha's hand trembled as she tried to hold her weapon on target. She pulled the trigger with her middle finger, and the heavy assault rifle bounced. The pain shot through her entire arm, but she managed to put those rounds onto the APC, even though they ricocheted off the armor. Inside, the gun crew turned the autocannon on her, and deadly shells as thick as her arm flew over, around, and next to her head, any one of which would have disintegrated her, before they streaked out into the desert and exploded.

Kane had a brief moment before the APC turned Daisha into vapor.

"God, I hope this gun's loaded," he said, jumping behind it. He could see the movement behind the cracked viewports when they spotted him.

They tried to retrain the full weapons package on the SPG-9 before Kane fired the 1960s-era anti-tank gun.

"Please, Lord, let this be armor-piercing," he said when he pulled the trigger. He watched as the 73mm rocket lethargically jumped out of the tube like a wounded duck. It puttered and dropped a few inches as it struggled to gain altitude. “Go, you son of a bitch!” he shouted.

The main propellant ignited just as Kane dove backwards off the truck. He hit the sand and rolled to the side, out of the enfilade fire that came a second later from the APC. The rocket and the SMG-3’s fire passed each other in flight. The 73mm rocket found its mark, striking six inches below one of the viewports. The thick steel armor plating was up against a miracle of modern warfare, the Monroe Effect—which was a high explosive warhead that superheated its copper core into a jet of liquid molten copper that could defeat virtually any steel armor with mythic ease.

The older, up-weaponed, armored personnel carrier rocked violently as its internal fuel tanks ignited. Nothing could stop the molten copper.

Kane had bolted across no-man’s-land and ran into Daisha before they fell to the sand and all hell exploded around them.

Daisha tried to get up after the first round of explosions, but Kane pulled her back down. “Secondary explosions!” While he covered her. More ordnance exploded, rocking the ground around them. The APC’s last moments were a bizarrely brilliant blast of color that lit up the sandstorm.

Kane held Daisha for ten minutes before they got to their knees. Covered by a blanket of sand and debris, they looked at each other and laughed until the next round exploded, and then they ducked down.

They dusted each other off, and Daisha said, “Samir! Could he still be alive?”

Daisha ran to the end of the line. The APC was an unrecognizable pyre, a burning pile of ragged steel on flaming melted tires. Kane stopped at the other burned-out vehicles, surveying what remained of their dead occupants—all killed by men who had no concern for anyone's life, not even their own.

Kane poked through the wreckage with the nose of an AK 47 he pulled off a dead militia man. He searched as best he could the smoldering wreckage.

He shouldered his assault rifle and pulled out his Beretta.

The voice of a survivor came from the column of wrecked vehicles. It competed with the noise of destruction that was all around them.

"Cover the road." said Daisha, and she began looking around. She stood directly over the trunk of what was once Samir's Mercedes.

"Can you give a bloke a hand?" The words came out of nowhere. Daisha tried to locate the source, then turned to Kane. "Kyle, give us a hand?"

Kane kicked the trunk latch several times.

"Hey cowboy, take it easy; it's a classic."

The trunk lid popped open, revealing Samir behind the body of a militiaman, covered in blood and soot. In front of the angry Egyptian lay the body of another militiaman, still clutching the AK-47 scope Samir had offered him.

Samir climbed over the man. "Poor bastard shouldn't have taken the window seat."

Daisha and Kane exchanged glances and laughed. "How the hell did you two end up in there?" Kane asked.

"This guy was standing right next to you when you were under the lorry, so I waved him over. I was trying to distract him with the free scope when that APC rolled up. A few seconds later, I saw its autocannon train its barrel on us. I jumped into the open trunk, and all hell broke loose! I got the better seat."

"Contact!" said Kane. He was looking out past the burning hull into the desert. "We've got inbound. Two, possibly three, vehicles, probably technicals with more militia, maybe two klicks out."

"Let's go," said Di.

Kane nodded anxiously. "Yeah, it's gonna get real crowded around here, real quick."

Samir's first step almost ended in a faceplant; Daisha and Kane grabbed hold and pulled him along.

"Grab my duffle from the trunk," said Samir. Di grabbed it. "And the gold from the back seat—please, if it's still there." The two helped Samir back to the only vehicle left standing: the Hilux technical with its patina of bullet holes and the aged SPG-9 recoilless rifle.

Daisha looked at Kane and nodded. She let go of Samir and searched the dead militiamen. She pulled out a set of keys and fired up the truck. Kane pushed Samir into the middle, then piled in.

Di hit the gas, and the truck fishtailed back and forth. They sped down the sandy, dust-covered road to Rafah.

The militia pulled in right after them, and one of the approaching Hilux technicals broke ranks, veering off into the desert around the roadblock. They followed Daisha, Samir, and Kane as they sped away half a klick down the road.

"They've got another damn Dushka!" shouted Di. "Gotta be at least six of them in that truck."

The small pickup in pursuit was overloaded and out of balance, and it swerved all over the road. Like a scene from the original 'Rat Patrol,' the Dushka gunner was hanging on by the machine gun's handles. He managed to fire off a few rounds before the truck spun out into a roadside ditch.

Daisha shouted, "Thank God that idiot doesn't know what he's doing. If he'd just slowed down, his gunner could've run a line of 12.7 right up our ass!"

With only a hundred meters left before they entered the town, the gunner managed to unleash a burst of fifty rounds, which snapped and popped as they zoomed past the Hilux.

Samir jerked his head around. "Just one of those rounds hits us, and we'll be burnt falafel!" he shouted. A second later a round burst the back window of the cab.

"I'm trying to concentrate, Mr. Criticism," said Daisha as she calmly tried to see through the shot-up windshield. "Guess they're back on the road!"

"Ease up, Di; if we go off this road, they'll erase us just for kicks," said Kane.

"Is everybody a damn critic?" she snapped. She tried to use her rearview with its naked woman air freshener swinging back and forth.

"How very religious."

The city of Rafah came at them rapidly, reminiscent of postwar Berlin. Blocks of burned-out buildings stood alongside brand-new fast-food joints, while art deco apartment complexes bustled with children playing out front, all surrounded by mountains of rubble. Everything was just a 155mm artillery shell away from becoming its own pile of debris.

Daisha flew into town, constantly checking her rearview mirror. At the first cross street, she yanked the wheel hard, sending the truck into a screeching left turn. Two hundred meters down the block, she made another sharp left, causing the anti-tank gun to swing around like a top.

"We may have lost them; it's an abandoned part of Rafah!" Samir exclaimed.

"Premature," Daisha replied. "This is Gaza, and they are Hamas. They have eyes and ears, spotters and snitches everywhere."

Before Daisha could respond, an RPG-7 fired from across the intersection flew over their hood and obliterated an unattended street vendor's cart on the other corner. The explosion sent mystery meat kebabs out in all directions.

Samir jumped out and ran down to the corner to check the wreckage. "Oh shit, that looks like my friend Dinesh's cart!" he shouted.

"Get back to the truck, and take cover!" Kane yelled. He turned to Daisha. "Don't those vendor carts all look alike?"

"Not to him."

"He still owes me 3200 shekels for that cart!" Samir protested until gunfire strafed up and down the block and sent him back to the cover of the truck. It took out what was left of the shattered windshield and blew off the passenger-side mirror.

"Steam, I see steam, Sami," Daisha said. "We lost the radiator."

"Are you crazy? That's the least of our worries; we're in a box canyon, a dead end!" Samir shouted.

Kane shook his head. "Don't tell me he's a fan of westerns." He pulled a 73mm rocket from the truck bed and loaded it into the SPG-9. Bullets struck the truck and the concrete facade behind them, but Kane stayed focused, located the building, floor, and window before he fired another rocket. The explosion blew out the walls, and the entire three-story structure, already badly weakened, came down on whoever was shooting, ending the discussion.

"Spin the truck around, Di," said Kane. "We can use it."

Daisha reversed and k-turned the truck around. The battered but mostly intact Hilux now faced back toward the intersection.

"Stop there, Di," Kane said. "I've got a plan."

Kane picked up a piece of concrete and asked for Samir's belt. Samir obliged and handed it over. "What's wrong with yours, Kane?"

"I gave it to you, along with twenty grand worth of gold, remember?"

Kane removed the SPG-9 from its mount. "Inside that box are some rounds; grab them."

"I'll watch for militia," Daisha said, bolting to the corner to take cover inside a blown-out storefront.

Kane leaned the gun against an abandoned building. He placed two anti-tank rounds on the floor of the driver's side. Samir watched as Kane secured the wheel and positioned a concrete block on the accelerator. The Hilux revved while Kane gently wedged the anti-tank rounds between the concrete block and the bottom of the front seat.

"Wait," Samir cautioned.

Daisha was running back from the corner, shouting, "They're coming; they are one block out!"

Samir rushed to the passenger door and retrieved the canvas duffle he had asked Di to bring. He pulled out two H&K MP5s and magazines.

Kane looked at Samir in surprise. "We could have used those back at that Hamas roadblock, man."

"Sorry, Kane, you didn't pay for those; someone else did."

Kane shifted the Toyota Hilux into drive and jumped back. Samir watched as the vehicle slowly ambled toward the intersection.

Kane called out, “Sami, help me with the gun; we gotta take these assholes down.”

Samir turned and followed Kane to the gun. Kane propped the SPG up on a concrete barrier and aimed it downrange at the intersection.

“Load me, Sami!” Kane shouted.

Sami picked up one of the cardboard tubes that held the 73mm rockets. He took a step and nearly dropped the rocket out of the front end.

“Holy shit, Sami!” Di exclaimed, reaching out to catch the rocket just an inch above the concrete. “Get control of yourself, man. If you drop that, we’ll all be wearing molten copper wings.”

“Now, Di!” shouted Kane.

Daisha jumped over to Kane, slid the rocket into the gun, and slammed the breach closed. She tapped Kane on the head. The first vehicle, filled with Hamas, pulled into the intersection and stopped.

The Dushka gunner opened fire on the empty Hilux, ambling toward them. He shot up the cab and managed to blow out the right side front tire. The wounded Hilux limped towards them. Kane fired the SPG-9 and watched as the rocket’s low-pressure exit from the barrel was followed by its wounded duck imitation before its rocket fuel ignited. The timing wasn’t perfect, but like horseshoes and hand grenades, the rocket struck the rear of the empty Hilux with a resounding bah-boom. A chaotic domino effect ensued. When the 73mm rocket hit the Hilux, it collapsed the molten core with such heat that it sliced the gas tank open, causing an explosion. Gas splashed onto the other Hilux as it cartwheeled through the air. The entire mess landed in a giant fireball and turned the intersection and both Hilux technicals into a bonfire. The pressure wave blew Kane into Samir, into Daisha. Shrapnel followed the pressure wave and shattered the last remaining windows within a square block of the intersection.

“I hope they took pictures—for the insurance,” said Samir, trying to push Kane off him. He pulled Daisha up along with himself.

Standing together, they watched the massive bonfire in the intersection. "Sometimes a plan just comes together," Sami remarked.

“You’re preaching to the choir. I can’t believe it worked. Now, gather up your stuff, and let’s get across the intersection and into an alley,” Kane instructed. The three jogged past the inferno, amazed by the amount of heat it was putting off. They started to run when Dushka rounds began to cook off. It was not odd to see people run through the streets of Rafah, especially when explosions and gunfire echoed across the city. They ran for five minutes before Samir stopped. He fumbled with his crushed pack of Camels. He had managed to save a dozen halfies.

He lit up and began a search of a wall. He was looking for the loose plank that he knew was there as a part of a sophisticated storefront that served as topside cover for the tunnel systems twenty, thirty, or even fifty feet below the surface. There were hundreds and hundreds of bombed-out, boarded-up storefronts, which provided the perfect cover for the tunnel systems of Hamas that ran throughout Gaza.

“Come on, follow me.”

Inside was a bakery showroom, its back wall blown out into the kitchen. The former bake shop had taken a large-caliber shell dead center, and blew the glass cases and a concrete wall back into its kitchen. Ovens, cooling tables, and the walk-in were in a mangled pile.

Kane stopped Samir in front of the wrecked ovens. “Let’s grab one of those H&Ks, Sami.” Samir narrowed his eyes at Kane. “What, you have your Beretta?” he retorted.

“Come on, Samir, we’re in enemy territory; we need firepower.”

Samir shrugged, then nodded reluctantly. He handed one of the submachine guns to Daisha along with a bag of clips.

“She’ll respect my property,” Samir said. Daisha took the weapon and stuck her tongue out at Kane. When Samir turned his back, she handed it to him.

Samir looked at her, hurt.

“What, Sami? He’s the universal soldier; I’m just a spy.”

"7000 shekels, my friend. Be cautious; I can get only 3000 for a used model."

Chapter 24

Rafah City, Gaza. 14:00

Samir led the way through the bake shop and into the adjoining space, which was crisscrossed with fallen beams and slabs of hanging concrete.

"Whoa, Sami, this place looks like it's going to come down on our heads."

Samir ducked under a couple of beams and made his way to a door on the opposite side.

"The tunnel crews work under the cover of night to stabilize buildings. Not many IDF soldiers would think to do a walkthrough in a place like this."

Kane and Daisha examined the dilapidated door beneath a crumbling concrete lintel, where plaster and cement dust covered everything; even the floor looked undisturbed.

Daisha stopped Samir with a question. "What's our cover story for wanting to leave through a tunnel?"

Sami thought for a second. "I'm helping you pick up vaccines in Cairo."

"Are you sure this is the place, Sami?"

"Yes, Dr. Lewis, this is the place. These people are master set builders—good enough for Bollywood, I think."

"You mean Hollywood?"

"What's that?"

"Never mind, lead on, Samwise Gamgee," said Kane.

"There are some booby traps, I think, so follow me closely."

The three continued to the back wall of the building, where Samir ran a hand along the flat surface. He felt a slight depression and pushed in. A thousand-pound concrete wall moved, pivoting open like a five-ton vault door.

"Be mindful of our hosts," said Samir as he stepped down into the darkness. Each of them carefully followed. Step by step, they descended into the cold and dark until they reached the bottom, a large space cut deep into the bedrock.

"Cold for Gaza, especially this time of year?" asked Kane.

Samir smiled at Kyle. "We're going deep into the ground. It keeps the scorpions out. Please, do not move when the lights come on, and for God's sake, stay quiet."

Khamundi's timely request came seconds before the three were blinded by a bank of bright halogen lights.

"Put down your bags and step forward two steps," said a voice in Hebrew.

Kane whispered to Samir, "How do you know these people?"

Samir kept smiling and whispered back, "If I told you, you wouldn't be here. Now shut the fuck up."

Another massive concrete wall, pinioned in the middle and spun open. On the opposite side stood three Egyptian men in khaki jumpsuits holding short-barreled AK-74s.

"I sold them their weapons," said Samir, not so much to brag as to remind his trigger-happy guests who he was, "real Russian 74s."

Two of the men flanked the team, while the boss, a big man who resembled the second coming of Zorba the Great—with woolly eyebrows, a massive silver mustache, and a great bald head—stood in front of them.

"Samir, you old gazma!" shouted Al Noori.

"Abed, you old son of a goat."

"Why are you here in my humble tunnel, my brother?"

Sami turned to Kane and Daisha. "This is Abed Al Noori, the owner and operator of this

fine transportation hub—along with his not-so-silent partner, Hamas."

Kane and Daisha nodded as Sami introduced them. "These two are aid workers. They are traveling with me to Cairo to pick up a shipment of black market vaccines. It's for the camps."

Abed listened carefully. "So you're going with them through the tunnels?"

"No, I'm going to drive my taxi across the border and pick them up on the other side. They need transportation but don't want to risk the IDF confiscating the vaccines at the border."

Abed hugged his old friend from their Palestinian Authority days, a fact Samir hoped would stay quiet. Al Noori reached out to shake Kane's hand. "That makes sense. Their passport and work visa stamps must be perfect, with no unexplained trips." Abed looked at the pretty woman in the red and white keffiyeh. He considered shaking Daisha's hand but knew there were fundamentalists among his crew.

Kane moved to grab the duffle bag, but Abed beat him to it. He took hold of it and ushered Kane and Daisha down to the lower level of the tunnel, calling for the railcar from the other end of the line.

Abed shook hands with Samir, and the two parted ways. Kane and Abed walked down a set of switchback stairs, fifty feet into the ground. The lack of discussion created a tense atmosphere.

The engineering was impressive. The stairs led into a large central room carved into the bedrock. Parts of the area were reinforced with heavy lumber and concrete blocks, while other areas were just bare rock, all excavated with picks and shovels. The IDF conducted scans with ground-penetrating radar and had laid motion and sound sensors in the area along the border. There was no opportunity to use heavy equipment to dig or work on the tunnel. The IDF even went so far as to flood the area and fill the tunnels with seawater.

A small group of workers stood waiting for the small electric-powered train to return with the second half of the Cairo shipment. The crates and boxes stacked along the bottom level platform were black market goods ready to be counted and sold at a ridiculous markup to the poorest people in the world.

Emerging from the dark maw of the tunnel was a set of small-gauge rails. Two men paused in their tasks and stood at the railhead as a line of small flatbed cars, stacked high with smuggled goods, was backed down the rails toward the platform.

To avoid detection by ground sensors, everything was kept quiet. The men wore headlamps as they unloaded cases of contraband American cigarettes, boxes of infant diapers, and dozens of cases of French and Spanish wine.

Samir motioned for Kane and Daisha to climb aboard one of the small flatcars before he negotiated with Abed for their fare—along with a carton of Camel cigarettes, ironically made with fine Egyptian tobaccos. He pulled down a couple of folding bench seats in the last car of a ten-car line. Abed called out for the driver to prepare to take the two passengers to the other side.

The driver swung out of the lead car, an aging electric engine. He was missing an arm below the elbow and walked with an angry gait toward his boss, Abed.

"What the hell is your problem, Abed? I'm finished for the day!"

"Get your ass back on that train and take these two to the other side!" Abed snapped, turning to one of his henchmen. "Lazy Pakistani thinks he's back in the Taliban commanding men."

Kane's ears perked up. Without turning to Daisha, he whispered, "Taliban—did I hear that right?"

The man passed Kane, and their eyes met for a long second. Kane refused to look away, knowing that would be an admission of guilt. Of what—it didn't matter. He fought the urge to swallow hard, his racing heart quickening.

"Don't look now, but that one-armed man is or was a Taliban," Kane said. "I think he knows me."

"What?"

"Running into someone I messed up on the job has never happened. At least, I don't think so."

"I'm going to neutralize the threat."

"I'm coming with you, Kane."

"It'll look too obvious. Can you cover me from here?" Kane replied.

"Roger that, Kyle. Don't die, please," Di said, taking his arm. Their eyes met before Kane slid out of the open railcar and made his way toward the arguing men.

The one-armed man had his back to Kane as he approached the four.

"When do you think we can get this thing rolling?" Kane asked, trying to sound casual. "We're on a pretty tight schedule, and—"

His instincts screamed that he was going to have to fight. The one-armed man turned, and Kane saw the hatred in his eyes—eyes he would never forget.

"I prayed for this day to come, soldier." His words were slow and filled with venom. "I've envisioned torturing you a thousand times before."

Kane raised the MP5, ready to fire, when he heard a sound behind him. He turned to see a fifth man, one he hadn't accounted for, standing over the still-seated Daisha, a Colt 1911 pointed at her head.

A second later, one of Abed's men grabbed Kane's MP5.

"I will have to discuss Samir's choice of friends," Abed said. "In Gaza, betrayal is a one-way ticket."

"He had no idea," Kane replied.

The one-armed man, Faheem Mohamed Salima, struck Kane with the butt of his century-old Enfield MKII revolver. Heavy and still carrying the steel ring on the bottom of its handle, it knocked Kane to the ground.

The narrow-gauge railcars slowed to a stop at the end of the tunnel. Kane's head rested in Daisha's lap, and Abed sat across from them, his nickel-plated East German Makarov 380 pistol pointed at them.

Abed smiled at Daisha, revealing a half dozen glittering gold teeth. "It's strange how one meets his destiny and the road he takes to avoid it," he said.

The train stopped with a jolt, and Faheem jumped out, hurrying back to his prisoners. He aimed one of Samir's MP5s at Kane.

"Now we will kill you with your own weapons. Fitting, isn't it?" Faheem said.

Abed frowned. "Not in my tunnel, Faheem. If you must, I caution you: there is a fortune to be made by ransoming these two. But if you insist, take them out onto the sands and do as you will; it is your right."

"Get up, American capitalist pig; meet the fate Allah has ordained for you."

"Let the girl go. She has nothing to do with me or anything I've done."

Faheem raised the butt of the MP5, attempting to strike him again. Kane lunged at him, only to be halted by the barrel of the submachine gun.

"Go ahead, Navy SEAL; meet your god in this hole in the ground."

"No, Faheem!" shouted Abed. "This is my tunnel, and you work for me. I have decided that we will ransom the SEAL. You may shoot the woman to quench your bloodlust. The Americans would pay a tidy sum to get him—"

Before Abed could finish, Faheem turned the MP5 on his boss and shot him in the mouth. He fired again, killing one of his men who reached for a weapon. The other two raised their hands in surrender.

"We will kill them both on the sands of our people," Faheem declared, motioning for the other two to drive the train. He sat across from the Americans.

The bright sun blinded Kane and Daisha as they emerged from the tunnel, but the seasoned smugglers had donned their sunglasses.

As Kane's eyes adjusted, he noticed a line of razor wire strung across the top of the IDF concrete barrier. A tall sand dune stood between the tunnel entrance and the barrier. The two men pushed Kane and Daisha against the steep dune.

"I never thought I'd die like this," Daisha said.

"We're not dead yet, Lady Di," Kane replied.

Faheem stopped thirty feet away and called out, "Do you have any last words?"

"Yes," Daisha said, surprising Kane. "I would like a blindfold."

Faheem threw up his arm in disgust. "She wants a blindfold," he said to one of the men. When neither of them moved, he yelled, "Get her a damn blindfold!"

One of the men tore a strip from his Kaffiyeh and hurried to Daisha's side. He started to put it on her, but she took it from him and shook it out as he walked back.

"Any other delaying tactics?" Kane whispered with a forced smile.

She leaned in closer to Kane. "How about a cigarette?"

He nodded and shouted, "How about a cigarette?"

"No!" Faheem shouted. "You die now!"

The two men raised their assault rifles, waiting for the one-armed Faheem to give the order.

Kane raised his hands. "Wait, wait, I want to call my wife before I die. I have this new iPhone 15 and—" He pushed the SIM card all the way in as he pulled the phone from his pocket.

Faheem paused the execution and ran the sixty feet to Kane's side. He tucked his bulky Webley Mk VI pistol into his belt and grabbed Kane's phone. Dashing back to his firing squad, he noticed the phone ringing. Faheem glanced at the screen, then walked back toward Di and Kane.

"It's Washington, DC!" Kane shouted.

Gleefully, Faheem exclaimed, "It's America!" He swiped to answer and held the phone up. "I will show your death live to the infidel world."

Kane turned to Daisha and yelled, "Get down!"

Confused, she asked Kyle, "Now?"

"Yes!" shouted Kane as he pulled her down. He landed on top of her at the same moment a Hellfire rocket dropped out of the sun at Mach 1.3. Faheem made recognition at fifty feet away, and he didn't have enough time to stop the grinning before it detonated six inches from his face.

The blast vaporized the grinning Faheem and sent a pressure wave radiating outward. It was a huge fireball that enveloped the former Taliban commander in flames so hot, it evaporated every molecule of his body. The AGM-114's shrapnel blew out followed by a wall of sand from the blast crater that covered everyone and everything.

The two tunnel workers that were far enough away to survive got the same treatment. They came too under almost a foot of sand, and when they climbed out of their holes with their beards, hair, and clothing scorched and still smoking, they screamed and ran in terror, convinced that some supernatural phenomenon—Abed's Jinn—had come for them.

"It's Abed! We betrayed him, and he comes for us in in the form of a jinn! He vanished, Faheem! Abed's a Jinnnnnnnnn!" shouted the men in. "The Americans are Jinn! Runnnn!"

"He is of flame and air, capable of assuming human or animal form," said the other man as he sprinted away.

"The ground continues to shake. They dwell in the stones, sand, and ruins—underneath the earth.

Jinn delight in punishing humans!"

"Let's get the hell out of here."

"What the hell is going on!" shouted Daisha as she pushed herself up. "Get off me—you're crushing me, you oaf!"

Kane got to his feet as sheets of sand fell off him and Daisha. "The sand dunes are collapsing all around us!" Kane shouted. "The tunnels are collapsing!"

Faheem's men froze in their tracks. The sight of a fierce, steel-toothed snout attached to an iron giant that surged up and over the dune. It drove them into what was left of the collapsing tunnel entrance. It was 80 tons of Merkava battle tank that shook everything for 100 meters, and it was barreling straight down on top of them.

"That was a freakin' miracle!" shouted Daisha as she brushed the sand out of her ears. "A Hellfire dropping on top of our enemies."

"It was your phone. When I pushed in the SIM card, it dialed the same DC number that tried to peg us down out in the desert. They probably had an MQ-9 drone in high loiter over the area. I'm sure the drone was programmed to go weapons hot the instant your phone joined the network."

The tank stopped at the bottom of the dune.

When the main hatch popped open, the pair expected to see an IDF soldier poke their head out, but instead, it was Samir Khamundi wearing a tanker's helmet. He climbed out, grabbing hold of the machine gun barrel.

"Oh my God," said Daisha. "How many lives do you have?"

"Wrong deity, Daisha. It's Allah, and Mohamed is his messenger!'" shouted Samir from the turret of the Merkava, wearing a broad, toothy grin as he slid off the futuristic-looking battle tank. Major Mordecai Ben Davidson of the IDF followed Samir.

The two surveyed the puddle that was Faheem.

"Firstly, I never trusted Abed; I wager he tried to ransom you."

"He did," Daisha replied, "until the pile of goo over there shot him in the face."

"I suppose the Hellfire missile detonation gave you our location," said Kane.

"It certainly did," Major Ben Davidson confirmed.

Samir turned to the Israeli officer. "My apologies, Major; this is the SEAL I mentioned."

The Major extended his hand. "As I understand it, you will need a ride to Tel Aviv."

Chapter 25

Tel Aviv, Israel. 16:00

Kane and Daisha looked down on Gaza as the UH-60 Yanshuf helicopter, a Blackhawk variant, ascended to 10,000 feet for the sixty-five-mile flight from the Philadelphi Corridor, the narrow strip of land between Gaza and Egypt, to Tel Aviv.

Kane had left Major Faheem's Enfield as a memento. "Even at 10,000 feet, I can see the gross disparity between the desperately poor majority of Gaza and Hamas' wealthy minority."

"How do they get away with it?" Daisha asked. "The people of Gaza could easily overrun their Hamas oppressors."

"Few people, regardless of how desperate, would be willing to charge into the line of fire of a heavy machine gun," said Kane as he looked out over the med.

The helicopter reached its maximum altitude and began its descent into the mini-metropolis of Tel Aviv. The pilot landed on the rooftop helipad marked with an X. They were met, patted down, and then escorted by a phalanx of armed soldiers.

Kane was led to an interview room directly opposite the office of Ygal Moskowitz, the director of Mossad's Counter Intelligence Bureau. Daisha was taken to another room on the same floor. Both carried incredibly important information and waited to be interviewed.

Unbeknownst to Daisha and Kane, they were being observed by Mossad's expert psychological profilers, capable of identifying any signs of subterfuge or dishonesty.

These experts were far more accurate than the best lie detector professionals. The interviewers took notes until, before long, Ygal Moskowitz—a short, round man who would barely stand out in a room by himself—introduced himself to Daisha. He didn't seem like the handshake type, so Daisha didn't bother.

The eyes behind Moskowitz's old-school tortoise frames were lifeless. It was a gaze that told Daisha Ygal had been in the Middle East spy game for too long. Too many lies, too many lives taken, people murdered, sent on missions he knew they would never return from. The eyes of a man who understood that peace and absolution, regardless of the state of the world, would forever elude him. It was a dangerous flaw.

Daisha described, in terms a fellow spook could understand, what had happened since the meeting at Tavern on the Green.

Kane, sequestered in another room, was asked virtually the same questions. A half hour and two cups of coffee later, he was brought into Moskowitz's office, where Daisha had been sitting quietly by herself. The Mossad director slipped into the room and exchanged banal greetings before taking his seat. He immediately excused himself after an assistant handed him a note.

Daisha and Kane were alone. "What do you think?" Kane asked.

"I can only hope they believe us," she replied, leaning into Kane. "You know they're listening to us?"

Kane laughed. "That's pretty much a given with you people."

"That is true, Mr. Kane, and yes, we are recording you," said a deep baritone voice from behind them. Kane turned to see a shorter, stocky man whose thick build filled much of the bottom half of the doorframe.

"Prime Minister Benjamin Netanyahu."

“Bibi, to my friends."

Kane's surprise was evident. Momentarily speechless, he jumped out of his chair and crossed the office. Two bodyguards blocked his way until Bibi nodded. They shook hands, and the legendary Likud leader was a match for

Kane's dominant presence despite their obvious height difference.

A political bull, Bibi the Bull… He'd probably win a death cage match with Idi Amin.

The prime minister escorted Kane to his seat, then bowed in front of Daisha and shook her hand.

"We've prepared for an attack," Netanyahu said, "as you can well imagine, but this was far more audacious than I expected. This is beyond the planning capabilities of Hamas or Hezbollah."

"There's a reason for that, sir," Kane replied. "This plan came from the US."

Daisha leaned forward and placed her hand on Kane's arm. "This is my area of expertise, Lieutenant Commander."

Kane nodded. "She possesses a tremendous amount of knowledge from a wealth of information, and the trick she learned was to separate the musings of the lifetime paper pushers and wannabe door kickers from the purposeful disinformation leaked by the scheming deep state—case officers and operatives who had seen too much and were always plotting from inside a universe of one, which birthed incredible tales of the unlikely.

BiBi raised his hand. "Daisha can sift through the noise to find the gold; that's her gift?"

Kane started to say something when Di jumped in, 'It is, Mr. Prime Minister, and the agency, in concert with members of the Senate, Congress, the judiciary, and the military—the globalist uniparty, and in this case, the entire executive branch—is working tirelessly to gain control over Western democracies through open borders and voter fraud, a CCP specialty. The deep state are the foot soldiers of the uniparty. They have their generational anchors sunk so deeply into the fabric of the federal government's culture that no controversy or group of controversies could drag them into the light. A significant portion of the annual budget was siphoned off using bogus congressional bills paying billions to bogus NGOs. Now the Chinese blackmail politicians, agency bureaucrats, and the deep state using stolen taxpayer money defrauded through the State Department or the BS congressional spending."

Bibi's expression turned thoughtful. Before he could ask Daisha a question, she said, "It is this axis of evil behind this attack on your people, and worse, they've devised an endgame, firing on their own people with captured or black market IDF weapons so they can overwhelm your government with international outrage. Mr. Prime Minister, the mainstream propaganda outlets will paint you as an international war criminal and call for your arrest."

Daisha could see she had shocked one of the most well-informed people on the planet. "I knew Biden was a coward," Bibi said. "I didn't know he was so treacherous."

"This plan is Iranian, to be implemented by their Hamas proxies, but all of it has come from the CCP's MSS playbook."

"Their attacks have mostly involved rockets used to draw us in or divert our attention from other areas. I was quite surprised by the Russian APC roaming Gaza, and even more amazed you two managed to defeat it."

"The APC probably came from the black market, provided by a man like Al Mazari, a former CIA asset, and possibly still is, at least up until earlier today of that piece of armor. If it hadn't been for the inexperienced crew, we would have been food for the scarabs," Daisha replied.

"Our field commanders will be shocked by that bit of intel," Bibi said. "We moved a Stryker Brigade into forward tactical positions. Our armored divisions, staged in strategic locations, are ready to move as necessary to the conflict zones, all reinforced by attack helicopters and fixed-wing elements if needed," he continued. "The border incursions outside of Gaza and the border with Lebanon are a diversion. I spoke with my J-GID contact, and Jordan is clean. Gaza and the Bekaa Valley—that's ground zero."

"Any shots fired?" Kane inquired.

"As a matter of fact, we caught a brigade of Hezbollah regulars coming across the border through several of their tunnels we identified several weeks ago. We struck their command and control center with a series of cruise missiles.

We will eliminate the threats," he glanced at his watch, "very soon."

"Tunnels?" asked Kane. "How extensive are they, and who built them?"

BiBi raised his eyebrows. “In Gaza, tunnels are extensive. The concept of tunnels in warfare is throughout history, almost always in siege warfare or in one-off covert use. China is the first to use tunnels in war as a major tactical and strategic element. The CCP brought their tunnel warfare technology to the Korean War, the Vietnam War, Iran, Lebanon, Yemen, Gaza, and their chemical warfare proxies on the US southern border. It began as a distinct component of the Chinese communist ‘s PLA in the 1930s war to resist the Japanese before and during World War Two.”

“Not surprising, Mr. Prime Minister," Daisha said. "There are bureaucrats and politicians at work in the U.S. government that are actively, seditiously, working to undermine all democracies worldwide.” She looked at Kyle. “I know I sound like a broken record, but most people don’t know; they don’t realize the country that builds your cheap stuff is also actively murdering children and adults in a multitude of ways on their run up to World War Three.”

The prime minister looked at Daisha, then Kane. "We've known about it for a long time."

She nodded. "As you know, the avenues of power are no longer clear and unambiguous. There's no telling who has been bought and who hasn't."

Netanyahu walked around the office and stopped behind the desk. He sat in Moskowitz's seat and said, "I made the decision not to reveal you as our source regarding the invasion."

"So it's up to us to get the story out?" Daisha asked.

"Someone has to do it, and who better than a decorated Navy SEAL and a CIA case officer with a clean record?" said Netanyahu. “But be aware, they will tear your life apart and stomp around inside it until it’s unrecognizable.”

"So you did some checking?"

"We have the Mossad; I'm sure you've heard of them."

"We have. I believe we ran into a couple of them at a certain hotel in midtown Manhattan."

Netanyahu's reaction indicated he had not. When his gaze shifted to the office door, Daisha understood Moskowitz had returned, and the entire mood of the room changed.

Netanyahu looked at Moskowitz and said, "I cannot admit nor deny the involvement of the Mossad."

Daisha shook her head and smiled. "Ghislaine Maxwell, the madame and Epstein's Mossad handler—her work is stored around here somewhere, isn't it?"

Netanyahu started to laugh, while Moskowitz looked down at the floor and said, "We believe this is tabloid nonsense."

"I believe in speaking truthfully when a once-in-a-lifetime opportunity presents itself," said Daisha. "The globalist jackals are everywhere."

Kane said, "Who can you trust in your own government, Mr. Prime Minister?"

Netanyahu narrowed his eyes at Kane. "There's an El Al flight that will touch down at Newark Airport at zero dark thirty, I believe you say. I suggest you be on it."

"Just in time for the meltdown," Daisha remarked. "Okay, we'll drop this bomb on the Washington Brahmins ourselves, but in our time."

"Let's get to it," Kane said. Daisha was trying to get Kane out of the office before Netanyahu lost his sense of gratitude.

"Okay, okay; thank you, Mr. Prime Minister," Daisha said. She turned to Kane. "It's back to flying coach."

"Do you mean back to the back of the plane, flying coach?"

The not-so-inside joke set everyone in motion. The pair stood up simultaneously and shook hands. The prime minister left with his security detail, while the director of the Mossad, Ygal Moskowitz, motioned for Kane and Daisha to follow him out of his office.

"Please feel free to contact me when you return to the States. I would love to hear firsthand about your experience dropping that bomb."

Kane stopped just before the elevator. "Di, hold the elevator; I have to ask the Prime Minister for a favor." He ran off before Moskowitz could stop him.

Kane rounded the corner just beyond Moskowitz's office, and two steps later, he was confronted by two bodyguards, who pointed their Jericho 941 pistols at him. "Mr. Prime Minister, I have a request."

Netanyahu leaned in and said, "Mr. Kane, you have a lot of chutzpah, and fortunately for you, that’s something I hold in high regard."

Chapter 26

Newark Airport, Terminal C, Newark, NJ. 01:30

The El Al flight landed back in the U.S. after midnight. It had been almost twenty-four hours since Daisha or Kyle had any real sleep. After passing through customs, they headed to the parking garage to pick up a rental car.

"I left Angus a text, but he's gone silent after running interference for us in midtown," said Kane.

The pair found themselves on the empty parking deck of Terminal C, where a group of car rental agencies occupied offices at the opposite end.

Daisha had already taken a seat on a nearby row of benches. She flashed Kyle a smile, and he nodded. "You sit, Di, and I'll get us a car."

"I'm sure my email accounts have been flagged," she replied. "It's been four days since I checked them last."

"Be cautious; whoever called in that Hellfire in Gaza is seriously trying to shut us up. I'm sure they're looking for us."

She sat among the myriad pieces of old gum stuck to the pavement around her. "I guess this is the point where nicotine gum just doesn't cut it."

"No, I guess not," said Kane, yawning and stretching before he jogged off.

***

He completed the always tedious rental process using his fake documents, pocketed them, and jogged over to his rented Denali. The clock on the dashboard read three in the morning.

As he approached the benches and found them empty, he checked to see if Di had moved. She was nowhere to be found, and a sick feeling grew in his gut. Reflexively, he reached for his pistol.

"Shit. It's a hell of a time to be unarmed." He scanned the area. "Daisha, where the hell did you go, girl?"

Kane put the large SUV in park and began to search the area. He considered involving the Port Authority Police as he walked briskly toward the elevators. He was surprised when the doors opened.

Two men in black hoodies and balaclavas, and armed with silenced Uzi machine pistols, stood in front of him. Kane started to back away when one of the assailants, with a deep Eastern European accent, said, "There's nowhere to go, squid." Another added, "Turn around and check your six—you gavano."

Kane recognized the Russian word for "shit." He slowly turned, and standing behind him, bold as brass, were two more black-clad marauders. One of them was pointing a gun at Daisha's head.

"Not again," Kane said. Daisha was crying beneath her duct tape gag. Anger surged within him. He turned back to the two men in the elevator. "What the hell did you do to her, you animal piece of shit?"

"We had a little fun with her while we waited for you to come back, suka."

"You sociopathic bastard! If you touched her, I'll kill every one of you pieces of shit!"

"Now we'll settle some old scores, sooksin."

They exchanged curses until one of the two men holding Daisha approached Kane and tried to cuff him. The two wrestled briefly until Daisha cried out, stopping Kane. He turned and saw the other man holding a knife to her ear.

"Stop! Just let her go. Don't hurt her," he pleaded as he allowed himself to be cuffed. In a sudden burst of energy, Kane delivered a powerful mule kick to the man's groin before he could cuff up his left wrist. He charged at the two men holding Daisha. One squared up against Kane while the other kept his knife at her throat.

Daisha saw her opportunity. She drove her heel into the shin of her assailant and simultaneously slammed her head into his nose. He released her for a moment, and she was gone.

She ran with the speed she had once possessed as a Division One track athlete in the 400 meters at Columbia.

Her assailant stumbled after her, but the chase was futile as Daisha accelerated down the ramp. Kane hooked the other man in a horse collar and slammed him to the ground. The sickening sound of a melon cracking against the concrete echoed through the parking deck.

One of the men raised his Uzi and aimed at Daisha but stopped when his boss said, “Not here, gavno.”

“Go, girl! Hell yeah!” he shouted, spitting blood and cursing. “Fuck these Russian bastards!”

Four of the men wrestled Kane onto the pavement, and they all joined in putting the boots to him. The last thing he saw was the parking deck lights, which reminded him of the Bangkok fight club.

One of the masked men approached Kane, limping heavily. “Just like a weak American, you caved at the sight of a woman being hurt. I purposely gave you the opportunity to escape. It was her or you. Freedom or this. Predictably, you chose chivalry, you fool.”

He knelt next to Kane, blood pouring from his mouth and nose, and said, “There are a few people who want to speak with you, not the least of which is your current, soon-to-be former employer.” He looked at the others and shouted, “Idti, idti, let’s move!”

Tires squealed on the upper parking deck of Newark’s C Terminal.

Three dark SUVs rolled out into the highway traffic, embarking on the long journey through New Jersey to rural Route 17 in New York State.

The highway stretched for miles with meandering medians until they reached their exit, where the deep glades and tall, pine-covered mountains of the Beaverkill River Valley swallowed them up.

The three vehicles refueled at a station next to the Roscoe Diner before navigating the winding, sometimes washed-out roads of Beaver Kill, Trout Town, USA.

The headlights of Medved's caravan traced the river as they raced through the dead of night, paralleling the fast-moving Beaverkill River, filled with the treasure of rainbow, speckled, and brownies—beautiful trout as big as a man's arm.

Castle Skye, an early 1900s replica of a Scottish Highlands castle, sat abandoned on a bluff overlooking the river. The reconstruction was massive and elaborate and, until recently, a work in progress.

The new structure, a stylish dacha called Riverstone, represented the architectural version of a restomod. The restored and modified building, with three stories of imposing fieldstone construction, featured turrets, parapets, and vaulted slate rooflines.

The trucks drove through a massive stone archway, flanked by opposing witch-hat turrets that had guarded the entrance for over a hundred years. The SUVs rolled over the white-stone gravel courtyard, triggering motion sensor lights that transformed night into day. A row of ghoulish gargoyles, brought in from a castle in the Carpathians, gazed down on the caravan as it lined up at the side of the courtyard.

The loose weave of Kane's hood allowed him to assess the courtyard as he was pulled from the SUV. He stumbled down a set of concrete steps to an entrance. The electric eye was tripped, causing the thick Lexan doors to whoosh apart.

Two men dressed in combat black emerged from the secure sublevel entrance, carrying CZ75 machine pistols.

Kane's hood was yanked off, and he squinted against the brightness. As his vision adjusted, he was astonished to find himself in a vast underground complex that rivaled anything he'd seen during his years with the Seals. Closest to him was a briefing center equipped with a line of large flatscreens, map boards, sand tables, and rows of theater seating. A dozen smaller spaces, including offices and conference rooms, were sectioned off by thick glass walls.

A mass media and communications center featured a 180-degree wraparound wall of flatscreens displaying news feeds from every outlet across the globe. An impressive armory housed a vast array of weapons: AKs, FN FALs,

Glocks, Colts, Uzis, Sigs, Armalites, Brownings, Springfields, Barrets, Smith & Wessons, Dragunovs, and some weapons, like a Cheytac M200 .408, he had never seen in person.

He realized the wide variety of weapons was intended to confuse and obfuscate rather than establish any kind of usable standard.

An armory beyond impressive, especially in New York State, the home of vehement anti-Second Amendment policies. It begs the question: Who's paying whom?

Kane turned to one of the soldiers guarding him. "Yo, Boris, what is this place? Looks like Yuri Gagarin's basement," he said sarcastically. "Someone's got some juice."

"Shut up, Yankee asshole!" one of the guards shot back.

"Whoa, an intellectual."

"Shut up, sooksin."

"This is where the magic happens," said Medved, who had walked in from the extensive workout facility. He rested his injured knee. "We represent the tactical brilliance they couldn't conceive of on their own. Elites across the globe are trying to return the world to the dark ages—an age where the wealthy can do anything to anyone, steal anything, and face no fear of retribution. Where the people are nothing but serfs."

"And that's what you want for your people?" Kane shook his head.

Medved pulled a prescription bottle from his pocket and swallowed a handful of pills. "I would say no, but it's the system in today's Russia. I choose to work with the power, not against it. The great revolution was fought to lift Russia out of the dark age, but after eliminating every honorable revolutionary, the revolutionaries became the oppressors and reinstated the dark ages in Mother Russia."

"So, you've given up hope, Medved?"

"You had a chance, Kane, to be part of this. You and I could have led these men, and you too could have become rich beyond your dreams."

"This—this bunch of mercenaries acting for the benefit of billionaires? I'd rather be dead."

Medved laughed. “You won’t have to worry; these people will grant your wish.”

“Stop speaking in gibberish!” Kane retorted arrogantly. The guard next to him delivered a cheap shot to Kane's kidneys, doubling him over in pain. Medved cursed the man.

Kane dropped into a chair, gasping for air. He watched Medved hobble away, a smile creeping across his clenched teeth. “I’m glad to see your recovery is going well, asshole. What was that you downed—oxys, a little morphine?”

The same thug next to Kane wound up to hit him again, but this time Kane beat him to the punch. Handcuffed, he threw a flying elbow into the thug's groin, then kneed him in the face. The thug's nose exploded like an overripe tomato.

A volley of stun-gun darts struck Kane from behind, knocking him to the floor. Cuffed, he began twitching like a fluke on a party boat. Once he stopped spasming, they threw him back into a chair and zip-tied him to it.

A man rushed up to Medved and whispered in his ear. He turned to Kane and said, Alas sooksin, you’re wanted upstairs. Keep him cuffed in back and clean him up before you take him upstairs."

Kane found himself in a large ballroom, facing a bizarre Dali painting: The Face of War.

Too much parallel computing going on in that guy’s head.

Kane pulled at his shackles, cuffed to a heavy wooden chair and placed in the center of the elegant space.

He tried to get up, but the effects of the beatings, the boots, and the kidney punches, on top of four or five taser darts, had weakened his legs. He struggled as the double doors at the end of the hall opened. Several men in tuxedos walked in, passing Kane as if a man beaten and shackled to a chair were part of the furnishings.

“Hey—hey, you two, come over here,” yelled Kane. Both continued past him as if he weren’t there.

“Hey shitheads, come back here. Your mother—”

Kane’s words were cut short by the sound of dozens of men and women, a crowd, that filled the room behind him.

Must be the open bar. Free drinks brings them in like flies to shit.

The entire group of thirty to forty men and women walked around and past Kane again, as if he weren't even there. Not one of them glanced at him.

The last four men through the double doors were carrying crystal snifters and smoking cigars. They walked up to Kane and encircled him. He had never met these men before, but they seemed to know him. The way they walked, with a certain air of confidence, told Kane they were American elites.

"Well, well, look who we have here," said Chuck Bogner. "This is retired Navy Commander Kyle Kane, the asshole who poured a bucket of sand on our operation."

The other three nodded and glared at Kane.

"I'm sorry, gentlemen, you have me at a disadvantage."

Bogner chuckled, "We certainly do." All four men laughed at Kane's situation.

"That there is Mr. Warren Trask," said Bogner. "He's a deputy director somewhere in the CIA." Trask sneered at Bogner. "Relax, Warren, he's at his *last supper*." Bogner turned to Cole James and introduced him as director of the FBI. "And I'm Charles Bogner, senior advisor at the Defense Intelligence Agency."

"Wow, a real cornucopia of scumbags and traitors," Kane retorted.

"That's some real false bravado, Lieutenant Commander, or should I say Lieutenant Commander retired? I imagine you've figured out that we as a group pushed to have you cashiered out of the Navy."

"Our original plan was to see you in Portsmouth," said Cole James, with a hateful look, "but that old fool Corbett called in some chits and—"

"And you fucking killed him for it," Kane interrupted. "I knew there were rats involved in that shitshow. Your fucking prints were all over it. I just didn't know who you were. We sure put a crimp in your little plans, didn't we?"

"A minor setback," said a woman behind Kane. "Carrie Gould, Mr. Kane, I work for the NSA." She made her way around him. She was tall, with dirty blond hair and a shapely figure. She extended her hand to shake Kane's and laughed. "My bad, Mr. Kane; I see you're indisposed at the moment."

The four men surrounding Kane, smoking their cigars and slugging down Armagnac like drunken lords, laughed at Gould's sarcastic jab.

Gould put her arm around Kane's shoulders and stroked his bloody, matted hair.

"Easy, Carrie, he's not your type," said Trask. The four men chuckled. "He bats from the wrong side of the plate, honey."

She pulled back, as if from a hot surface, and turned to Trask. The playful look on her face had vanished. Trask's casually cruel comment was the same game he played back in James' office.

"I guess that takes me out of the good old boys' club?" Carrie said, attempting to brush off the indignation.

"Not at all, Carrie," said Chuck Bogner. "We just had to be sure whose side you're playing for, if you get my meaning."

"I understand your clumsy, ham-handed double entendre, Chuck."

Cole James approached Carrie and stood well inside her personal space. "Carrie, you wanted to be part of the club. You gotta be able to take the heat. No one's judging you; it's just locker room talk."

Carrie looked at the other three and smiled. Thoughts of her home being bugged ran through her mind. "I know; I was just throwing a little shade your way. I wanted to see if you cretins could handle it."

Trask and Bogner laughed as they pulled Carrie along with them on their walk to the bar.

"Come with us, young lady," said Trask. "There's talk of a high-stakes poker game breaking out," he added.

James remained behind with his captive. "This is your last night out, Mr. Kane. Do you have any questions?"

"Yeah, what is this place, and why am I here?"

"I guess it doesn't matter. Telling you anything won't go beyond these walls. You're going to die here tonight.

Through a series of serendipitous events, you have decrypted a fully secured laptop and the files involving our operation."

The director of the FBI took another snifter from a roving waitress. "The Kennedy assassinations—that was a coup d'état. An unqualified success by any standard. You can't imagine how many decisions have been made under the rubric of that operation. Its success has emboldened countless administrations to do the unthinkable."

"It was the CIA, wasn't it?" Kane said. "JFK was going to shut the agency down and end the Vietnam War. The Dulles-controlled deep state of the 50s and 60s put an end to that, and so we the people got a clay-footed LBJ, who quit as soon as he could, with the writing on the wall that if they could kill a president as popular as Kennedy, killing him would have seemed like a public service."

"Very good, Mr. Kane. You live up to your profile as a very cerebral grunt," he replied, looking at his fingernails. "And that's rare."

"Tell me, Mr. Director, what does the current coup look like?"

"It's complicated," James said, "but I'll tell you this much: the plan began with two billion dollars being passed via proxies to the ever-malleable Hassan Mudgizzen. At that time, he was a chair at the London School of Economics. We specialize in elite capture and candidate selection—scrubbing their backgrounds and putting them in play."

Cole took a long pull, belched, and continued, "He started passing this money to Hamas, Yemen, and the other proxies. The CCP has them all on retainer."

"Why didn't you just use Iran?"

"They were ready to play their part, providing direct action in response to our disinformation. So, these militia groups were in play along the borders of Israel; the trick was getting them to cooperate. Today was supposed to be launch day for the attack. From a hundred dispersed points along their respective borders with Israel, they would make their incursions. Most of them were diversions, drawing fire from Israel's reflexive response. It would make Israel feel vulnerable to their neighborhood bully to the north. They would respond as they always have—by attacking military installations inside Lebanon." James smiled and thoughtlessly flicked his cigar ash onto the inlaid parquet floor.

"Nice touch. So using stolen and black-market Israeli weapons fired by your foreign fighters in IDF uniforms at civilian targets in Gaza and Hezbollah in Lebanon, which will kill thousands of their own people in their hospitals, their schools, and their civic centers, was all good with you people?" asked Kane.

"Don't forget government buildings and the odd orphanage. That was Trask's idea. We'll leak it to our mainstream media that Israel committed war crimes and atrocities, and they'll run with the shocking footage of the carnage and, the best part, the identifiable wreckage of Israeli missiles and rockets. That's when Iran attacks."

"Incredible."

"To put a fine coat of shellac on it, I was going to send an FBI forensics team to verify it. That was my little addition."

"What happened to Daisha?" asked Kane.

"I don't know if Warren would tell you this, but she's alive, at a CIA safe house. They're trying to decide whether to eliminate her or deprogram her. You know, *Jason Bourne* her. It's nasty; personally, I'd rather take the 9mm option."

"Deprogramming? Using the old MKUltra techniques, or do you have something better?"

Cole James shook his head. "Some of the old ways are still the best. You have no idea of the vast power of the federal government, particularly the intel agencies and my FBI. There is so much technology and talent arrayed against you, not just here in the U.S., but across the globe. You could never have succeeded in taking this public."

Kane shook his head. "The U.S. will never let that happen."

"We are the U.S., Mr. Kane. The deep-state administration will slow-roll help, and when it does, this country will be left desperately vulnerable. And that, my boy, is phase two."

"At some point, China will make a move on Taiwan, and the U.S. will threaten a response, going to DEFCON two. That's when the true deep-state operators will take the football away from the man and seize total control of Washington."

"What about our allies?"

"Germany, France, and Italy—none of them have the stomach for war. Britain will not back the U.S.; they're all on board with insane migrant invasions. It's globalization. Hell, they're arresting people for being mean on social media. If the story leaks, we have buy-in from our paid operatives around the country. On our orders, they will cause internal strife here and across Europe, rendering their unstable forms of government in a state of perpetual no confidence. I've always thought their governments were created more for tabloids and pub tongue wagers than for the people."

Kane was amazed at the level of sedition this federal employee was discussing.

A minute later, two new people walked through the double doors in front of Kyle.

"You're fucking kidding me!"

"Is that any way to greet an old friend?" said Roland Moreau.

"Guess it's too late to take you up on that Monaco vacation?" Moreau said nothing but made his way to his guest. "Ygal Mosckowitz? That's goddamn predictable."

"Commander—Mr. Kane, nothing is ever as it seems."

"I guess not. A Mossad director turning on his people."

"We can't sustain our position in the Middle East, Mr. Kane, unless we are willing to compromise," said Mosckowitz. "I'm not alone. Look at all the Jews who turn their backs on Israel."

"Are you trying to convince me or yourself? The CCP has financially backed the radicalization of Islam, and they us antisemitism to cover up their actual target, the US, and your on their team. You're fucking lucky my hands are handcuffed, or I'd got through you like a hot knife through butter."

"I know, I would too, Mr. Kane. Some things are just not what they seem."

"You people keep saying that, but everything here is as it seems. You're turning on your own people, Ygal, as if they haven't been through enough."

Carrie Gould could be heard as she made her way back to the center of the room. Her loud voice was a bit more inebriated than earlier when she approached the group.

"Mr. Moreau," said Carrie as she slurred her words and clumsily tripped and fell forward. Her drink splashed out. She managed to catch herself on the back of Kane's chair, almost knocking it over. She struggled to get up. "Oh my, I seem to have had a bit too much to drink."

"Ms. Gould, perhaps you should consider a cup of coffee or a trip to your room," said Moreau.

Carrie Gould nodded, her head bobbing drunkenly. "I think I'm going to be sick!" she muttered as she passed Moreau and Mosckowitz.

Trask and Bogner approached Moreau a minute after Gould, having done little more than refresh their drinks.

"Gentlemen," said Moreau, "please enlighten us: what's so humorous?"

"Ms. Gould got drunk on two scotches."

"That seems odd; her workup, as I recall, indicated she could hold her liquor. Two drinks?"

"Medication interaction," said Bogner. "It's happened to me before."

"That's fine, Mr. Bogner. I'm sure it's a worthy tale, but we have a point of order to address," said Moreau, stepping back. "We don't want to keep Mr. Kane waiting."

"Director Trask, who's going to kill our guest—Mr. Kane? According to Sun Tzu, it's a rare honor to destroy your enemy," said Roland Moreau as he looked at Kane with contempt.

Kane smiled back. "I believe Sun Tzu said, 'Never put your enemy in a corner.'"

The room full of guests closed in around Kane. The men and women of the cabal, the elites and government officials

—all of whom benefited from CCP corruption—circled around Kyle Kane.

From the crowd emerged a lanky Persian man. He strolled up to the group surrounding Kane. His dark, deep-set eyes grew ominous as he approached the enemy of his country's kleptocratic theocracy. He had a long scar that ran from his ear to his pointed chin.

He drew an ivory-handled Colt 1911 from his suit jacket and held it at his side.

"Governments are like babies: an alimentary canal with big appetites at one end and no sense of responsibility at the other," said the Persian.

Warren Trask, well into a bottle of Chivas, looked at Cole James. "Did that guy just quote Ronald Reagan?"

Bogner grinned and replied, "Yeah, he tried, but I think he messed it up."

Davood Shirazi was an assassin for hire, known throughout the Iranian black ops community. His nom de guerre, the Persian, was adopted after he left the Quds Force to pursue a career as an assassin in the U.S. His current employers were certain members of the globalist movement.

Shirazi approached Kane from behind, raising the classic Colt with its hammer drawn back. He pointed it directly at the side of Kane's head and stared at him for a few seconds. The scene at the Cigar Emporium flashed in his mind.

He lowered the gun to his side and took a step back. He stared at the side of Kane's head. "I killed your boss, Admiral Corbett, and I had you in my sights in Virginia."

Kane bristled at his words. "You killed the girl, Colleen, in Manhattan."

"I warned you in the alleyway that I would kill you. It's my duty to kill you, and now I am going to do it."

Kane turned to face the Persian with steely eyes. "Excuse me, but who the hell are you?"

"Do you really need an explanation, frogman?"

"If these are my last moments on earth, I believe I deserve one."

"If you worked in the shadows like many of us in this room, you would know me."

"I got that part, jackass!"

The assassin smiled and shook his head. "You have incredible élan. It is a shame to have to kill you shackled to a chair." He looked at Moreau, Trask, and then Cole, saying, "I am here to bring order to a world that is spinning out of control. I am, in many ways, like the Indian god Vishnu, the destroyer of obstacles."

The Persian leveled his pistol at Kane's head again, even pressing the barrel to his temple.

Kane flinched as a single shot rang out. The report ripped through the crowd, sending people screaming as they ran. Only one person fell—the destroyer himself.

Kane's actions were a blur. His right wrist restraint was unlocked with a paperclip placed in his hand just as Carrie Gould crashed into him.

His left wrist dropped to the floor, free from the restraint. He grabbed up the Colt 1911 and pointed it at anyone who moved. Everyone, even the so-called intel warriors, was frozen with fear. He considered double-tapping the person to be sure.

"Don't waste your rounds." He turned the gun on the others, scanning the entire room.

"Over here, Lieutenant Commander." It was Carrie Gould, cool as a cucumber, holding a pistol on the group. She stood ramrod straight in jeans and a leather flight jacket, adorned with all the patches and insignia she had earned flying jets off U.S. carriers.

Gould had gone to her room and retrieved her personal Taurus G3, 9mm, with its seventeen-round magazine.

She stood next to Kane, admiring the cuts and bruises on his face. "What do you think, Mr. Kane? Should we shoot them all and let God sort them out?"

"Tempting, Ms. Gould."

She turned to Cole, Trask, and Bogner. "You simple sons of bitches! You bugged my home to get blackmail material so you could twist me into one of your go-along lesbians? A Moreau puppet? This Texas girl doesn't play that game."

"Carrie, you are way out of your depth," said Cole James. Carrie smiled, struggling to control her urge to shoot him in the kneecap.

Moreau looked at the pair with disgust. "Thirty armed men will converge on you in seconds. I suggest you put down your weapons!"

"I don't think so, Rollie," said Kane.

"I'm speechless, Ms. Gould. Is there a plan?"

"We're making it up as we go along, Roland," said Carrie, pointing her pistol at Moreau's chest.

"Consider yourselves lucky; I'm not cold-blooded like you."

The two backed out of the room. "I'm really okay with you shooting him, Carrie, but we'll need to move quickly. His security team is just below decks."

"I know; I paid them a visit just before coming to get you. I shorted out the electromagnetic control sensors on all the basement doors."

"You're good," said Kane. "Where'd you—"

"An electrical engineering degree from Annapolis. Now follow me." The recently resigned senior NSA department head led Kane out into the central hall.

"So, what's our exfil plan?"

"I don't have a vehicle; we all came up here by limo."

"They have dogs; we'll be hunted down in the woods."

"Roger that. The courtyard's a killing field."

She pointed up. "It's the roof." Kane followed her to the grand staircase. "Do we have a way off the roof?"

Up two steps, on the way to the second floor, Kane raised the Colt. "Contact right." Carrie ducked as Kane fired once, dropping a rover security patrol. "He was ready to fire; I had no time."

"No worries here," said Carrie.

"I've got six rounds left," Kane replied. Gould handed him her pistol. "I have sixteen left." She took hold of the larger, heavier weapon.

"It's got a kick," said Kane.

"Not my first rodeo, Kane. Always use a large caliber for a large-caliber man."

"I have no doubts."

"How did you get a chopper out here?"

"As I was touring the basement facilities," said Carrie, "I clipped this." She tossed Kyle his wallet. "Inside was a card, a GGIG card, with a name and a number written on the back. I thought it was worth a shot."

"Don't tell me, Regimental Sergeant Major Walsh; you called Angus Walsh?"

"That's him. It sounded like he was drunk. He's a bit of a wild man, right?"

"Without question. He said he could get us a helicopter."

"Can he fly a bird?"

Kane wasn't sure how to answer that question. "He's an old-school SAS operator, and those guys are cross-trained on everything."

Carrie smiled. "A nuclear sub?"

"Sure." He scanned the second-floor hallway at the top of the stairs. "He's one of the good guys."

"But can he fly a helicopter?"

"Walsh was twenty-five years in the SAS; his father was SAS, and his grandpappy was a Chindit—British special ops royalty. Angus has been cross-trained on so many weapons and platforms that there's no telling what he can do."

"Chindit?" asked Carrie, scanning left to right.

"Chindits were British long-range guerrilla units that scared the hell out of the Japanese using sabotage and surprise attacks. They fought to survive in the deadliest mountain jungles in the world—Burma."

Kane paused again, listening for any sign of the enemy. "Back then, the spec ops guys were mostly bare-knuckle brawler types." At the end of the hallway, Kane pointed to the stairs leading up to the third floor. "Did you hear that?" The commotion on the first floor urged them to move up.

"That's Medved and his merry band of assholes." She checked the corner at the top of the third flight. "How did they get out?"

"They probably re-juiced the doors," Kane said. "The door bolts released, and they're out."

"We gotta move," said Carrie. The pair stood on the top floor landing.

"Was Angus drunk?"

Carrie pointed Kane down a third-floor corridor. "Sober as a church mouse," he said.

Barely a step off the landing, a rip of automatic gunfire tore into the plaster wall behind them. Carrie pushed Kane out of the way as rounds zipped past his head. He changed elevation, dropped into a squat, and leaned out around the corner. He fired four rounds downrange, catching a staggered pair of mercenaries halfway up the staircase.

Carrie sprinted down the hall, turning halfway to the corner. She stopped and dropped into a shooting stance. A second later, she fired the 1911; one shot snapped past Kane's ear, dropping one of the mercs who had leaned out into the hall. Kane tapped her on the shoulder as he passed.

The pair rounded another corner of the building. The muffled sound of a helicopter's rotors could just be heard overhead.

"He's here!" shouted Carrie.

"Son of a bitch, Angus, you beauty!"

"We're not the only ones hearing it."

Gould spotted the steel ladder first. It was tucked inside an alcove and bolted into a wall at the end of the corridor. "Roof access."

Kane didn't wait for an invitation. Gould was with him, stride for stride. They reached the access point, and Carrie shouted, "Up the ladder, sailor!"

Carrie understood that chivalry was useless in a firefight. Kyle climbed the ladder while Carrie fired another round and jumped on. Kane was halfway up when he heard Carrie take a hit; she let out a yelp.

Kane looked down just in time to see Carrie fall from the ladder.

"Goooo!" she shouted.

Ignoring her, Kane slid down the ladder. Carrie raised her Colt .45 and fired two rounds downrange. Kyle dropped into a shooting stance next to her and returned fire.

Without a word, he grabbed Carrie around the waist and lifted her onto his shoulder. She had the presence of mind to fire another round down the corridor before Kane pulled them both up the ladder.

He muscled the former naval wing commander through the access hatch in the roof. The mercs had run the length of the hallway and begun firing through the hatch.

Kyle searched for a way to secure it. He saw that it latched from the inside and cursed. His eyes fell on the catwalk that ran around the roofline.

Shivering in the raw chill of the Catskill Mountain night and in great pain, Carrie pulled herself up against the cold stone of the parapet wall. Her oxygen saturation was racing her blood pressure to see which would bottom out first.

Kyle ripped off part of his sleeve and grasped Carrie by her upper arm. He leaned her forward and lifted her shirt. What he saw dashed his hopes.

"How bad is it?" she asked, blood pooling in her throat. She coughed once, gurgled, and spat out blood.

Kane's eyes told Carrie everything she needed to know. She groaned when he packed the wound.

"Take the pain," she muttered under her breath.

"I'm going to get you out of here, Carrie. Keep pressure on the wound." He kept one eye on the roof access.

Carrie reached back and pulled her hand forward. "Dark, pulsing blood, Kyle. I'm fucked."

"Keep pressure on it, Commander!"

"It's okay, Kyle," she said, shivering. "I don't believe in sugarcoating a bad ending. My ticket's been punched—you can't change that." She coughed up more blood and spat. "Dark blood tells me it's the liver. I'll be dead before I get on that bird."

"No, we can do this!" Kane said forcefully, fighting the same helplessness he felt the night he lost his daughter. "I'm not leaving you here."

Carrie raised the Persian's Colt 1911 and handed it to Kane. "It's got two rounds left. Give me back my Taurus. I'll buy you some time before—"

The roof hatch popped up, and one of Medved's men tried to push an AK through the crack. Carrie shot him with the Taurus. She smiled at the sound of his body hitting the floor.

"That felt good."

"You'd make a hell of an operator, Gould."

"Not my idea of a good time, sailor, running through jungles with a bunch of swinging dicks. Personally, I'd rather walk the tiers in a women's prison for supermodel first offenders. Now that's—" She coughed up another mouthful of blood, struggling to speak.

Kane smiled at her. He slipped the clip out of the Colt, checked it, then slapped it back in. "Time for some serious fire discipline."

He leaned over Carrie and straightened her up. "If you see my baby girl over there, tell her I love her." Carrie tried to smile, but the darkness of tunnel vision was closing in.

The same suppressed whooping echoed in from the west until it filled the sky above them. Kyle looked up in disbelief at the bizarre-looking matte black cylinder that dropped from the night sky.

Carrie grabbed Kyle's hand and said, "Tell Lizza I'm sorry. Tell her I love her!" She let go and, with the last of her strength, urged, "Now move, sailor!"

Kane stood, unaware of the tears rolling down his face.

Fifty yards away and one hundred feet in the air, the strange hybrid vertical lift aircraft with four articulating rotors hovered in the lee of the massive stone structure, just off the edge of the roof.

Before leaving, Kyle put his hand on Carrie's shoulder. "You're a hell of a warrior, Commander Gould!" He saluted her, then turned and ran down the flat roof.

A volley of shots rang out from the courtyard below, some striking the parapets while others whizzed past Kane as he ran. His blood-soaked torso was visible from below, and twenty laser sight dots traced the path of the fleeing man.

AK's a great rifle—if you're fighting in a phone booth, you assholes. He returned fire with his last two rounds. It was Angus or nothing.

Ahead of Kane, like a magic carpet, the wavering helicopter ladder beckoned. A side door swung open on the stealthy, radar-evading craft that bobbed in the windy night sky.

The ominous barrel of a GE Minigun slid out and locked into place on the port side. It spun up with a sound like hell's own sewing machine as it spat out great balls of fire. Six thousand rounds' worth of spent brass hopped and danced across the deck, and the delivery of so much 7.62 mm full metal fury ravaged the courtyard and those foolish enough to remain in the open.

For those who did stay, it became a killing field. White stone gravel chips and blood spray filled the air as bodies exploded around the courtyard.

"SHHHIIIITTTTTT!" shouted Kane as he ran off the end of the building. The launch sent him over the edge of the stone parapet. He could barely make out the ladder in the darkness. Everything moved at high speed until he made the jump; then everything for Kane slowed down.

The nylon ladder, with its carbon fiber rungs, swayed back and forth. It dangled in front of him like the brass ring on a merry-go-round. Kane willed his body to stay aloft long enough to grab it, and when he felt he had reached the apex, his mind flashed to what was sure to be a bone-splintering death.

Fate being what it was on any given night, with swirling winds and unpredictable rotor wash, the rope ladder swung in his direction. His right hand missed the first rung and passed through it up to his elbow, and when he flexed his arm, the momentum whipped him around like a rag doll. He managed to hold onto his lifeline, and his body swung out into the dark ether.

He pulled himself up using just his arms. His pulse raced like a wide-bore needle was pumping adrenaline directly into his heart. The aircraft was pulling him laterally, and he struggled to stay on as he was dragged through the branches and pine boughs of the old-growth forest.

When they cleared the gunfire, Kyle climbed the last ten rungs and came face to face with a smiling Angus Walsh. "Aye, Laddie, nothing like a grand entrance."

"Turn this bird around, Angus; we have a man down on the roof!"

"Did I miss something?" He handed Kane a headset. "His name is Mac Harris."

"Mac, take us back over the chateau. I don't give a damn! We have a man down on that roof!"

A GE 214 Microgun was mounted on the opposite side of the aircraft. Kyle pulled the hatch open and locked the Microgun's door mount into place. He pulled back the charging bolt. At that moment, the X4 Super Kestrel made a hard bank, sending Kyle and Angus sideways and almost out the door.

The aircraft screamed back over the treetops, and Kyle pushed the swivel-mounted gun out into space. Kane shouted, "Weapons hot."

The 5.56 mm flamethrower tore into the castle. At ten thousand rounds per minute, Kane paid his respects to Moreau's CCU mercenaries, who had charged back out of their revetment.

The extreme experimental aircraft executed another aerial Batman turn, and Kane shouted into his headphone mic, "Hold over the main gatehouse."

Kyle spotted Carrie Gould still propped up on the stone battlement of the roof. She sat across from the roof access hatch with the pistol in her lap. He watched as she tried to raise the weapon. Her arm shook as she barely lifted the gun off her thigh.

"She's alive. I'm going down," shouted Kane, tossing off his headphones. "Angus, get on the microgun and keep those pricks busy!"

"Roger that, Lieutenant Commander."

Kyle swung out onto the rope ladder and looked down. Using only his arms, he performed a hand-over-hand maneuver until he reached the bottom of the thirty-foot ladder. His stomach twisted into a knot when he saw a dark figure, seventy feet below, round a ventilation shack just feet from Carrie.

Kane recognized the shadow. "The fucking Persian."

The wraithlike figure approached Carrie's blind side. Kane tried to shout, but his voice was drowned out by the rotor wash.

The assassin stepped in front of her, and Kane reached for his sidearm, only to realize it was empty. He signaled to Angus to shoot as Medved stepped closer. The assassin pointed his weapon at Carrie and paused to look up at Kyle, smiling—a sick, sadistic grin. Kane threw the Colt, but it clanked off the parapet, just feet away.

The Persian fired at Carrie, emptying his entire clip into her. Carrie's slender body danced under the near point-blank rounds. Torn apart, her limp body fell to the catwalk, her eyes still open; they stared up at Kane.

He climbed back into the chopper, unable to help the woman who had just saved his life.

Insane with rage, his mind spiraled into a dangerous place. As he jumped behind the microgun and charged it, he called to the pilot, "Get me a shot at that fucker!"

The Persian had reloaded and began firing at the Kestrel, laughing the entire time—right up until Mac Harris spun the nimble bird around and aimed the Microgun's barrels at his position.

The microgun was leveled, and fire roared from its five barrels. The Persian tried to run, but Kane was on him. He unleashed a line of red-hot tracers across the stone parapet, striking him in the back as he dove headfirst into the open roof hatch.

Kane emptied the last 200 rounds from the 1,500-round ammo box into the roof opening.

Angus reached over and eased him back off the trigger. "Kyle, you're dry running the gun. It's a loaner."

"You got more ammo, Angus?"

"Yeah, six more boxes of experimental 7.62 incendiary rounds."

"Hook me up, Angus," Kane said as he jumped over to the bigger, more destructive Gatling gun. "Mac, circle the structure until I tell you otherwise!"

"Roger that, Lieutenant Commander."

Kane imagined Mac was an Air Cav vet the way he handled the bird. Rounds dinged off the X4 as it banked hard in a circular pattern just above the treetops. Angus loaded the minigun, and Kane set about destroying everything in sight. He blew out windows and doors, collapsing entire sections of its walls. The incendiary rounds turned the century-old rafter system into a sky-burning pyre. Then, Kane turned his rage to the vehicles and outbuildings.

He spotted a row of six 500-gallon propane tanks above ground and raked them with fiery orange rounds. The explosions lit up the night sky across the region.

The pressure wave pushed the Super Kestrel twenty feet sideways. It took every bit of Mac's thirty years of rotary experience to keep them steady. The stone castle became a fiery shell as Kane turned to Angus and said, "Here endeth the lesson."

"Only for the moment, Laddie. There will be people coming for us. We need to get the hell out of here."

Chapter 27

Stewart Air Force Base, Newburgh, NY. 22:00

Angus' buddy Mac Harris, who turned out to be an RAF helicopter pilot and chief weapons engineer and test pilot for Arch Angel Armaments, brought the experimental helicopter in at treetop level. He touched down just outside their research hangar.

Angus and Harris wiped down the chopper with Kane, and the three men tied it down.

"Do you think they'll know we borrowed the bird?" said Angus. They both laughed. "I don't know, 20,000 rounds of advanced prototype ammo spent, and no test data to show for it, and more than a few bullet holes in the fuselage—"

"Don't forget the additional four and a half flight hours on those four GE T700 turboshaft beauties," said Mac as he pointed over at Kane, who was staring out into the night.

"What do you think?" asked Mac. "A couple of pints of bitters?"

"Yeah, I think our friend over there could use a couple—and a couple more."

The three men made their way to Mac's favorite watering hole, the Bierhaus, which featured dark woods coated in decades of heavy lacquer and busty, dirndl-wearing waitresses who could carry half a dozen liter steins in each hand. Mac ordered a couple of beers from Verena, who was standing at the waitress station.

As they settled in, the big screen replayed the Manchester Derby. A Breaking News banner flashed across the screen. It reported:

"Four of America's highest-ranking intelligence officials are missing tonight. Cole James, FBI Director; Warren Trask,

CIA Deputy Director; Charles Bogner, Defense Intelligence Agency Director; and Carrie Gould, former Navy combat pilot and Counter Intelligence Deputy Director with the NSA. All are reported missing and believed dead after their private boat sank in the Bering Sea. They were booked on a chartered fishing boat out of Kodiak, Alaska. Staffers described it as a working vacation."

Walsh turned from the big screen to look at Kane's face; his friend wore a thousand-mile stare. For those familiar with it, it was a PTSD effect common among people who had witnessed too much—too much violence for a human mind to process.

"And so the chess pieces begin to move," said Angus as he got up from his chair and headed to the bar.

"Where are you headed, Angus?" asked Mac, motioning for another round.

"I'm going to see a man about a horse."

Kyle looked back at Mac. "I've got to thank you, Mac; you guys were the fucking Air Cav today."

"I'm sorry we couldn't save Ms. Gould. Was she your girl?"

"No, she was—she was seeing someone. A real committed relationship, from what I could tell. Tell Angus when he comes back to keep a bag packed; we've got some work to do."

The End

www.ingramcontent.com/pod-product-compliance
Lightning Source LLC
LaVergne TN
LVHW010636110826
845149LV00014B/2856
9781966625797